© Matthew Chamberlain

Amelia Gray is the author of five books, most recently *Isadora*. Her fiction and essays have appeared in *The New Yorker*, *The New York Times*, *The Wall Street Journal*, *Tin House*, and *VICE*. She is a winner of the New York Public Library Young Lion, of FC2's Ronald Sukenick Innovative Fiction Prize, and a finalist for the PEN/Faulkner Award for Fiction. She lives in Los Angeles.

ALSO BY AMELIA GRAY

Gutshot

THREATS

Museum of the Weird

AM/PM

"A great novel of character: the story of a real woman's real grief and survival . . . Gray's characters devour the world through their senses, a voracious, bodily quality that's a gift in writing the story of a woman for whom meaning began in the body. . . . Though it uses gifts already apparent in Gray's work, *Isadora* also marks an evolution: Here, Gray's prose is enriched by a profound tenderness. . . . *Isadora* is a heavenly celebration of women in charge of their bodies."

—Ellie Robins, *Los Angeles Times*

"A stunning meditation on art and grief by one of America's most exciting young authors . . . Gray is a gutsy, utterly original writer, and this is the finest work she's done so far. *Isadora* is a masterful portrait of one of America's greatest artists, and it's also a beautiful reflection on what it means to be suffocated by grief but not quite willing to give up."

—Michael Schaub, NPR

"[Gray's] sentences are painfully precise. Thrills come from telling gestures and original thoughts rather than plot twists. . . . Isadora is so confounded by her fame and grief that she's in the dark about her own emotions, even as her expressive dances capture the world's attention. Gray portrays that great irony in heartbreaking detail and psychological acuity, her language hinging lyrical flight with wry directness. . . . The novel's greatest test is also its greatest strength. You might not like me, it says, but what do you know of extraordinary grief?"

—Josh Cook, *The Washington Post*

"Gray makes [each character] and their suffering tremendously compelling and allows each of them moments of great sympathy. . . . [*Isadora*] is the most deeply sustained of [Gray's] books to date, the most epic and ambitious. It is a brutal novel in many ways, completely unrelenting in its depiction of pain, yet that makes it exhilarating, too. Gray is a fearless writer, a writer willing to look into the most profound darkness and find strange, compelling music there."

—Gayle Brandeis,
Los Angeles Review of Books

"[*Isadora*] achieves something far more ambitious than documentary fiction. . . . *Isadora* is a portrait of a revolutionary artist who endures extreme misfortune and the flow of history, a novel whose depiction of a world on the brink of horror and atrocity feels utterly contemporary, but it is also a novel about writing, about the creation of literary art. . . . This is what is known as 'making it look easy,' which Amelia Gray has accomplished to the utmost."   —Brooks Sterritt, *San Francisco Chronicle*

"Intricately spun . . . For every raw, grisly passage, there lies a frolicsome wonder at work, and we are treated sentence by sentence to [Gray's] irrepressible exuberance. . . . Gray can confidently change the steps halfway through, and it's not until you're knee-deep in the weird, the wonderful, the absurd, that you realize you have danced your way far from any recognizable home."   —Hilary Leichter, *BOMB*

"A stunning work filled with profound emotional insights and downright splendid prose. Indeed, Gray's sentences move with a natural cadence that mirrors Isadora's philosophy as a dancer. With each movement, Gray gradually reveals the ambitions and losses of her characters."
            —Aram Mrjoian, *Chicago Review of Books*

"Like its subject, [*Isadora* is] full of contrasts and contradictions, a story wrought with complexity and understated humor that lives comfortably in the nuanced, darkened corners of experience."
            —Megan Burbank, *The Portland Mercury*

"*Isadora* is a moving exploration of the way sadness threads through a life, stitching it into new forms and figures as strange as they are resilient."
            —Margo Orlando Littell, *Manhattan Book Review*

"Gray displays a wide range of versatility in her dance literacy—often in surprising, pleasurable ways—but she is most eloquent when describing Isadora's connections to other people. . . . [*Isadora*] has passages of great beauty, exhilarating savagery, and humor. . . . *Isadora* transcends the realities of its individual characters to focus on the ties that bind them."
            —Kristin Hatleberg, *The Culture Trip*

"[A] deeply inquisitive and empathic story of epic grief . . . Historical novels about artists abound, but few attain the psychological intricacy, fluency of imagination, lacerating wit, or intoxicating beauty of Gray's tale of Isadora Duncan. . . . Gray, performing her own extraordinary artistic leap, explores the nexus between body and mind, loss and creativity, love and ambition, and birth and death. The spellbinding result is a mythic, fiercely insightful, mordantly funny, and profoundly revelatory portrait of an intrepid and indelible artist."

—Donna Seaman, *Booklist* (starred review)

"Captivating historical fiction . . . Gray does a terrific job of depicting not just the bereavement of a mother but also the bereavement of a mother for whom life is a source of fuel for art. . . . A novel equal to its larger-than-life protagonist." —*Kirkus Reviews*

"Gray's striking, sensual language is perfectly suited to her visionary protagonist, and the novel shimmers with memorable prose."

—*Publishers Weekly*

"Gray isn't the first or the last novelist to take on Isadora Duncan's outsize, groundbreaking, tragic life. But she might be the weirdest, in a good way. Gray's stories have tended toward fabulist absurdism. Her treatment of Duncan in the wake of her children's death by drowning is relatively conventional—half-crazed first-person narration intercut with the perspectives of those struggling to keep Duncan's life together."

—*Vulture*'s Spring Book Preview

ISADORA

AMELIA GRAY

PICADOR
FARRAR, STRAUS AND GIROUX
NEW YORK

ISADORA. Copyright © 2017 by Amelia Gray. All rights reserved. Printed in the United States of America. For information, address Picador, 175 Fifth Avenue, New York, N.Y. 10010.

picadorusa.com • instagram.com/picador
twitter.com/picadorusa • facebook.com/picadorusa

Picador® is a U.S. registered trademark and is used by Macmillan Publishing Group, LLC, under license from Pan Books Limited.

For book club information, please visit facebook.com/picadorbookclub or email marketing@picadorusa.com.

Designed by Abby Kagan

The Library of Congress has cataloged the Farrar, Straus and Giroux edition as follows:

Names: Gray, Amelia, 1982– author.
Title: Isadora / Amelia Gray.
Description: First edition. | New York : Farrar, Straus and Giroux, 2017.
Identifiers: LCCN 2016045035 | ISBN 9780374279981 (hardcover) | ISBN 9780374712587 (ebook)
Subjects: LCSH: Duncan, Isadora, 1877–1927—Fiction. | Women dancers—Fiction. | GSAFD: Biographical fiction.
Classification: LCC PS3607.R387 I82 2017 | DDC 813'.6—dc23
LC record available at https://lccn.loc.gov/2016045035

Picador Paperback ISBN 978-1-250-18309-5

Our books may be purchased in bulk for promotional, educational, or business use. Please contact your local bookseller or the Macmillan Corporate and Premium Sales Department at 1-800-221-7945, extension 5442, or by email at MacmillanSpecialMarkets@macmillan.com.

First published by Farrar, Straus and Giroux

First Picador Edition: May 2018

10 9 8 7 6 5 4 3 2 1

FOR LEE

April 1913: the world enjoys the prosperity of modern days. Though the Great War is only a matter of months away, Europe blossoms with invention, artistic achievement, and social change. With little sense that a world conflict lies just around the corner, the growing middle class savors the feelings of peace, prosperity, and optimism.

Isadora Duncan has situated herself at the center of it all. Born in California, she convinced her mother and three siblings to join her in Europe at the age of twenty-two: the year was 1899, eve of the twentieth century. The Duncans arrived in London the same year the RMS Oceanic made its maiden voyage and Marconi transmitted a radio signal over the English Channel.

In a time when dancers laced themselves into corsets and audiences worshiped the rigid precision of ballet, Isadora made her life's work a theory of dance which claimed that if the ideal of beauty could be found in nature, then the ideal dancer moved naturally. At twenty-six she gave a lecture in Berlin called "The Dance of the Future," which derided the "deformed" muscles and bones of the world's finest ballet dancers and decried the tragedy of restriction at the core of the genre. She urged her growing audience to consider the art and ideas of the Greeks, whose concept of Platonic form underscored Isadora's assertion that art must strive for the emulation of nature. Her dances, appearing outwardly to be simple waltzes and mazurkas, sought to capture in their ease of movement the vital, visceral expression of beauty's purest form.

Isadora was an instant sensation, reveling in sensational press, and she rode her reputation to glory. Barred from some theaters for performing in a tunic and bare feet, her intuitive, innovative skill found her an early audience in Vienna and Paris, London, Moscow, and New York.

Her acquisition of lovers was equally prolific, and quietly remarked upon in polite society. In 1906 she gave birth to Deirdre. The father was Gordon Craig, a director and stage designer she called Ted; four years later, she gave birth to her son, Patrick, with Paris Singer. A relentless capitalist, Paris was buoyed by the Singer sewing machine fortune yet haunted by his father's success, a reminder of which could be found advertising nine hundred stitches a minute in every shopwindow in the modern world. Paris offered Isadora the possibility of reconciling her ambitious ideas with her fiscal reality, and although their partnership was marked with explosive arguments, they were happy together in the years after Patrick was born.

In the early days of the twentieth century Paris and Isadora gallivanted around Europe, children in tow. She worked tirelessly, giving performances and lectures and throwing parties that went on for weeks. With her long-suffering sister, Elizabeth, she created her first schools, which would instruct a generation of dancers in the type of natural movement that grew into modern dance. With that, the family took on the arduous task of building an artistic movement.

April 1913: Isadora Duncan is at the height of her power. She finds herself teetering on the cusp of a great change, both in her own life and in the world. An energy builds around her, a feeling that fascinates her and informs her work. She anticipates that an artistic revolution will emerge from that energy, and that she will stand at the forefront of an era devoted to the sublime.

Unfortunately, she is mistaken.

ISADORA

DUNCAN CHILDREN
DROWN WITH NURSE

**Little Girl and Boy of American Dancer
Hurled with Automobile
into River Seine.**

CHAUFFEUR LEFT POWER ON

**And Car, Running Wild, Carried Them to
Death—Mother Terribly
Stricken by Loss.**

Special Cable to THE NEW YORK TIMES

PARIS. April 19, 1913.—A pathetic tragedy, which has cast gloom over all classes in Paris, took place in the suburb of Neuilly-sur-Seine this afternoon, when the two beautiful children of Isadora Duncan, the American dancer, were, with their Scottish governess, carried by an automobile, running wild, into the Seine River and drowned.

Isadora Duncan, who had been spending the week resting at the Trianon Palace Hotel in Versailles, came to her town house this afternoon. Although a drizzling rain was falling, she decided to send her children and the governess back . . . in a hired automobile.

The car appeared in front of her villa in Neuilly at 3:30 o'clock. The children, dressed in white fur coats and gaiters, were conducted to the automobile by their mother, and, having been fondly kissed good-by by her, jumped merrily into the car.

The French chauffeur started off, the mother waving as the vehicle drew out of sight. It had not gone more than a hundred yards when the driver, coming out on the Boulevard Bourbon, which flanks the Seine, had to pull up to avoid collision with another car. The engine stopping, the chauffeur descended and turned the crank. Apparently, by an oversight, he had left the first speed gear on, and had no sooner started the engine than the powerful automobile shot across the road, the driver leaping swiftly aside and narrowly escaping being knocked over.

On the other side of the road there is no parapet separating the river from the road, only a gentle grass slope running from the sidewalk to the river's edge. As the car sped down the bank shrieks from the two children and the nurse were followed by a loud splash as the automobile plunged into the river and sank in thirty feet of water.

Not a sign of the car appeared above the surface, and after a few seconds the eddying water became tranquil above the grave of the children and nurse.

PROLOGUE

The little one ate toast and cheese and kissed the cloth with buttered lips. The older chose a soup and sipped it plaintive from her spoon. Napkin in her lap, poor love, ever obedient, white lace twitching in the breeze. This crumb-coated pair, arms lifting for Mama, only know to take in love and churn it out again, offered up still warm from the soft shell of their delicate hands.

What is love but fingernails and backward glances? Picking the pills from the lace laid square at her neck, the girl smooths with spit the cotton rose pinned over her heart. White socks and soft shoes, sleeves like diving bells. The tailor blessed this dress and wished her well, stitching her name into its seams: Deirdre, ever serious, minding her manners while the grownups talk.

Her brother, Patrick, fresh as cut grass. Buttered baby in a high seat, soles of his kicking feet soft as a calf's new cheek. Flour-skinned in curls, knowing without lesson the whole of love in golden waves. Patrick of the rumpled pleats, framed in red wicker. His sweetheart mouth! That handsome hair!

He fusses when his toast is gone and gnaws the cloth his papa presses to his face.

There's a winsome Pop, collar sharp and tied. The man feels most at home in a city that bears and shares his name, a proud piece of him inked on every calling card, cut into doorframes and hanging signs as greeting and deference in one: Paris. He came here as a sweet young man and grew to become as hungry and moneyed as the city itself, as damp-spirited in the mornings, as shining after dark. He skims the paper's late edition, twisting his thick ring as he reads. Black onyx in gold, a gift to himself for his most recent birthday, rare only in the sense that he usually doesn't need an excuse for extravagance. The resident men of Neuilly-sur-Seine retreat at the sight of him. They crowd the corners, hands to their lopsided mouths.

The body is a column. It begins with each foot steady in the dirt, rock-long fastened to the ankle, shin to knee bearing the pelvis, that busy fulcrum, friend to the waist, spanning wing from root, the cup of power and the seat of it. The belly and back, jaw to the trunk, its sternum a wagging tongue. And there, buried in the rib like a line of charged powder, the solar plexus. Its ray powers far-flung satellites of the hands and mind, belly and breast, shoulder and sex, willing the feet to move. Any café in the world is a crowded constellation of these rays, a sea of waves, cut with men bearing cakes and tea on silver trays agleam through the drizzling spring.

The head waiter distinguishes himself immediately from the rest. The tallest among them, he works the patio on his toes to avoid ladies' skirts and discarded silver, dogs using their own thin leashes to strangle themselves among chair legs, baguettes upended from inexact baskets, three pigeons angling at a forgotten slice of steak, a nosegay trampled to a purple smear, a pat of butter rolled in a grime comprised of chalk dust from the specials board, the dried mess from a practical-minded prostitute, and half a handful of sand from Sausset-les-Pins hitched on the suitcase of an old man who has just this afternoon returned, for the last time, from the sea.

The waiter leans benevolent, a cyprus over scrub, gracing the service with a subtle pot of tea, its silver spout an extension of his hand. He slides a cup without comment out of baby's reach. His vest cinches with a polished clip, but he is otherwise unadorned: collar loose at the gentle skin of his neck, shoes free of hook and eyelet, hands bare to the unlinked cuff of his whites. His chin cradles the thin rind of his lips, browline carved with the blade of a boning knife. He draws a silver file from his vest, easing crumbs into his cupped hand before he slips away.

Following him means keeping close as he goes, dodging lesser staff as he vanishes to all but the one tucked into his wake.

The two of them glide inside to find a slick-walled cave of bolsters and peeling paper, a pastry case flanking one wall. A bulb strains to light an empty booth where a pile of cloth napkins await folding beside a bowl of soup.

By the booth, a bannister, from which a painted white birdcage hangs. Two wood-carved lovebirds touch beaks in a permanent state of distant affection. The stairs rise to another floor, growing darker, windows painted shut beside another set of stairs that lead in silence to the attic, where the wet jewel of a rat's eye glitters to witness the single cot and basin in a room where the waiter sleeps. The day the others find the head waiter dead, they will bury him in the back under a sack of flour, and the rats will bring their own dark offering.

The waiter examines a haze of sickly tarts under glass, selecting a square of lemon cake to place on paper lace as a warm hand lands gentle on his gut. He tries to go, but it holds him still. The hand moves with enough leisure to belong to him, but with his own two in sight, this third is curiously foreign. Searching for a witness, he finds only the wooden birds.

The strange hand is joined by a second, and the pair slide across his slim hips. In watching the birds, he misses his silver file slipped away, a souvenir, before the hands twin themselves around his trunk, spreading to root at his waist.

The lemon cake shudders on its tray as a woman arranges herself before him. The waiter sees her shoulders, broad and bare, stretching two ways her smooth expanse of skin. His father, who sold cavern stones to sculptors, once found by touch a precious marble and laid it into his hearth as proof of his skill, a daily lesson for his boy, born with the man's ears but not his gift, dull-eyed in the cradle, like a fish his mother said, but here it seems the son has found a monument to make any stoneman dash rasp and hammer to the ground—

On a sunny street in the Paris neighborhood of Neuilly-sur-Seine,
Paris Singer takes a dire inventory of their flat

None of it turned out as he had imagined. He blamed this on his own
distraction, which kept him from looking too closely at the details when
his agent found the place. There had been problems at the time with the
property in Paignton, and in the way a simple pendulum swing can describe the boundaries of a man's entire life, his attention to one meant
neglect of the other.

In the Paignton home, which his father had named Oldway and
lately had come to live up to its title in the failure of its various fixtures,
Paris had sunk months into work. There were problems with the old
foundation, sun-stained paint flaking on the tennis court, plans for an
updated garden, which would need a season to seed—there would be no
spring party, the girls would be disappointed—and all of it had made
him eager to find something simple in France, somewhere close to
the theater district, but not so close that they were sleeping in the wings.
He wanted it ready to move in, large enough for the children to have their
own room.

He allowed his local agent to convince him to look for furnished flats. Working out the details personally would have ensured a more precise result, but his agent made the point that as much as they all would have liked to see it, they truly didn't need the chaise to be covered in worsted serge so that Isadora reclining might resemble a handkerchief laid across the breast of a royal officer. Paris meant to trust people more, and as an exercise, he allowed the local man to make the arrangements.

And so, of course, they arrived in November to find his rented flat on the drafty third floor of a thin-walled walk-up, the soft wood of the stairs sinking under their feet. The entry door was painted thickly shut in its frame and he had Isadora and the children stand back as he threw his weight against it, cracking it open to reveal a junkman's collection of furniture and fittings scattered across a dismal set of rooms, a cemetery view on two sides, and an ominous spot on the kitchen floor that smelled strongly of kerosene. In the children's room, an old window had been jammed open and nailed into place, ensuring that the street's black ash would leave a leaden crust on their beds and a ribbon of filth would ring the tub after every bath. The only advantage was a view of the river, which wound its way across the west-facing windows. Isadora seemed to appreciate the jagged strips of half-torn wallpaper, speaking brightly of the bohemian aspect and going on about her early days in Europe, though later, when she couldn't find a proper punch bowl, she sank into a malaise that required three days and a trip to Printemps to cure.

They stayed through the winter, stuffing rags into the children's open window to keep out the cold. The nurse reported that the children had invented a game they called Urchin, wherein they covered themselves in soot from their toy chest, and spent many happy hours cleaning the fireplace. Patrick was too young to understand the game, but Deirdre was an observant one, and though the nurse tried her best to press *Little Lord Fauntleroy* and other mannered texts into her hands, she was interested only in the children she saw in alleys, speculating constantly about their lives and begging their humiliated nurse to introduce them. Deirdre had naturally decided that the other children were also playing a game, that they already had their breakfast and would run around and dirty themselves heroically like this until they were well tired, at which point they might find their nurse and go home to have a rest before afternoon lessons.

Leaving Isadora to deal with it all in her disinterested way, Paris spent most of February addressing labor concerns at the factory in London, but he returned again in March, hating the flat even more on his second arrival. It was worse than a hotel, where at least the things were cared for and a pleasant anonymity greeted him each morning. In a hotel, broken dishes would be cleared and thrown away, but at the flat, Isadora liked to keep shards of china in a paper bag on the counter. She talked of arranging the delicate filigreed pieces to make something even finer than what was broken, but she had no technique for it, and the bag ultimately gathered more of the ever-present black soot, as it waited for its chance to upend shards over whichever child found it first.

The accident happened early in the afternoon, after lunch. Paris had enjoyed a satisfactory pot-au-feu with beer. The other patrons exercised their usual theatrical shock over the children seated among them, but they all looked away when Paris turned to confront anyone directly. Isadora seemed near tears when she returned from the ladies' room, and he understood in her expression the feeling of endless scrutiny.

With lunch coming to an end, they worked out the schedule for the rest of the day. She wanted to return to her studio, citing some vague assignment that would keep her there for hours. It was obvious when she wanted them all to leave her alone. But Paris didn't want to be saddled with the children either—quite literally, as ever since Ted Craig had uncovered a pint-size saddle in some filthy Florence shop, Deirdre took every opportunity to strap Paris in and goad him across the hardwood. So he ordered their nurse, Annie, to take them home for a nap, and he trusted that she would tidy the place before he returned.

The afternoon settled, they parted with kisses. Isadora went one way up the street, Paris went the other, and the children went with the nurse to their death.

He would learn almost right away. He hadn't even sat down behind his heavy desk—a pity, they would have to move it back to England—when he saw from his window an officer running up the road, pushing gentlemen and ladies aside and sprinting knees-up like the anchor in a four-man relay. The door downstairs swung open, and he heard the man taking the stairs two at a time. As the steps came closer, they grew curiously softer, and there was a strange silence until the officer burst in, at which point the noise of the room returned, accompanied by a low humming tone that reminded Paris of the waterlogged feeling of coming out of a swimming pool. He was tapping his own head curiously as the man delivered the news.

He gathered his things, canceled his afternoon meetings, and followed the officer back to the flat. Though the officer would later report that Paris had been terribly dignified about the whole thing, there wasn't a single noble urge in his mind at the time. It was relief he felt, as plain as day. The tragedy he knew would ruin him had come at last, and he didn't have to dread it any longer.

The children and their nurse had been riding in the back of the car when it stalled. There was some trouble with the engine, an issue Paris had known about and should have had fixed; he and the driver had briefly spoken of it the week before, passing the time.

And so when the car stalled that afternoon, the driver thought nothing of it. He left it in gear when he got out to crank, and it wasn't long before the engine roared to life. The car lurched forward; he had failed to block the tire or account for the angle of the road. The driver leapt away in terror as the whole cursed thing rolled its three screaming passengers across the street, lurched over the thin ridge of curb, and tipped face-first into the river, where it bobbed once and sank like a fat stone, ten meters down.

The officer told him all this on the walk between office and flat, having taken the report from the driver. He seemed particularly pleased about the fat stone bit, the officer did, and opined that the whole automotive craze was perhaps too dangerous for women and children.

They arrived at the flat to find that half the city had come to gather and were walking from room to room in their street shoes. Someone set out a plate of hasty sandwiches, and Paris watched in humiliation as everyone took appraisal of the place. To distract himself from their judgment, he tried to remember the old catalog of fears he had once felt for the children's safety. The bag of broken plates, for example; he always thought one of them would turn it over their heads, ceramic shards working into their eyes. He was certain that Patrick would squeeze himself through the open window or that Deirdre would choke on a button in the back of the closet where she liked to hide. When they went off with their nurse to the park, he thought of the mangling lower branches of the trees, of steep drops from rocky ledges, and he was never fully soothed even when they returned home as safely as they always had. Isadora always teased him for his concern, but in the end it was as if he had known all along.

The room's nervous conversation dwindled to silence. Isadora had arrived on the arm of one of the neighbor ladies to find twenty strangers staring back at her. She put her bag down by the door and looked around, uncertain why everyone was there, and why they all seemed to be waiting for her to speak.

"But where did they go?" she asked.

The women around her collapsed into hysterical tears, and she reached for them, confused. Paris thought she had lost her mind entirely, but it turned out that her question was only natural; the neighbor who brought her said only that the children had gone.

Finally, someone told her, whispering in her ear as she brought her hands to her face. She stared at Paris as though he were a stranger to her, and in that moment, she was a stranger to him as well.

The room started up again, as if everyone felt ashamed by their own witness. Paris was swept away by the details of the coming days. There was the official inquest, the coroner's report. The press had a particular interest. And then the public events; there would be a viewing, a ceremony, an interment.

A downstairs neighbor kept trying to get Isadora to eat something, and though they all had lunched not an hour before, it seemed crucial to the woman, who came to Paris in tears, pleading with him. He added it to his list of things to do, along with selecting the music for the funeral program and setting up a meeting with the coroner. The neighbor insisted on following him into the children's room and watched while he dug among the dolls and books until he found a cup from Deirdre's tea set, rubbing the soot from it with the corner of her bedspread and leaving a black mark on the quilt. This further upset the neighbor, who fussed over the mark, spitting on it and rubbing it onto itself, which only served to set the stain.

Defeated, the neighbor turned her attention to the little cup, remarking that confronting Madam with the child's things so soon might damage her in a permanent way. Paris dismissed the idea. Miss Duncan would be all right, he said, careful to stress her unmarried name as he always did with people he didn't trust. The formality inspired a comfortable decorum. And anyway, he reasoned to himself, Isadora was far too strong to be felled by a symbol.

Finally the woman left, taking the teacup with her and leaving the quilt behind for the maids. He heard her calling for Isadora in the other room, employing a tone of voice as if she were trying her best to coax the other woman into a cage.

The press report arrived with the late edition, and someone read it aloud: The three victims could be heard screaming pitifully for just a moment before they went silent, and though a number of men dove in after the car at their own peril—Paris knew this to be true, having personally shaken the wet hands of those would-be heroes—their actions came with no result. The current was too strong, the water dark and cold.

Hours passed. Women poured wine into Isadora's teacup, and she drank it daintily, asking for more. They presented her with tarts from the shop below, which she mostly ignored. When she refused food on the second day, they mixed a little melted butter into her wine and she took it just the same.

While she was turning up her nose at cheese and charcuterie, Paris dealt with the inquest against the driver. He thought that learning more about the mechanical failure behind the accident would bring him some peace, but it only troubled him more. He returned again and again to their casual conversations about the engine, and remembered saying nothing on other occasions when he saw the driver leave the car in gear. He pitied the man, who was no doubt grieving in a lonelier room, his children looking up at him with wide and wondering eyes that would soon enough hold the knowledge of what their father had done.

Through it all, the flowers. They came by the cartload, and visitors arriving with their own bouquets were instantly shamed to silence by the cut garden that greeted them, every countertop and closet in full bloom. Isadora made a path through a pile of white lilies on the floor, calling for more wine in her little cup, though she knew full well where it was kept and could pour it herself if she wanted. It disturbed Paris to see her so obedient, but it did give him the freedom to arrange things without her looking over his shoulder.

The days bled together. He thought pleasantly of an hour draining into a surgical tray as he prepared himself for the coroner's early report, which arrived in a crisp ivory envelope. Inside, he found a description of the water in the children's lungs and the fact that they were discovered clutching Annie, which Paris took to mean they had learned enough of death to fear it. It wasn't specified in the report, but he heard from the coroner's assistant that the strength of the nurse's grip in death was such that two men had to use an iron bar to pry her off the children, that the prying broke both her arms, and though she had been dead for twelve hours, the coroner still set them in splints as if they might somehow mend.

Paris wanted to keep Isadora from all this, and so he saw to it that she spent her days writing letters and taking a series of luxurious baths, which seemed just fine with her. The women kept her teacup filled until she was quite well tippled, and soon enough she took on the affect of a lesser monarch receiving dignitaries, propped up in an overstuffed armchair, to hear condolences from friends and neighbors, gossips and well-wishers, officers, and aspiring members of the artistic community, everyone coming through to say their piece and touch her hand. She entertained them all, swaying a bit as she fingered a golden tassel affixed to the hem of her robe. He watched her from a distance as she smiled gently at her guests, speaking of the children in a low voice, as if they were only asleep in the other room.

19 April 1913
Teatro della Pergola
Ted Craig, Direttore
Caduto dalle Nuvole
Firenze

Teddy—

They won't let me leave but I realized I'm free to write to whomever I like and nobody else will do, my dear. All men are my brothers and you always were, even in those early days when you snuck into my bed, like a brother so sweetly you did lay your hand, and so I must ask you to make a study for me from a few simple materials.

This favor is something I ask most seriously of you, most reverently and relevantly as Deirdre's father, which makes you a brother greater than blood to me; brother of my heart, which governs my blood. I hope you will return a full report care of Paris Singer at our flat in Neuilly. Only write his name and they'll find it. Nothing is too much for the afternoon mail, Teddy, you know that as well as the postman.

I assumed you're working late and so addressed this to your office. I suppose you're arranging Rosmersholm as an Egyptian temple, Eleonora

Duse your kohl-lined Rebecca; so much to enjoy in Italy, the whole population of Florence are actors and one gets to watch these lovely scenes in shopwindows all day long. I hope you're having fun and not in too much trouble. I'm sure May keeps you in clean cuffs and hot meals, bringing lunch to the theater herself; something thin, a broth, which you'll pour on a plant behind the building the moment she goes. Now your image is clear to me—wrapped in a light coat, fumbling for your cigarettes. Hello, my dear. I hope to send you some stagings I have been working out in my mind, which you should find highly appropriate once word arrives of what happened. Condolences given and received, you need not mention, I'm so tired of hearing them!

Keep this letter and consult it on your way home; you'll have to make a quick stop. On the tram you could perhaps meditate on the idea that we are dear friends now and owe much to one another, and I have not lately asked anything of you. I can remember the last time we spoke, over lunch, when Paris and I were passing through and you focused sullenly on his vest as if you had just ordered one for yourself in precisely that color, and May was there, happy to drink our champagne and curse us quietly—do send my regards—and at that pleasant lunch I could have allowed Paris to continue his interrogation on our early years, forcing you to speak of those nights in Belgrade, but I kept conversation blithe and lively, on some silly subject—that's right, the preparation of eggs, regarding which I am sadly ignorant—and while May went on about warm coddling you touched the tip of your shoe to my ankle and I knew it was in thanks. But you see, I would never force you to suffer a thing I would not readily suffer myself, and so you must realize the importance of this letter and its simple but essential requests.

When you arrive home, drop your bags in the hall and sort out your folios in a way that will ensure you won't be thinking of them for a few hours at least. If May inquires, say you're clearing your mind with an afternoon stroll. You might have some pet name for her, Lump or Dolly, which you should employ so that she returns to her book on benign nettles of the East Indies.

Before you go, however, you'll need to sneak upstairs and find one of her heavy woolen dresses in the old style, which surely she packs in paper in a trunk at the base of her bed or perhaps hangs in an armoire—search your memory to recall when you've seen her lifting the lid on a long box, the kind you might use to ship long-stemmed roses. Remember the ones you brought to the Tavaszi? In a box with precisely those dimensions but not quite as nice, you'll find a dress—take the whole box if you like and your mackintosh if you fear a storm. (No, no of course, not a single fear! *Sans limites!*) And a pair of her shoes, any will do but ideally something at the back of the closet; she keeps the ones that pinch her feet, and when she sees they're gone she will be secretly relieved. Some people are only truly glad when the course has been changed for them, so they can complain all day long and wonder how life spins so swiftly out of their grasp. Perhaps you could leave the house now, as you read this. I cannot bear the thought that you would be delayed even a moment, even to the end of the paragraph, to the end of this line.

The trick then, once you've gathered these items and brought them to the riverside—sorry, yes, all the way to the Arno—is to find a place somewhat secluded, perhaps up a bit from the Vespucci bridge, where those sweet trees overhang the water and there's a bit of shore. I never thought I would have time or reason to sit and think of every river I have ever known, but here we are and I've found I remember a surprising lot of bridges walked in love and solitude, waterways discovered in those sweet brief moments when I first arrive in a new city and try to take it in before it fades into my memory of every other place. Hopefully you brought your mackintosh; it's possible, now that I think about it, you'll be out there for a while and you might like to take a seat on the wet ground. I remember your mack hanging flanklike in the Moscow flat, proper soaked after one of those nights, ho-hum. We were so young! Though you brooded too much to ever be truly.

I trust you're at the river. You can imagine my jealousy; all we have of nature here are flowers. When the man tried to deliver more we begged him to take some away, to drop them on doorsteps down the street or perhaps to other towns if he could, but he returned, his load untouched. Nobody wants the curse of them. They were a comfort before every room was packed with dahlias and creeping vines, white roses and tulips in jam jars, chamomile stinking up every corner, mums balancing on the sills, an entire bedroom packed with lilies I can't bear to witness. The table is set so tight with peonies it appears to have elevated three feet and grown thick enough to make a fine funeral bed, needless to say this has ruined peonies conceptually. We've run out of space for gifted condolences and can only accept simple words which, as everyone has swiftly found, are not enough.

The stain of death sets at once. I thought at first that if I could only keep too many people from knowing, perhaps the few of us who did know could will it out of being, as if the whole thing was my own anxious invention, an illness I spread to others, a curse that knowledge had borne and only ignorance could reverse. Now it's too late, of course. The florists, finding their entire stock depleted, began to bind dandelions and breadbox poppies from their window boxes with leftover twine, pasting calligraphic sentiment on wooden cards, *Praying for You in the Storm, My Dear* and similar, soil flaking from the stems, a clutch of weeds wilting in newsprint—one thing the papers are good for lately, to wrap a junk bouquet. The man refused to take them back so we pried a board loose in the ironing cabinet and started shoving them behind the wall, and once that space was full we backed a dresser up against it and commenced to filling the drawers with gifts of food, which I personally plan to forget. Three weeks from now, the caretaker will hopefully smell it.

Thinking of You at the Arno. What a lovely postcard you would make! Never mind the circumstances, I'm sure you'd think of me all the same in such a pretty place. The bank is low and grassy, its small stones washed over. Earlier I drew cold water for a bath and observed it both lying in it and resting beside for some time but could not get the same sense as the actual rushing thing. Of course they pried open the door once I really got to splashing.

This powerless ignorance is making me feeble. I hope you will forgive me for involving you in all of this. My questions are as follows:

1. How heavy does the dress become when soaked in the water and would it be quite impossible to move while submerged and thus saddled?
2. Of the shoes, do they shield against the shocking cold or do they only sink like stones?
3. What is the quality of vision underwater? Does the sunlight find some straining use?

4. What is it like to be fully submerged? Does the rushing aspect lull the senses, or do you panic when you lose the surface?

Use your senses in roles both protective and investigative to explore the environment as best you can. I wonder about the reeds and the rocks, the sense and sound of the current, and the quality of the dress, if it would snag on things underwater or ward off hazards like a woolen shield. There's so much I don't understand, you see, it becomes impossible to sleep even with a strong sedative. That old dress will see some destruction in the process, in case you were wondering why I enclosed the money. She won't miss the shoes.

Paris is meeting with the men from the cemetery now, sorting everything out. A very convincing act of practical diligence. But if there is anyone out there who might understand me without pity, it is you, Ted! If you were here, you would help me escape, and we would run to the river to find the answers for ourselves. There is so much we must learn!

Paris manages the mourning and generally keeps himself occupied

The condolences would need to be organized. There were six hundred cards and letters by his estimation and counting, from old friends and dignitaries, patrons of the arts and former lovers, and the mothers of students. Propriety demanded that each one receive a response, and Paris estimated that it would require forty-four hours of work from an assistant he would need to hire for the purpose. He began to price it out, idly, on a notepad, while his guests talked. The assistant would need skills in both penmanship and composition, which would mean a surcharge over the rate he paid his usual secretary, who would take down shorthand all day but couldn't compose an original sentence to save her life.

Isadora's sweet sister, Elizabeth, arrived and stood quite still by the door, as if instead of coming in, she would very much rather be tasked with holding everyone's coat and hat. She was taller than Isadora and nearly as lovely, though she had a loping limp and a bad habit of averting her eyes that made her seem to hold hidden judgment on any group. She was a fine teacher, and Paris was impressed with her work managing the Elizabeth Duncan School in Darmstadt, a program that was nominally hers though it was funded by him and supported ideologically by

Isadora. Her man Max Merz was with her, looking very much like a coat and hat himself. They huddled together as Paris approached.

"Darmstadt weeps with you," she said, taking a quick step forward to embrace him. The strength of the Duncan women was always a surprise; Paris was not a small man, but he felt squeezed like a bellows through every one of their embraces. After a while she released him, and he caught his breath while she frowned with the same expression she might direct toward a particularly complex jigsaw puzzle.

"There is no more heartbreaking loss than the loss of a child," Max said, adding: "we came as soon as we heard."

It occurred to Paris that every one of his guests, on the walk up to the flat, must have worked out the first thing they would say when they arrived, but nobody had thought beyond that. Perhaps they assumed a litany would be presented in return, the details and minor gossip they craved laid out for their enjoyment. Paris resented this lack of forethought; he himself suffered the type of mind that was more likely to pursue in advance every avenue of conversation to its inevitable dead ends, its detours around the weather, scenic routes past politics. But he tried to be patient with Elizabeth and Max; they were family, or close enough.

"Your love for them remains as enduring as our love for you," he said grandly. "Come now, join us." He sent the both of them into the main room and went back to work.

A little planning would avoid a larger inconvenience later on. He resolved to store the children's things locally until he decided what he would do with them; perhaps an auction for orphans, or a sale. And then there was the problem of where to send Isadora. She couldn't stay in the city, that much was clear; the scrutiny would be too much for anyone. Perhaps he could arrange to have the sisters sent away after the service. An island on the Mediterranean would be ideal, somewhere restorative and pleasantly Greek. Elizabeth could plan a historical tour.

They would do well on Corfu. He would check the hotels for availability. The women would take in the sunshine and the good sea air. Perhaps their brothers could accompany them. Gus was arriving shortly from London, having canceled his tour, and would appreciate the chance to extend his travel without the arduous work of presenting any ideas of his own. Raymond would likely return after the funeral to Albania with his young wife, where he had convinced himself he was of some use to the refugees. Hopefully he would arrive in time for the service at least. The siblings were something Paris could arrange around Isadora like a defensive line ringing a city under siege. It was settled: he would send Gus and the sisters to Greece while he closed the house.

He turned his mind to the rest of the week. There were notices to write, and statements to the press. They needed to formally dismiss the inquest against the driver before the attention on it got out of hand. He had to source the proper clothing for the service, likely for everyone. Isadora could wear the dress she had worn to his mother's funeral, and they could find something to fit Elizabeth for both the service and her upcoming trip to Greece, as her traveling clothes were stained and her slight valise suggested that she had forgotten to bring a change. The children would wear white. Patrick could wear his christening gown if it still fit—they had both sprouted up in the past month and Patrick had gained at least half his weight as his hems had all lately seemed too short, even after the woman let them out. Paris suffered, imagining his boy's baby-fat arms squeezed painfully into the white sleeves of the gown, though it would only be painful to witness. None of it would hurt the boy, of course. Nothing at all would hurt him ever again.

19 *April*
Teatro della Pergola
Ted &c &c DA LEGGERE PRIMA

Ted—

I'm having a little trouble imagining anything outside of this bath, which at the moment is taking on the clammy temperature of human skin. Happily there's enough of a sill to write. A religious woman recently advised me to picture God as a kindly spirit cradling me in His palm but I could only think of the old grocer down the street who insists on sweating every piece of fruit in his dirty hand. Here in the bath my sense is distant and weightless, like a girl on a Ferris wheel who climbed out at the highest point, clutching a beam to gaze wistfully at earth and sky, unable to choose one or the other and waiting for the wind to make the decision. I do believe I have lost my grip.

Before they haul me out of this water, pack me into a black drape, and roll me into some airless church, I wanted to send you a little theatrical staging. (No mood for dance at present.) Still waiting for your response on the previous, though perhaps you're too obedient. I would like your thoughts on the following as well.

Consider HECUBA, daughter of the king, mother of Troy, finds her
children murdered after no fault of her own, as far as I can recall:

ACT ONE. Hecuba paces her chambers fore and aft, her sense a
mounting dread. The floor's rut suggests she's long gone fore and aft
like this, fore to choose a glass from a tray, something to shine on
her gown, and aft, turning the fruit over in her hand—a dressing
gown, something linen—before placing it on a sill, and fore, holding
herself close, arms wrapped round her trunk, an apple tree lonely for
her fallen fruit, and aft, watching the door as we all have once or
twice but held, fore to her trodding path, her mind's line with the
wooden slats, and aft her trinkets are fore strange despite their standard position sapped of the aft she saw in them before, when the man
enters with the body of her son, drained of blood and drowned, his
body which she sees first as her own but then, her son, her boy, she
falls over him screaming, every sense wrenched by force, sorrow
stuffed through lungs and hauled from her mouth, she barely takes
a breath before they bring her girl, her sweetest only girl-child,
run through with a spear, and between boy and girl a pool of traitorous bloody water seeps into the path her feet have carved. We live
to fill the rut we've made. More screaming at this point, end of
ACT ONE.

ACT TWO, her home has burned to smoldering ruin, drifting ash. She
wanders the scene, tracing her son's name into the char of the frame
and her daughter's into the hearth. *But where did they go?* Coming to
her knees, she tries to bury herself, slowing as she sees the futility and
turning over onto her back.

The audience shifts in their seats. Hecuba rolls onto one side and
falls asleep. The men and women of the audience murmur and watch
her even breathing. They menace the evening's program in their hands.
A man calls out from the third or fourth row, a startling sound. Someone groans—a woman, disturbed at her proximity to the scene. She
fears the theater's influence on her own family, her small children, for
what young mother isn't wary of witchcraft?

The groaning spreads across the group, rising in tone and volume until the crowd as one makes an oceanic vocalization, a crashing cry, gripping the arms of their seats and swaying to stand. They rush the stage and pull the actress into the gallery. As they take her into the darkness, it's impossible to tell from her expression whether she means to fight them off or not.

Elizabeth holds court in the flat on Rue Chauveau, an unfortunate view of the river visible from most windows

Isadora brought another letter out from the bathroom, seeming unaware of her own nakedness and trailing wet footprints that burst their bounds and sank immediately into the dry wood. It appeared she was already drunk, though the guests hadn't yet finished their morning coffee.

"Go back in," Elizabeth said, shaking the water off the letter her sister handed to her. It was addressed to Ted like the other three. No storm could keep her from that snobbish son of an actress—who as of late had gone a bit husky, if press photos were to be believed. He had never been kind to Elizabeth and had once remarked in front of everyone that he suspected she exaggerated her limp to appear more interesting. But no matter, he was a glorified set designer who had an idea that he understood theater because his mother had forced him as a boy to busy himself sidestage.

Isadora obeyed the order and returned to the bathroom, walking as slow as a queen, and they all saw the petulant shake of her naked rump as it rounded the corner. Elizabeth was annoyed to see Max making a point to look away. He obviously didn't know any better, having met

Isadora only a few times in person, but acknowledging her scenes only served to extend them further.

Paris would be away at Père-Lachaise all morning, leaving Elizabeth to manage the rest. She wished it had been the other way around; she used to love walking through the old cemetery, a beautiful wild garden lined with the apartments and marble bins of the dead. She liked to take an apple with her, fantasizing that she was an enchanted princess with the power to revive the suitor of her choice by spitting a single black seed onto his monument.

It would be different now that the children were there, she thought, and realized with shame how flip she had been, playing fairy games with the thousands interred. This was punishment for her easy attitude. But it was better, really, to feel it now; otherwise she would have mentioned her stupid game at a party, and the gentleman she was talking with would turn and walk away and later she would learn that the man's dear father was under a slab on the Chemin du Bassin. Shamed, she would never have a chance to explain herself, and never would learn if it was grief he was feeling, or simply the knowledge that she would never, ever choose someone's old dead kin over Oscar Wilde.

Elizabeth turned her thoughts to the conversation at hand. It was her responsibility to host, as Isadora had spent most of the afternoon in the bath, but the formality of the job bothered her. She felt like an arbiter reporting for duty, a docent tasked with clarifying biographical detail and ensuring nobody ran off with the silver. The visitors—all strangers to her—had been talking idly of the children for hours, pausing for long stretches of silence and starting up again. They spoke with tender familiarity despite the fact that none of them had ever actually met Deirdre or Patrick, children being generally not invited to the performances and parties. Max told a story of having once witnessed the children at a reception, which included a heavily embellished conversation he claimed to have had with Deirdre as an infant.

Of course, Elizabeth didn't have much more experience. The only time she met Deirdre, the girl was more of a sentient bean than a human child, and she had never met Patrick at all. Still, blood being stronger than knowledge, Elizabeth was declared bereaved-adjacent and given a wide conversational berth. She half-listened in case talk turned to dance or to Germany, or general thoughts on the quality of sunlight in Père-Lachaise. The whole morning had put her in a bad mood. These strangers had arrived with breakfast and stayed through the morning. It was too late to put out a guestbook now; they would hate her for her thoughtlessness. She desperately wanted them to talk of something other than the children, the accident, which she was doing her very best not to think about. But she could never change the subject and risk showing her callous core to her guests. Perhaps Isadora would come out again and do something truly unbalanced, harm one of the guests or herself, and they could enjoy a thick hour of speculation about her sanity. Elizabeth was hoping for a scene. It would be something to do.

A busy café across from Père-Lachaise Cemetery, spiced tea highly recommended

The burial man asked to discuss details over breakfast, which put Paris off right away. How could a man in his field not have the good sense to meet with the bereaved in private? But Paris determined to soldier on, not having any other choice and anyway wanting to keep an open mind. Père-Lachaise was the best cemetery in town, as far as he knew or cared. Surely this man Étienne was aware of the subtleties of his own industry.

He watched as Étienne tipped the counter girl a silver franc and squeezed through the dining crowd to claim one of the delicate chairs wedged in the corner. He was a large man, made larger by the confined space. Pinned there in the corner as he was, it seemed as if he were preparing himself for the crypt.

"We all of us express our sincere condolence," Étienne said, shifting his body to lean the bulk of it against the back of the chair beside him. The man occupying the other chair frowned and leaned forward to make room. "To know the love of a child and then to lose it is an unimaginable tragedy."

"Thank you," Paris said, looking around. "I wasn't expecting this café to be quite so bustling."

Étienne lifted the croissant to his face and smelled it before taking a bite. "There is no comfort in the world at such a loss and no comfort in others," he said. "You can only look to a God, who you find to be ever distant, and turning away." He took a sip of his hot cocoa, which had been served in a wide-mouthed teacup.

It was early still. Their fellow patrons were a mix of men who seemed to be on their way to work and men without a clear destination, all dressed for the office but idling over the paper or chatting among themselves. It was impossible to distinguish any of them by rank, and they each seemed uniformly satisfied with the morning.

"Of course we will spare no expense," Étienne said, fingering the filigree of the other chair. "Not in the service, the viewing, or the processional. The very best for all. Along those lines, you might consider again the beauty of the *sépulcre familial*? The family crypt, in Père-Lachaise, has no equal. Only there will you know an earthly monument to mirror the splendor your children have found in Heaven."

Paris found himself imagining Deirdre and Patrick playing in a heaven set up like a cemetery, hiding behind headstones and tall trees.

Étienne wrote a figure on a bar napkin, pushed it toward him, and turned to look out the window, where a pair of women rushed by, bundled against the morning. "Unimaginable," he said.

Paris could appreciate a salesman. His father had considered himself an inventor first and would have papered the parlor walls with blueprints had his wife allowed, but he was a salesman at heart. Another man botching a patent application was the only reason Isaac Singer arrived first to market, the technicality saving him from a life spent peddling his nine-hundred-stitch-a-minute marvels from the back of a scrapyard truck. He might have been happier, but he wouldn't have been nearly as rich. Isaac well earned his own marble mausoleum, which he commissioned long before his death so that he could personally express his displeasure at the work. This skepticism was the most useful trait father passed on to son, so while Paris could appreciate a salesman, he would not suffer a fool.

"We have decided to pursue your crematory service," Paris said, folding the napkin as if he had spat a piece of gristle into it.

"Your wife, then," Étienne said, pressing two fingertips to his broad lips, "she is not a Catholic?"

"My wife," he said. From his breast pocket he drew out the cheque that would secure the service. "Miss Duncan is the mother of my youngest child. She is the singular mind behind an artistic form that aims to usher in a new kind of movement. She is a great many things, but she is not my wife. You might spend your days among relatively silent companions, but I'm certain you know better than that."

The other man coughed so heartily into his cup that the cocoa splashed back onto his face. Watching him clean himself, Paris worried for a moment that the man was innocent. But no Frenchman would lay down a silver franc without motive, and the counter girl looked guilty enough for the both of them.

Étienne picked up the cheque and folded it crisply in the middle, marking the seam with his thumbnail. "Of course," he said, with the nonchalant attitude of someone who had been given a trivial piece of information, the cost of oranges or similar. "Miss Duncan was a vision at the Châtelet."

Paris thought back to the performance to which he was referring. Sitting in the Théâtre du Châtelet was rather like being held at the center of a beating gold-gilt filigree heart. The gems on the ladies' gowns spangled the room but Isadora was the brightest of all without a single bead or ornament, able to consume and process the electric light before sending it in waves across the assembled crowd. Étienne may very well have been in attendance, though tickets were expensive enough that he would have to be skimming something from the cost of every burial. Paris watched him unfold and refold the cheque before tucking it into his breast pocket. It was good to know with whom he was dealing.

The social mourning continues at the flat on Rue Chauveau, hazy with cigarette smoke

Gus arrived at last, beating the afternoon's light rain off his coat by the door and ducking down for a kiss from Elizabeth. Word of the accident had arrived in London before his first matinee, and he found himself stifled, gasping through his longer monologues as if there wasn't enough air onstage. In hindsight it lent some legitimacy to the character of Narcissus, the thought of himself so delicate in his own mind that even a moment of silent contemplation by the pasteboard stream took his breath away. And though the trip to Paris was an incredible expense, he undertook it immediately, reasoning that he had been meaning to go anyway and that Margherita, heavily pregnant, must have been craving some time alone, for when he told her he was going, she went to her room and locked the door.

Elizabeth took his coat, a very nice camel hair he had bought the moment he arrived in France with the last of his up-front money. He was pleased to see his sister appreciate its quality. "She's in the bath," she said. "Come say hello to everyone."

He looked over her shoulder to the crowd in the sitting room, which looked like a strange spiritual meeting: the ladies in black, the men holding their hats on their laps. None of them seemed to be speaking, though when he looked closer, he saw one of the women directing something toward her folded hands. "Who are they?" Gus asked.

"I don't know," she said. "If you introduce yourself, they might tell us."

Elizabeth was such a nervous creature. It had been years since he'd last seen her, on tour through Germany—Margherita was only his costar at the time—and though Gus felt impossibly older, he found his sister very much the same, peering around the corner as if anticipating an attack.

Someone brought a plate of smoked salmon in from the kitchen, and the guests leaned forward to pick at it.

"Buzzards," Gus muttered. "You know, if you didn't want to ask their names, you could have put out a guestbook."

She winced. "I think some of them are promoters."

This immediately improved his mood. "Maybe they will be interested in bringing my show to town."

"Not every moment bears an opportunity, Gus."

He shrugged, watching them eat. "You'd be surprised."

"I hope they won't stay overnight," she said. "The man is supposed to bring the children here tomorrow morning, and then we'll all go to the cemetery together."

"Which man?"

"The man from the morgue, with the children."

"How macabre!"

"He insisted. There is some artistry involved in their presentation, apparently. Paris spared no expense."

"They'll most certainly stay to see that."

She sighed. Clearing her throat, she got the attention of a few of the guests, who were swiping the last pieces of salmon through a dish of crème fraîche. "Look, everyone," she said, "Augustin is here."

Teddy—

They've laid them out in the sitting room. The sitting room! Two doves nestled together on the chaise, two halves of my broken heart drained of all its blood.

You must imagine it though I'm certain you'd rather not, and I must describe it to you though I would obviously rather forget. This is the duty of the living, the curse on those who must walk on as the dead find their rest. You should find a quiet place to sit backstage, perhaps near that cubby where you hide the gin.

Paris insisted Patrick wear the gown we bound him into for the over-wrought teatime we called his christening and had a white dress found somewhere for Deirdre. He wants to make sure we won't be barred from the parties thrown by the devout next season, always the best parties around. I do remember your mother bought Deirdre's first christening dress, and all complaints aside I did like that dress, and I do hope she is well, your mother, I miss her very much, send her my love, all of it! Box it up!

After a long morning of dread and speculation the children were unboxed and brought in holding hands. Two men had to maneuver them awkwardly through the door, tipping their bundled bodies upright like a conjoined set of porcelain dolls before laying them out on the chaise. Fortunately I was asleep when they arrived and only heard these details later.

Elizabeth woke me to say they were in the other room, and I was very confused, thinking for a moment that it had all been a terrible dream. Once I remembered the morning's itinerary, I was afraid to move for fear I would be sick. I thought that perhaps if I could convince Elizabeth I was ill, she would let me stay in bed, but she pulled me to my feet, talking of getting things over with.

She helped me into the other room, and I saw them there, holding hands. The men who arranged them couldn't have known, but it was precisely how they tended to sleep, holding hands like that, one leading the other into a dream.

I stretched out face down on the floor and crawled to them as if it were one of our games. We loved our games very much and had some favorites which retained their charm no matter how often we played. Patrick had an after-dinner habit of hiding under the table and startling the adults, which of course was great fun whenever we had a party over for dinner. The first time he did it, the nurse tried to pull him out and he screamed and kicked at her and the second time he actually bit her, catching a tender place on her hand between her thumb and pointer. He was a toddler then and half-feral. She went to whip him but I made a small scene, stripping to the waist and offering my back in his place, and ho hum! Of course we had all been drinking some, even Annie, who burst into tears and ran to the bedroom where Deirdre was sweetly reading. Following Patrick back under the table, I saw how the wooden legs made a strange forest and the funny way the feet shuffled about depending on their owner's mood.

Patrick was the observant one, though Deirdre could better articulate; she often interpreted his tantrums. I could picture the two of them as adults, traveling to cities where she might give lectures on artistic invention before he took the stage to introduce his choreographed masterworks. They held the very best of all of us, you see, and none of the awful bits.

The two of them holding hands were silent as I crawled to them there in the parlor—*naturally so*, Elizabeth would say later, *and one would hope*—but everything has felt so impossible lately that in a strange way anything seemed possible, breath and movement not the least of it, not even from the dead. I felt a strange peace when I approached them and none of the horror I feared, for it was the two of them there with me and there was no strangeness in it. I kissed their bellies and held their sockied feet and my hands grew cold as theirs seemed to warm. There was another possibility, that everyone was fatally confused; perhaps the water had merely shocked the life temporarily out of them. If warmth could return, then breath would not be far behind, and holding them close might inspire some life. As their bodies took on more of my heat, I began to think we might meet mild-blooded in the middle. We could take this show on the road! How strange we would be, how unique! It was only when I tried to take their clasped hands in mine that I found I couldn't pry them apart.

It wasn't a natural bond, despite how it seemed. They had been forced by the undertaker into this little play of clasped repose. I felt the hard ridge across the baby skin on the backs of their hands where he must have tightened a belt. When I tried to separate them, I found to my horror the line of pale thread that stitched their palms together, holding Deirdre to Patrick and keeping them there. They were sewn and sealed with casein glue, fixed for the viewing.

Poor Deirdre! Who hated sticky hands and, despite our pleas and threats, was always dunking them in her water glass to clean them. And poor, sweet Patrick! Who never could be held in place, who even in his sleep roiled like a restless sea.

A keening scream spread swiftly from my body to reach the walls and floor. It made a residence of sound echoed through my empty core, my ribs a spider's web strung ragged across my spine, a sagging cradle for the mess of my broken heart.

Their flat on Rue Chauveau, every light on past midnight

They were teaching one another deeply inappropriate songs of Irish mourning when Paris arrived back at the flat. He was about to cast them out on their asses when he saw Isadora's blissful face, her telltale half-sleeping sway. He was drunk too, only modestly, having stopped on the way home for dinner, where he was easily steered toward a bottle of fine Bordeaux. Gus and Elizabeth had both grimaced up at him with expressions of suffering saints, but hours after he said good night and shut the bedroom door, it sounded as if they were happy enough to lead the singing. Elizabeth's man was there, and Paris tried earnestly to remember his name. He had known it before. They were all dressed in black for the funeral in the morning, and they would surely stink uniformly of cigarettes and whiskey by the time they piled into the pew beside him. And cheap perfume; one of their visitors seemed to have marinated in the stuff like a chippy sardine. Retreating to the bedroom he could smell her through the pillow he pressed to his face.

Rolling onto his back, Paris stared up at the ceiling. He could never sleep when others were awake, a habit he learned as a child. His father worked through the night on his patents and, on realizing some altering detail or improvement to his plans, would cry out, startling the dogs and children and throwing them all into a frenzy. The breakthroughs had a terrifying ecstatic quality, and Paris would slip out of bed to watch from the top of the stairs as the man mopped at his face, muttering *Draw the stitch by the shuttle* or *Frame the friction surface, of course of course*, and pacing the length of the kitchen. Isaac Singer's children—there were twenty of them at the time—quieted their sniffling to hear the incanted phrases as they one by one returned to sleep, dreaming of production lines. Paris stayed awake the longest, not daring to leave his perch in the stairwell, ready to spring into action if any of his father's sounds turned out to be the death throes they seemed to portend.

Hard work was a necessity at the time, if the Singers were going to improve their lot there in upstate New York, where bitter cold was met with an exceptional bitterness among people and his father was eager to escape life as a factory warden. Isaac kept his promise to make his name and never return, but the old homestead would always mean something special; as a grown man in New York, Paris often found himself walking idly north from the Singer building on Broadway, as if a magnet were drawing him back to Pittstown.

It had been quiet pandemonium all morning at the flat. The undertaker had apparently delivered the children's bodies in a massive wooden box, something that might otherwise store an oversize wreath. He finally left once every single one of the guests had plied him with enough compliments to his craft to last him the season and enough money too, of course, from Paris.

Everyone had their hand out lately: the officers who kept a crowd from setting up camp in front of their flat; the men who dove in after the car and came to offer their condolence along with a passive remark about leather shoes after a soak; of course the clothier in Italy who had stored Patrick's christening gown and the tailor as well. Ted Craig had contacted him to ask for money to travel, and Paris threw the wire out before fully considering it, though he was satisfied, thinking about it later, to find that his thoughts on the matter were the same.

A glass shattered in the sitting room, and there was a second of silence before they all screamed with laughter. Paris had the uneasy sense that he should be out there with them, that his absence would be seen as indifference, but he had already taken on the responsible role. If he went out now, they would quiet down, sweep up the glass and apologize. He hated the position he had placed himself in, relegated to his bed like a dog.

Isadora's voice rose with her sister's, the two of them braying "The Parting Glass:"

> *Of all the money that e'er I spent*
> *I've spent it in good company*
> *And all the harm that ever I did*
> *Alas it was to none but me*
> *And all I've done for want of wit*
> *To memory now I can't recall*
> *So fill to me the parting glass*
> *Good night and joy be with you all*
>
> *If I had money enough to spend*
> *And leisure to sit awhile*
> *There is a fair maid in the town*
> *That sorely has my heart beguiled*
> *Her rosy cheeks and ruby lips*
> *I own she has my heart enthralled*
> *So fill to me the parting glass*
> *Good night and joy be with you all*
>
> *Oh, all the comrades that e'er I had*
> *They're sorry for my going away*
> *And all the sweethearts that e'er I had*
> *They'd wish me one more day to stay*
> *But since it falls unto my lot*
> *That I should rise and you should not*
> *I'll gently rise and softly call*
> *Good night and joy be with you all.*

Of course, it was hardly notable that they would drink to the children. Only a few months back, Isadora had led everyone in toasts to their own health, the health of their friends and enemies, the health of persons known and unknown, to good fortune and moderate, bad fortune when it comes at the right time, to improvements in science and the arts, to sustenance and glory, the shipping trade, its sailors and captains, to moments of leisure and industry, to vital literature, good strong liquor, chocolate Napoleons, the human spine, oil and vinegar, fiscal irresponsibility, half-decent sunsets, the comfort of surrender, loyalty, cartography, friendship, and easy evenings. She could go on all night.

Paris turned his thoughts to the morning, which would arrive soon enough. He would hire a second car for the siblings. They were all set to arrive at the cemetery by eight, which meant he would need to start trying to get everyone up at sunrise. At the chapel, they would have to suffer through a visitation and another viewing. He would give Isadora a few minutes alone with the children or else he would hear about it for months—his coddling, her precious privacy—and then they would all go and have lunch and put the whole funerary business behind them. No life in it.

The crematory room at Père-Lachaise Cemetery, where in the confusion of the proceedings someone allowed Isadora to sit unattended with the children

Of course they have a flooding problem. Once Étienne with the gastric eye burped his way through basic condolences, fiddling with the chain to balance the pin weights of the cuckoo clock in his office, I should have called for the car, written a note with varied apologies, and slipped out the side door, keeping my eyes trained forward in an only slightly conspicuous way as I slapped the color back into the children's cheeks. But duty makes a sturdy trap, hard to escape in the best circumstances, and so the three of us find ourselves penned in by death in a half-lit basement as upstairs they deal with a backed-up toilet. A stinking thin wash of sewage flows the length of the marble hall, finding the linen draped across the table on which the children are laid out. The dark water draws swiftly up the material, fluid ruin here again to remind us of its power.

Their bodies, despite the heat of the room, are even colder than before, refrigerated for the pleasure of their guests. Deirdre once set her bare feet on a skating rink and drew them back shrieking, but Patrick has steeped his whole life in palm-tested bathwater and never once met the cold which has him now. He shouldn't have known pain for years, protected until young love had him sobbing shamefully into fistfuls of spring roses. The world feeds us sugar and then crushes us in a single afternoon.

I find myself passing the time with sweet and familiar thoughts, like a tourist wandering through a grocery store stocked with items from their hometown. I think of Deirdre's pink toes curling against the skating ice, having removed her shoes and socks. She was meticulous, like Ted, and she liked to keep a list of all the items she had enjoyed on any given day:

> three dresses (long)
> two dresses (short)
> doll (rag)
> doll (straw)
> playing cards (half deck)
> clasp from Mother's sandal (brass)
> one lizard (wooden)
> orange peel
> cinnamon stick
> shoelace (half)

Happily she bore none of Ted's grumpy neurosis, caring for herself with the same detached interest she gave her inventories. She was thoughtful with her things, always searching for her special woven purse in which she kept her special pieces—buttons or perfect acorn caps, a doll's porcelain leg. She had that purse with her always; now, her treasures speckle the floor of the Seine like nonpareils on a cake.

But where did they go? I should have run before they told me. To the train station, riding to the farthest stop, to Russia! Finding transport further and further out until I was cradled in the wild like the stone in my own throat, exiled to a land where the children were neither dead nor alive, and in that permanent uncertainty I could live and work. I have built my world around the feeling of being tipped forward on my toes, gathering with outstretched arms the whole of life as a harvest and releasing it without a moment's moderative thought to the potential for that energy's extinction. But here it is, proof of the world's end.

Étienne asked me to knock when I was ready to go but I'd prefer to stay forever. This is the columbarium, the interment room serving the entire cemetery, a city block of souls. Urns stacked to the ceiling hold the dust of a thousand dead, and the room is ringed with names, each tin plate meant to convey wealth to those who have never truly known it. In this dark hall, countless men and women wept with bitterness because they came to realize the mistake they made in thinking their love was stronger than death. The children and I are the central exhibit in a museum of failed hope.

I always thought that if I suffered enough in service of Art, if I laid down my life to please the world, I could live in peace. Now I know that the world will consume everything in its path. Art is not even an appetizer to the horrors of the world. The world consumes horror itself and savors it and is never sated.

My mind turns to regret, an emotion that has lately found an endless quarry in me, my mind's darkest tunnels bearing cartloads of salt for the wound. I torture myself with particulars. There was my choice of café, when cold meats at home would have sufficed. There was our very presence in France, which had seemed so necessary by a schedule of debuts and the promise of a new school. There was Annie, hired because her thin waist gave her quite the look of a lady; my bind to pride of impression despite all my talk of classical simplicity; my flirtation with the waiter, which clouded my intuition and sent me away distracted, embarking on a self-satisfied nap rather than my usual afternoon walk through the neighborhood, where surely I would have discovered the accident, stripped off my clothes, and gone down to save them. There was the practice I neglected in honing my intuition as a mother, as I've heard that good mothers know their children's thoughts even when they are far away; my waste of this intuitive practice on art; my inattention and laziness, which resulted in three deadly items of blind trust—in the hand brake, an item of such frailty; in the man who operated the brake; and in the world, to keep them safe. The evidence of my own failure lies in state before me and will be interred this afternoon in my heart.

The children and I suffer the indignity of one last waiting room, where my gown makes a cornered shadow. Soon enough they will be introduced to a chamber blackwalled with a sudden fire. What silly thing is art to fire?

This is our last chance to escape. If we found a car, we could make it to that country home we once visited, that friend of a friend's place with the small pond and pasture, a single sweet passenger train chugging by once an afternoon. Her name escapes me, the friend of a friend with a tray of lemon fizzes, silver cups sweating in the afternoon, the sweet little pond in tall grass, the children fascinated by a dying oak tree, the black lightning of its bare branches. If only we could leave here and travel back to that afternoon! We would arrive in these ill-fitting clothes, Patrick squeezed pathetically into the gown his father insisted on, owing to the expense in shipping it from Rome and its inherent blessings; Deirdre in a white dress the maid brought from storage, upon inspection clearly unwashed, with spots of fruit pulp at the collar from the day she insisted on blackberries for breakfast. How satisfying it will be to thrash that idiot maid! If it were her own child, she would have scrubbed that dress so well, the lye would rise up and fill the room, and everyone would come away from the casket with raw-rimmed and burning eyes, and there would certainly be no idle talk of the weather.

All this time I've been ignoring the other spirits in this hall. Dull and crowding, these ghosts hang around though they could take up residence anywhere: in the center of their childhood homes, above an old lover's bed, drifting through a lightning storm curled around the lightning itself, chasing it to its earthly end, crushing life and scorching a place on the earth. Despite all their freedom, they float obediently beside their own cubbied ash. Maybe spirits can enjoy only as much energy as they brought to life; most of them wasted their time on the planet and are damned to commune dully with similar ghosts, taking the days in measured sips, as on some broad human veranda.

Étienne in a coughing fit excused himself for what he declared would be our final moments together. But the three of us know these moments are not final: this is only the first shy conversation of a new phase. We've passed the deadline the risen Christ set in pushing aside the stone, which means I have to push aside the thought of them in some awful cave, soiled and sobbing, taking up their burial offerings and toddling into sour darkness so black that their eyes strain and soften, finding with their searching hands the occasional dead canary, which would feel to them like a rabbit's foot.

The children are alive, in their way. They persist, subtle and dormant, and their souls are tucked safely in triumvirate Mother. They have become the winter earth, which grows without our knowing.

After the ceremony, Paris finds himself kneeling before a rather unsettling depiction of the Seven Holy Brothers

Guilt, Paris found, was a sturdy emotion. It could keep for years in the temperate climate of memory, stacked like a hearty cheese among moldering rounds of love and fear. Guilt constructs a narrative: the old woman puts down her fork to think of a girl she shunned on the walk from school. The man pauses on his threshold to remember a dog he tortured with a firecracker twenty years prior. Guilt makes its own punishment: the woman buys ribbons for the children she encounters at the park, but they run from her, screaming; the man nurses a scrapyard mutt with rice and milk, wiping the stained mange around its mouth and crouching down to try to catch some expression in its eyes. But guilt is not a logical thing, a series of weights to balance. It is a carousel, hand-carved with all the choices its uneasy rider could have made. Here he insists they walk; here he checks the brake; here he sends their mother in place of the nurse; here he sends himself. The golden rings slip from his hands. He will reach for them forever.

Étienne had tried to bring some color into the children's cheeks with a chalky rouge that made them look as if they had perished in a circus accident. He was compensating for the unnatural color by rouging their arms and legs until Paris made him stop and wipe it all off. Étienne complained that the children looked far too dead, which was fair enough.

Isadora would surely complain later that there wasn't enough emotion at the service. There had been far too much for Paris, though; it seemed to him as if everyone were weeping, from the ushers handing out programs at the door to the drunks those ushers cleared off the burial monuments before the Mass began. Everyone in attendance held a handkerchief to their eyes. The chamber strings wept as they played "Death of Ase." The tears fell on their instruments and charted milky paths through rosin dust to well at their wooden lips.

There was some trouble with the fire downstairs, where Isadora had insisted on being left alone. Upstairs, Paris made a studious effort to pray as the bulk of the crowd greeted the family and left. He chose a neglected corner of the chapel. On the other side of the room, a pair of attendants started sweeping the floor. Finding he had nothing much to say, Paris picked himself up and went outside.

Elizabeth and Max shook the last of the hands as Raymond shuffled around in his robes like a dimwitted priest. Most of the guests had already left, along with Gus, for the bar. One of the few remaining carried a flask from the night prior, which he offered around. Paris drank and washed it across his gums. It was flat champagne, and warm.

He found himself looking to the horizon, in the general direction of Florida. He thought of his wife, Lillie, who kept a small house near the ocean and was raising their children there. He wondered if she still thought of herself as his wife; surely so, with a reminder of him at the end of her name and four more at her table. At that moment his girls were likely reading in the sunroom, having just gotten up and ready for the day. He found himself wondering why he left his old life, considering all that leaving had gotten him.

After the children are taken away, Isadora addresses the residents of the crematory hall

Damned ghosts! Only the living can know me. You wailing mothers and widowing men, moaning about like children, playing at sadness as if you can even recall it. You hazy physicians can't harm me any longer, you snake-oil spirits. You would lock me in a white-walled cell, but you have no weight to throw against me, do you! I will bind and curse you, and torture you with a lesson you can never learn. Only try to move your arms to greet me!

The baby stretching to take the world delivers a performance to which the rest of us can only aspire. Watch in wonder at a baby freshly born. Our book of natural movement has been buried so deep within us that its pages have become general, merging ten into one, those first perfect movements fading into the story of our first words.

Simply stretch! You could pay good money to learn this simple pose, but no amount will buy you ease. Your fear builds a thick foundation, and when you try to stretch, your solar plexus makes a fist in the core of your body as shoulders and throat seize above as if hung from far-strung wires.

Every gesture of surrender is built from control! At shoulder level, raise forearms, hands extended gently from the wrists. Taper the movement in each hand like a conductor drawing a phrase to its end between forefinger and thumb. The movement fails you! The disease of twitching logic ruined your hands the day you learned to write your own name. A curse of cursive! Your own mind drags you into its ruin and locks you there for life! Only death releases you from the prison you built yourself, and now look at you, wishing only to stretch.

Goodbye, dull spirits! Practice three times daily and you might begin to feel it. If you can will magic for me in exchange, I beg only one thing: that in the moment the water was pressing in on all sides, their fear was gone, and all that remained was the sound of their own heartbeats thumping in their ears, my babies knew once more the comfort of the womb, the ease of being carried through the world.

The ride home is delayed by an accident between a tram and a horse

The horse laid out on the pavement was draped in flowers. Its rider, picking himself off the sidewalk, was also formally dressed, and declared to passers-by that he had just come from a wedding and had lost his hat. Weddings bothered Elizabeth. The false finality troubled her, the optimism of death parting a pair who would more likely be destroyed by boredom. Funerals, on the other hand, were always a strange comfort. At least they delivered on the eternity they advertised.

Raymond had arrived after the service began, strolling into the memorial hall in his tunic and sandals like a drunken Aristotle. He and Elizabeth never had much to say to each other, rather preferring to level a mutual judgment that satisfied them both. The service was uneventful, sweet even, with a charming small chamber group. Isadora made them all wait for the cremation, and the family obliged as even the most stalwart guests and most of the press went home. When Isadora came back up from the columbarium, she saw Raymond at once and threw her arms around him. He always was her favorite. His late arrival forgotten, he seemed happy enough to leave with his sisters while the men sorted out the last of it. Max stayed behind as well.

Isadora claimed that she wanted to have something to eat, but when she got into the car, she lay down on Elizabeth's lap and fell asleep.

"The service," Raymond said.

"It was lovely," Elizabeth said, "so lovely."

It had been lovely enough. She had found a guestbook at last and taken it out to the gate for the reporters to comb through, aiding them with the spelling of names. One of them had asked if the grieving mother had danced during the service, and Elizabeth delivered a withering glare that was apparently interpreted as a confirmation; people worked hard to support the ideas they already believed. They were hungry for examples of Isadora's callousness, but Elizabeth hadn't suffered that callousness in silence her whole life just to give it away.

"So lovely," Raymond said, as if he had been there to see it. "It was just what they would have liked, the poor babes."

It was a bizarre supposition, and Elizabeth disagreed sincerely that the children would have liked one second of the funeral, but she didn't want to start a quarrel. Instead, she stroked their sister's unwashed hair, finding an ornamental comb that must have been placed in there days before.

It was impossible to know what the next year would bring. There was the question of Isadora's touring schedule, which Elizabeth immediately felt low for even considering; of course it would be scrapped, and any upcoming seminars and lectures as well. Singer was sending them both to Greece, and Elizabeth was happy to go, knowing what it would mean for Isadora and anyway needing a vacation herself. Max could return to Darmstadt and manage for a few weeks without doing too much permanent harm, and Paris would support them all financially in the venture so long as Isadora didn't cross him in an actionable way.

The accident on the street had drawn a crowd. Men were running up to help the passengers of the tram, which had partially tipped and was leaning dangerously against the curb. The man with the horse was asking if anyone had seen his hat. The poor horse might have broken its front legs, though it was hard to tell from a distance. Elizabeth missed the old carriages, with shades that could be drawn over their windows; trapped behind the accident in the backseat of the touring car, she felt like the grand marshal of a sadistic parade.

In Elizabeth's lap, Isadora snored. Last year, she started including press clippings in their recent letters, letting them speak for her; the critics were astounded by her latest work, dances that seemed extemporaneous but which reviewers witnessed her execute again and again, every performance flawless, her students frantically notating in the wings. The social reporters tried to turn the public focus to minor scandals, such as Raymond wearing his toga on the streets of New York, but nobody among the Arts pages could ignore the fact that she was doing the best work of her life. This was a key moment in Isadora's career, which made it a key moment for them all. And now every venture, every lesson, every curtain would need necessarily to pause.

"And with good reason," Elizabeth said. Raymond startled but didn't respond.

Through the front window they could see the horse's legs jutting up from the street.

"Looks bad," Raymond said.

"How is Penelope?"

He gave a dolorous shrug. "How are any of us?"

"You don't have to be so dramatic."

He turned to her, and she saw that his eyes were red-rimmed and sunken. "The children are dead," he said, his voice ragged. "They're dead."

"But your wife is still alive," she insisted. "We are still alive." She wanted to say more but stopped herself. It was impossible to reason with any of them. Everyone wanted this crisis to bring life to a halt, to stop the Earth from turning while they found some sense in sunlight, but Elizabeth knew better. Understanding the road that lay before them wouldn't make it any easier to walk. They were obliged to take one step and another, stumbling over themselves as the larger dance was revealed.

On the Greek island of Corfu, the craggy jewel of the Ionian Sea
and a favorite of Kaiser Wilhelm, who used his holidays there to pursue
amateur archaeology

Clouds upon clouds. The quality of air by the sea suggests some process by which the whole of the atmosphere is scrubbed, wrung out, and hung up again. Endless layers of fresh-washed clouds press upon one another, each of them as thin as a veil over a woman's body, over her face.

Corfu bears a steady flow of visitors on holiday, and a few sailing skiffs lashed to the low port welcome the daily ferry. It's quieter out of town and nearly catatonic on the farther beaches, where locals claim the rocky grottoes and lay planks to span the rocks like fingers on an ancient hand.

Elizabeth walks with me, the two of us arm in arm like old friends. She holds the jar of ashes I gave her and limps along sad-eyed, so kind to take a leave of absence for a grand adventure with her darling sister, whom she loves very much, clearly.

Yesterday we made a slow tour through the market and bought yards on yards of rose-colored silk. I paid the vendor before she had a chance to bargain, and she was cross with me for the rest of the day and said I only hate money because I have lately been spoiled. The silk was worth the fight, and we both wear lengths of it wrapped around us today, bound up by cords I found in the armoire. It drags along behind as we shuffle along the sandy path toward a promised scenic view, obedient to our guide.

Elizabeth requires some help as we go, ever unsteady on her bad leg and faking it just a little for sympathy, less than she used to. She plucks my hand off the raw place inside my elbow where I've been scratching. Pressing the spot with her fingertips, she comes away with a bit of blood on her fingertips, which she wipes on her own forearm.

It wouldn't do to stay in France, so Gus and Elizabeth gathered me up like our old days on the road. Memories! Our world was cradled in the pocket of a slingshot drawing back, and anything would send us flying.

In Greece we crawl like sullen ants. Elizabeth hopes we will soon return to normal, as if life can pause and begin again, a singer who lifts his hand to stop the music while he clears his throat. And so we make these convalescent motions by the sea.

Our old guide farmed this land and knows it. The path switchbacks endlessly up a steep hill, ridges jutting out where he grew kumquats and olives and some grapes. The path is edged with white stones the size of a woman's kneecaps floating in bathwater. His working days came to an end when an accident inspired his children to intervene, and now he sells a walking tour twice a week to tourists, promising some ancient artifacts along the way.

He introduced himself in Greek and Italian but insisted on English for us, though it is unclear if his knowledge of the language extends beyond the script or even if it includes the words he speaks at all.

During every pause in our walk, he launches into his speech, stretching in two directions to hold his wooden walking sticks, which he hangs between like the flag of an economically depressed nation strung up on a windless day. "The white cliffs cut a dra-matic sil-hou-ette along the shore-line," he says. "Simple to see the an-chor point 'fore the pier, har-bor to Ulysses, har-bor to Glad-stone." Each word lines up like an officer for inspection, remarkable in their uniformity from one to the next. It's possible he worked out the way the words fit together, by sound, memorizing them without knowing their meaning. His syllables emerge unnaturally fused, like babies conjoined at the skull.

He faces the sea: "The cliffs take their white co-lor from sand and stone which com-prise. One may see the gods them-selves to take a sun-shine trip on this path." The wind carries his words past us and over the rocky crag separating us from the water.

"Fruit and flo-wer abound on our kind isle." He spits onto a wall of stones that restrain a fat olive tree from falling four stories to the sea below. The three others in our touring party—gentlemen in spotless jodhpurs—list behind, throwing pebbles and pointing at times at the hills. A viewer from afar might assume they were watching a funeral march, an old man escorted to the next world by two draped angels with his faithful sons trailing behind.

Things would have been livelier with Gus, but his preparations for the day took too long, and we had to leave him at the hotel. He has al-ways been a deliberate man and careful with his things, taking hours to line up his morning supplies, inspecting the brushes and blades. Every picture of Gus features him cleaning his glasses. When he was a child, he scrubbed his wooden toys with a rag until he ruined the paint and was punished. It's better to leave him to his own devices as the rest of us go on with our lives.

The cliffrise extends a few hundred feet above the audible mess of foam and fish dashing against stone. It is a churning machine, an endless sound, soothing only in how it consumes all other sounds, inspiring a pleasant hypnosis; the sirens calling from their rocks may well have been the rocks themselves.

Sister says we're almost there, clapping in a manner meant to be encouraging. We've fallen behind the guide, who went on fifty paces before realizing our distance and now waits for us, his head lowered against the wind. The walk is pitiful work, but at last the path comes to an end at the cliff's edge.

Between us and the sea, a huge white stone in the shape of a horseshoe extends a few meters out, curving gently into blue sky. The width allows one person at a time to walk single file and observe the view. Sand and softer stone must have once held it tighter to the ridge, but heavy rains have washed it all away to reveal the promontory arch. Around the perimeter, a slack chain swings daintily between three upright posts. The flat sea stretches out before us, a banquet table cleared of its plates under a wash of electric light.

From a deep pocket in his vest, the guide produces an orange. "Please step to the rail, be a guest to my land, ob-serve the earth's boun-ty," he says, carving a thick rind of flesh with his thumbnail and flicking it off the cliff's edge, examining his thumb and then the fruit before splitting off a wedge and popping it into his mouth. "Miss," he says, addressing the both of us together.

"What fun," Elizabeth says, taking a healthy step back. The men excuse themselves down a side path. The red-haired one gave me a frank smile at breakfast back at the hotel. His skin is the color of a cloth-bound archive, as if cutting him open would release reams of pages. Bury all boys, burn the earth, and pave a road over the lot of it.

The guide stretches his walking stick to prod us forward.

"All right," I say. "I'll do it."

"Ob-serve the earth's boun-ty," he repeats, going back into his pocket and coming up with a pair of figs this time, months before season and green as grass. He chews one of them without seeming to register its bitterness. "Be a guest to my land," he says.

The wind roars vertically up the cliffside. The horseshoe stone is more precarious than it looked at first, bits crumbling sideways in the wind. I wonder how quickly the surface of the sun would end us were it to fall upon the planet, if we would have a moment of fear or pain or even a sense of warmth before we were crushed into the void. My hand catches the wind when I reach for the chain. The guide ejects a green knuckle of pulp over the edge, and it sails awhile before falling.

Elizabeth calls out bland warnings, seeming not to understand the simplicity of one step and another, as in all things, gaining ground, leaving only footprints to suffer the company of the fools who didn't try. The chain jangles on its rail, which rises only to mid-thigh in a way that would aid a fall rather than hinder it, turning a body right-side down. And so the things designed to keep us safe will kill us in the end. Such is life! Such is every day of life.

The guide continues, so drowned by the wind that I have to read his lips:

"Ob-serve the boun-ty of the earth, your step under-taken by only the bold-est man in the face of gods"—this amalgam presents itself, its meaning unclear—"boun-ty step and brave the farce of God." He says more, which I can't register.

"What's that?" I call out.

Sand scatters across the path. They sent the children's ashes after the service, and I insisted on taking them with me to Greece. Of course I wouldn't leave them with Paris to dump over some garden. I claimed I would release the ashes here, but as the days passed, I wanted them closer and closer. I was greedy for them and didn't want to share them with the world, and so when the time came to take this walk, I gathered ash from the fireplace into a jar from the kitchen. Elizabeth will see them go and feel some comfort, and it will stop her from asking me what we must do with them.

The real ashes have another fate: when I can get away with a sprinkle or a pinch, I take them in, bit by bit. I mix them with my food and drink. I feel exceptionally heavy these days, saddled down with potatoes and fish dunked in butter, my gut stratified with filo and sweet wine, courses taken at midnight and all hours of the day. It has come to be that I can eat only when the flavor is attended by the subtle ash of the children in my mouth.

The sun's steady burn dulls my vision to striations of gray and black. A sickly blue vein tries to creep across my squinting eye but is stopped by the relentless light, a swift and brutish elimination, so that every object within the walled city of my gaze is stripped of its variegated charm and bundled in soothing stone. The wind shifts to roar across the arch, bringing the guide's voice with it. "This is what she did," he says. "Think of this woman Sappho on the altar of love—"

Elizabeth runs up to him, shouting something and throwing her arms wide, the pink sail of her dress unfurling as she wraps both arms around his waist. They engage in a strange scuffle, where she seems to be trying to pull the man's staves away. I suppose she has never held much affection for Sappho.

"The broken heart's only cure is the leap," he calls, struggling against her grasp. "Feet bare on the warm stone! The sen-sation of that final flight—"

Elizabeth releases the man and rushes to the rail. She calls my name and speaks in a steady stream, and from what I can hear, she is accusing the man of inventing a story to keep people touring his old pasture, dismissing his apocryphal story for lack of romance, and insisting that I should already know that the true pleasure of life is in waking each morning to slice an apple, to enjoy a nice strong coffee with your dear and loving sister while brother reads the news aloud, stories of brave men saving women from burning row houses, of explorers on intrepid journeys to various frozen norths, all of them living to tell the tale. She reaches for me, calling my name.

It's fine it's fine, our ticking clock insists, it's fine, says steady heart and mind made for finer things than daily life; it's fine, the smallest parts declare, it's fine, rays screaming from the open breast; it's fine, the water a slab; it's fine, it's fine, a bird in the cage worth three in the car, it's fine my dear, it's fine!

The men have returned, waving their spyglasses like copper cudgels. One of them holds a dead squirrel bound at its feet with red twine. The man with the squirrel is handsome enough, with a flat nose as if broken by a punch. They stop and take in the scene, all of them smiling in the same deranged way, which must mirror my own smile. The squirrel watches from its dying eye.

Elizabeth's foot drags a gentle half circle in the dirt, its sandal cutting a scalloped edge. It makes a nice counterbalance with her arms, which reach for me; I must want to live if I'm motivated enough to think in choreography. The men watch her limp and pull herself onto the arch.

"Come on," she says. "Think of the good piece of meat we'll have for lunch."

"You know I don't take meat with any meal."

"Let's go," she says, trying to sound reasonable though her hands are shaking madly. On the other side of the world, Mother feels a chill down her spine as someone tries to take her place.

"I'll stay here for a while longer, thank you."

"Look there! Your shadow has already come down and is heading home for a rest. See it going down the hill?"

Sure enough, darkness leads.

"The water is cold along the strait," notes the guide, who has come up beside us. "Warm wind all through the year, many beach-going days."

"Oh shut up," Elizabeth says.

The men watch with amused disinterest. I'm snagged by their hooks, suspended on an invisible line. I'd rather they throw me back, my wounds healing in salt water, but they have darker aims. They want to flay me while I'm still alive, working their hands into my gut to find golden locks of hair and sandwich crusts and ashes, baby teeth and rattles, soft shoes and acorn caps. Open me up and find the full strata of my love! Serve it on a piece of toast!

Their hotel on Corfu, over a series of heavy meat courses prepared midday
for the tourists

"You would not believe our adventure," Elizabeth said. Lunch was served, the last dregs of morning chased off by steaming plates. They returned to find Gus in the parlor room, where the hotel kept its collection of overstuffed furniture smelling faintly of dogs. Gus had apparently not moved all morning, even when the kitchen staff came in to lay down a tablecloth and settings for the meal.

The staff had been overextending themselves in the kitchen to make the tourists feel welcome, and the heavy courses seemed to trouble Isadora, who had been off meat for some time, eating fish and vegetables like the principled little sophisticate she was. It made Elizabeth uncomfortable, which she expressed by making an aggressive effort to eat everything served and remarking often on the fine quality of the food. She swiped a forkful of steak through a sopping pile of mashed potatoes. "Wonderful," she insisted to nobody in particular.

"Look here!" Gus said, folding the newspaper around a photograph. "Our darling immortalized in stone."

Sure enough, the marble muse resembled Isadora very well, reaching to touch the sky beside Apollo, who seemed to be teasing her with a length of sculpted silk. The frieze had been three years in production for the new Champs-Élysées theater. Bourdelle, its sculptor, had come by Isadora's flat so often with his sketchpad that even his subject tired of the attention and encouraged him to go on working while she slept, her arms stretched above her on the bed.

Gus examined the photograph, sampling a kumquat from the center bowl. All of the Duncan siblings had been scheduled to appear at the opening ceremony, and the lilies the sculptor sent to the flat after the accident included a subtle note expressing the hope that he could offer his condolences in person soon enough. It was a disappointment to miss the party, but of course it couldn't be helped.

Gus deposited a bit of macerated kumquat into his napkin, examining the pulp before folding the napkin and placing it daintily aside. "And *Jeux* premiered, the sporting motif. Can you believe they pushed it through?"

"It was a fine walk," Elizabeth said. They were drinking wine from extravagant silver goblets. "If you wondered at our late arrival, we were simply enjoying the morning air and then a bit of the afternoon air as well."

"Can you imagine the reception, though? A tennis match!"

"Our guide was so funny," she said, patting her sister's arm, as if some gentle handling might inspire her to remember a fonder version of events.

"The dancers in sporting flannel. Avenue Montaigne would have burned on that alone ten years ago. And the ménage!" He removed his glasses, picking up one of the blue-striped linens to clean them. "My God, they'll hang Vaslav from a rafter."

"You've been away from Paris too long. Everyone likes a scandal now."

He tongued a bit of kumquat in his teeth before employing the napkin on it. "I suppose you would know, stuck in Germany. I wonder if he got his car crash in, it doesn't mention. Was it an aeroplane? My word." He dug at the kumquat with the napkin, ignoring a lady seated nearby, who observed him in silence for a moment before covering her open mouth and turning away. "He wanted it to be three men, you know. I wonder if he even presented the idea. Do you recall him saying?"

Elizabeth rolled her eyes in response. After a few days of Gus she missed Raymond's guileless sensitivity, his ability to weep over nothing. She wished she could combine her two brothers into one man, practical in all things, with a caring and awareness for others. It was as if the four siblings had inherited a different quadrant of their mother's heart, and each looked upon the other three as strangers, though they were separated by nothing more than a membranous wall. Elizabeth decided to change the subject.

"The guide held himself so strange," she said. "Between two tall sticks. You would have laughed and laughed. Of course we were just trying to stand upright ourselves after all the fun we had last night, isn't that true, love?"

Isadora was looking off. At Elizabeth's question, she took up her fork. "A straightjacket could barely keep me together," she said, spearing a carrot.

"What a week to be away," Gus said. "*Sacre du Printemps* next. Stravinsky himself came and showed us all the score one afternoon in London. He really did! Don't make that face, it's not flattering. I was sitting with the orchestra when he brought it out. He had the working score bound up in a case secured with three locks. We all came and had a look. I'll never forget how quiet they all were. The oboe hummed a bit of it but trailed off, and there was no other sound but the composer turning the pages. The principal violin sat down and started writing a farewell letter to his family. And now we've gone and missed it. Will you look here, later this month—" He went on like that, down each item on the bill at the Champs-Élysées, moving on to the revivals and other acts of small significance at the Grévin, then the Palais-Royal, a one-man show featuring a man Gus swore he knew, though not well, he admitted.

He was going through the student work they were missing at the conservatory as Elizabeth waited for him to lift his eyes. At last he did, buttering a second slice of bread.

"We are missing nothing in Paris," she said.

They both looked at their sister, who was staring dully at a curtained window.

"Of course," he said. "Of course not."

Morning lay behind them, paving the way for an afternoon of cards and visits from other guests of the hotel, which, if the previous week had been any indication, meant suffering through stories from dowagers about long journeys by rail, mistaking in the Duncans a sympathetic audience and launching into complaints of filthy conditions and the true lack of white flour, and at every stop sad, strange women selling faded bolts of fabric, the women's flesh matching the material so cleanly they both might have been woven the same day and would all crumble into linen dust the moment they were touched. The old tourists clearly failed to see their own resemblance. They shook as they spoke, as if the trepidation that came with age had manifested in their bones.

The dowagers tended to make their rounds the moment lunch was over. These women could talk all day about how similar every place looked to them, how unremarkable every parlor, and how much they missed their home every time they dared to leave it. One of them was working her way to the table to begin just such a story, dabbing the blood of a rare steak from the corners of her mouth. Elizabeth saw her coming and excused herself to the other room.

*Without Elizabeth to entertain, Gus does his best to make conversation
with the little genius of the family*

The headache wasn't helping, though Gus found some relief pressing the
sockets of his eyes with two fists. "Luminous shards," he said. When
he opened his eyes again, Elizabeth had aged fifty years, smacking her
lips as she started in on a story about the Dutch East Indies. A full minute passed before he realized it was one of the other guests of the hotel,
the woman who had spent much of the morning trying to engage him
in conversation while he dozed by the window.

Isadora was watching the woman with an expression that suggested
she was trying to solve a complicated mathematical problem. The old
woman was telling a harrowing story of survival in a hotel with only one
chambermaid.

"You've been having headaches?" Isadora asked, watching the dowager but speaking to Gus as if she wasn't aware the other woman was
talking at all.

"All morning long," Gus said.

"Maybe your body could properly breathe if you weren't stuffed into
a winter vest."

The old woman started in on a story about Charleston.

"You don't like the vest?" Gus asked.

"Your shirtsleeves billowing out like that makes your torso look like a chimney."

"That's precisely why I like it."

She adjusted the strap on her tunic, an elegant rose-hued silk. "It's as if your internal organs have chosen a new pope."

The old woman was picking at the carrots from Elizabeth's abandoned plate, squinting at each piece before bringing it to her mouth.

Isadora took up the silver creamer and lifted its dainty lid to smell it. "You should pray to Saint Lucy for vision. Send word to your patron in London that you have come to consult the saints. Perhaps he will be inspired to send a little advance. Money always helps me with my headaches."

Wrinkling her nose, the dowager excused herself from the table.

"Don't tell Elizabeth," he said, folding his paper and placing it before the empty chair, as if to suggest that the seat was saved for a man who would appreciate the daily news better than either of them possibly could. He took her hand. "I was thinking we could go on an adventure."

"But Gus, isn't life adventure enough?"

Across the room, Elizabeth and a cluster of Italians were looking through an album of photographs brought down from someone's trunk. All travellers want a witness, Gus always said, something to put their stories in context. Without one, they became strangers to themselves. "I've been reading a book," he said, watching the men. One of them broke from the group and strode purposefully across the room, his retreat drawing her frowning attention.

The Italian approached with a smile and took the empty seat. "Your sister is a candid woman," he said.

"Hullo there," Gus said.

"Very illuminating, in truth." He reached for the discarded newspaper. "I wanted to make your acquaintance as well. But oh—"

In hindsight, it might have all been avoided. Realizing his desire for a thing the moment it was desired by another, Gus tried to take the paper before the Italian got to it. The other man drew back, and in the confusion, one of them tipped a forgotten cup of tea across Isadora's dress. All three stood at once in an ovation to the moment, reaching for place mats and cloth napkins to soak up the tea, a strong floral variety. Everyone in the room stopped to watch as a healthy quarter cup of it seeped across her.

The men did more harm than good with the soiled napkins from lunch, leaving behind blots of oil and crumbs. A bit of the sour fruit Gus had spit out earlier dotted the very tip of her breast. The Italian desperately reached for a book from a nearby shelf, opened it at random, and pressed its pages to Isadora's hip. "Dear," he said, "oh dear."

Isadora, in the middle of it all, seemed the least bothered. She looked down at herself, where the soaked thin fabric stuck wetly to her skin, revealing with no subtle shading the expanse of her left breast.

"That won't do at all," she said, and if she hadn't had everyone's attention before, she got it with that. One of the dowagers slumped forward in her chair. Elizabeth put her head in her hands. Someone laughed in the other room, having already heard the story. Isadora exited the room with a flourish, and if she had returned for a curtain call none of them would have been surprised.

Upstairs at their hotel on Corfu, unseasonably warm and not much by way of windows

A fat old rug runs from one edge of the hall to the other, folding over it-self at the doorways to the guest rooms and offering thick shelter to ciga-rette ash and flattened crumbs, obliterating every hard corner and giving anyone walking through the hall the feeling of a blood cell squeezing through a fat vein.

A woman once worked the pedals of a loom broader than her spanning arms to make this lovely rug, easing back at times to rest on a rolled rug of lesser quality, one of her own early attempts. The finished product was sold or loaned or given in good faith, and the woman was paid or thanked or allowed to remain alive to make another, and the rug continued to exist beyond its creator's desire to know it. My body may move gracefully without attention but cannot move artfully without intention, and so my art will die with me. A certain sturdiness is asked of me! I am rug and woman both.

Our hotel suite is a well-stocked womb. Some Monastiraki Marie Antoinette had a glorious fantasy of what a French hotel should look like, and it shows on the tin trays stocked with useless little carved pieces, elephant figures in ivory and amber, and empty perfume bottles shaped like cut jewels and smelling of cinnamon and mold. The old armoire splinters at the base, but they did a fair job of patching it up with wood glue and covering the rest of the damage with a few strategically placed hatboxes. I removed six pinecones from a biscuit tin in the bathroom, poured in the childrens' ashes, and found they have taken on a pleasant woody flavor.

Removing my wet dress reveals in the mirror a slab of noonday flesh, belly puckered above the mound, strong legs drawing down to a pair of ankles that could stop a door. Under the thin skin of my doubled tit, fine blush organs hang sweetly from their skeleton frame. Arching back and bending forward, I go hand to feet in a dancer's hanging stretch. My bones complain, but the organs go along with their alignment turned entirely upside down. My liver and heart work some magic to keep themselves from tumbling out of my mouth and pooling on the floor. My body is proof of resilience and witness to it. Even if I had leapt from the cliff's edge, the men who fished me out would find me buoyant and bound, my heart and lungs intact in their human raft, holding out against the invasive attentions of fish and waterfowl. Deep in my stretch, my spine begins in gradations to ease.

Once during a period of nagging injury I was treated to an impromptu demonstration by a doctor, who held a rat's cleaned skeleton as he spoke. The animal evolved for a life of labor, he explained, tracing his finger along the bucked bridge of the rat's spine, showing how the bone and its attendant bits were supported by the four legs, the brain sending simple telegraphs to the heart and tail. But humankind, the doctor said, was unusual among nature. He tipped the rat so that its front paws reared in surrender and showed me the stress it placed on the hips. Mankind is born to bear its own faulty frame. The skeletal ridges of the human spine do their level best to lift the brain. Every one of us is born in balance, everyone stands to crumble.

Fingertips to floor become hands pressed flat and then, breathing with the body's need—draw in like a bulb sucking blood from an infant's mouth, hold and expel, the lungs compressing—the arms slacken and cross, wrist to elbow laid gently on a rug trimmed to uniformity, a million dyed fibers experienced all at once. This pose requires stillness, steady breath, patience, strong circulation, and a general stubborn nature. One panicked inhalation will send you falling back, and the brain's rational suggestions of surrender will have you stumbling over your own feet. The heart pounds, desperate to pull its blood back from the extremities. The solar plexus thrums.

What would it mean to follow my every impulse? I need to make water and without a second thought I follow my need, making copious water gloriously down both legs right onto the floor, something I haven't done since a performance years ago when I was heavily pregnant and too stubborn to feel shame. This time there's a strange freedom to it, and I watch it pool atop the rug for one arch moment before it sinks in all at once, the poor rug lying there as quiet as a lady and allowing it.

The door rattles, Elizabeth behind it entering. Crying out in surprise she hauls a quilt off the bed and throws it over me as if I am a pan on fire, adding such sudden weight that I collapse into my own mess, saying, "The sibling relationship!"

"They're weeping over your memory downstairs," she says, her judgment only slightly muffled by the quilt. "What are you doing under there?"

"I was just asking myself the same." A musty warmth under the quilt contains and cultivates my own animal odor. "Feeling rather ratlike. If only you had brought a cheese."

"The Italian is torturing himself with shame," she says, lifting the corner of the quilt. "You should come down and speak with him. He is a sculptor and says you are one of his greatest inspirations."

"I won't forgive him until he replaces my dress."

She tucks her head inside. "Everyone saw it happen and they laughed and he is ashamed."

"Very dramatic!"

"And you'll catch your death, running naked around your room."

"Could you have my mail forwarded to this quilt? I rather like it actually."

She crouches close as she did years ago when we were children, our hair frenzied across the blanket which served as stage and ceiling both. Our cloth dollies were dressed as we were, in salmon-colored nightgowns, and we would press them side by side to dance the *pas de deux* from

Blomsterfesten i Genzano, the ladies' promenade. Mine did an aggressive polka while hers, *en pointe*, offered the porcelain hand sewed at the tip of her rag arm and coyly drew it away. Then the solos: Elizabeth took hers by the head and twisted to wind the cloth body up before releasing it to spin underneath, the simplest execution of a *tour en l'air*, suggesting that the ideal form requires a freak quality of brain-based gravity anchoring gyronic limbs, overshadowing the technical perfection of my doll's *grands jetés* and creating a new and unsettling standard over which we would viciously fight, the performance forgotten. On one occasion she forced me to swallow one of the porcelain hands, and we had to wait days before it could be sifted out of the pot, rinsed, and sewn back on in secret, and still mother noticed and reprimanded us in her weary way, looking around for something to punish us with and ultimately having us shell walnuts for the rest of the afternoon.

Elizabeth's balconet nose twitches as she both smells the air and gives the appearance of smelling the air, an air of smelling, her theatrical gesture felt more than seen in the half dark. "Are you drunk?"

"I don't feel well. I'm coming down with something." Saying this makes it true—a weakening in the lungs.

"Fine, then. Come out when you're ready and not a moment sooner, lest you give the impression that anyone else has the least say over your mood, and thank you very much for dragging your brother and me away for a season to prove your point."

"Please send my deepest apologies to the Italian and dry his tears with your left tit."

The door opens and gently closes, and it seems she has gone, until I hear her sharp sigh and then feel the pointed little toe of her shoe, which lands well into my midsection before I can tense against the attack. The door opens again and slams. Elizabeth always has her say in the end.

Rolling onto my back to splay my gut to the morning air like a sunning crab, the quilt my seaworthy shell, my mind snaps at a morseled krill of a thought: Deirdre would have taken strong exception to this nakedness, her offense brought about on a child's boundless moral grounds—surely taught by some well-meaning nurse trying to keep her clothed in public— but sweet Patrick would have crawled in with me and played moo-cow until the bell rang for supper.

The whole cremation process came too quickly. Perhaps there was still some sense of life in them, some flickering pilot light; if we hadn't turned them to ash, they could have had the dignity of a gradual death. They could have held hands in a marble crypt and eased themselves into the slow way of the dead, which is so foreign to young life, keeping one another's secrets as they eased down onto the stone. I shouldn't have agreed to burn them, Paris made me do it. If it were up to me, they would be in there with a bell to ring in case we made some kind of mistake.

I spy with my good eye a rolled stocking tucked in the springs under the bed. It contains one of the crystal sherry glasses from downstairs, as thin as a fallen leaf with winnowed glass spurs. I've found rye makes a better friend than sherry, brown liquor being a warming spirit and rye as warm as a rug distilled to its essence. The stocking's patient mate behind the bed holds the pint.

A dram for the pair! Tippled to the crystal brim and raised to catch the light for a solemn oath:

> Blessed be my children, LORD—
> Bless'd be their hearts and the soft flesh of their hands.
> Bless'd be their hands in the hands of their white-capped nurse.
> Bless'd be their bathtimes.
> Bless'd be their wailing times and the curls framing their tears.
> Bless'd be the noses given by their fathers—one puggy, one
>   sharp—and the hearts given also.
> Bless'd be their shits up the backs of cloth pants to make a rind
>   above them.
> Bless'd be their spelling lessons and smocks and their books and
>   dolls, their traveling trunk.
> Bless'd be their dimples and the pinked flesh of their mouths.
> Bless'd be their mouths saying Love.
> Bless'd be their Love.
> Bless'd be their games made up with curtain cords.
> Bless'd be their hands, their mouths, their flesh,
> And bless'd be the flesh of my children, LORD—
> AMEN—

The story of a Viennese boy who became a German man, thanks in unlikely part to Benjamin Franklin

When Max Merz was a boy, he wanted nothing more than to grow up to become an intellectual. He was ten years old when he first had this idea, studying English under the casual tutelage of an American student who found in Max an eager pupil and extra income every other weekend at the Merz family grocery. To teach the boy clauses and tense shifts, the student loaned him a copybook featuring the writing of Benjamin Franklin. The words were designed to be traced, to hone penmanship rather than theory, but Max found utility in both. And so his very first experience with philosophy came to him in a new language. Florid and lush, Franklin's paragraphs bloomed in his own hand, the central tenets half obscured by his own understanding but slowly revealing themselves, the curtain drawing aside.

He began to take an immodest pleasure in his book each night, arranging himself by the lamp and touching the silver nib of his pen gently to his lips as a serious scholar might before tracing Franklin's words with passion and vigor, pausing at times as if he were inventing the ideas and then noting them swiftly, before they flew away. He repeated the action, laying sheet after sheet of parchment over the original and tracing until the words were etched onto the page.

Max loved the feeling of writing more than the process of thinking, and it was immaterial to him that the words he put down were not his own. He copied another page from memory, daydreaming of long nights at the dinner tables of his future professors at university. He would communicate with these men as equals and love them as brothers. Late into these intellectually rousing nights, the professors' young wives would pour themselves another thimble of port and smile at Max with the same tender look of sentimental pride they had once given their husbands.

Once he mastered every word and knew it all by heart, he took an empty notebook to a café. He seated himself at a straight-backed chair and copied the entire book from memory. It took a full hour to get everything down, including a short break wherein Max pretended to consult a menu. When he was done, he gazed at his work until eventually a man came out from behind the counter and chased him off.

Max took on more hours at the grocery and began making deliveries to collect an additional stipend. With his meager savings he bought a biography of the man, which included more of his writing. Franklin, who despite speaking of Austrians as stupid and swarthy, otherwise seemed like a worldly fellow. He pursued knowledge all his life. When he was twenty years old, he created a virtue list designed to keep the course of his mind straight through the wickering ways of adulthood. Even as a youth he appreciated silence and order, chastity and industry. It was as if he knew how powerful he would become.

Max enjoyed the biography, but the copybook remained his most faithful friend. He kept it under his pillow, sneaking a secret glance every night after he pressed his hands together and made the studious murmurings of prayer.

Keeping it close was his first mistake, he realized in hindsight; it would have gone completely ignored had he kept it stacked on the table with his ordinary school materials. His second mistake was in how he reacted the morning his mother found it.

She was changing his bedsheets when she found the book under his pillow and an unopened tin of tobacco under the mattress. She left the tobacco tin on his desk but brought the book to him, holding it pinched at the base of its spine like a rat she intended to thrash against a wall. His heart broke to see it like that, and he burst into shameful tears, further dismaying his mother.

Frau Merz was a devout woman, and hated idolatry in all forms. She was horrified to see her son following the dark path; as Nebuchadnezzar worshiped Daniel, so Max worshiped this American politician. Something would have to be done.

She pushed him into the backyard, where the first thing she saw was the bucket of muddy rainwater she kept by her vegetable garden. Taking him by the back of his neck and forcing him to his knees, she ordered him to put his beloved copybook into the bucket. He refused, hoping for a simple slap in the face, but she was coursing with horror at his betrayal and duplicity. In one motion, she tore the book from his hands and plunged it into the water herself, and when the pages touched the murky surface Max screamed as if bitten. He pleaded with her, sobbing, but she took both his hands and made him hold the book down until the bubbles quieted.

Finally, she let him take it out. The words had gone cloudy and slipped from their bloated pages. Max bowed his head and was sick. His mother watched him clean himself off, her anger turning to shame. As a kind of consolation, she allowed him to bury the book beside the turnips and left him alone while he said a few final words.

It would cost him dearly to buy his tutor a replacement copy, but the worst part of it all for Max was the feeling that he was burying Franklin himself, a man who had already suffered the indignity of one death and didn't deserve to suffer again. He scraped the earth over the ruined book with a sad little spade—his mother used nothing larger to tend her garden—and, wiping his face with a dirty hand, resolved that he would commit thenceforth his strongest-held ideas to memory so as to keep them safe. There in the garden, chewing on a carrot he had accidentally unearthed in the interment, Max made an oath in the man's memory and with the man's words: *Lose no time.*

Elizabeth returns downstairs to find the mood completely ruined

If anyone could make herself sick by willing it, it was Isadora. She was cruel with the power she held over her own body, the despotic ruler of a nation constantly on the brink of civil war.

Lately she was such a bother, but Elizabeth could remember a time when this power had served them all well. For years, when this party or that got too tight and someone had to answer the door to make apologies to the police, Isadora was the one they sent to play the virgin up late with her studies: *Of course, Officer, I'm only grateful you arrived* and *yes, these are all my friends from school, won't you come and join us for a tipple?* Whenever she met someone she wanted to impress, she would mirror their expression until they mistook her for a friend. Isadora was working so hard to make everyone believe she was unwell that she had likely convinced herself, but Elizabeth would not be fooled.

Romano was still too embarrassed by Isadora's dismissal, so Elizabeth left him to sketch by the window, blinking hard, as if he had a physical compulsion. Artists were so delicate, the men especially so. The Italian reminded her of her brothers, who had been dear boys and fearful of strangers. Perhaps it was how they were raised. Their mother involved them all in her anxieties and put on an elaborate show for Mass before divorce shamed her away from the faith. But even after they no longer had anything to dress for on Sunday, she heaped velveteen expectations on her children and treated them with an extraordinary care, which taught them to be extraordinarily careful.

Elizabeth remembered her gathering them all around the dinner table to tell them there was no God and no Santa Claus, that they had only themselves to guide them. Elizabeth as the oldest knew better than to believe this, having witnessed both transubstantiation and Christmas stockings, but Isadora took the note to heart and announced that she would find herself a job. That was how she started teaching dance, though she was only eight years old at the time and the mothers who brought their children by seemed more interested in child care than instruction. The family business was started, and everyone found their life's purpose. It was just in time, since Daddy had gone to Los Angeles, promising more ice cream on his way out, which poor Raymond would ask after for years.

Mother landed on her feet, as she always did. She doubled down on their training in Greek myth and encouraged them each to pick a muse: Raymond chose Clio for her books; Gus chose the globe and compass of Urania; Elizabeth picked dancing Terpsichore before her sister had a chance; and Isadora, pouting, went with Melpomene. They left California, and though Mother was right there with them from the trip to Chicago and then New York and eventually London, the Bay drew her back; she was a child of the Gold Rush, and never lost the foolish idea that glory was there for those patient enough to wait for it.

All to say that Romano, with his sentimentality and easy tears, had immediately felt like home. He and Elizabeth had enjoyed the Victorian photo album together, laughing at the clothes their grandmothers wore in their graves: leg-o'-mutton sleeves, funny old coats. Next to the pictures, Elizabeth felt like a goddess, bending solicitous in her tunic to hear Romano's stories of home, its mild surprises of climate. Even though he asked after her sister and she realized his angle, she still played along, answering questions about their working life together.

When he expressed his sorrow for the children's accident, she pretended not to understand his Italian. He repeated his condolences in

English, and Elizabeth looked back down at the photo album as if she could turn the page on the entire discussion. But it got even worse; Romano excused himself to speak with Isadora directly, and then the whole thing happened with the tea and she brushed him off. It looked for a moment as if he would follow her up the stairs, and Elizabeth had to hold the arm of her own chair not to spring up after him.

She found herself hoping that Isadora really was sick with something that might keep her in bed for a few days, long enough for the other hotel guests to lose interest. Entertaining strangers was bad enough without everyone bringing up the past. Elizabeth thought of the reception line at the funeral and how relieved she was to shake the last few hands, not realizing then how many more condolences she would have to work through, an endless line.

Their time spent between America and Europe, which Isadora chooses to remember with an abundance of fondness

A life in hotels!

We landed in New York and took a room big enough to lay out two mattresses, Mother on one and the four of us on the other. Most mornings, we rented out the room to teachers of speech and rhetoric, the students working through their fragments and surely wondering about the mattresses, which were leaned up against the wall as if the room had gone sideways. The students would clear out before we welcomed the afternoon's dancers, and then Elizabeth was so personable with the girls' wealthy mothers that they hardly noticed the condition of the room. We could have put up partitions and sold the early evening hours to boarders on the graveyard shift who needed a place to collapse, or laid panels of scrap over the beds and served coffee to patrons seated on the floor. Of course hindsight always reveals the best route. I always think of that first room as being just above Carnegie Hall, though this may not have been true; an old neighbor did play a viola most evenings, and in New York a proximity to greatness was always easy to imagine whether it was real or not.

After some success we moved the school to an unfurnished gallery in the Windsor Hotel. Gus found a dinner theater and Raymond found a library. The Windsor gave us a good deal on the expansive front room, in part because they wanted a cosmopolitan display and also because they hadn't yet had curtains installed. Mother, Elizabeth and I taught our barefoot dance to a growing brood, and we all did our level best to ignore the men leering from the street.

We believed that natural movement was the only path toward an ideal of beauty, and we pursued this idea seven days a week. It was around then we began encountering a certain type of dismissal from the mothers of our students. The mothers would wonder aloud why we didn't simply teach ballet, as we clearly had an aptitude for it. It was true, and Mother was even classically trained, though if ballet required a license, she wouldn't even know where to find a modern handbook to study.

These women—and it was always women who felt obliged to correct us—had apparently decided that there was one track on which artistic merit might run, making orderly stops to pick up and deliver their daughters. Ballet would transform their ducklings into graceful swans or at least cygnets in the corps. They couldn't understand the appeal of putting up master-class funds for mastery in a new form; it looked like artless play to them, no matter how many pages of notes we presented.

That was always the trick of my method. Even at the beginning it presented a simplicity that appeared simple. Watching the girls skip to cross the stage or bend to adjust a strap on a sandal, their mothers felt a nagging sense of familiarity. They could hold ballet at arm's length and leave it behind when they left the room. But this wasn't something they recognized from the ballet; they were watching their very own youth dance before their eyes.

The self-loathing rich were worst of all, having padded their nests with a working knowledge of technical dance. They hated to see their girls at ease, furious to feel conned into watching something they had already lost.

For us, the Windsor was a disaster even before the fire. It was a place of quiet cruelty, where even the man who unlocked the door for us in the morning looked down on us. When the place finally burned, Mother led our last few charges out, holding hands, and Elizabeth remarked in hindsight that at least none of us were hit by the ladies jumping from their penthouse windows.

We wouldn't stay where we weren't wanted, not for longer than a season. We had protected for too long the idea that New York would hold our fortune, but the hotel disaster showed us that if you can make it in New York, it means only that you've made it in New York, a city that holds as much loyalty to its residents as a child holds to a smooth stone in the presence of a pond. And so we hopped that pond to London, where we assumed our artistic merit would be given its due.

The only thing due to us, it turned out, was a few months on the street. We had more promise than money, which didn't work for anyone, and we were wild, our public scenes inspired by beer but made truly possible by the fact that we had already known some success, although we hadn't yet learned that success for artists isn't a permanent condition but rather one which must be perpetually reinvented.

Mother was there with us in London but refused to witness the spectacle. She kept to park benches during our first rowdy jags, no doubt wondering into the cricketing night how much she would give to return to the old days, though certainly those days weren't much nicer and we were at least out finding our fortune instead of waiting for it to happen upon us.

She began to quietly harbor the hope that some young man would arrive and marry off one of her lovely daughters. This was uncharacteristic of her; though she suffered through a true Victorian divorce and all the shame that accompanied it, Mother had nevertheless begun to make the mistake of thinking things were better when she was married. She had been scorned daily by Father's infidelity and his financial misdealings, but at least she had a roof, and the gossips were always so keen to know about her life that she could occasionally mistake them for friends.

She was still a handsome woman and charming enough, and we were humiliated daily to find her sitting with some young clerk or barrister who was eager to meet her beautiful young daughters and horrified to find us holding our own shoes and picking feathers from each other's hair. Sometimes they would give us a little money out of pity, which was the worst of all, but we had gotten far too used to food to ever give it up and so accepted what we were given.

Between this occasional charity and a brief nannying job on Elizabeth's part we pulled together enough for a locking door in London. Sleep
at last! Or so we thought. The hotel offered a shockingly low rate, and
soon we found why; the room was situated directly above a newspaper's
printing house, which would come to life around midnight when they
started work on the morning edition. The industrial roar shook us all
awake the first few nights, vibrating our series of stolen ceramics to the
edge of their shelf before they each dropped without ceremony to the
floor. After a few weeks of this, only one piece remained, a palm-size figure of a woman cast in porcelain that Raymond had nicked from a vendor of sentimental wares. She was our prize, sentimentality being in high
regard for us at the time; poverty always was attended by a kind of desperate magic. We started keeping our porcelain goddess under the kitchen
table, and every night she danced across the sloped and shivering floor.
Eventually we grew accustomed to the printing press. I even invented a
seizing dance to honor the goddess, but nobody much cared for it, and I
stopped performing it by the time we were booked outside London.

We moved from London to Paris to Munich. Hotels were such a condition of life that it began to feel as if I lived in a cursed room that changed
nightly, shifting furnishings and fixtures, swapping out occupants and
altering the view from its windows to confound me every morning.
There was always something to contend with in the hotels, which marked
the city for us forever. In Athens, a pair of brothers paid Gus and Raymond to fight each other until they were too bloodied to tell who was
who. In Vienna, a red-haired girl came to my bed one night and said
God had asked her politely to murder me.

I remember it as a happy time, but those were precarious days, and
total collapse was always near. Home was where we paid to stay, and
there was an unstoppable vibration under us, something out of our
control moving us from place to place. Newspaper ink makes me sick to
my stomach to this very day.

Those weary first days of success were plagued with the suspicion
that my career might be better served in New York or Budapest, perhaps
taking a more serious study of the body, adding upward of eight hours
each day by replacing the evening bacchanals with theories of being
and tall glasses of cold buttermilk. Every day I convinced myself I was

wasting my time wherever we were, so any move at all could be made on a whim. I would decide to put on a series in Athens, and our traveling circus would pull up its stakes, load out the room's elephants, and head for more lucrative markets. But the same show followed me no matter what, with a varied supporting cast and the same directionless longing playing the lead.

In France, Singer closes down the apartment

It took a month to get them all out. Paris tried to be polite at first, apologizing for the lack of coffee or breakfast, but the guests thanked him and remarked that they weren't much hungry anyway. They slept stretched out on the floor and went down to the café for butter pastries. He recognized some of them as fellow patrons of the arts, men he knew only in profile from their seats at the Palais Garnier. At first he appreciated the distraction of their presence, but as time passed, his opinion changed. They had become tourists to his tragedy, inserting themselves into his grief. Once it was clear they wouldn't heed his subtler cues to leave, he hired a pair of women to clean and close the apartment, with the idea that his guests could take on the monthly rent once he was gone.

The women arrived with a cartload of supplies and immediately got to work on the kitchen. They scrubbed and polished and shook out the rugs. Someone had gouged a hole in the parlor wall, but one of them revealed a pot of mastic and repaired it while the other pulled furniture away from the walls and scrubbed the baseboard corners. Their noise cleared a few visitors out, but not everyone got the message, and soon enough the cleaning women were herding ten stalwart guests from room to room as they went.

The children's room was the last to be closed. The stalwarts milled about like the party guests they were, thumbing through the picture books and going on about the children in reverent tones while the cleaning women worked diligently to remove the soot from the walls.

Night came on, and the guests still wouldn't leave. The cleaning women had gone home, having better things to do. By then the guests were clustered in the entry hall, enjoying an endless conversation about the worst cafés in the neighborhood. Exasperated, Paris bid his guests good night, claiming that the place needed to be fumigated. They looked at him with surprise and disgust, as if they weren't the vermin he was trying to remove. He heard someone remarking on his rudeness as they were heading down the stairs. Paris regretted his tone, which was sharper than it would have been had he taken a stand at a more appropriate hour. Entertaining hadn't been the salve he had hoped it would be. Everyone wanted to try grief on for a little while, but nobody wanted to claim it.

In the morning, the cleaning women returned. He had them empty the ashtrays, scrub the bathroom, wipe down the silver and pack the children's toys and clothing into a pair of trunks. One of them pried the nails from the window in the children's room and hit it with a mallet until it unstuck and slammed shut with such force that it cracked the glass.

They washed the floors while he went through the bin of correspondence that had accumulated by the door. There were a staggering number of cards and envelopes, some addressed to him and some to Isadora, never to both. Paris would be busy through the season, inventing thoughtful phrases to give his assistant in response to the longer letters. Because Isadora would no doubt prefer to keep her letters sealed, wrapping them in a black ribbon and tucking them under a stack of folios to be forgotten, he would deal with hers as well.

One of her letters came from Harry Kessler, Ted Craig's patron. Paris opened it, remembering Ted's wire asking for travel money. Kessler's letter was pleasantly perfunctory, featuring short, clean lines of regret and support. Paris appreciated a man who could keep sentiment within its rational bounds.

Gus and the women had been on Corfu for the whole month, no doubt enjoying the summer breeze and other island pleasantries. Elizabeth had wired to say that Isadora had taken ill and he should come to see her. He considered it, but decided for the moment that there was too much to be done in France. He would have the trunks put in storage, his own things sent back to Oldway. Happily he wouldn't have to worry about the furniture, and the landlord would forgive the bail on the place. They had done such a good job of showing it to the neighborhood over the past month that it would be rented out soon enough. Once things finally wound down, Paris would turn his attention to the weeks and months ahead in England, improvements to the building and property, and long evenings passed mercifully alone.

Isadora's sickbed on Corfu, where illness threatens jovially to level her

If I was wrong all this time and there is a life after death, I can entertain the celestial crew for hours by describing every detail of this two-bit hotel room. Sad furniture crowds around the bed, and while the hotelier made such a presentation of the private bath, I would rather have a soak in front of everyone if it gave me witnesses to the spiders. The bathroom has a single porthole window, only large enough to fit my arm through. Outside, gulls dive sideways into hell and wheel up carrying bits of charmed fish.

Perhaps I am convalescing in the inferno, in the ring of suffering where the damned beat rugs with tennis rackets and roll wooden carts up endless cobblestone paths while a meaningless siren drones on and on, and just when I can't take it anymore, the siren fades to a disappointed moan and the ferry plank bangs onto the dock to allow its passengers to disembark. The charm of this port wore off within an hour of our arrival, and now, after a month, I would rather be curled up in muddy water at the bottom of a well.

My nurse has been sampling from the dish of kumquats by the bed while I sleep. She thinks a fruit here or there won't be noted, as if the sunny still life wasn't the only bright spot in the room. Every time I wake up, another fruit is gone. Then again, there is no such thing as a still life, as even paintings are only as still as conditions allow.

The nurse is very old and squints at the thermometer as if it's whispering something to her. If she even saw the biscuit tin of ashes on the bathroom sink, she must have dismissed it. She would never throw it out, considering her resistance to cleaning, which seems class-based and rather fixed. And so the children remain in their tin by the porthole window, the only place in this awful room with a partial view of the sea.

The hotelier scrambled to care for me in my illness, not wanting a dead woman to mar his hotel's curative reputation, but his effort is half staffed; I remember seeing my nurse working last week in the hotel kitchen, basting a roast with the same close attention she now gives my thermometer. She seems kind enough despite the fact that her black linen cowl gives her the impression of a friendly hooded Death, and she seems optimistic about my persistent cough despite the fact that it's getting worse. Bedrest hasn't killed me yet, and so therefore I must be stronger, but as of late, I only feel weighed down by my own weight. They say sunlight is good for your nerves, but too much of a good thing will drive anyone to madness. It's hard to tell how much sun the old nurse has gotten, if she accepts only a slice of it through narrowed eyes on her walk to work or strips naked at noon and lies out on the roof, but either way, she's stealing the fruit.

"*Ilekobathee*," she says, replacing the pot under the bed and laying a cool cloth on my forehead. The joints clip inside her wrist as she shakes the thermometer down, the sound of small stones. She's talking to herself, aware of the silent and useless nature of her audience. She's even older than I thought, on closer inspection, an age where a birthday should mean a parade around the town square followed by a long nap, her bed surrounded by her largest and most pleasant family photographs so that if she happens to wake in the middle of a sudden gasping death, they are all there, in their best clothes, sepia-toned or folded down the middle, but happy to see her, smiling down in groups of two and three on the dresser or the windowsill, gazing with bravery and love at their dearest daughter, their friend, their sister, there with her at the end as they promised they would be.

The nurse has decided I will be washed, and so I am washed. She hauls me up by my armpits to get my back, where all week I've suffered an insect bite like a half-buried stone. She scrubs at me with her salt-stained cloth until my skin is raw, then leans close to pick something off my side with her fingernail, then scrubs some more. Soap flakes float in the gray water of her dish. Wringing out the cloth, she wipes her hand on the quilt and draws from her pocket a yellow copysheet from the Marconi office:

PARIS MAY 16 I DUNCAN LYING SERIOUSLY III AT CORFU

An error in the type made my illness into a triptych. Consider the triple scene Teddy could design: left panel a dancer bent back in *cambré*; middle a mare with her foals; far right some waterscape town featuring residents, warring general against the Turks. Folding the page, I tuck it under the pillow, where it wraps around my silver flask. "We can expect some letters, then."

She responds in Greek, *Ilekobathee*.

"Maybe a visitor or two if they can stand the ferry."

Taking up her cloth again, she scrubs my breast, where one wiry curl springs like a coarse weed, having resisted my plucking, nothing on this earth as persistent as a nipple's single hair.

Oh, imagine if I had the audacity to die! The ladies would have to bring out their black again. At the children's service there was so much bad behavior when they thought I wasn't looking, but Étienne was paid off easily and reported it all. Jules and Gabriel apparently came only to make the papers, chatting with the reporters and spelling their names for the write-up that would come in the social pages. Yvette signed her name for the reporter as if it were for an autograph book. Only Albert Calmette was a friend and refused to give his name. Years ago he wrote a critical piece on the Ballets Russes, calling Nijinsky's body hideous from the front and even more hideous when seen in profile, and no matter what injuries life will surely bring, I will always have that happy morning reading his takedown over toast and tea. I kept that delightful piece tacked to my dressing room wall for a month, until Nijinsky himself stopped by and I had to quickly hide it behind a lamp. I felt guilty for a moment, but he was coming only to see the size of my dressing room and also to ask me to tell Gus to stop contacting him.

The nurse lifts the pillows to prop me up for lunch, arranging my body like a waxwork. She brings the tray, on which she has arranged a thin cup of broth and a palm-size cracker burdened with figs and honey. At my funeral, Gus will give an overlong oration from behind a shroud and Elizabeth will manage the recital, the girls all dancing in black. It will be a dear performance. Raymond will arrive too late to offer much beyond tears before decamping again to Albania, where he is cementing some philosophical movement among the refugees. Mother will write a note to the priest a few months after the whole ordeal. From his flat in London, Paris will put down the paper and look out at the busy street before taking his dinner in his room.

Ilekobathee.

Of course the reporters didn't ever name Paris when they wrote about the funeral, despite the proof of our love draped in white roses. The weight of these will always rest squarely on my shoulders.

The nurse plucks the fattest kumquat from its perch and places it on the tray like an ornament. Christ's sake, it was perfect. My limbs lack the strength, and words may as well be etched on a block of ice for all the good they're doing us.

Really, though, Paris would as soon plunge a paring knife into his palm than take a meal in his room. He's a glorious depressive, and hiding away would deprive him of the chance to brood in public.

My nurse is patient with her spoon, but her hand quakes with age and inattention, the tremor enough to bail most of the chicken broth port or starboard en route to the mouth, pale limonate buttons weeping across the bed. When it reaches me, the spoon holds only a foul memory in warm silver. She eyes it with dread, as if dark magic has willed the liquid away.

"That's fine," I assure her. "I'm so tired." When we children fell ill in California, Mother would bring in hearty fistfuls of bougainvillea and jasmine, depositing the flowers into our beds. We thought at first that they were meant to be a comforting distraction, and in a strange way they did have their use; the petals would stick to our arms and legs and make a gummy cast, and swaddled in the rotting material, we felt warmed and comforted. It would be years before she confessed that she was only expressing a morbid practicality; at the first sign of every rash, she was prepared for us to die, and so gathered our funeral flowers. She would always seem surprised and unsettled each time we got better, but then another would fall ill and she would bring in the flowers again. Eventually a few of the neighbors decided she was a witch and left a basket of stones in our garden. It all gave illness a magical quality, and death seemed to spite her preparation by staying away. Perhaps I should have dressed in mourning from the day my babies were born.

The nurse keeps watch over her patient, who is running a high fever,
convulsing at times, and lately has begun to groan

Marta yawned, looking out the window. The long days had been no good, not worth the extra money. She was missing her usual routine with her friends, who on cooler afternoons liked to go and collect glass around Kanoni. At that moment they were surely gossiping on the beach, admiring the day's collection.

But Marta was stuck inside, all on account of this woman, apparently an American dancer. The dancer had been warbling insanely in English and Italian all week, and laughed through tears streaming down her face. Her fever was very high. It was unusual, and Marta thought a few times that she might try addressing her in Italian but decided she would prefer they continue their acquaintance without conversation. The rambling looked like a real mental break, something Marta could well recognize; her own mother had been hardy and well until one evening when she stood up from the table, declared that she was a dark angel cracked from the egg of the world, crouched down on the floor, and died.

The dancer certainly seemed on the verge of mental collapse. She would hold suddenly still and narrow first one eye, then the other, like a slug squirming on a twig after a day's slow rain.

"*Hasfyn*," the dancer murmured, appearing at first swollen and then deflating, a strange old stain on the pillow making a brown halo around her head as if her ears were leaking a dark fluid—"*Hasfyn, eymsotied*"— falling asleep so quickly that Marta leaned forward to check her pulse at the wrist before gathering her things to go. She dropped a foot back into a quick curtsy to Elizabeth, who was brooding in the hallway, and excused herself to the kitchen, where an olive oil cake was waiting for its walnut glaze.

After a few featureless weeks, Isadora remains ill enough for her siblings to almost worry

Something was off about the furniture, Elizabeth decided. The wood was so dry she could feel the desire it held for her skin's own moisture. She wanted desperately to rub a teak oil into the dresser, as close as it sat to the sun and salt air. Cover the wood and keep it fine, that was her thought. If it were up to her, they'd oil up the desk, the armoire, and the bed frame as well. They could fit a cloth cover on the heavy oak door, another for its brass knob and the filigree on the base of the bed and the glinting pulls on the desk. It's a sad task indeed to keep the old things nice but sadder to see them go.

She couldn't bear it and went back out to the hall. It was almost worse out there, where she felt like a draped statue guarding a crypt. She pictured herself cast in marble and posed in an attitude of standing penance, head removed at the neck to make a place for birds. One fat pigeon would take up residence, his feathers blending nicely with the marble as he watched over the women and children laying down flowers, mistaking Elizabeth for her sister, their sweet students saying prayers for successful recitals, dropping to their knees to sop up with their own hair the perfume they poured onto her stone feet, so fully unaware of their freedom, their ability to shake the ash from their coats and go for a cup of tea before scattering like seeds to find enough obligations to fool anyone into thinking that time was something to be endured. They would all leave, eventually, and once the paths cleared and the last mourners had gone home, a gardener would take up their wilted gifts and toss them over the far wall. But Elizabeth would remain, standing in witness because witness was her destiny. She couldn't leave if she tried.

There was a shuffling sound at the end of the hall and Gus arrived, dragging two parlor chairs up the narrow stairwell. In the hallway, they could be close enough to her fevered agony without being directly accountable to it. Gus had found a book among the stacks of newspapers in the coatroom and was enraptured, as if he had never encountered a book before, reading the pages again and again and making notes shamelessly in the margins. Elizabeth leaned against the pitted velvet rise of the armchair and rested her eyes.

"Listen to this," he said, tipping his head slightly back in the way he would deliver a monologue and lifting the book up to his sightline. "'It was different out upon the rose-tinted waters of the central lake. It boiled and heaved with strange life. Great slate-colored backs and high serrated dorsal fins shot up with a fringe of silver, and then rolled down into the depths again.' Isn't it wonderful?"

"Heavens. What is it?"

He showed her the cover, one of his adventure books. "There's an entire half-hidden world that we have never known or seen in the Southern Hemisphere. Can you imagine, all of us on a low barge, a reeded shelter in the center with provisions, schooning deep in-country?"

Elizabeth imagined fish cutting through shallow water, fins like knives lodging wetly in the soft wooden hull of the boat.

Gus flipped back to an earlier page. "We would refer to things as In-Country and Out-Country. I'll need to look that up. It would be a real adventure." He showed her a sketch he had made describing the dimensions of a raft. He had spent a lot of time drawing the various fauna on its flanking shores.

"Let's get one thing clear," she said. "You've been reading a fiction with scattered scientific terms, and now you believe you are prepared to pilot a low barge."

"No, no, listen." He found his place again. "'Lord Roxton rushed forward, rifle in hand, and threw it open. There, prostrate upon their faces, lay the little red figures of the four surviving Indians, trembling with fear of us and yet imploring our protection.' You see?" he asked, keeping his place with his thumb. "They need our *help*."

The hall was warm and humid, which made it feel as if they were seated in a chafing dish. The cook insisted every afternoon on roasting carrots and potatoes in the French style and, in doing so, humidified the building, swelling the floorboards from tea to sunset. Elizabeth had wondered why the thick air hadn't made its way into the bedrooms until she saw in the doorframe a layer of wooden clapboard, which meant the front rooms had been a hasty addition. The building was a long way from the painted stone she remembered from Athens and had imagined when this trip was suggested to her. The whole place had the feeling of a swallow's nest built thicker by new birds, and it ensured, as did the differences in climate from room to room, that the building groaned with every breeze and shuddered whenever the cook closed the oven.

Elizabeth felt some affinity with the place. Her joints never quite agreed with the salt of the sea air, despite her physician's recommendation that she immerse herself in thalassotherapy as a practice whenever possible for the health of her hip and leg. The physician had claimed that the climate would ease and comfort her, but she found the effect was quite the opposite; an afternoon on the beach made her feel internally powdered.

"Stop reading that trash," she said. "Don't you have a pregnant wife to attend to in London?"

He looked up. "What does that have to do with anything?"

"You're so overcome by the details of your own life that you need to go insert yourself into someone else's. What need do native people have for an actor?"

"That's exactly it," he said. "The arts. Leisure. These people have so many troubles I could so easily solve." He was chewing his nail as he read, an ugly habit. "Anyway it's the stuff of manhood, that's why you don't find an attraction to it. There's a romance portion too, if that helps."

"I'm not interested in any romance portion."

"I should send it in to the sickroom, then?"

She snorted. "You'll be sorry if this turns out to be her deathbed."

"Oh, come on. She's only having a bit of fun with us. Remember the week in London when she claimed to have the flu? She saw so many doctors in private I thought she would contract syphilis and pass it to us through the toilet seat."

"My God, Augustin."

It was true that Isadora had invented illness in the past, but Elizabeth knew it was different, because her sister didn't have the energy to deliver her usual cruelties. Just after she gave birth to Deirdre, she requested a private visit from her Dear Friend, the Great Italian Actress Eleonora Duse; it would be many years before Isadora stopped introducing her like that. Word was sent, and her Dear Friend, the Great Italian Actress Eleonora Duse, arrived a few days after, apparently having nothing better to do. She went to Isadora's chamber, and they were alone for only a few minutes before Eleonora emerged again, holding her face as if it had been slapped. The rest of them rushed in to find the new mother propped up with pillows in her bed, the babe at her breast, preening like a satisfied cat and claiming before anyone asked that her guest had tried to suckle the other teat. It was a naughty rumor, one delivered with the intention to instantly spread, yet Eleanora returned the next day, walking proudly through the crowd of whispering visitors, and half an hour later the two of them were walking arm in arm around the garden, pausing at a bench to embrace like lovers reunited, one pulling the other laughing to the grass, out of sight of the line of shocked employees watching from the windows, the baby having been handed off to a nurse.

It was most distressing to see Isadora so ill. It seemed to herald a worrying new trend. Elizabeth remembered the week before, the sight of her sister at the cliff's edge, the uncertainty in her expression suggesting that if only they came a little closer, she would recognize them as old friends. Alone up there, her hand wavering back to find the rail, she seemed complicit in their judgment, ready to confess her sins before they pushed her off. She may very well have been drunk.

The walls heaved and swelled. Elizabeth heard the Italians laughing outside as they came up the road. Romano had been very sweet to mostly not ask after her sister, mentioning her only once with an easy smile that suggested he didn't care if she lived or died.

Elizabeth thought guiltily of Max for the first time in a week. Ever since he returned to Darmstadt, he had been sending daily telegrams updating her on the school, but she couldn't make it to the office every day to receive them.

"My sweetheart would be displeased to hear you selling me on this tropical adventure," she said. The days seemed shorter on vacation, late mornings and early supper.

Gus looked up. "Who is displeased? The Italian, you mean? What's bothering the Italian?"

"Max Merz, for God's sake. You've met him twenty times. He was at the funeral."

Her brother frowned. "Max Merz."

It was his cruel idea of a joke. A few months before they met, Max denounced Gus's *Oedipus* revival publicly at a summer recital, going on about the failures of the adaptation as an aside to his introduction as he mopped his forehead with a cloth. It was all written up in embarrassing detail in the local paper, the greatest surprise being that a reporter was at the concert at all, though he could have also heard the story from a friend. Later, Max would try to claim that it hadn't been a personal denouncement, that he took issue with the Oedipal myth itself, its familial cruelty and vengeance. But the damage was done, and Gus would always insist on subsequent encounters on having forgotten the poor man.

"Ah yes," Gus said. "I'm sure Herr Merz would be additionally disappointed to know you were not buried in the anatomy books he sent with you to prepare for your advanced class."

"I shouldn't have told you about those."

"Perhaps he has already written you out of the payroll for insubordination."

The teasing annoyed her. Max was working diligently in Darmstadt, obedient to his work and to her. Isadora couldn't be bothered to manage the school as long as it was turning a profit, and so Max enjoyed the freedom to try out his little ideas, such as having the girls skip their afternoon cookies, performing deep lunges between sips of tea.

Elizabeth rotated her ankle in a slow circle as she studied the door, half listening to her sister's clotted cough. "You never complained when he picked up the round," she said at last, but Gus was no longer listening. She turned her attention to the door's brass hinges, thick cast in a twisting rope pattern and secured firmly with small bright brass screws, giving the old wood a gilded look despite the fact that it was too pale to be oak or maple and, on closer inspection, was splintered at the base where it ran against the rug. Perhaps it wasn't as sturdy as she thought, a hollow pine. "What do you think that is?" she asked.

"Bronchial infection," Gus said, turning the page. "She'll be just fine. We'll make our journey to the Mighty Amazon at the end of the month."

"Confusing it with the Mississippi should prove to be the least of your troubles."

"I suspect they're at least comparably mighty." He closed the book and stroked its leather. "I forget that you're not the adventurous one."

"You're calling her adventurous now?"

"Her parties begin in the city, continue on the docks, and end on the Nile."

"Yes, but try convincing her to get off the boat. Try to bring her to a show that's not her own." They were all dismissive of ballet, but Isadora could be really insufferable about any alternative, which she regarded as a personal attack. There was one road to glory, as far as she was concerned, and it would be paved with stones she laid herself. She seemed to dismiss the idea that she might be building over someone else's footpath or grave.

"I'm feeling my age too keenly," Gus said. "The only antidote is adventure. Come now, before you ruin the game for everyone."

"I will not be the Lewis to your Clark this time."

"Well, for one thing, you would be the Clark to my Lewis."

"There's too much to do at the school."

It was true: the one letter that arrived from Max spent three full pages detailing the school's problems, the personal funds he had poured into advertising and the return they had not drawn. Because he was short on staff and had to teach chorale and theory both, he was forced to arrange the classes to create one long day from sunrise to sunset. A second pianist would ease the burden a little; the new girl he was considering could cover the chorale to allow him to focus on theory. Elizabeth remembered his insistence upon chorale, which she had been against to begin with. At the letter's close he asked after her trip, which Elizabeth took to mean he missed her. He was a man of deeply subtle insinuation.

Gus found another book to read from the pile at his feet. "You should task Herr Merz with the whole operation," he said. "Give him the school, have him write us a cheque every month. He would be happier to know he could have control of everything, and you would be free to pursue your own interests."

It was too bad Gus didn't care for Max, as the two men had a lot in common. They both had tender hearts, for one, and in the way of tender-hearted men, they felt most comfortable delivering cruelties both egregious and mundane. Elizabeth remembered their first holiday in London, when the family sat down to Christmas breakfast to find that their special oranges had been stolen overnight. Their mother worried that a citrus-motivated thief had broken into the room until Gus admitted he had eaten them all at midnight while the rest of them were out caroling. Apparently, after making fun of the whole venture for hours, he was upset that nobody had invited him.

Max was the same way. A sore loser at party games, he once interrupted a garden-party Ludo match by throwing a crystal goblet at a fountain with such force that its shards cast a wide and irretrievable arc, landing in planters and scalloped patches of sand, the force and range of his throw ensuring that there would be bits of his bad temper embedded in the landscape for generations. Their hosts insisted with an abundance of grace that they were glad to know his glittering hazard would become a permanent feature of their daily walk to the garden, for the shards might catch the light and remind them of the sea.

Elizabeth gave a sharp sigh.

"What's that?" Gus asked.

"I'll check on dinner."

"Tell the cook that if she serves another consommé, I will set a fire in her room."

Elizabeth hoped Romano would be having coffee downstairs as he often was around this time. She thought again of Max, not quite her suitor after all these years, but certainly not her husband either. He had agreed a little too enthusiastically before she left for Greece that they should take the next few months to discover themselves more truly, addressing what that meant to their romantic or business partnership on the other side of her journey.

And in truth, she found herself appreciating him more during her time away, despite her little distractions. Max's fits and scenes were precisely what distinguished him from other men, with their invitations for afternoon strolls, their thin lips and wringing hands. The ordered depth of Max's anger attracted her, a library's worth of grievances organized in the heavy card catalog of his mind. His principles placed him in stark contrast with her family, who seemed not to have enough of an attention span between them to hold a grudge longer than an hour or two. Limp and elastic, bored by sport and usually drunk, they conspired to invent rifts with anyone foolish enough to wander into range and lost interest before the night was over. Isadora was the worst of them, a hissing flirt. She was ill at ease until she had inspired a row at any given party, stepping over the wreckage of another courtship or marriage as she picked her teeth with the lady's comb. Isadora would hate Max if she ever cared enough to learn his name.

Max tries to remember his first meeting with Elizabeth, eventually recalling an injury to his pride

As a young man, Max liked to keep up with the cafés in the old town, placing a coin on the counter of the Landtmann or Central and finding a good seat, stroking his budding beard as he eavesdropped on men at nearby tables discussing the rational mind. For months he could only smile in the direction of their voices, eyes filled with envious tears.

Finally, he'd gathered the courage to start a conversation with one of the men, at first so quietly that the words could not escape the glass lip of his coffee, half phrases bobbing in the overmilked sludge.

He befriended the man, who eventually made a vague promise that in a few weeks he would take Max to an afternoon salon with the famous psychoanalyst, a party at which this man had a standing invitation. The man used his promise to Max as an excuse to speak often about the event, describing how brilliant scholars would roar through a series of posits in the center of the room, tugging passionately at their own hair as they thrilled the crowd. They were all in competition for the favor and praise of the famous analyst, who might reference offhand the greatest ideas of the evening in his closing improvisational speech, a subtle crowning that would follow the victors for the rest of the month. There was also sup-posedly a coffee cake so delicious that the whole afternoon ended with a genial sweetness and the combatants left as friends. The man reported all this in earnest. He would bring Max, of course, at the earliest avail-able time, the next one for certain.

Max took this to heart and cleared his meager schedule in the event his invitation might come without warning. He spent the morning of the salon—they were scheduled the first Tuesday of each month—pressing and then carefully rumpling his shirt collar and running expan-sive exercises on the piano to boost his confidence before practicing his diction and extended eye contact with the wary patrons of his father's grocery.

He quickly came to the unsettling realization that he didn't actually have any ideas of his own, only Ben Franklin quotes memorized from his old copybook. He made it his daily work to find a point of view, even-tually settling on the idea that physical strength could be linked to mental prowess and if an entire culture could take on a serious study of calisthen-ics and weight training, their minds would be prepared for a mastery of mathematics, science, and the higher arts. He worked through these ideas behind the counter at the grocery, and the ladies he rang up carried home their fish and eggs and prepared the evening meal thinking of the boy in the store who seemed so pale with longing they assumed he was lovesick, or perhaps he had been injured lifting something heavy; it didn't seem that he could handle much. But they assumed it was weakness brought about by love and pitied the poor girl he was in love with.

Every month at the appointed hour, Max arrived at the café to find his friend already there, dressed in the precise intellectual style: a long woolen coat in all seasons, with a watch pinned smartly to his vest, leather gloves clasped in one hand, and scholarly papers rolled in the other. Every time, his friend offered up an excuse for why he wouldn't be able to bring Max with him that afternoon. First, the gathering was closed to extra guests; the next one had to be delayed for a holiday. An-other was closed to men under forty, for they were discussing death, and the analyst didn't care to hear what the young men had to say. The ex-cuses were humiliating for Max, but his unreliable friend was the only hope he had of early entry into the scholarly set, so he took the rejection with a grim and patient smile.

His invitation kept coming, along with the excuses: the meeting was canceled for weather, and then the coveted guest spot was given to another man visiting from Paris or London who had arrived unexpectedly on the evening train but would have to be accommodated, the implication of this unknown friend's importance understood to all. Sometimes the visitor would actually be brought into the café and paraded before Max, as if to illustrate the bearing of a true scholar—his canvas-bound books, his uneven smile—and Max would be forced to shake his replacement's hand, before he was left to the serious duty of filling an evening with nothing but time.

One such evening, when the group was set to discuss the anal impulse in a closed session, Max had settled in for a long evening alone when he saw a woman on the other side of the café, sitting so poised with such a pleasantly blank demeanor he thought for a moment that he was looking at a mannequin in the window of the shop next door. But then the mannequin came alive, and he watched with wonder as she ordered a slice of cake with milk.

Watching the lovely young woman was a nice distraction from the day's disappointment. He felt his own awkwardness and wished he had learned to roll cigarettes—his old tobacco tin remained unopened as punishment and reminder—but the woman didn't seem to notice him, seeming perfectly content without any distraction, not even a book or newspaper. When her dessert arrived, she ate with careful satisfaction, tipping her slight chin up to observe the framed pictures on the wall. There was something so peaceful about her, which transformed the café into something wholly different from the dull room it had become to Max. He found himself wanting to know her.

He had been well trained by months of rejection at the hands of his friend, and his introduction in hindsight was very straightforward. He took a seat without asking, demanded to know where she was from, and then guessed before she could respond that she was visiting from out of town.

Somehow she found him charming despite his bad manners. She

was in Vienna for the month with her sister, who until recently had been dancing with Loie Fuller. He learned that they were traveling artists and scholars in their own feminine way, and would he like to join the two of them for luncheon later that week? He would.

The woman had a strange intensity that made him feel pleasantly observed. He guessed from her halting French that she was from Tulin, one of those lovely towns along the Danube, and he was heartily surprised when she corrected him to say she was from San Francisco, a city that brought to mind an image of a hot air balloon rising in a clear sky. Elizabeth was the first American he had ever met, and between her and Benjamin Franklin he got the idea that Americans were kind and industrious, thoughtful and serious; it wouldn't be long before his opinion changed, but this first impression was like a thumbprint on warm dough.

Elizabeth was a beautiful girl, as graceful as a reed in water, with thick dark hair secured at the nape of her neck. He loved how she dragged her left foot behind her like a reluctant guest, and he looked forward to the evening it would be appropriate for him to offer his arm. She would lean on him and right herself, and they would make a handsome couple walking down the sidewalk, which would have been recently doused by dishwater. A bit of washing soap would attach blithely to her dress. It would all be very nice.

Max found himself thinking often about Elizabeth, and when it was time to leave home, he looked to her school for potential employ. That first evening also paved the way for their romantic life together, which he always appreciated for how it was built, on a communion of ideas. From the very start he knew that conversations with Elizabeth would give him more knowledge of the world than he would gain sitting at the feet of any famous thinker. Her thoughts were so plain to him, so easy to interpret. If she described a landscape, he could understand its nature in her simple description; she spoke about all of life in the same easy way, whether she was thinking about dinner or arguing for the necessity of physical affection. She lived in the world as a familiar guest. He could find in her life a rationale for his own. And that was how Max fell in love.

Elizabeth spends the afternoon hiding from her family

Though the hotel had been designed in the same grand European style as the city hall and various residences up and down the main street, the other buildings had been kept up and now stood proud over the hotel, which had long ago fallen into the disrepair standard to coastal towns. Elizabeth kept meaning to ask the owner about the building's history but had been put off by his small dogs, who hurled themselves endlessly at birds in the courtyard despite the constant material presence of the door's inlaid glass. The door suffered a shin-level smudge, and guests suffered the strangled sounds of the dogs' desperate attempts to escape.

A large kitchen down the hall operated in a constant state of minor chaos. From breakfast through supper, the kitchen supervisor leaned against a counter and repeated tasks to three women. He was a thin man and seemed not to have benefited much from their cooking. Elizabeth understood well, not benefiting much from it herself. Attempting the French method meant chucking their standard honey-drenched pastries in favor of scorched béchamel and the youngest cook's attempt at macarons, which emerged from the oven dense as stones and leaked a marbled wet stain onto a porcelain tray while the girl went into the pantry to cry about it. The others pitied Elizabeth's limp and allowed her to sit on a high stool by the open door, giving her napkins to fold. The youngest came back to practice her English as she stood by the stove and frothed an innocent bowl of eggs in preparation for some extravagant culinary failure.

"How is your mother feeling today?" she asked, tapping her whisk on the bowl's metal edge.

"My sister, you mean."

"Yes, your sister."

"Mother is in California, and last I heard, she was not leaving her neighborhood."

The girl frowned. "Your mother?"

"My sister is fine. They're all fine, thank you."

"You are welcome." They were very agreeable with each other in the way of two people without a common language. At the stove, the thin man lifted the lid to smell something bubbling and turned to scowl at one of the cooks.

"A stew for dinner?" Elizabeth asked.

The girl turned the eggs out into a bowl of dry goods. "Carrots, roast stew, leek," she said. "Tomatoes consommé."

"Gus will be pleased."

"Augustin," she said. "Isadora. The famous family."

Elizabeth wondered how long after Isadora's death the school in Paris would be able to continue. She certainly couldn't change the name and take it on herself as she had in Darmstadt; it would be a lesser copy no matter how much success she found. Perhaps they could keep Isadora's name if they had her stuffed and propped up in a corner. If one in twenty mourning visitors signed up for a lesson, they could continue operation through the fall semester, and there would be extra revenue if the pilgrims left flowers fresh enough to be resold.

"Where are you from?" Elizabeth asked, shifting her weight to lean against the counter, resting her back. They had been in residence one month already, but she had just thought to ask, at this rate she would never learn the woman's name. She considered assigning her one.

"Corfu, the island."

"But where were you born?"

The woman pointed to her feet, as if she had been ejected from her mother's womb right there on the tile.

"You were born in the city?"

"In Korkyra, yes."

"It's very peaceful."

The woman shrugged.

"Quiet, you know, very calm," Elizabeth said. "I imagined a trade city when it was first described to me. Great ships going out with oils and spices. Maybe that's Athens, though. There is a solace here in the beautiful secluded coves. We took a tour to the high point and looked out over the water, which was a blue I've never seen from any coast. I think it's a quality of the light that imbues it. And then there's the air, which feels freshly transported from Olympus. All of it offers a real meditation, a thoughtful feeling, you know. Peace is all of that. That's what I meant when I said peaceful."

"I was not confused," the woman said.

"Oh."

They sat awhile in silence, Elizabeth tracing a line on the countertop where a piece of tile had cracked, following the line with her fingernail to the mortar. The woman certainly could have made it clear that she understood the first time. It was rude to make a guest feel foolish. She considered alerting the owner but then thought of the dogs clamoring over her dress.

"Your style is very current," the girl said, and Elizabeth realized she had been frowning down at her tunic. Isadora made her wear it to satisfy her own idea of Grecian authenticity. That was embarrassing enough, but then some of the women mistook the costumes as a fad from Paris and followed their lead. Soon enough, half the women in town were in short-sleeved tunics and sandals and the other half were deeply envious. It inspired an unmoored sensation, and the young soldiers who had begun to arrive from Serbia observed the classical maidens and surely felt as if they had tucked themselves into a greatcoat pocket of history, jostled around in time along with the scraps of varied revolutions and the philosophers' lesser posits.

The Italians filed in through the kitchen door, wool pants pulled over their swimming gear. Their arrival drew the subtle dismay of the cooks, who wordlessly moved their meat and produce to far counters as the men lined up for glasses of water, depositing their canteens in a sweating pile by the sink. Romano was among them, looking cool and dry. Elizabeth supposed that while the others swam, he had remained onshore, giving an intensive lecture on Garibaldi to a seabird.

The kitchen supervisor had already begun to clear his throat and advance, bowing slightly, gesturing at the food and at his watch, indicating everything still left to be done and the fleeting time they had in which to do it. The Italians accepted apples and decamped to the dining room. Elizabeth followed them out and sat with Romano as he opened his sketchbook.

It was impossible to talk to Romano without two thousand years of sculptural art history serving as a tedious chaperone. Every topic was ushered into his mind past brooding men and Madonnas cast in the certain bronze of the era, under *fleurs* of classical frieze, horses and cherubs and birds in flight, until at last it reached the head office, at which point he would roll his eyes, deliver some pronouncement, and send it back down. His father's sculptures—for his father was also a sculptor and apparently very well known in Italy—held court in his son's mind and made for a talkative gallery. As a result, Romano always seemed distracted, burdened as he was with thoughts of men greater than himself. And women, she supposed, as well.

"The light was fine today," he said. "It seemed to melt a little around the point where the water met with the sand. Not at all like yesterday."

"It was too bright yesterday?"

He grimaced. "Too flat."

"You sound like a painter."

His friends had set up a game of bridge in the dining room, relocating the silver and plates to another table. The thin man headed for the pantry, strangling a dish towel as he went.

"How is the patient?" Romano asked.

"Stronger every day."

"It's funny," he said. "I find myself afraid to bring her up, as if she's a ghost I might invoke by speaking her name."

"How Shakesperean of you." She thought of Hamlet moping around the castle for months before his father arrived. Perhaps the guards had set the whole thing up to bring a little excitement to Denmark.

"She seemed strong a week ago," he added.

"When she's well, you can feel her in every room. The chandeliers shiver."

He seemed impressed, so she continued. "Why, Isadora once held an audience in such a trance, they woke to find they had moved en masse from their seats and killed a cat in the alley behind the theater."

"How thrilling," he said. "It would be an honor to speak with her."

"I prefer her bedridden, honestly."

She was embarrassed to realize she had said this aloud, but Romano was distracted, watching his friends. One had gotten up to ask the kitchen for *caffè coretto*, and the woman set to arranging a tray with short cups and sherry glasses, unwrapping a bottle of grappa. They had brought a stovetop *napoletana* to the island and spent a good amount of time instructing the women on the proper method. The women listened patiently as the device their grandmothers owned and used daily was explained to them, and they pretended to take notes on the precise amounts of coffee and water and the character of the grind.

Romano liked to feign embarrassment on behalf of every man in his party, but when they stood to leave, he would follow them out like an obedient dog. Elizabeth appreciated Romano as a kind and thoughtful man but saw his false fraternity as cowardice and hated him for it in the way one hates a pretty mirror in which one only sees oneself. She touched his arm, and he stopped sketching the office dogs until she moved her hand away.

"It was a good season," he said.

"Where will you go next?"

"The others will return to Milan and I'll spend some time on the coast, at the home my family keeps during the summer."

"That's a true shame," she said.

"Every season comes to an end."

"Your departure, I mean. We were becoming such good friends."

He frowned at one of the dogs. "And I haven't figured out the light," he said. "If I can't understand simple light, forget about stone."

"It's the same light wherever you are, my dear. Only your angle changes." She shifted her chair closer, almost touching him again. "You see, it's different from where you sit. The beam enters the window more fully."

One of the women placed a coffee and a grappa between them, and he turned his attention to the cup, turning it so that the handle faced her, and then him, and her again. He was a careful man. She could imagine his mother cradling him as a child, pressing her lips to the fine hair of his eyebrows, moving breakable objects to higher shelves, her boy making his way through the world with a halo of fine things just out of reach.

"We are good friends," Elizabeth said.

"Indeed. You and your family, when your sister is well again, are welcome in my home. My parents keep the house on the coast. My father—"

"That would be wonderful, but we would never impose." This wasn't true at all; her family was happy to impose. She thought of the rowdy time they all had spent with a second cousin who put them up in Marseille for a month before saying kindly and then more pointedly that the South of France might need a season off. "Thank you for the invitation, but I am needed in Darmstadt."

"Such an American sentiment," he said, and gave a short laugh that sounded precisely like the first abrupt sounds of a boiling kettle. "Nobody needs anybody in Frankfurt."

"You know, comparing Darmstadt to Frankfurt is like saying Yonkers when you mean New York City."

"Yonkers!" Pushing too hard on the first syllable, he flattened the vowel as if the city were home to brick walk-ups stuffed with hay, chickens squawking from open windows.

"I have no patience for Germany," he said. "All their great halls rising over empty streets. It's a towering hymn to the dead. The stonework alone is enough to crush the spirit."

"Poor Romano, was your heart broken by a beautiful German girl?"

"Even the ghosts are lonely there."

"Complexion like milk, smelling of soft winter wheat?"

He sketched an errant line on the dog's tail and rubbed it with his thumb, cursing to himself. "I marveled at the facelessness of its people, and of its women, of course."

"Why, you're blushing. It must be worse than I thought!" She couldn't stop herself from teasing him. "She ran away with your dearest friend, and the two of them went on a motor trip around the country. You could only imagine the depravity!"

"Something's off with the grappa, don't you think?"

It was clear he wasn't enjoying the joke, but Elizabeth didn't care; his agitation thrilled her. "After they married, your friend and your lost love set up a farmhouse in Havelaue, and he paned the windows with a blue glass in the precise shade of her eyes so that when he looked to his garden, he could be reminded of her beauty as she slept."

"Yonkers," he muttered. "What a world."

"And see, you'll talk and talk of a place you don't know the first thing about and remain totally silent on items of your intimate acquaintance."

"I only have to wade into cold water before I've had enough."

"That's exactly right. You're not brave like Jules Verne, who went twenty thousand leagues in search of the vastness of the sea."

He tossed his head back, as if the very idea of Jules Verne were so repellent that he needed to be physically distanced from it.

"The vastness of the sea!" he said, a little louder than he must have meant. "It's impossible for you to know it."

Elizabeth was ashamed, but his friends only looked over and laughed.

"Why, I saw the vastness just this morning," she said a little louder, trying to save face with the others.

"You go to the sea and watch the boats," he said. "The waves, the fins of little fish, the garbage washing against rock, sea foam, disturbances in the sand, tracks your feet have made. All those things, you know. You never know the vastness itself."

"I stood alone in the early morning hours, when there were no boats and no footprints besides my own behind me, and I felt a stark emptiness in my heart."

"It is not possible! You might have felt some condition of vastness, but if you had actually understood it, you would have lost your mind then and there. You would have walked until your feet left the earth, and there would be no more of you."

"The thought that I would end my life over your invented idea is as offensive as it is absurd." Feeling wild, she reached right over and took a sip of his coffee.

"A fact," he said. He waited for her to replace the cup on its saucer before he spoke again. "I saw it happen once. A woman standing on the shore, just as you did this morning. She was wearing a long muslin dress and boots in the old style. This was some years ago, on the Italian coast. I was watching the woman, and the woman was watching the sea. She never once turned around, as I assumed she would. Later I realized that she never moved at all, not shielding her eyes against the sun, not shifting her weight from foot to foot. It seemed from the position of her head that she was gazing toward a particular point in the distance, though she was not observing the horizon line. I watched, foolish and helpless, from my balcony as this poor woman became acquainted with the vastness."

"What happened to her?"

"What happened? She went face-first into the water and drowned before anyone had a chance to save her."

Elizabeth gasped. "But why?"

He shrugged, stirring his coffee with a small smile.

"You could have gone after her."

"I tried. I sprinted to cross the balcony and down the stairs to a switchback trail that went all the way down to the boardwalk. A thumbtack on the road went right into my bare foot, and I didn't notice it until much later, when I was changing into dry clothes before I visited the police station to give my account. The infection I suffered later was so aggressive, that thumbtack nearly put me into my grave. Let me see if I can—" He turned slightly in his chair to lift his foot from his shoe and slipped off part of his sock to show her the mark. "Here it is."

"And the girl?"

"I was too late. She was gone so quickly, it's as if she were dying even as she fell."

"My God."

"Yes, she was already very dead." He seemed ready to say more but paused, gazing down at his pencil as if he were trying to estimate its weight. He looked up at her and then to the other men. She leaned toward him, and they were quiet for a moment, his lips nearly touching her cheek.

"My friends over there say that violence is the only balm for suffering," he said. "They believe we must baptize this world with fire. What do you think about that, Miss Duncan?"

She looked over at his friends, who were flirting with the youngest kitchen girl, giving her sips of grappa. In Elizabeth's experience, it was the men who blustered about who carried the least potential to harm.

"Did you know her, the girl?"

He righted himself, disappointed. "I kept seeing her around my neighborhood after that. I thought for a while that her ghost had returned to haunt me, but it was another woman in a similar dress."

"How awful." Elizabeth didn't at all believe in ghosts but knew how an idea could pursue the mind like a restless spirit.

"For months I would see the neighbor woman at parties. She wore three iron peacock feathers clipped in her hair and so resembled a creature who had landed in the midst of a conversation, peering around the passing plates for scraps before she would fly again. At last I approached her and told her that she resembled a dead woman. She didn't like that at all, as you might imagine."

"What was her name, the one who died? Who were her friends, her family? Had she come to the shore on holiday?" Elizabeth noticed the thin man watching her from the kitchen. She lowered her voice. "You must have asked around, learned more about her tragic life."

He shrugged, looking away.

Elizabeth had more questions, which she decided against asking. What in her life brought her to stand there that morning, facing down the infinite? Did her family turn from her in her final hours?

"There was a Mass at some point in the little county cemetery," he said. "I decided to walk there but I accidentally set off in the wrong direction and didn't realize until it was too late. I came upon a remarkably smooth stone on that walk, which I still have."

"You could have met her family."

He shook his head, refusing to face her. "You're asking me to carry this woman on my back. A burden like that gets heavier as you go, not lighter."

Elizabeth looked at Romano, and in looking felt as if she'd seen him for the first time. He was a nervous man, fidgeting with his sketchbook like a boy in school. She wondered how long she would have to sit with him before she could reasonably escape and go back upstairs, where Gus was likely sleeping upright in his chair.

Her time on Corfu felt governed by a clock marking only the hour. She thought of all the people she had met: the women baking bread in the kitchen, Romano's friends shouting over cards, Isadora's old nurse upstairs, the European doctor lurking about, the thin man, who held his shirtfront back as he tasted the soup. She wouldn't miss any of them when she went away, and none of them would spend even a moment wondering if they would miss her. Each of them would fade in the others' minds like paper dolls in a sunny window. They would be relegated to the recesses of faulty memory along with an old recipe for crepes and Anna Pavlova dancing the dying swan, her flapping, desperate *port de bras*, faltering toward the crowd and away, panic in her darting eyes and none of them moving to save her.

Interminable Corfu, where illness attended by island climate makes everything feel packed in cotton

The main trouble with convalescing by the sea is the sea itself. They wheel you out onto a veranda and the brakes are set to face the trenchant sun, under which the blue expanse stretches merciless and uninterrupted save for some sad boat. It's fine for a morning, but after a few weeks, any reasonable mind loses itself to mundanity, searching the scrubby hills flanking the bay and activity therewith: a stag picking through breakfast, a blustering thing that could be a bird on a branch or a man's handkerchief. The hills seem to lurch forward, a landslide in perpetual motion, your weary eye accustomed to weeks with nothing available to read but the ceiling's plain fortune, a crack in the slab suggesting six more months of illness and a shifting foundation also. Worse yet when you start to wish those hills would fall.

We've given ourselves over to a new life. I feel rudderless without a schedule, and Elizabeth's school surely languishes without her. To think, we were once so thrilled for the venture in Germany! The studio was such an expense, the materials of its making infused with a kind of mania, though at first it was all well disguised; the wood and lacquer

were our first scent of freedom. We were consumed by our desire for independence. It was very American of us, though it was precisely the same
desire our father kept as his traveling companion when he vanished in
the night. The Oakland Council on Development hung a banner declaring *Progress!* over a burning beachfront as if they'd planned for the
old boardwalks to dry to tinder before the outrage of some reckless spark.
In leaving, we made to deny the connection we felt to fire and fathers
both but came to realize soon enough that these tragedies would always
repeat themselves one way or another.

The studio in Darmstadt seemed at last to be the tragedy we were
looking for. Construction alone nearly drove us to distraction, inspiring
enough screaming fights between myself and Elizabeth that we had to
tell the neighbors we were rehearsing a performance centered conceptually around Irish mourning. There was a materials issue; the studio's
rosewood floor required passage rites from British New Guinea and
weeks of steady work from a carpenter who spent the first three days with
his ear pressed to the wood, listening for its nuance before he unpacked
a single sanding block.

Despite our terrific fights, and despite the opening we threw with
strawberry cakes and enough champagne to float the city, it soon became
clear that the studio wouldn't be very much fun. The neighbors, who all
arrived empty-handed for the party but promised to enroll their daughters,
soon found that business had not returned enough to invest in private
lessons, that group sessions might have to wait until spring as well, when
everyone surely would have a little more time and energy, and anyway
the girls' mothers just spent all that on toe shoes for ballet and would
hate to throw them out after so little use, &c. We found ourselves trying
to insinuate on a huddled community looking at one another for cues,
ready to humiliate anyone who dared to step out of line. Change required
courage, and courage, it seemed, required change.

The other lesson of Darmstadt has been that every great idea is diluted
by its creation. Elizabeth claims that they are making improvements in
enrollment because her lover insists on teaching the girls to sing. He has
some foolish thought about giving them things to lift into the air, as if their
movement lessons are not strenuous enough. And so my grand experiment
floats out into open water.

"There's my dancing girl," the doctor says, sneaking up on me again. Taking up my cup, I quickly finish the last of my whiskey and cold coffee. The doctor is Parisian, and apparently he jokes over dinner with the other guests that he was imported specially for me. Really he just happened to be in the hotel when my strange illness came about, and he took the opportunity to work. He volunteered despite his wife's plaintive objection that they were on holiday, that without his droning mundanities, she wouldn't be able to properly ease herself into the absence of thought that helps to pass the time. I can imagine them on the ferry deck, his kit wrapped in a woolen blanket on its own chair, the three of them enjoying the afternoon.

"How is our national treasure feeling this morning?" he asks.

"Very well, thank you." I'm so weak lately, in truth. I remember a dinner outside Milan, along the Naviglio, good heavy food and plenty of wine, and for dessert a rum chocolate salami with walnuts. A piece of marrow was roasted in its bone and brought to the table with a great offertory feeling, the charred thing sizzling on its plate. It smelled so rich and savory, but I couldn't bring myself to eat it. The marrow seemed too vital, a fundamental pudding. I watched the others spread it on thick slabs of bread. I should have spooned my portion up, blessing the beef for the chance to savor its primordial fat, licking it clean and gnawing the bone, absorbing every bit of its power to store it for this very moment.

"Madame Grunet and I passed an evening last night with your siblings," he says. "Augustin has the most fantastic idea about a real adventure, one that promises to take him—now hold on, we agreed on little movement and none of it sudden—"

Gus will have to find us another bottle. "Have you seen my brother this morning, Doctor?"

"You really shouldn't touch the terrace rail, my dear. Better to keep your hands in your lap. I've taken on the study of metallic properties as something of a personal project. I'm convinced that dark metals like this"—he raps the rail for emphasis before wiping his knuckle on his coat—"cause a frenzy of the germ population."

When he leans in to examine my teeth, I worry for a moment that he might catch the scent of brown liquor before remembering he is partly so agreeable because he lacks the observational skill that physicians before him have employed to ruin whole afternoons. "The metal heats over the course of the day, you see, and develops a viral compound. Elderly and infirm, such as yourself, should avoid contact entirely. I plan to publish my findings soon." Elderly and infirm! He should know; his face is draped with soft folds of expressive skin, and he has a paunch that reveals itself against his clothes when the wind blows directly at him. His belly strains against the tight expanse of cotton, pressed and tucked like a buttoned sheet.

"All right then," he says. "Let's see those gums."

"And how is Madame Grunet?"

"I hope you might meet her. Even after all this time she still finds ways to charm me with her little thoughts. Last year we had a luncheon with Frantz Jourdain, and by the end of it he had invited us to a private showing of the Salon d'Automne. I'm not sure if you know him, but Frantz is not a simple man to charm." He continues on like this, working his way through the endless proof that cultural capital requires. "Of course, I destroyed it by taking the wrong position in the gallery. My wife wouldn't look at me for a week, but I'll stand by it, the art world lately is a waste of the time and money of generous men."

"I mean to say, tell me about Madame Grunet herself."

"But I was," he says, confused. "What else would you like to know? She was born in Nice—"

"Is she plump, Doctor, or very thin? Is her complexion pale or ruddy?"

"You want to know her weight?"

"You are a man of bodily science, sir. You should be pressing your ear to her breast every morning and palpating her entire form once a week."

"She is a lovely woman," he insists. "Her easy nature is a comfort to me. But she is nothing like the women I knew in my youth." He touches my shoulder and keeps his hand there. When I look up at him, he grimaces, seeming rather constipated by emotion. "God help me," he says.

And so the gallant emerges, tapping the dust from his hat as he listens for the opportunity that roused him. So deadly dull to be proven right.

"It's no matter," I say. "Mother told us when we were children that truly there was no Santa Claus and no God, but only ourselves to guide us." If he'd like to touch me I can do him one better; laying a hand there under the doctor's long coat, I find that He is risen indeed.

"You seem warm," he says vaguely. "I should find you a lighter covering."

"I am very warm."

"It won't do," he says.

The currents this morning are so slight they seem washed over a pane of glass. Ships at the horizon line roll by on miniature wheels.

"Sit and enjoy the water with me, Doctor."

I can see he's considering it. The silver tray of his heart holds two brown tincture bottles, each offering their own opiate. The first is marked Desire and the other Virtue; one clouds the mind and the other turns the stomach, but they have the same general effect in the end.

"It's important for you to regulate your temperature," he insists, removing his spotted hand from my shoulder and concealing it shamefully within the other. Certainly all of us grow ever older than we wish, despite our gay protests that our younger years were sloppy in construction and poorly lived, that we really would rather sit in the shade while the others go exploring. We must be careful, as our slackening skin can take only so much before it sloughs off into a wrinkled heap at our feet.

"I have another question, Doctor," I say, working him over with my hand. "Let's assume that what we know as the surface of the sea is actually a churning wall, particles emerging for air and light before cycling back down to meet the rocks and crags. A spray of sea might escape to the beach only to sink down through the sand, or become a vapor and live awhile as a cloud before dropping again." My hand wanders down his thigh and back up. "All the while, waves like these are crashing all over the world, on every beach, as they have done for all time. How much time will pass before every germ of the sea has been observed?" His sex fits snugly in the span between my thumb and forefinger. I wonder why there isn't an initiative to measure the worth of every man by length and pin it to his collar along with his blood type and major fears.

"You need some water," he says, clearing his throat and removing himself subtly from my grasp.

One of the boats rolling across the horizon line skids to a halt and drops from the face of the planet.

"I so value our little chats," he says. "Thank you for thinking of me."

"Thinking of you? Sir, I pity you."

"Well then, yours is a Christian pity and I am grateful for it."

"Christian pity is a weakness that drives a soul without sense or worth."

"Madam?"

"Christian pity," I say more carefully, "is a weakness that drives a soul without sense or worth."

"The Christian life creates its own worth." His coat lopsides as he thrusts his hand into his pocket, fondling himself thoughtfully.

"As a man who has avoided the kind of authentic experience that might cause you to better know your own faults, cowardice should be dear to you."

"I fear you've taken on a fevered tone, Madam."

"And you pity yourself most of all. How ordinary. Will you send my brother by when you find him?"

He bows, despite himself, and finally leaves.

The sea turns a cut of surf onto the sand. A barge rolls by as I lean forward to lick the balcony rail, coming away with salt and sticking dust, the very flavor of independence. A defiant death! The greatest death of all.

Elizabeth better appreciates a new romance by relentlessly comparing it with an old one

Romano saved a seat for her at breakfast and they ate without much conversation. At one point he remarked that ten people had died in a train derailment in Germany and they spoke of it in distant terms.

It was a simple morning but a pleasurable one, and Elizabeth found herself preoccupied, thinking of subtle ways to appear more elegant, holding her shoulders down to elongate her neck until she felt a strain in her collarbone. Max never liked to talk about the news, but Romano seemed content to spend the morning on it, going over every detail and adding his own commentary.

She thought back to when Max came to their new school in Darmstadt. He had arrived very hat-in-hand one afternoon and declared himself ready to become part of the movement. She had enjoyed a nice weekend with him some time before, in Vienna, so she let him in. Isadora was away at the time but he took to Elizabeth as if she was the true genius, actually sitting at her feet to listen to her stories of New York and London and all the way back to Oakland, the house, her father. Her life seemed endlessly fascinating to him. When she asked him for stories about the cafés and his parents' little grocery, he always changed the subject back to her. He intimated once that he had gone to an intellectual salon hosted by Sigmund Freud but he seemed unwilling to speak on it more, and she appreciated how he didn't seem to hold much interest in famous people. That was the season he wrote a lecture on the power of a woman taking charge of her own mind in a move she suspected later was meant only to court her. She was flattered and so ignored the little ways they disagreed, including his personal disdain for the daily news, which he dismissed as gossip and speculation, even the political pages.

They grew closer on an early faculty trip to a lake near the school. The girls had wanted to go swimming, but the teachers decided it would be inappropriate to go together and so waited until their charges went on a shopping trip for ribbons or candy or whatever it was girls bought with the pennies they found.

At the waterside, the teachers set up towels and unwrapped their lunch, grapes and bread and hunks of cheese. There were five of them in total, all women, save for Max, who glanced around at times to see if anyone else on the beach had noticed his good fortune. He unbuttoned his shirt and was naked to the waist, and though he spoke often of the necessary physical strength of women, Elizabeth noticed that he was padded with a generous layer of soft flesh, pouting tenderly at his breast. But it was his attention that charmed her; he made her a plate of food and repeated for the group a story of a recent kindness she had given to a student.

The other teachers went down to the water, and he stayed with her, reading a book while she watched everyone swimming. There was a group of boys playing on a large floating pallet, something that must have fallen off a fishing boat. There was not quite enough room on the pallet for all five boys to stand, and they climbed all over one another, waving to their friends on the shore. Soon enough they realized that if one of them shifted his weight, the others had to drop down to keep from falling in.

They grew bolder, hurling themselves across the way. One of the smaller boys was launched into the water and the others howled with laughter, slapping the board with their open palms. He made to pull himself up again, but when he tried, the others kicked his arms, leaving him to swim in sad half circles. Elizabeth watched the little boy as he paddled around his friends and called their names, and long after that day, she remembered the look on his face, so surprised and hurt and yet smiling all the time as if he was in on the joke.

Isadora remembers first meeting Singer at the theater Gaîté Lyrique,
the interior of which was warm enough to forgive the
miserable wet snow

He arrived on paper first, cardstocked over red dahlias, special delivery from a land of gentle sentiment I had glimpsed only at galas where my honorarium for the evening was just a drop in one of the buckets under the sculptural ice flanking the ballroom floor.

I find a gift of flowers has as much potential magic as spontaneous flight or traveling time, coins in the mouths of fish or new shoes for good girls. When they surround the dead, they protect the body for a few delicate days from the earth pressing in. In life, they bind any pair and bless the union with evidence of spontaneous life. And so yes, flowers for all occasions and particularly before a show, serving as a nice reminder that fortune favors the fortunate.

After the dahlias were presented, the courier apparently delayed for twenty minutes, making conversation with the stage manager before knocking on the dressing room door again to present the card:

PARIS SINGER,

PAIGNTON.

It was a particularly good season for dance, and a general feeling persisted around the city that if things continued to build, we might end the year with untold advancements in art and science, ushering in an era of human dignity and love. I performed in the center of the great hall of the Gaîté Lyrique, with the audience standing all around me. Tall windows looked out on the snow, and a compass star pattern laid into the wood made it feel as if I were dancing across a map of the world.

I must have been doing a Chopin show that night; endless Chopin at the time. Before having the pianist begin, I liked to stand in silence for a full minute, taking in my audience and breathing with them. I hoped they would each feel I was inventing the program on the spot for them, when in reality I had practiced every move in sequence for weeks, including the walk to my mark and the ease with which I would ask the pianist for a certain movement or cadenza.

Eventually the spontaneous feeling came to work too well, and I found myself needing to prove my own mastery, which made the whole enterprise lose some of its magic, but that came long after that winter in 1909, when magic was in high supply.

After the performance, Paris came to my dressing room door and waited patiently outside while I tidied up: tunics thrown off and on again, two boxes of gifted chocolates stashed in a long drawer, a side table cleared of stage powder and blush, three pairs of street shoes and their attendant stockings placed in a smart line by the WC, a square of paper soaked and swabbed around the basin, newspapers deposited in the wastebasket, and the page with the good review brought out and tucked under the vase of dahlias. The flowers were so freshly cut they seemed to pulse with life, presenting themselves shamelessly and giving the room a frankly sexual cast. Finally I threw the door open to reveal Paris Singer, a gleaming pillar taking the form of a man, and anyone who has never fallen in love with a fresh stone pillar has not spent enough time among them.

A pillar! Ducking through doorframes, hair-curling Ionic, the centerpiece of every room and broad as a horse at the shoulders. I wanted to hand him everything I owned and climb onto his back. This fresh Lohengrin could have sailed in on a swan for the pride of posture he brought to my dressing room, and in his presence I saw all the broken-down things pressing in: the rusted latches of cabinets, smudged half-drunk glasses, a galette crumbled on a cloth, all of it wilting before him. The flowers bent deferent. He seemed to be everywhere at once; we had barely settled into conversation when he had to get up and shake the hand of the boy who interrupted to announce the time, and later he stopped in mid-sentence to remark that he had looked in on the child care at the theater and found it quite sufficient. He was curious about our life on the road and my local students and asked a hundred questions; he had children of his own, he explained, four girls with their mother in Florida. I appreciated his subtlety. Later, when Deirdre was brought into the room, he gave her a piece of hard candy from his pocket as if he were her grandfather. She called him Papa right away and I didn't try to stop her, as every man over forty was her daddy back then and mine as well.

Paris, son of Isaac, descended from myth at the helm of his father's fortune, Isaac Singer's banquet so opulent his children could only hope to find the energy required to consume a thin slice of it. They were obliged to smile gamely at parties while people looked around as if Isaac himself were standing just beyond the conversation. Women told Paris of dreams they had where his father came to their beds, flanked by a double line of sewing machines, coated in the golden dust of invention, making violent love to them among reams of hemmed trousers.

He didn't think much of it. Women were thrilled by the idea of Isaac Singer, particularly the lower classes. Every sewing machine rolling off his factory line was destined to save the life and livelihood of a woman somewhere in the world, a gift of forty extra hours a week and healthy backs and hands with which to enjoy those hours, and Isaac was the warden who set them free. He had twenty-four children when all was said and done, four boys and twenty lovely girls, and Paris liked to think that he was the one born with the most business sense. He seemed to lack that charming desire sons have to kill their fathers and merely wanted only to exile from his own heart and mind the patriarch who was, by all accounts, also very tall.

Like a transient picking through garbage, I've selected from memory a few fresh prizes and left the remainder to rot. I've kept nothing of our first conversation that night, which surely went beyond my performance or the flowers, the fine performance space; it's hard to say and better to forget. Without the dull details fogging things up, we can exist forever as in a museum diorama, standing forever in a perfect state of admiration and anticipation. On the left, our captain of industry, ticker tape to his shins, frozen mid-stride before a painted stretch of free land; on the right, our heroine, barefoot on a waxed wood floor, laurels draped about her shoulders. We would have had a better chance in a museum like that, with a pane of glass between us.

When he said farewell that night at the Gaîté Lyrique, I thought that was it; there seemed a mutual desire to keep that first meeting sacred by never repeating it. But he arrived again despite himself the next evening, taking his place in the *grande salle* as if it had been built around him. His vest fit like a ream of brocade stretched over a grain thresher, its machine heart driving rows onto a field. The room was strung with garlands all the way to the lamps flickering at the high ceiling, and the room below was warm and glad when I came in to dance. We forget the cobwebs in the chandeliers until they disturb the light.

The series I did that night was modeled after the *Titeux Dancer* draped in terra-cotta at the Louvre, which Gus and I had sketched one endless afternoon on the museum's benches. I remember now, it was Chopin, and six of my younger students formed a supporting corps. That evening I chose a tunic the color and weight of skin on a glass of milk, and when the children padded around in their frantic circle—too loud, darlings, let's work on that in the morning—the folds drifted to reveal just a glimpse of my strong thigh, the tension built by the leg's steady line only slightly eased by the billowing fabric, steel to stir the fold. The girls smelled of clover, and their movement contained as in a shallow dish my own scent of coffee and dark beer.

We made a storm of human energy. Having the crowd stand through it was a little cruel to the ladies, but it allowed us to create more of a clear contrast: bare feet supple and lithe around shoes and heeled boots, flaunting our freedom against their constraint. They were meant to feel their own feet aching. Though I had done it that way for years, nobody seemed to understand what I was going for until that night, when Paris Singer took off his dress shoes.

He didn't make a fuss about it, holding toe to heel to remove one and then the other while remaining upright. It seemed as if he didn't want to disrupt the performance, moving slowly and watching me all the while, and I was the only one who saw him do it. He stood beside his fine dress shoes. It was the sight of him in his trouser socks that made me realize we would make a child together. He would continue to surprise me though never quite so sweetly.

The girls held hands, and little Deirdre on one end earnestly shook a tambourine for the finale. I lifted a basket of flowers overhead and drew navigatorial lines with my feet, turning half circles from the knee. A few of his dahlias were slipped in to say hello, and I turned my head as if I were too timid to regard his gift straight-on. Of course, shyness is an invention of the state and as easily forgotten as its representatives. Though the whole of it might later be rendered harmless in watercolors, it was not a harmless moment. It was the moment Paris and I truly understood each other. He was in the center of that compass star, and cardinal north drew him to me. If only the rest of the floor had fallen away, leaving the two of us alone in the world.

We sent Deirdre home that night with the children of my wealthiest patron, a friend to Paris to whom he showed no fear or deference. The man had two girls in my school, as gawkish and somber as cranes, with the emotional thrift typically inherited with wealth. But they were sweet to Deirdre when their father told them to be, and they gave her little flowers they had plucked from a centerpiece. The girls went off to play, and Deirdre was gone before I could tell her to wash her face before bed and not to trust those other girls.

It wasn't much later that night that Paris and I escaped the party and ran laughing down the stairs, bursting from the heavy doors to find the icy rain laced with thin strands of potential. His hands were so soft I could have pushed my fingernail into his palm to see it emerge from the other side, but he was strong, and he carried me gracefully over the water which surrounded his car in a perfect ring.

He had ordered the car to be filled with flowers and they were blooming up the back window and encroaching on the passenger bench, thousands of stems piled without water. The air inside was lush and as thick as a jungle, petals soft against my bare arms, pollinating his cuffs as he pulled me near. The thorns of lesser blooms prized bits of my tunic into their thicket as I kissed him.

We were gin soaked and immortal, and ready for a grand adventure. I turned to watch the night jolting by through the fogging windows. We crossed the Boulevard Saint-Martin, past a woman who stood on a wet trunk waving her arms, either calling out for help or advertising the bill of some show, nobody paying her any mind either way.

On Corfu, the unlikely appearance of Paris Singer seated at the foot of the bed

I should be thankful for the fresh sheets. The old ones were stained and gritty, scattered crumbs from breakfast and a few books splayed around. But I miss the smell of my own illness, my sickly nest. Soap makes a slick and unnatural perfume, it makes me forget my own body, and I come to wonder if I have lost myself in a dream.

Paris reads aloud from a newspaper, opining at times as if the editorial board is located somewhere between his ears. I must be dreaming. The fever broke overnight in a drenching sweat, and in the ensuing hours I received more swabbing down from that damn nurse than a standard workhorse. The girls in the kitchen downstairs have been saying I'll be up and about before the end of the week, and I do seem to be doing better, despite wanting very much to prove them wrong on principle.

A leather valise resists against his calf with the day's plots and sketches folded neatly on top: banks and bridges, dark beer with lunch, and an afternoon nap. We ought to have plenty to say to each other, many potential apologies, and plenty time to fit it all into an eight hour dream, but as how it happens in moments like this, the foundation is laid with simple slabs.

"Hullo," I say, as dull as a brick. "You're here."

He shrugs, his presence being natural everywhere. "You came to me in a dream."

"So you've arrived to even things out."

This interest in fairness is a well-established trait. He likes to count the number of times a couple invited us to dinner and multiply that figure by some determiner to find the value of the gift he would bring to their wedding. In business, he is aware not only of who picked up the bill, but of the quantity and occasion; four beers on an early lunch is reciprocated with an engraved pen given as a gift to sign the contract, while a fine bottle of champagne warrants an invitation onto the *Iris*, his white-winged yacht. Equivalence as a social concept rules his life, and so it follows that he would trade my visit to his dreams with his own, his suit pressed despite the journey, his facial hair far too well-groomed to be real. Already the light seems to bleed through him; we should get to the point before I wake.

"Darling," I say. "Draw near to me, for I am dying."

Paris gives me that old look of patient dismissal, the same look he employs to return untouched baskets of rolls to the waiters unacquainted with his preferences, informing them in his polite but firm way that he would eat bread when he was poor.

"You're dying?" he remarks. "You look well enough."

"But you've only just arrived. You find me in a grave state, sitting in the grave itself."

"Your grave has lovely clean sheets then, and three meals daily." Taking up his paper again, he considers the foreign press. "The nurse said your fever broke last night, and you might be able to have a little breakfast already today. She says it was quite a fast turnaround, actually." He takes hold of my foot, giving it an encouraging little shake.

"But it's not possible you talked to her, she hasn't come in yet."

"And you've made two healthy bowel movements since your fever broke, praise the Lord." Holding my foot against its attempt to escape, he rubs its arch with his thumb. "I know you might believe the world ceases to turn outside the bounds of your experience, but they're all gossiping endlessly about you downstairs. One of the girls in the kitchen has serviceable English, and the older ones know Italian."

"They haven't spoken a word of Italian to me!"

"You'll be dancing to cross the room when we shove off at the end of the week."

I pull my foot so violently out of his grasp that the bed shakes. "You're joking."

"It's past time," he says. "Elizabeth has selected a lover from a group of rowdy tenants, and Gus is preparing for an expedition down the Mamoré. They're drinking the island dry between the two of them. The kitchen has worked its way straight through the wine, and two bottles of rye have gone missing from the front office."

His image splits clean in two, speaking in perfect unison. The man on the left gazes nervously at the one on the right. "All this is happening on my tab, I'm sure. I'll receive the bill consolidated from the hoteliers and dock merchants in the spring." Paris makes a strange set of twins. I picture them screaming in a pram.

"We can't go now. Gus only wants to sit and speculate, he'll never make a trip. And Elizabeth would never enter into a casual dalliance—" I am overcome with a coughing fit, extended only slightly to garner sympathy from the visitor, who nods as if a worldly concept is being expressed in phlegm. "With whom?" I manage.

"I'm only relaying information I heard from the girls downstairs. They had quite a bit to say, as you might imagine."

Unfortunately, shooting the messenger would require taking aim twice. The man on the right would be easy enough to strike, but his alter form shifts to watch the bed from different angles, menacing his newspaper in his hands.

"Don't give me any trouble on it," says the man on the right, ignoring the other. "You said you needed time to think, and now look, you've had a month and a half to do nothing but turn your thoughts over and over. Come, let's get you back to France. You'll shock them with a solo series and set up a new school after that."

What would be the use in contradicting his method? Paris prides himself in downswing investment. And anyway, welcoming grief as a friend has only made it friendly, and now it has outstayed its welcome, settling into my lungs. Paris has been off overseeing enterprises, and planning my recovery while he's at it.

Men like Paris, which is to say great men and kings of industry, don't just happen on this personality; they practice it from the moment it's engendered into their boyhood. They mark plans on scraps of paper they steal from their fathers, binding the loose pages with twine and calling it juvenilia. As they grow older and more romantic, they write sprawling love letters to themselves disguised as fiction or philosophy. Great men anticipate their own greatness and consider almost every angle of it; except, of course, how their greatness will appear to anyone else. A woman might as well be alone when she is alone with a great man.

Women pursue their own legacy in ways far more subtle, hedging their bets with culinary skills or self-effacing charm, though the etiquette lessons we suffer through don't do us much good if we're dead before we get a chance to enjoy the parties thrown in our honor.

Paris goes back to his newspaper, waiting me out. Beside him, his shadow seems smudged at the edges like a hasty sketch made out of proportion, his torso wielding the dark wings of his shoulders. The shadow man glares with simple loathing at Paris, who ignores him, talking aimlessly of autumn in New York.

Surely you don't believe him, I address the shadow man. *He's only trying to convince himself.* The shadow man bares his teeth. He is a dog beside the great man, beaten and cowering, neglected by his master. He looks hungry. He wrings his bare hands, which I notice are missing both the onyx ring and the wristwatch Paris bought to seem more like an airman despite much preferring the piece in his pocket with its heavy gold chain.

I have seen Paris Singer's shadow man only once before. It was after a long dinner with friends, wherein a case of wine may as well have been poured into the toilet for all the good it did us. One of the men was engaged in an argument with a light fixture, which nearly came to blows. A woman locked herself in the bathroom and could not be cajoled to emerge again, and three girls nobody knew were singing Christmas carols beautifully while everyone yelled at them to stop. Memory draws a curtain over these nights, which might begin in the city but really get going when someone suggested we go sailing.

The first time I saw the shadow man, it was after that long dinner, the night that German fought a lamp and lost, as I recall. I can't remember for the life of me who the man was, but the lamp was a beautiful old brass piece with tassels hanging from the shade, apparently imposing enough to start a quarrel. Paris gazed at the man strangling the lamp. He looked at each of us in turn, as if forcing himself to observe the human scene would allow him to describe it fully to an interested third party. The women had moved on to fellowship-style hymns. A plate of ice cream melted into a puddle on the carpet. Someone was scraping candle wax from the wall, and I had just begun a serpentine dance to the accompaniment of a fellow playing a toy piano when I saw the shadow man appear for just a moment beside Paris, his eyes skewed and loathing. I feared him and was glad when he absorbed back into his host, at which point Paris excused himself, lifted one of the heavy sash-weight windows at the front of the room, stepped out onto the ledge, and jumped, dropping two full meters to the road below. We had been fighting bitterly all week, so I declared *Death to Tyrants* and went back to my dance. Someone rushed to the window and reported that he had fallen hard but lay for only a moment before getting to his feet and running down the road. He turned the corner without so much as glancing back.

It was an unusual move for the man typically content to serve as grand marshal to our little parade of disordered malaise. We all gossiped viciously about him for the rest of the night, and though I would claim in the morning that I had harbored a secret concern and gone out to search for him while the rest of them slept, the truth was that I lodged a few of the worst jokes at his expense and even pulled some secrets out of the archive, such as the fact that he wished most of all to be rid of his father's house in Paignton, and also that he fully believed that in a prior life he had been a dire wolf.

He was gone for two days, returning on the morning of the third wearing a new suit and bearing a bolt of velvet that I made into a touring curtain. We never spoke about the rest of it. After that, I encountered the shadow man only in my dreams, his sullen gaze following me through the labyrinth.

Though Paris and the shadow man both seem to resent their presence in the room, neither attempts to escape; Paris wouldn't fit through the window, and his shadow probably doesn't want to fall into the sea and have to contend with the divisive properties of jetsam threatening to spread him without distinction across the strait.

Paris recites a few ferry departures and connecting trains. We could go through Brindisi and take our time working through the hills, resting before we arrived back in the city. I feel a tempting pleasure of a new hotel: the staff and their labor, the soothing course of daily tasks.

A quick knock precedes Elizabeth with the basin. She comes in midway through a monologue about my health and has already asked after the sore on my rump before she sees we are not alone, startling so violently she nearly dumps the whole liquid operation in the process. "Paris," she says.

"I am having a dream," I explain. "This is a spirit man and a shadow man in addition."

"Hullo, Elizabeth," one of them says.

"Good Christ," she says, setting the basin down and bracing herself on the counter in a pleasantly dramatic way, Elizabeth not typically given to dramatics. Perhaps she has taken a lover after all. "And so in this dream," she says, "I am bringing in a bath?"

"Apparently so. I'll say honestly that your presence destroys any sexual element that might impose itself on the scene, but the way things were going, he was more likely to hand me a gourd filled with secrets than take me in his arms—"

"I have not arrived in a dream," he interjects, dubious but insistent, in the same tone he uses when he doesn't fully remember giving an order to a member of his staff but has not quite decided to commit himself against the idea of it.

"You probably did," Elizabeth says. "We are already bound on the vector of her whim. Doesn't it follow that we would be called to serve in her sleep as well?" She looks him over. "You look like you came straight from Ghent."

"I was trying to remind her of the merits of France."

"How perfect!" she says. "Come to my dreams next with a croissant." She wrings out a rag. "Now, Isadora, quit shifting about, you'll exhaust yourself. Let's see that great wide forehead of yours." The rag is pressed in turn to my forehead, cheeks, behind my ears, the nape of the neck. The shadow man seems preoccupied. Elizabeth talks at length about her day so far, but it's possible to gently shift her voice out of the conscious mind, much like one could push an old, worn brick back into the wall from which it had begun to hang. "Never mind me," she says.

Paris has always had a funny way of watching people, as if he is trying to determine and absorb their secrets. The shadow man is even less subtle about it as Paris roams the room. His shadow's eyes rove across my rounded shoulders and the curve of my breast through my dressing gown, which I further cover with the blanket. He licks his lips.

"Not much of an opportunity," Paris says, tapping the window glass.

"If you could carry some of that breeze to the bed, it will be the first I've felt in days."

"We should have them move this armoire," he says. "It's blocking a second window entirely."

"There's a second window?"

"They told me you were enjoying mornings on the terrace until the doctor determined that the chance of infection was too high." He looks me over, and his shadow cackles to see my discomfort. I hate the both of them.

"I'm starting to get the sense you've already interviewed everyone on the island. Are you sure you wouldn't like to have a sample of my stool?"

Sensing the storm, Elizabeth makes a subtle exit.

"I only wanted to make sure they were taking care of my dancing bear," he says genially.

"And moreover, you're blocking the light." He makes a better door than a window, but his presence is a door in itself; the hotel accepted the promise of his eventual arrival as implied credit on the account, which came to include meals and lodging both, afternoon tea and sundry items, including a small crate of wine that was far too sweet, which they would not allow us to return. They extended the credit to include my medical care, but the material cost mounted, and the nurse had her own expenses— she kept speaking of a family to feed, as if they were all kittens trapped in a crate—and though the hotelier was of course honored to serve, and in serving support the arts, there was, in the end, the question of the bill. The manager was well pleased to see Paris coming up the street that morning. He did very much resemble his father, whom the owner had seen in advertisements in the foreign press, the inventor hovering in an ink frame above his newest machines. Paris goes through life thinking of money the same way he thinks of the train schedule.

"Come back with me," he says. "They're calling for you. I have three bound parcels of personal letters, most of them well-wishing."

"Show me the ones that call for my immediate demise."

He laughs, frowning, which makes him seem very Parisian.

"Mills is bored at Oldway," he says, changing the subject by bringing up employees and property, the two things he knows very well are my least favorite subjects. He could fill a book with the people on his payroll and pass it off as the yearbook representing a class of homely misfits. "I've begun to think he's inventing architectural extremities in order to occupy his mind. He just sent plans for reinforcing the ballroom floors to hold more people than either of us have ever met."

If he's going to insist on conversation, let's make it something substantial. "Have you been to Père-Lachaise," I say, "to see the children's memorial?"

This straightens him up. "I have not."

"Because you couldn't bear it."

"I could bear it fine. I simply don't see the point when any corner of the city could be imbued with their spirits. And anyway, you have the ashes, unless you've lost them somewhere." He comes and smooths my hair against the pillow, speaking gently. "Perhaps you were right, we should have buried them. Mother's crypt is visited by mourners every day, and there is a stone to lay the flowers down. My sisters go there for guidance."

"They say any grave is right twice a day."

He leans back and observes my bed, as if calculating the cost of labor required to have it dismantled and rebuilt as a homesteader shack, the kind of place that might forever remove him from conversations such as this one.

"Ashes are so economical," I add, trying to soothe and attack him at once; nothing so intricate as a good fight.

"If you didn't want me to visit, you could have sent word to the effect."

"I wanted you to come," I insisted, the sentiment falling flat because thoughts of him in truth have only just arrived to replace the blankness

I felt after observing the ceiling and walls and the palms of my hands for weeks and, when thoughts of the palms become too much to bear, turning the hands over to observe their slight scars. That quackish doctor declared on his way out that my rest cure would be best confined to the bed, and when the meager surroundings exhausted me, I reluctantly entered the confines of my mind. At first I couldn't stop going through the details of the accident, half-regarding the scene in memory as one might observe a room of cheap and embarrassing furniture. I could only distract myself from those thoughts once I realized that each mole on my forearm had a twin and that every one of those twins could be grouped into fantastic swarming colonies all over my body.

"I'm here now regardless," he says. "And you'll come back with me to the city if you know what's best." The shadow man edges slightly toward the window, his eye bulging as if it were being subtly inflated.

"I would rather throw myself into the strait than return to some depressing play at life."

"I came all this way for quite a cold welcome, then." His broad attempt at guilt doesn't fool me for a moment. Likely he scheduled this trip to fall between a trip to the coast and the dedication of a factory. Factories must be so dedicated these days, with all the work they do!

He sighs and goes into his bag, as if my attitude has forced him to do this. Finding a letter, he tosses it onto the foot of the bed, and I have to draw my own aching body forward to reach it. It's marked from Berlin, from Harry Kessler, Ted's patron.

"I thought you might like to have it," he said.

"And you already opened it, of course."

"It was addressed to both of us."

"Declaring love and fidelity on behalf of Teddy, I'm sure."

He's really sick of me now. "Stranger things have come in the evening post."

It is impossible even to begin reading the perfunctory lines. Everyone seems to have taken these messages as an excuse to display their calligraphy lessons, assuming their little notes will be preserved in my archive. True sentiment is hard enough without all the fussy stags and whorls of fine penmanship, and most people can't be bothered. Harry's cardstock is so thick that I have to lay it flat to rip it in half.

Paris watches me do it. "That's all then," he says, gathering his things. His shadow cowers. "I come to find your family beleaguering the Greeks, running up an outrageous tab you have no intention of paying—"

"Excuse me, we have every intention—"

"—and you haven't thought to ask me how I'm getting along."

"But I can see exactly how you are, Paris! You're working out my concert dates for fall."

"You may prefer to own this entire tragedy," he sneers, "but I'd like to remind you I was there for it, too."

"You mean for the funeral? We didn't see much of you at the flat, except for when you came home drunk."

The shadow man unhinges his jaw, and a sound emerges like a runaway train bearing down on the room. Paris has always had the power to cut me down, and now he has plenty reason. I am an unarmored creature, as soft as gelatin, with just a few poison spikes in my arsenal, but I will deploy them if I must.

"Perhaps you could console yourself with your more legitimate children," I say, the words flying like slipped brakes, the steward leaping for a grassy bank. "Or you could go lie in your precious family crypt and discuss the subject with your mother." The cars bear down and ram through the wall, scattering clapboard and glass, books and plates and wooden dolls soaring into the open air.

"I believe we are done here," he says.

"Go on then, get out."

He picks through the wreckage in search of his dignity, lifting his hat from where it landed on a pile of crushed metal. The shadow man follows him out.

With the both of them gone at last, the quiet morning returns. I can look forward to many hours of contemplation about how perfectly shaped grief is as a private venture, how melancholy can be played for an audience, but true grief should be guarded and held close. Grief is the only hope for the poor soul flailing in water, the only stone the body can hold that might have the weight to sink it.

Elizabeth remembers her triumphant return to New York in 1899, after her first unlucky months in Europe

Even with the unpleasantries of ocean travel—the disorienting motion in windowless quarters that made her feel as if she were stowed away in the inner ear of a swimming giant—it was hard for Elizabeth to ignore a particularly buoyant feeling of optimism. The ship on its second passage smelled of paint and fresh-stained wood, and the oiled deck gleamed as bright as the jaunty stacks. Even the dishes in the dining hall were perfect, every plate and saucer bearing the name *Oceanic* between a pair of hairline blue rows.

She was in steerage with three Celt girls who were traveling to pursue life in America. The girls were twenty years old and new to the open sea and spent every night green-gilled and moaning as the ship rocked itself to sleep. When a sailboat rolls on the waves, you see yourself as an object on the waves. When the ocean liner does the same, however, it's as if the whole world is tipping from its axis and the rest of your life will have to continue on this horrible canted course. The gut is the last to adjust, aligned longingly with the old horizon while the rest of you hangs onto a rail for balance.

Elizabeth relished the chance to travel without her family. Isadora had always been the mallard topping their chevron, and they were all ducky in her wake, but they were in London not two weeks before it became clear that beyond Isadora's little lecture tour on the function of art—which she had surely booked on the basis of being twenty-one years old and so charmingly preoccupied with Nietzsche that the audience had to restrain themselves from running up to pinch her cheeks—there was no work lined up and no contacts to speak of either. Mother and the boys were fine going along with it, being optimistic and easily fooled. They would all go from theater to theater, begging to put on a matinee show. Eventually the shame of it wore Elizabeth down, along with the helpless sense that Isadora was their only hope for success.

In London, she had nightmares of the cattle boat that brought them to Europe. Every night she was forced to remember how they suffered on soiled bedrolls over a hundred quailing beasts, hooves like plug iron slamming against one another as the animals screamed in fear and agony, terrible human screams. Every morning the deckhands pulled at least one broken-necked milch cow from her pen and hung her from a boom over the water, skinning her before dropping the denuded carcass into the sea.

She remembered the sad end of the largest steer, who had spent the last days of his life in a horrible state. He kept mounting the poor lowing cows, killing three of them with his violence, but he was allowed to remain general in the pen because there was no room to move him. The Duncans were trapped right beside him for days, separated by a few thin planks. They watched the carnage unfold, weakened by simple witness, by the sight and sound of death and the river of blood flowing from the wounds he opened on the backs of his hapless mates. At last the doomed thing kicked a supporting beam and took down the deck above, crushing himself and ten cows and breaking the leg of a sailor who had sworn that very morning over breakfast that this was his last cattle trip. In the rubble, the man was filled with such fury at the situation that he found the trapped steer, bowed his head over it, and took a savage bite out of the animal's neck. Elizabeth would never forget his wild eyes when he reared back, chewing as if he hadn't eaten in weeks, fresh gore blooming down his neck.

It took the rest of the day to dump the dead animals from under the fallen deck. They had amassed the sea's population of sharks following in a carnivorous mass. Isadora had insisted again and again that bovine ghosts were following the ship as well, until Mother told her to shut up, and pointed out that if there truly were ghosts, they would scatter to haunt the city once they arrived in port.

Elizabeth believed there was something to her sister's eerie observation. One thing was clear: they had built up enough bad luck to keep them from ever finding steady employment in London. They failed to find work in performance, public or private instruction, or mending, although they didn't try very hard for the mending, as nobody but Gus was very patient and he didn't have the tactile skill. They failed to draw notice dancing on the street, invisible next to buskers who used tricks and animals to hide their own inexperience. After dinner, Mother went to the corner below their room—once they finally found a room, its own sad story—and asked well-heeled men on the street if they might bring their daughters in for an afternoon lesson, remarking with her usual mix of prescience and delusion that one of her girls would one day be quite famous and would command performances in the great cities of the world as a beloved inventor and curator of her craft and the other one was also very sweet. It was lucky enough that she wasn't thrown into jail on any given night for her solicitation, but it seemed the men only pitied her.

Mother liked to look the part of a lady even when she played it less convincingly, such as when Father left for good and she screamed threats and accusations to his receding frame, clutching their children to her skirts and inspiring in them a mutual wail that alerted the neighbors but inspired no sympathy from its intended target, who was only meaning to escape criminal debt as efficiently as possible and would be a dead man soon enough without anyone's help. Elizabeth had to push the thought away; speaking ill of the dead was a low act and could turn luck away.

This interest in luck was her only souvenir from Europe, and she pinned it to her heart. Before she needed fortune so desperately, she would never have guessed at all the things she could do to alter the odds: touching the left hand of a child could bring in money, for example, while rolling a spearmint leaf between cheek and jaw usually worked to conjure up a hot meal. She discovered the trick with the spearmint on their third week of stale biscuits; if she had only known, she would have plucked the plant bare weeks prior.

Ultimately, it was a way for Elizabeth to protect herself. She couldn't bear to think that the inattentive eyes of fate—or worse, her sister's free-wheeling whims—might control the family's destiny and her own. So she did small things when the thought occurred. She thanked the butcher while focusing on the number twenty-four and walked quickly past financial institutions, ignoring their front door and repeating her mother's maiden name. She skipped the third step on rainy days in favor of the second and fourth. It was important to perform every superstitious act that came to mind; each premonition was surely placed there for a reason and so deserved her attention and respect.

Her strategy had reaped some small reward, for though cattle saw her to Europe, the fresh sheets of steerage would carry her home. She had been wise to keep in touch with the ladies whose daughters she had taught in New York, sending long letters with dark and dramatic retellings of their adventures and hinting politely at the trouble they continued to endure, her idea being that one of the ladies might see fit to write a cheque in the name of old friends. Before long, she was shocked to learn that her favorite of them had been moved to tears by her story of hardship and was offering to wire return passage and set Elizabeth up in the maid's quarters to teach her five daughters again. The girls had been remiss in their training and were turning wayward; if Elizabeth would consider returning, she would be rewarded handsomely indeed. The letter arrived while they were living above a printing house that gave her those terrible nightmares of the cattle boat every time she managed to fall asleep, so the choice was clear. Isadora only protested to remark that Elizabeth gave up too easily, but relented on the grounds that her sister would be teaching the Method, which meant they would be diversifying on two coasts.

It was a soothing thing to say that hardship made her stronger, but she wondered if it were true. The Celt girls were so gentle with one another, so open with their laughter and tears. Elizabeth would look in the mirror each morning and try to smile as those girls did, but she could not even approximate it.

She returned again and again to the question as they drew closer toward

New York's hearty three meals a day. If her goal was an innocence in expression, it would be better to take nothing from heartbreak or horror but the knowledge and ability to avoid those routes in the future. A horse dying in the street did nothing to enhance her experience of a waltz. Isadora felt differently, and would rather fall to her knees, rub her face in the slab of its shuddering hide, and call it an orgastic experience of death in the midst of life, but it was a dead horse in truth, and as it became a sodden pile of grist under traffic, it served only to muddle the potential for the pure expression of ideas such as joy and faith, gumming those bright concepts up with such a palette of bleak shades that no light could struggle through.

Perhaps it was only a function of her personality. Elizabeth hated her own good memory, which dogged her with sentimental images. She was nothing like her sister, who could gather herself up from any corpse and ask about supper, and in the same way find in congress with friends and lovers a fleeting glimpse of life's pure energy or whatever she wanted to ascribe to that moment, but then was able to discard the entire exchange like a pair of ruined slippers on her walk home from the party. There was a way Isadora had of engaging on levels spiritual and emotional and physical all at once and then pushing aside the entire interaction as if it meant nothing to her. Meanwhile, Elizabeth was dull and forgettable with men and women both and then agonized over those stilted interactions for months.

There she was, making slow passage back to the city that had thrown every impulsive terror at her and etched them into her memory. At least the passage was fine. The *Oceanic* boasted a dining hall with chairs rather than hard benches, serviceable biscuits with every meal. She might have gotten second class out of her patroness if she hadn't spoken in such detail of the low life to which she had become accustomed in London, but she also might not have return passage at all; anyway it wasn't so bad, the biscuits soaked in tea, plenty of time to think on the details of the new school, and the Celts were sweet and plaited her hair. The *Oceanic* found steadier days, and they eventually caught a favorable wind, all of it a sign of how simple things could be, for the smart and good, for the lucky.

15 June 1913
Teatro della Pergola
Ted Craig, Direttore, cavoli riscaldati
Non troppo avanti, Firenze

Feeling a little better here in Greece and not a moment too soon, as our bill is only paid through the week and they'd like very much to open the rooms for the high season. Gus has passage booked to South America; he's acting out of stubbornness now, having heard that none of us thought he would actually go. He still wants me to join him, but I believe I'll stay in the region. Raymond and his wife are calling me to Albania, which is closer than Peru, quieter than Paris, and cheaper living too. I'll be away for a while from the common post, but before I packed my cards I thought I would write.

You have done much work with the myth of Orpheus adventuring into the Underworld to save Eurydice. I would like to present an alternative story to appear in your program notes:

EURYDICE—
Who was well acquainted with the Underworld and had begun even to see its charms, such as the soothing human groan from the lake of the

damned and the bleeding walls cool against her face. Her hosts brought her pomegranate seeds and allowed her to sit sometimes on their dark thrones, which were comfortably warm, heated from lower floors. She and Persephone found they had so much in common, both of them happier alone than in company, both frolic-shamed and made to feel small. They both spoke of the world above as a tedious play they were happy to escape halfway through, its dramas a distant memory.

All to say Eurydice was thriving, and though she knew it would happen, her heart still sank when Orpheus arrived. He stood before her in his robes from the last time she saw him, as if he couldn't be bothered to change. The garlands he brought her withered as he approached, dry petals dropping to scatter.

She had rehearsed her refusal for months, but the Moirai compelled it to slip her mind, and even though her friends and lesser demons wept and tried to hold her back, she agreed to follow him up to the surface again; to life, which had gone on without her.

The two of them began the journey at once. She tried to soothe herself by studying him, and mirrored in her motion his slow-lifting foot, muscles in the standing leg made to support and span the other, touching toe before heel to the black sand, his foot's powerful arch soaring the length of his step. The strength of the living was already a mystery to her; the dead hardly move, not seeing the point.

Her reluctance mounted as his steps fell slower and slower; she watched them, shivering already against the cold wind made to feel colder by the comfortable heat at her back. The morning light burned her eyes as they passed the virtuous pagans, and she knew they were almost there.

But then a miracle happened. He came to a stop at the step that would bring them into the light for good. It was a blessing she couldn't have ordered up more perfectly herself, a moment of grace. Some goddess smiled upon her when Orpheus stopped and turned around.

She couldn't believe it. He was silhouetted by the light behind him, and at first she wasn't sure. Only his howling sorrow confirmed the curse was broken. They were close enough to touch, but would never touch again. She was surprised to see the agony in his eyes. The look on his face, how he hated her! It had all become clear at just the right time.

Damned forever, she felt herself relax. There was nothing Eurydice feared so much as life's dull potential, and now it was gone forever. She laughed, despite herself, as the goddesses of violent death dragged her down, his face fading into the senseless light of the living. The truth of it became clear to her as she lost sight of her beloved: the Underworld would be her only home until the end of time. She wept at the thought. She simply couldn't believe her luck.

On their final morning on Corfu, the lover witnesses a dream

The sun cut across the blanket, soaking the wood in beams. A fat housefly fell through the open window and tangled itself in the curtain for a moment before going out again. Romano, watching from the bed, felt keenly sick for home.

The two of them had most of the day before the ferry arrived. They would take it together, parting ways in Italy. Romano regretted not having the chance to spend much time with Isadora, but Elizabeth had made it clear that he would have to choose one or the other. He only wanted to sketch the dancer. Isadora had a classical figure, it was a singular opportunity. But he relented, not caring enough to make it an argument.

The trip was a success overall. He was grateful to have met Elizabeth and passed a few evenings with her, time spent pleasantly for them both. He listened to her sleeping talk, stroking her thigh as she repeated, again and again, *I hate her, I hate her, I hate her.*

II

On a mail ship en route to Constantinople, gateway to the Holy Land,
a ferry bears mail, rust, Isadora, and her sister-in-law

On closer observation, the opportunity for which has been ample in close quarters, I discover that Penelope is a plain woman. She's sweet enough, and a capable translator, but her stubborn shyness has kept us away from the other passengers, and she seems perfectly content playing endless card games and having no fun at all.

The trip to Turkey was her idea. Her brother in the Samsun Province is retiring from military service and dramatically requests one last visit before he dies, despite the fact that he's not quite forty years old. She promises to write me later on and tell me if he was ill or only joking.

The Dardanelles offer up a steady scene, featuring minor forts, low hills and brush flanking antiquity Troy. We watch it pass, the motor of the ferry we've named *Hippocampus* chuggling mildly along. The children are safe in their box, which I carry now in my lap just in case there's a leak below deck. We had some trouble in Albania when one of the men carrying my bags thought there was food in the biscuit tin and made to pry it open. I traded Penelope the old tin for a lovely little carved wooden box made to resemble a book. It was less conspicuous among the hungry, so nobody would bother me and I could eat in peace.

Penelope brought the cards, an oversized set. When we play rummy, she invents stories for face cards—the queen's dogwood lover, the traitorous prince—and it's easy to tell her hand by her expression. I would insist we play for money if she wasn't already financing the trip. "When you've seen one coast, you've seen every coast," she says, discarding.

"That's not true. Look there," I say, pointing at a grove of olive trees where a woman wraps a wide bolt of mesh around the trunks, securing them with thick black ribbons. "Every coast is new, and we are made new in witness, and so we find them infinite and within them our own multitudes."

We sit in silence, and I try to excise from my mind an image of her reading a book on local politics while Raymond makes elegant love to her.

"Fair enough," she says.

The southern bank has been close all day, and earlier we witnessed a vague but strident celebration near Chanak. On the captain's orders our charming young first mate inquired after it, speaking with a drunk in a pleasure skiff who was lighting Catherine wheels and throwing them overboard, where they immediately extinguished in the water and sank. The drunk reported that the Bulgarians pulled out of Adrianople and the men were returning to celebrate.

It lifted spirits on our barge. The captain had been eager to leave Albania that week over a bad business deal. He sailed despite the skirmishes to the west, and it was clear he planned to claim much bravery through the strait, though we haven't seen any soldiers, and the most dramatic moment came when he spilled a bit of garum on his trousers, making him smell for the rest of the trip as if he slept on the docks. Bravery made for a better story. After the news was relayed, the captain and his mate embraced, pounding one another on the back, gazing to the far shore and peerless victory beyond.

Penelope was less pleased, though she tried to put it on Raymond. My brother is the kind of man who throws his weight against his own uneducated speculation, claiming his gut has some desire larger than lunch. It drives him to lose spectacularly in games of chance, but in times when the real world goes against his romantic ideal, as in the case with his protracted engagement with the refugees in Albania, he can usually rely on a kind of righteous momentum to carry him through until too much peace and prosperity dampens his spirit.

In Albania, Raymond and Penelope wore their tunic and sandals every day and misinterpreted everyone's discomfort as deference. When the Albanian men refused to band together under his guidance and build a symbolic temple to Hera, he turned to their women, ordering Penelope to give them some industry. Together they installed thirty women weaving for show and creating a passable product, the tapestries selling for a few times the local rate to traders who appreciated the unique sentiment behind the work over its quality. Every rug and runner came from women so eager to earn money for a hard loaf of bread that they didn't fight Raymond's claim that this new style would be useful in a broader sense, an investment in the same genre as studying a language or taking an extended trip to a foreign country and staying just long enough that the narrow roads would feel as plain as home—which was precisely what the women were already doing, of course, though not by choice, working long days, their mothers' rings sewn into their clothes. And Raymond sold them the bread.

In their tent, set back twenty meters or so from the beach, Penelope kept a waterproof travel case for her books. Most were either translation texts or unbearable allegories on the responsibility women have to their husbands told in the hazy context of literature, but under those she kept a few slim volumes from the dark philosophers, including a worn copy of the *Dionysian-Dithyrambs* in German. From the tent I could see Corfu across the strait and missed my sickbed there. Penelope gave casual morning lessons to the children in her patient Greek, and I did my level best to sit among them and listen to her stories without looking at the children directly.

After one such lesson I cut my hair and threw a clump of it toward the ocean, and though the wind blew most of it landed on the rocks, it was a powerful moment. Penelope took the shears and fixed a spot in the back, and then she must have found a way to alert Raymond because he didn't even glance at it when he arrived for dinner.

My time in Albania forced me to sit under their scrutiny, our quarters close enough that they must have spent hours walking around the camp in order to exhaust the topic.

I'd like to go to Manisa, to see Niobe in the cliff, for Niobe defied the gods when she presented the fortune of her loins to the city of Thebes and the gods struck them down, her seven boys and seven girls killed before them all. And then Niobe—who really should have known better, that sort of thing happening all the time—wept until the gods shrugged and turned her into a stone that remains even today, seeping rainwater, denying her even the comfort of death.

"Constantinople by nightfall," Penelope calls out, stretching out with a strange pelvic thrust that comes off somehow both morbid and crude. The *Hippocampus* was set to arrive earlier but slowed to bump an old junker into port. We have to shout at each other over the noise of the other boat's failing engine. Penelope wraps a deck blanket around her as if the noise is a physical assault. "What's that?"

"To Manisa! Niobe!"

"Manisa! Why not a nice bed! Dinner to the room!"

"We could hire a driver!"

The junker's engine sputters and quits. "Absolutely not," Penelope says in the strange silence.

"You could come with me, before you see your brother. It would be fun."

She observes my hand, which has come to fall on her thigh.

I have a brief but compelling fantasy of slipping between the hull of the *Hippocampus* and the junker we're pushing into port, the delicious feeling of my body pressed to the edge of witness before being crushed into simple oblivion. The thought bobs alongside us for a while and sinks in our slow wake. We will have Constantinople by nightfall, another city of children living to spite the dead.

Max thinks fondly of Elizabeth as he memorizes a list of things he will accomplish in her absence

First there would be improved calisthenic and weight training for the girls. That was the most important item, and crucial for his work. He would look over the piano accompaniment and ensure that Trella had enough alternates, and he would talk to her about the changes to the curriculum while he was at it.

He meant to research a proper nutrition schedule. Lately he had begun to suspect that the very young and very old had different needs, and found that he himself could subsist on less and less. Surely the girls would benefit from heartier portions.

There were miscellaneous duties as well: he wanted to arrange a mountain trip after spring recital; the lake was too filthy to take the girls. He needed to consider new choreography for summer and organize the chorale program, perhaps around Verdi and Gounod, and reform the kitchen area to include space for a tea service. If he focused, he could do it all before Elizabeth returned later that week.

He found Trella at the piano in the rehearsal room, her white gloves folded beside her on the seat. She had confessed once that she found her fingers to be too stubby and so insisted on the gloves anytime she wasn't actively playing the piano; apparently she was soothed by the sight of the white keys lengthening her fingers, which explained the many hours she spent practicing as a child, when most children were happier to go out and play. Max was charmed by her insecurity and her adaptable nature, and besides, her fingers really were somewhat short and the gloves gave them a good look.

She was marking something on the page when he walked in, and seemed in no rush to finish the thought before she looked up to acknowledge him.

"Herr Merz," she said.

He sat down beside her on the bench. "Frau Venneberg, I trust you are passing a satisfactory afternoon."

"Very much so, thank you. The girls were a little tired from their morning exercise, so I let them take the rest of the hour."

"That's precisely what I wanted to address."

She had been altering dynamics on the sheet music, he noticed, pulling everything back to subtler phrasing. He handed over her gloves and waited for her to slip them back on.

"I have a theory I've begun to pursue in earnest," he said once she had them on again. "You've heard me speak of it in the past."

"The one about giving the girls lots of muscular wrinkles to smooth out the wrinkles in their brains?"

He cringed. "The idea that physical strength can better serve them in the higher arts and in a mental capacity, yes. I'd like you to incorporate some elements of my theory into your classes as well."

"But Herr Merz, I only accompany the dancers, I could never change Frau Lang's orders. Unless you're referring to chorale, and I can't imagine what you would have them do then."

He thought of Frau Lang, who had shouldered the burden of beginning and advanced classes in Elizabeth's absence, teaching the school's forty students with a spirited charm. The three of them had managed well enough, though reserves were stretching a bit thin.

"Chorale is a lost hour of their day," he said. "Think of ways to get a little more movement into those moments. They could do lunges while windmilling their arms, or swing bodily from the waist. While they performed their vocal warm-ups they could also warm up with toe touches or push-ups."

"Push-ups!"

"Or swinging leg lifts."

"Should I purchase a singlet?"

He hated her laughter but controlled himself. Any idea would meet its detractors at first. Ignorance needed to be set straight.

"Physical activity on the individual level only benefits the future of the world," he said. "You would be well advised to find its benefits for yourself as well."

"Oh yes," she said. "You're describing the Müller technique, yes? I read of it last summer—"

He stood from the bench a little more quickly than he intended, disturbing the balance and forcing her to reach for the piano with two hands, her gloves slipping against the rail. Flustered, he bowed to her and picked up her pages from where they had scattered on the floor. "I am not describing the Müller technique," he said, replacing the music, trying to find its proper order. "Damned pages. You don't number them?"

"They are numbered," she said quietly. "On the bottom."

He threw the pages down. "This is my own technique," he insisted, his finger quavering a few inches from her lovely thin mouth. "Swinging leg lifts," he said. "Or toe touches." He bid her a good morning and left her to tidy her mess.

Paris walks the grounds at Oldway, which is permanently under the kind of endless renovation that can be endured only by the wealthy

Gilbert took the Pommery Cup, flying a thousand miles on a Rhône motor. Paris found only a few sentences on the man's achievement in the middle of a longer article about recent feats of aviation, but it was enough to distract him with thoughts of his own future as a flying ace. Daydreaming was much more entertaining than reading the rest of the piece, which had turned to concerns for the safety of pilots and passengers, dismissal of the industry masked in a false concern for its pioneering few. Paris hated these cynics of progress, sour types who believed that they were owed an exceptional life and had grown impatient waiting for the hour it would arrive. Most salesmen had this precise attitude.

But simple salesmen failed to see that real success, lasting success, required industry so steady, so free of doubt and reflection that the inventors had to build machines out of themselves. Paris was only a formal acquaintance to hard work, but he knew this to be true. His father's friends claimed that he continued working even after he had expired; on the fateful day, his nurse found him slumped over his desk, pointing cadaverously toward a folder holding the unorganized plans for something his partners couldn't quite piece together until a man named Whitehill logged in the patent office his blueprints for the vibrating shuttle. White-hill won the patent by virtue of being alive, but destroyed this singular advantage when he was found quite dead off the road near Roussillon, the spokes of his bicycle glinting in the afternoon sun. It was a spiritual victory for the Singers, who looked to the future even in death.

His father was prolific across categories, but tended to tire quickly of his creations. Paris as an infant was left in the care and attention of a catalog of sisters. The girls crowded over him from the day of his birth, their eyes an irregular column of unpolished jewels twinkling on the peri-meter of his entire life.

He remembered feeling jealous of the girls. They were expected only to marry well and live as best they could, while he had the weight of the future. He sought for himself the comfort of successful partnership, but found in Lillie another set of disapproving eyes. Lillie hated Florida and hated him for bringing her there and forcing her to raise four girls in swamp heat, a thick layer of sweat under their high-necked shifts. They were all unhappy with him until the moment he packed up and left for Europe.

He tried his hand at a few halfhearted inventions, serums for sickly children and similar, always contextualizing his own meager success by reminding himself that sweet syrup was well and good but not quite as useful to the future of the world as mechanized thread. He saw between himself and his father an impossible divide, a canyon so broad and unreal he could think of it only in spiritual terms: he was the mortal descendant of a god, Tantalus betraying the secrets of the divine.

His attraction to Isadora was only natural. Men sometimes asked him how he could stand to manage a strong-willed woman, and Paris would sidestep the question, saying that all women were strong-willed in their way and that some were only more subtle than others. But the truth was that Isadora's industry was precisely what interested him in the first place. When he first saw her perform, he felt transfixed by a thousand moving parts. He wouldn't have been at all surprised if she had picked him up and draped him like a mantle over her shoulders. She seemed im-possibly strong, and he felt impossibly light.

Isadora gave him the balance he needed to focus on the things that most interested him. He found he actually enjoyed keeping up the family home at Oldway, its garden paths and halls, the feathered joints of its cornices and its wide stone floors. He liked catching himself in its broad mirrors, seeing in them a man always between tasks. He supervised the staff he hired to cook and clean the silver and keep wood in the fire and repair the foundation, which always seemed to have some problem. By the dumb luck of his birth, he was perched above the entire enterprise, occupied with a series of petty problems, the value of a single tea-spoon gone missing or the question of paint for the carriage house or the maintenance of the horse-drawn carriages themselves, which he had the men keep up with oil and polish despite the fact that he surely would never use them again unless Lillie sent the girls for the summer and the little ones wanted to play pretend. But that wouldn't happen, he reasoned; his wife always knew when to leave him well enough alone and anyway had no doubt surmised by now that he was cursed.

Every morning he spent an hour walking the property with his note-book, careful to mark down any opportunity to improve. His butler was cool and efficient, his chef good with last-minute needs. His gardener was easygoing, and willing to talk for hours on the finer points of polished stone.

Of course he was annoyed with Isadora for not coming off the island with him, but he reasoned that she would see his way soon enough. He was relieved, actually; without her, he could sometimes go a full minute without thinking of the children, two if he was well distracted by his sur-roundings. Lately he was spending more time with his art collection, work-ing methodically through the endless portraits, his sculpture garden, the artifacts from bygone eras in watercolor and oil. He passed his time like this, praying for the morning he would wake to find that the past few months had only been a dream, or rather a selective sort of nightmare, that he would wake to find that Gilbert had still won the cup, but the rest of it had been his worst invention yet.

Elizabeth, on her journey home to Darmstadt, notices the particular pleasure of factory air

Rather she recalled it, having been away so long. It smelled of freshly lit matches and steady work, and the haze drifting up from the smokestacks dropped a glittering summer snow, metal dust from grinding lathes. She breathed in as deeply as she could bear and felt it sharply in her lungs, scrubbing away the salt grime she had accrued by the sea. A fellow sitting beside her on the train remarked that the steelworks heated the ground so well that beautiful foliage grew all year long. They had Progress to thank for this, and she was well and truly grateful.

From her seat in the train's open car she could lean out and wave to men and women constitutioning at the tree line. Germany was so strong and steady. In New York, it seemed the moment anything was built, it would burn to the ground and they had to start again, and everyone tried to be optimistic about it as they filled another set of walls with crumpled newspaper. The proud old cities of Europe gave her a sense of peace and permanence, where bridges arched protectively over the same roads they had spanned for centuries. Max once told her of a book that predicted events nearly one thousand years into the future, but whenever she tried to picture the world he described, she pictured the gyroscopic whirligigs and motored tollways elevated one meter from the ground so as not to disturb the old familiar scene below.

She recalled the humiliating voyage she had made back to Europe after the failure of her makeshift school in New York. That damned city could burn for all she cared. Isadora promised to set her up properly in Germany, so she returned with her tail between her legs. But once the disappointment wore off, she came to appreciate her home in Darmstadt. Max was her first employee, and together they broadened the curriculum offering and began to build the business.

Elizabeth was heartened by her little solo trips, on which she felt an attitude of curiosity and pleasure her sister seemed to experience all the time. Isadora never questioned the tide, even if it was pulling her out to sea.

It wasn't so long ago that they were leotarded in pinks, learning ballet from Mother. Elizabeth was still young enough that her feet aligned and behaved on the same orders, a crisp fifth *croisé* to a lovely *dégagé effacé devant*. She moved through her stations while Isadora leapt like a stotting fawn through a *brisé* and back to fifth, landing with a perfect give in the knees, the look on her face matching the ease with which she expressed the posture. *Contact the floor*, Mother called, stomping time. Isadora yawned, hitting her marks.

Ballet would soon become as useless to them as Elizabeth's left leg, the connective tissue crumbling from hip to ankle like a rubber hose left in the sun. But she remembered those few sessions where they were equally elastic in body and mind, cushioned by the promise of their mutual success. She wondered if Isadora ever thought of it.

They say the other senses grow stronger on the loss of one. As her leg seized and stiffened, Elizabeth found herself becoming the most emotionally limber of the family—happy to teach six days in a row or to sleep on a pallet by the drafty wall—all so they might attend Isadora's greatness in London and Paris, supporting her as she went on to Constantinople. All Elizabeth knew of Turkey came from a photograph she had seen once of a fig market in Smyrna, the men in vests and fezzes. She dozed the rest of the way home, dreaming of postcard albums of foreign lands.

On landing late in Constantinople, Isadora and Penelope encounter a stranger who presents a challenge

At first the woman on the dock seems a statue or a spirit, gloved and veiled in black, draped in it, boots as black as the planks and drawing dark from her legs. The long black veil rests heavy over her face, coming well below her shoulders. I am a bride walking down the aisle to meet my own shadow.

She makes no move when the short plank is laid, banging so close beside her it could have caught her toe. A man emerges from the custom-house and guides her gently by both shoulders as he would move a sleep-walker, taking her place to greet the yawning travelers. The hour is long past midnight, the empty streets a cold welcome though it's still warm enough to melt a ghost.

My waist feels spiraled by a dry vine as I cross the bucking plank, which shrugs and sways buoyant under my feet; sadly, it seems the time has come for me to envy a plank.

The woman and I stand shoulder to shoulder as a silent welcome party, ignored by all. Penelope has found a veil to wear and hands me one when she disembarks but doesn't offer to help me pin it, going to talk to the customs man as I drape it inelegantly over my hair. It falls immediately into my eyes and I spend a while fussing with it before pulling it back to rest limp as a doily on my forehead.

Leaning to the side, I tap the veiled woman's arm. "Do I look like a sitting room sofa?" I ask. "Be honest with me, spare no kindness."

The woman's veil wavers. "A little," she says. "Did you meet my son on your crossing?"

I'm grateful she speaks English, saving us Penelope's smug translation.

"Unless your son was the ship's mate, there were no other young men."

"He is on the manifest. This ship has arrived from Sarandë at midnight on the last Friday of the month for ten years now, sometimes delayed by duties in the bay but regular in port, and he is arriving with the ship."

Penelope directs our trunks toward a car and lights a cigarette, cinching her long jacket against the heat as she stands away from the departing group, looking very foreign overall. She accepts everyone's well wishes with a humiliated wave.

"He is soon arriving," the veiled woman insists.

"There were no other young men," I say. "My companion is bashful. We only met a couple honeymooning from New York, an adventuring man who had never been to Constantinople and whose mother lived in Nanterre, a young mother and her child, and one older woman who declined our dinner invitation and may actually have quietly died after that, come to think, for we haven't seen her since."

It is that moment a handsome young man disembarks and comes to kiss his mother, unaware that he has the dark arts wholly to thank for his appearance.

"Raoul," she says without a bit of the relief I would feel in her place. "This kind lady kept me company just now while I was waiting. She says she did not meet you."

He does seem kin to a veil, with fine pale features framed by his black hair, his mother's smile lined with sadness. He holds what looks at first to be a striped card or a swatch of felt. On closer look, it is a single epaulet, which he hands to his mother. She holds it to her lips.

The man smiles grandly at me. "I heard you were aboard with the vomiting woman," he says, fixing his mother's veil where it mussed in their embrace. "This is a famous dancer, Mother."

"We should meet again," she murmurs, fondling the epaulet. "I would very much like to host a famous dancer in my home at any time." Her son offers his arm, and she takes it, leaning on him as they go.

How quickly the three of us have become Son, Mother, and Dancer, as clear as a call sheet. I find myself hating this woman, who held her vigil and was rewarded, so thoughtless in her luck and so ignorant of it. The two of them walk to the end of the road, looking about expectantly, as if love is a feast they've come to expect and a maître d' will shortly lead them to their table. There they go, arm in arm, hardly even hungry for all they get to enjoy.

A memory of Milan's old city in November 1909, a season plagued by a demoralizing amount of rain

Paris and I played a pretty Milanese family, and soon enough I was carrying his child.

I gave him the news once dinner arrived at his favorite table at his very favorite restaurant, in a district of family homes where talk above a whisper earned a thin glare. The owners didn't think much of me but had been so honored by the presence of Paris Singer that season that they engraved a brass plaque bearing his name and mounted it near the door. He was cutting into a jewel of fatty squab as I told him about the pregnancy and how I hoped to be rid of it by the end of the week.

He received my news in silence, his knife slowing to a stop. The squab was encased in a revoltingly sweet apricot gelée, which I detected from my side of the table, senses being keener at the time, and I was nearly sick right there as he speared a bite and brought it to his mouth. Indeed he always seemed the most thoughtful while chewing, as if a problem could be crushed in his jaw and absorbed over the course of some hours, its solution revealed the next morning in the toilet.

"It has already destroyed my balance," I said, gazing over his shoulder to avoid looking directly at the squab. The mounting sense of a second solar plexus had been building for weeks, thin as a matchstick but present and glowing. With Deirdre, Ted and I had felt nothing but love and anticipation, picturing a springtime child draped in roses. The idea alone had been more than enough to forgive the interruption to my work, and Teddy was beside himself with joy. Every night he would hold me and weep so inconsolably that I thought he had gone truly unhinged.

Paris was an older man and more practical. He had his wife and four school-aged children sunning themselves on the lawn of some bungalow in Miami. I thought of them only when I thought of any kind of future with Paris, which I rarely did; why trouble yourself with tomorrow when today is troubling enough? This new development had made me think of them, and I didn't care for it.

"You want to let the air in?" he asked, still chewing.

"I'm not certain what you mean."

He made a scooping motion at his trouser line, using the side of his fork as if there were anything he might excavate other than red wine and small birds. "The air," he said.

"You mean, you wonder if I might hire a midwife to open me up with a device, swab the area with a rag dipped in alcohol, puncture me with a bulb, and remove the affecting fluid and tissue?"

"That does remove some nuance." He took down the rest of his wine and called for another bottle.

"I can't imagine the woman performing it possesses any brilliant insight."

"And she's lucky, or else you would have to oversee every one." He set down his fork. "You know, my mother had ten children by the time she was your age."

"You're almost halfway there already, without my help."

"We were the joy of her life."

"And you don't seem to miss yours much."

"I don't have them wilding across Europe," he said, that old wolfish smile creeping around the edge of his mouth. I hate it when he smiles at me. "They are with Lillie, where they're safe."

"Safety! I was wondering what she offered, but that does make sense. What a good woman she is." Men resent nothing more than their own comfort and hate the women in their lives who offer it. They want safety from their wives and danger from other women, without realizing that all women risk mortal danger from strangers and live their lives holding that damage at arm's length, a cup that must never spill on the men they love, who meanwhile hate them for their feigned nature. This motherhood situation is even darker, as the mother grows in her body the architect of her own end; the child who doesn't kill her in childbirth will break her heart later on. Men have to manufacture this kind of danger, which comes so relentlessly to women.

"You could learn a thing or two from her goodness," he says, spearing a potato.

Paris had been racing cars by the aqueduct all day while I was at the doctor, dealing with one of life's more ordinary threats. Now he wants me to learn from good Lillie Singer, at her window with a book.

The waiter arrived and immediately retreated, bowing as if one of us had produced a small-caliber pistol and shot him in the stomach.

"You leave your students with your sister when you're tired of them," Paris continued, baring his teeth, "and it's better than how you treat your own daughter. You'll have Deirdre shilling before she learns to write. Put her in rags so she can play the beggar before she has to take on the role in earnest."

"You should be well pleased to escape me," I said. "Since you so clearly understand the dimensions of my failure."

He looked at his palms as if they could tell him the quickest route back to the hotel. A strange calm came over us both, in the charmed way it sometimes did when we tired of the argument at the exact same time.

"You contain within your quarreling frame a perfect machine," he said. "Come now, let's go."

He left enough extra for the waiter to afford psychological attention and we walked in silence all the way to the room, past the unfamiliar lift attendant who greeted us in English, clapping Paris on the shoulder as if he were a friend to whom money was owed.

In the room, we found the flowers had been changed, the empty bottles taken away. The curtains had been drawn to reveal the piazza, quiet aside from a drunk on a bicycle.

"I only wanted you to tell me to keep it," I said.

The man on the bicycle bumped along, weaving through the cobble-stone. He faltered and dipped the front wheel into a rut, jamming it to a sudden stop. Tossed over the handlebars, he fell in a heap under a light-post. We watched him struggle and go still.

It was cold in the room, colder than the street, where people had come to gather around the man. Paris brought me a blanket while the chambermaid lit the fire and showed herself out so silently I worried that she had flown up the chimney. The blanket covered me from shoulders to floor, curtaining around my feet to hold the air, the material as thick and rich as redwood bark. Outside, a pair of officers strolled up to the group gathered around the drunk, who was bracing himself to stand, bravely fighting the confoundation of a tilting planet.

Paris dropped to both knees, looping his arm around me to press his ear to my stomach. It was a pleasurable sight, the great man on his knees. We would not speak again of the procedure. In that way, the decision was made.

If only we could have stayed there forever, at the hotel window in Milan. The cyclist would melt into a pile of gears and brakes under the altar of our room, one room in a long line of rooms, heir to the next—I was bursting into fortune at last to find it was just another room—but this was the first moment I gazed into the future without an ounce of dread. The room should have been preserved as a monument and kept away from the public, and in the silence of days and months my body would swell to produce a child and he would be called Patrick, after no-body, and the three of us would remain forever there, looking out on the changing days. We would keep completely still, if stillness would keep us safe.

Putting off work in Darmstadt, Elizabeth sets to composing a letter to Romano in her mind

My Romano—*she began, and then scratched, as he ought not get the idea that she was taking liberties with the idea of courtship. He would send her a five-page letter addressing the point that no person could own another, and it would be the last she ever heard from him.*

Romano *was scratched for formality.*

RR *scratched for its locomotive aspect, though it was pleasant to think of the man carrying her merrily from one station of her life to the next. It had been a two-week affair, she reminded herself, plucking her own hand from the monument she had been building to their love.*

R *would have to suffice, suggesting enough familiarity and mystery both to intrigue him. The greeting sorted, she could relax a little. The next few paragraphs would obviously need to describe the weather.*

R—Do you remember our breakfasts out on the balcony? It was sunny and warm each time, with a slight fog and you so handsome across the table. There was coffee and endless bowls of fruit, and we ate like children, whatever was brought to us. I think of it often.

The weather here is fair, warm by the middle of the day. I realized you might like to picture my life in Darmstadt, and so first you must imagine my bedroom, with its slim single bed. Waking at dawn, I meet Max for tea, and we talk generally of the day. He's a good man and has these aspirations. I forget how simple aspirations are to come by, how free for anyone to alight upon. When I look at him, I feel like a child paddling around a raft.

But I was telling you of my day. After morning tea it's off to rehearsal. The girls have an affection for me, greeting me as Tante Miss as they line up against the wall to do their exercises. There's no barre, none of us having much use for it, though there are still plenty of mirrors for them to look themselves over and for Tante Miss to admire her profile as well. I've determined my left cheek is finer, though you might disagree, having seated yourself often to my right.

You might also like to imagine the view from our little studio, which looks over all of Darmstadt, its low, rolling clouds and an ocean of trees under which you might see a few people of the town walking or riding horses. We like our old-fashioned things here.

The girls are well acquainted with my drills delivered from the mirrored wall, against which I have lately begun to lean; the pain in my hip bothers me and saps my humor. I'm harder on them when I'm in pain. On those days, I make them run their drills until they cry out every time their bruising feet strike the floor, until they collapse and weep and then hobble out for a late breakfast.

We are considering costumes for a Summer Solstice performance, to which you are invited if you're interested. The pianist and I will dress as Theia and Eos. Even Max is being playful, though not much. I hope you are well—Elizabeth.

———————

*cut expansive references to weather—cut fussy & familiar allusions—
reduce formality—add mention of light & its uses—cut reference to M—
cut assumptions regarding imagination—add suggestion of desire—add
joking &/or teasing element—add element of seduction &/or interest—cut
allusions to age/infirmity—add playful element—add greater interest in
sundry artistic aims—*

R—Hoping you're well from across the way and thought you might like
to know about the scene here. It's warm all right but there's a soft morning light that filters through the leaves and comes to rest around the entire school, giving us all a glow that seems internal and everlasting.

I wonder what life has handed you in the months we have been
apart. Did you determine the proper ingress for the bronze? I'm so interested to have a glimpse of your current work, be it sculptural or on canvas or even on the page. I wonder if you are still sketching on the edges
of newspapers and if you are, might you do a sketch of me from memory
and drop it in the mail? I'm only curious. You might also sketch your
view which I am also very curious about.

Business as usual out here. We are all "gearing up" for a solstice celebration and the girls are preparing very amusing costumes. I feel and
harbor for you an intense desire that leads me at times to distraction.
Would that you might consider joining us for the performance next
month, and meanwhile I hope you are finding every comfort in your
mother's home. With affection—E.

*FOR GOD'S SAKE cut reference to intense desire—cut poetic reference—
cut invitation—add convivial feeling—add sense of mystery—cut allusions to curiosity—*

R—Can you picture the morning in Darmstadt? It's all cool air and
warm light. There are leaves and quick evenings. It adds mysterious depth

to my thoughts. Hopefully your own are progressing. I can early feel the chill of Autumn—E.

cut allusions to self—

R—Can you picture the morning in Darmstadt?

cut allusions to home—

R—Can you picture the morning?

At Oldway, Paris finds an unlikely guest in his stairwell

A few years back, Paris had gotten wrapped up in the excitement of an exhibition and accidentally funded a new wing at the Louvre. He bought *The Coronation of Napoleon,* depicting Napoleon at Notre-Dame, raising the crown of the empire over Josephine's bowed head. Paris had seen the image in a half-size reproduction and felt he had a sense of the piece, but there was such glory in the original, which was revealed to him in the museum's basement, the piece flanked monumentally by pillars of the ancient fortress, the dim light of the room drawing him closer to the painting itself. The processional cross lifted dead center meant to allude to the spiritual significance, but the real focus was of Josephine in the center, kneeling to receive such power. The whole coronation business looked like a supremely satisfying experience.

It had been a supremely satisfying experience to buy it, too. He felt none of the remorse he usually felt with large purchases, shuddering along with a new car negotiating rough road. With art, at least he knew his money had gone toward the appreciation of sublimity in the world. And at such breadth; spanning six by ten meters, the scene was life-size before him, as if he might only take a step forward and enter the hall. He was pleased with the piece, its size and importance, and it was only once it was delivered to Oldway in a crate hanging off the back of a lorry that Paris worried he might not find pleasure in the work itself. But time would tell.

After some delay he had it hung in the broad empty place on the grand gallery landing, a space on the wall larger than most sitting rooms, which turned out to be the perfect place for a gilt-edged window into the French Revolution. Jacques-Louis David had rendered hundreds of individuals to fill the frame, most of them supposedly recognizable from portraits hanging in various ancestral halls across France. Paris noticed that, while the principal players in the center of the scene were larger than life, the audience members in the dark gallery had been painted at their actual height, which gave him the sense he was standing among mortals in the presence of consecrated gods.

Once the painting was properly set and balanced, Paris began a daily study of it. He decided to observe each face in an orderly fashion, limiting himself to one individual per day with the idea that, by observing the gallery's varied expressions and moods, eventually he would have a fuller understanding of the work as a whole.

He started with Napoleon. The man extended the crown with an attitude of great power and grace, though with close attention it was possible to see how the angle of his offering matched the painter's earlier sketches, which featured Napoleon crowning himself.

The next day was spent with Pius VII. The pope was a fair-skinned man who blessed the proceedings with two fingers. This would have been a few years before his exile and a few more before the canonizing event in which he miraculously rose and hovered over an altar, a scene Paris would have very much liked to see. He had once read that Pius VII succumbed to an injury and died after repeating the names of the cities to which he had been exiled by the French. He tried to sense a grimace or sneer in the man's face in the painting, but the pope seemed resigned to the proceedings more than anything.

After those two, Paris counted one hundred and seventy-five figures, fourteen he knew for certain. Beside Josephine stood her immediate family and Joseph the Prince Imperial. There was Napoleon's sister, Hortense de Beauharnais, holding the hand of her oldest child, a boy,

Napoleon Charles, heir to the throne at five years old. He would be dead before the work was dry. There was the diplomat Talleyrand, and Joachim Murat. And there was Jacques-Louis David, studious over his sketchpad in the back gallery, artists always painting themselves into garrets.

Paris went from right to left, and the weeks passed quite pleasantly until he got stuck on the child, Napoleon Charles. He studied the boy for hours, unable to look away. The painter had gifted him with a strikingly optimistic pose; the boy pulled at his mother's hand as if he were actually straining to move forward, to walk without delay into a future that was already planning to leave him behind.

He had his mother's reed of a nose, but otherwise they could have been strangers to each other; actually Hortense bore a closer resemblance to her husband in the foreground than to the child they made together. Paris followed the line of sight, trying to determine if the boy was gazing at the crown or the ladies or Josephine's opulent gown or something else, Christ on the cross or the *Pietà*, the corner of which was visible and evoked the rest. He was struck by the thought of observing one work of art within another, the loss of dimension in the transition to canvas, ideas brought to bear by a different mind supported by an entirely different time. It was unsettling to think of how art, like invention, could be altered beyond its initial purpose simply by continuing to exist. Of course a painting could be destroyed, but the psychic damage of a regime change on a piece of art could be far more devastating. He pictured his family's sewing machines creating the uniforms of whole companies of men at war, the perfect stitched rows of enemy flags.

That wasn't the only similarity he found between art and invention. Though artists worked hard to elevate themselves—particularly when under commission, as he learned from every overserious painter who worked on his yearly portrait—he saw artists as the same breed as the farmers who came in from their country homes bearing sketches on brown paper for minor improvements to treadle mechanics. Artists and inventors both studied the extant form and found their own part. They were like children as well, watching the game for just a moment before jumping in.

He missed his girls, with their mother in Florida. Sweet Lillie, their mother; he missed her too, in a way. Neither of them had wanted the hassle or humiliation of divorce, and both continued to enjoy a fruitful partnership in truth, with the organization of many households to consider. If Lillie had dreamed of romantic love as a girl, she had long forgotten it by the time she entered into the marital contract with him. She was nothing like Isadora, who once demanded that a sofa be brought to her in a restaurant and, when her request was refused, ruined the entire meal trying to properly pose in a straight-back chair.

The painting began to consume more of his day, and he arranged a small table to be set up on the landing so he could take his meals there. He spent an entire week observing Napoleon Charles, and a second. He arranged the chair before the boy, finding that he could align his observation at the perfect angle for viewing his exact expression. The boy held a plumed hat, which his mother must have made him wear into the cathedral but forgot to mind, and in her distraction he slipped it off, exposing his fine curls to the assembled. Paris looked for clues of his impending croup. If he wasn't already sick, any sign in the painting would mean the artist had foreseen it, observing a little coughing fit during the ceremony, the worried expression of a nurse in the gallery. Those rosy cheeks might have been added after the boy was already dead, an awkward gesture made for his grieving parents.

Paris had always seen himself as a reasonable man, a Catholic in some circles, but with two major differences in opinion: he never picked up the rigorous superstition demanded by the faith, and he had never been able to bring himself to trust in an idea of a heavenly afterlife. Heaven, to him, had always seemed a kind of consolation prize for the living, a place where a glittering reward was promised for a meek and inconsequential life. He hadn't spent much time considering the question of heaven; the whole thing had a delicate consistency for him, as if the clouds were made from spun sugar.

His feelings changed after the accident. Lately it comforted him to imagine Patrick tottering behind Napoleon Charles as they explored the softer clouds behind celestial pulpits, playing tug of war with golden curtain cords and jabbing at the legs of the ethereal chorus under their robes before settling at the foot of the holy throne for a nap. Paris worried that the boys might have to contend with the flocks of angels, their thousand eyes bearing down in a wind of righteous judgment; he had never discussed the possibility with Patrick and feared in hindsight that he would be unprepared. Deirdre was usually patient with her brother, but the two of them would need someone to help them for those first few ageless decades. Napoleon Charles would be the perfect guide, explaining the thousand horrible eyes in a way that made the whole thing a game, the three of them eternal playmates in a gilded park. Patrick was so used to dancing and music it would all feel like an afternoon recital with better lighting. Paris hoped there would be a pair of sandals to suit his feet, and someone to ensure that he was served the food he liked. Most of all, he hoped that the boy wouldn't miss his home, wouldn't long for any of them in the way they longed for him, startling awake at night to remember his absence. It would be a major design flaw on the part of heaven if you arrived at last only to miss the poor mortals below.

Easing himself from his chair, Paris came to stand close to the painting, crouching to come face to face with Napoleon Charles. He was trying to find some kindness in the boy's expression, anything that might suggest he would be a suitable guide and not abandon his companions with a band of sophists. Paris reached out to touch the painting, drawing his fingers gently across the petrified slicks and divots. It was hard to tell for certain, but it did seem that the child possessed some headstrong nature, an old soul in his young eyes. He looked brave, but bravery was the least of it; he needed to be thoughtful, but not too serious, orderly and responsible but playful and easy in temperament, a fine and patient teacher and a friend. It was a lot to ask of a boy, Paris knew.

Preparing for dinner on the evening of their first full day in Constantinople

The lobby of the Pera Palace is warm and light by day, with soaring stone archways and six domed skylights, but when we checked in around midnight, the big chandeliers reflected themselves in the black glass above, and we felt trapped in an atrium at the bottom of the sea. Penelope insisted on using the elevator, though the bellhop noted that the motor was loud enough to wake other guests, and if she had ever ridden an elevator before, she certainly didn't act like it. Worst of all, once we were finally alone in the yellow light of the room, she removed her dress to reveal the thin swell of her pregnancy, the child making slow turns under the blood-strung chandelier of her heart, and I lay awake all night, staring at her from the other side of our shared bed.

Our room at least is very fine. The porter came by in the morning with a breakfast for eight and insisted that we keep it all, leaving us with tiers of sweet and savory cakes, pastry and pressed nutmeats, and breads dotted with sesame seeds. We lay in bed all morning and went down once for coffee, but we haven't yet left the hotel. It's as if we have been charmed to remain here. Dinner will be served at eight, and they've refused to bring it up to us, so we dress in the lazy way of ladies on vacation, half asleep in stockings, our arms too heavy to lift themselves into sleeves. Penelope sings a lullaby and brushes her hair, fondling her nightgown's half-imagined swell. I crouch beside the cart, my hips wound as tight as a ball of baker's twine.

The joint between thigh and pelvis shudders as if some magic has fused them, and not even a rich squat over the course of an hour offers ease from this choking knot. My bones feel bloated in the hot machine of my body.

Elizabeth would say it serves me right. The deep squat had become a vice, as easy as a tumbler of wine and just as necessary backstage. In a stranger's home I needed only half a minute and a chair to crouch behind. My tendons have slackened to their tensile limit, the wings of my hips peel toward the floor.

"Sounding rather witchy," Penelope says, pausing her lullaby to pluck a cake from the tray. "What are you incanting?"

"Nothing in particular." Reserves of slight energy collect in my wrists, and when she turns away, it is possible to gnaw at one vein or another, offering the blood within a gentle massage. Earlier she caught me licking ash from my fingers, the wooden book hinged open on my lap. She looked away quickly so as to not implicate herself in my insanity.

There generates in the hip points that demon neurasthenia, who threatens to steal my life away. If I don't address it quickly, the condition could seep across me and spread to harm the innocents in my life, Penelope and her unborn child. Consider the bleak welcome her poor baby would find, emerging from loving warmth into a haze. This tightness in my hips must be excised, or else nothing will stop me from fouling this world, death will not stop me, my buried body will poison wells.

With my fingers hooked round my largest toes, I am able to rock back and forth like a beetle on its back. Penelope turns from her dressing mirror to find my full wealth of flesh spread wide on the bed.

"Let's quit these cakes and go down for supper," she says.

"To hell with supper."

There was a time when my body would take on the condition of the surfaces it touched: strong and solid against the warm studio floor, then plumping itself wide enough to be indistinguishable from the satin cushions perched on an overstuffed bed. My feet would feel the road I ran across and know how each brick had come into being, the women who sifted the clay and the men who laid the stone. But now I feel estranged from that knowledge, distant from my body, and lonely for myself.

A mysterious Madame Candemir called before sunrise and left her card at the desk. We spent the morning wondering who she was, deciding alternately that she was a Bolshoi apprentice, then the mother of a stageman in London. Penelope thinks it unlikely that her friends in Constantinople would call on her, as she has been away for years and sent no word in advance of our arrival, anticipating that she would grow ill on the journey and would want to spend a few days in bed. Even now, feeling healthy and well, she seems content to braid and rebraid her hair like a girl, speculating on her callers.

"If it's a friend of mine," she says, "it must be a married name. I don't know any Candemir at all."

"I met a soloist once from Turkey, perhaps it was her." It had been at the end of a long night, when everyone promises to meet again.

"Raymond must have told his local friends to call," she says, shaking the braid out and starting again. "He must have sent word. But then she would have met us at the dock, and there would have been others—"

"Wait a minute, perhaps our caller was the veiled woman we met on the dock?"

"We did suggest she call."

"I think we've solved our mystery."

She picks up the card. "She's nearby, in Stamboul. We can find a driver."

"Could you help me stretch?"

She replaces the quilt where it has slipped away between my legs and gives a halfhearted shove to both knees. "You know, you could stand to explore a garment designed for this very posture."

"Harder, toward the bedposts, please. Pay attention."

She does what I ask, grimacing. "The simple cleanliness and comfort of bloomers," she says. "The hygienic aspect. You might consider it, is all." Her belly swells, quietly superior, against my shins.

Adjusting position to draw my legs aside serves to press myself more fully against her, with subtle violence, as if I could grind the cloth to shreds between us. I wrap my legs around her to draw her closer. She fixes her gaze on the headboard, thinking of Greece and her mother, the pair of them walking through poppy fields at sunset, poppy seeds all about, working into their hair and clothes, milled with the grain to make hearty flour, women raised on Adonis flour to be strong and sure. A shame such a woman is made pregnant by a lecherous dilettante with designs on philosophy but no real aptitude for it, and now, insult to insult, she finds herself trapped here with that lesser man's sister, a woman she has agreed to care for out of an obligation to a family she is beginning to doubt more and more by the day.

"All right," I say, releasing her and rolling to my feet. "Let's visit Candemir in the morning and bring her some of these cakes."

"All right," she echoes. She returns to her dressing table and brushes her hair for a while in silence before starting up again with the lullaby she sings only to soothe herself. The wooden book sits on the bedside table, waiting patiently for my attention. When we return after dinner looking for dessert, the pastry cart will be gone and I'll have nothing to eat but these ashes.

In Darmstadt, Max enjoys an opportunity to resent a gift

Max had been weaned from teat to tea and was never permitted any other beverage. As an adult, he collected tea and cultivated an exclusive interest in its finest delicate details, practicing its intricate methods with leaves sourced from premium importers.

Every pot of tea was a ritual, one his mother taught him long ago. He primed the cup with warm water and washed the leaves in their wire basket, pouring the first silty brew down the drain and viciously excavating his fingernails with a letter opener as the water came to a second boil. He monitored the steeping time, which varied based on the type of tea, and for most varieties placed a sugar cube at the bottom of the cup. When it was ready, he poured it slowly, steam fogging his glasses. Once the cup was nearly full, he topped it with a finger of fine chilled cream. The proper method would create a strata of sugar, tea, and cream, meant to convey a natural symbology: the cloud-soaked sky above spiced or subtle water above a sugar shoal.

He kept his teas in a series of airtight glass jars. Each of them had its own personality: the malty Assam, thin floral Darjeeling, white teas as crisp as a pressed shirt. And though his mother had been gone for years, a perfect cup brought her back, if only for a moment.

He tried not to think of his lovely delicate teas as he was presented with the coffee Elizabeth brought him as a souvenir from her trip to Greece. She prepared it for him in the kitchen reserved for instructors, muttering complaints to herself as she went: the water was too cold, the beans ground too fine. When she served it, he couldn't figure out what exactly had gone wrong, only that the result was very bad. Perhaps there was an unknown additional step required to prime a new filter; the Melitta had just come out of its box and still seemed unaccustomed to resting among the other dishes, let alone performing its strange function humped over one mug and then the other to produce this bitter result. Max was wary that she had brought it from a land not known for its coffee, but she insisted she had developed a taste for it there.

The instructors' kitchen had been added haphazardly beside one of the larger rehearsal rooms long after the school was constructed and they realized that there was no place for the five instructors to take their meals in private. If it were up to Elizabeth, they would eat in their rooms and never otherwise meet, but she relented after Max insisted, retrofitting a coat closet with a sink and counter and a small table. The only access to the kitchen was through the largest rehearsal room, where at that moment Frau Lang had a group of young ladies briskly trotting the perimeter in bare feet.

Elizabeth watched him across the table, fingering the rim of the new filter and wiping her hand on a pleat running the length of her dress. He hated gifted souvenirs, the act of imposing one's own sentiment onto another's life. And though he had put in his years grimacing through plenty of espressos in Vienna, this new gift came as a particular disappointment; he thought he had outgrown his distaste. He had gotten his hopes up when the fresh-ground beans smelled of earth and cherry, but the end result tasted blackened and was far more bitter than what he had found in the short cups of his youth, a thickly jarring interruption to the senses. He pictured cowboys in the American West supping the stuff around a dying fire, slicks of animal fat and ash floating in their shared pan.

The girls in the rehearsal room were still running as a group. By the sound of their footfalls, they had evened out, the faster girls taking the lead. Max made a note to ask the fraülein for a report of the best runners and for a list of the girls who had chosen to fool around.

"I believe it has been burned," he said.

She leaned forward, sniffing. "It's not good?"

"Something isn't right." He thought of the peppermint tea he could be enjoying at that moment, a sweet cup of earthly pleasure, plucked from a field of tender shoots. The coffee tasted as if it had been scraped from a plot of arid land farmed to the brink of function.

"Miss Venneberg informs me you have been altering her lessons," she said.

Elizabeth had put on some weight in her time away, he saw. There was a softness to her jowl and the curve of flesh over the puckered skin of her elbow seemed more expansive than before. He grimaced at the blank wall, precisely where a window would have been cut had he been invited to advise the construction crew. He imagined six men puzzling over an architectural plan drawn in dust.

"You might recall that the course instructions came directly from Isadora. She wants them to know Nietzsche's dance songs."

"They had been failing simple tests."

The girls next door were laughing, a sound that always seemed to make Elizabeth uncomfortable. "You had barbells delivered to the arbor," she hissed. "I saw the crates. Were you trying to hide them from me? I left a dance studio and returned to a gymnastic center."

"The students' vitality is of real importance," he insisted. "These activities do more than some exercises in movement. They cultivate their instincts and develop their will. They promote good character and ethical development."

"You're saying they'll be strong enough to lift a car off a baby carriage?"

"You yourself have said you are most interested in the future of these young ladies as they bloom into womanhood."

Next door, one of the girls skidded and fell into a heap, making a sound that drew the rest of them over. Elizabeth and Max had to continue in whispers to keep from being heard.

"In altering the instruction," she said, "you're altering the result we promised their parents."

"We promised them grace without qualification, and grace is what they will receive. That grace will simply be laid with a foundation of physical strength and mental power." He thought often of the cost of outfitting the girls in uniforms, something that gave them a greater sense of duty. He had hoped to broach the subject with Elizabeth on her return, but now, clearly, would be a bad time.

"Darling," he said, placing his hand over hers.

She frowned at their hands. "I should check on them."

"When I first agreed to teach at this school, you were pleased to read my supplemental matter on training. Strong girls can dance through the day with fewer injuries. They will be able to extend their practice. They will be happier, their skin will be bright and smooth. You can't know the benefits of something you haven't tried. Remember when you chose to trust me?" Max hoped she would remember the day he first arrived at the school, how desperately she had been searching for a curriculum master to bring them beyond dancing, how readily she had agreed to take him on.

She took their cups and rinsed them, not mentioning how he had barely touched his coffee. She tapped the filter over the bin, then laid a towel on the counter and lined everything up to dry. He appreciated the care she took with the dishes, as if she held some empathy for them. If she could find some of that empathy for people, they might be onto something.

25 July 1913
Teatro della Pergola
Ted Craig, La superbia viene davanti alla rovina
Ancora non sappiamo l'italiano, Firenze

Ted,

Hullo from Constantinople. My sister-in-law would like to stay all week in our hotel and soak her feet in milk, and I have nearly lost my mind trying to be rid of her. Please consider Niobe's story staged over the course of a charming afternoon:

ACT ONE. The curtain lifts on Niobe doling out the laurels. This is Thebes, the city square, where the mother sings the song of her children, singing of their strength and beauty. The children are grown, the youngest just now leaving home, but she's brought all fourteen to the square to show them to the assembled crowd. The citizens watch her and feel nothing, nothing!

Niobe wraps her arms around her friend Latona, who stands tense and unyielding through the verse about a full and happy home, a kingdom you have made yourself. All a harmless mother's pleasure, but it's the thought that counts with the gods, and these thoughts number fourteen damning pieces of pride in tailored robes.

Latona weeps to think of the babies she's buried, love's stillborn end, the handfuls of sand she ate in hopes that the same alchemy which allowed her two youngest to survive will somehow return the rest. They may not have been gods but they were hers all the same.

From the edge of the ceremonial square, the wall's old stones crumble at the touch of Latona's last living hope: Artemis and Apollo, her moon and sun, have an instinct their mother did not give them, a sense of justice which compels them.

They draw their weapons and go to work, drawing gore in a wash, a bloody gouache, painting the fall of pride. The lesson is written in the world's most durable ink.

The citizens look about with empty eyes. Those were better days, when the gods did the punishing for you and you weren't required to find the lesson on your own. They take all of this in, noting their own prideful acts, their displays of meat and grain. A woman crouches to rub mud into her sandals. End of ACT ONE.

ACT TWO. Curtain lifts to a scene of indiscriminate dead. Niobe wanders across the slaughter in silence. She turns to avoid a half-quiver of arrows fatally lodged in her oldest son, as though touching them might compound their grievous harm. The gods, of course, are gone.

She holds her own body as if she could lift herself from the scene. She slaps her own face, makes a fist and strikes herself. She tries to lift her oldest son, but he is too large. He slips from her hands, falling the kind of fall she feared from the day she first held him. She tries again, lifting one arm then the other, taking her boy up and dragging him away. She braids her oldest daughter's hair together with her own and drags her upstage.

This is the price of pride, the balance paid by love. Niobe continues like this for some time and has moved half of the bodies almost entirely off the stage by the time the audience takes pity and checks her into a sanitarium.

In Constantinople, an early-morning ride into the old city and a meeting with the mysterious woman, made less mysterious by daylight

The man we hired to take us to Stamboul loaded us up in his vegetable cart before Penelope could find the words to insist that despite all appearances, she actually wasn't a particularly pale variety of eggplant.

She sat up beside him on the bench, claiming that she could better direct us to our destination, which meant I had to brace myself in the splintered cartbed, hanging on to the cart's slim sides so I wouldn't fly out onto the road. He got us going at a good clip out of *Frengistan,* and the tourist ladies stepped out to promenade with their little dogs just in time to see us jolting by in the vegetable cart, curled reams of onion skin fluttering behind us like a comet's tail.

Our driver tips his hat at the ladies, muttering about the suffrage question in America and how he finds it relates to the concept of women traveling alone. Penelope only briefly attempts to translate, leaning back to add her own little notes, for example that I should not repeat *Frengistan,* the name I heard him use for the Pera district, because it's an ugly word that means "foreigner land" and implies a rather dim sentiment for the shops and hotels full of people who would prefer room service over fresh home cooking. Our driver goes on and on, not seeming to notice when Penelope falls warily silent, offering only the occasional half grunt, as if she were considering rejoinders but decided against all of them and then forgot the question. The pavement changes to broken stone when we cross to the southern side of the Horn, and we have to slow to the point that foot traffic overtakes us. Children run past the cart, slapping the mule and screaming. Penelope points out a patch of grass running alongside the road where a mother watches her baby outpacing us at a crawl. We might have made the trip faster on our hands and knees, but it would have deprived us of this view of the mule's asshole, bobbing perfectly at eye level.

Penelope heaves a sigh and leans back, holding the rail with one hand and her belly with the other. Her armpits have soaked through her thin dress, and sweat beads the downy hair between her shoulder blades, catching in her hammocked collar. Pregnant women have a look about them that suggests they've suddenly realized the world is too dangerous going on the way it is and it's up to them to stop it from spinning. I would pity her, but the ride is even worse in the back. Years from now, one of the springs will snap and toss the man's load into the street, bringing down his mule, and his first thought will not be of the years he spent neglecting the cart or the rust coming off the axle in chunks, but rather of the morning he offered two foreign women a ride. In his mind it will have been my weight on these springs that threw the whole thing off, and I will feel his mortal curse, if I am not already dead.

Six months ago this shuddering landscape folding out onto a staccato horizon might have laid in my mind the first foundations of a dance. Not to be defeated by this blankness, I set to considering such a movement: there comes a low running across the stage, shoulders lifting at beats incongruous with the music. Or perhaps there should be no music, only fleeting bars of organized street sounds, the orchestra hauling in a load of broken glass and pallets, buttons in metal jars calling across the pit about the price of sugar. The percussionist lights a fire in the bowl of his timpani and skewers meat from a plate to roast it as a horn player punches the oboist and surrounding members of the wind section are pulled into the brawl; the dancer must find sense in the action and follow it, crouching to rise at odds with her own body, thrusting her arms wide to gather herself up.

This is only an idea of movement, a theory out of practice. It is a fantasy of movement, and even thinking about it is enough for me to want to throw movement out entirely and replace it with sensation or idea or even song—scratch that, considering my singing—but anything, anything outside this fraudulent idea of dance. Choreography these days is wishful work.

We come to a rocking halt before a painted yellow door, the man turning to look over his shoulder before saying something to Penelope. She draws a few coins from her purse, but he leans over to touch her hands, which seems to shock her well enough that she allows him to push the money away. Now it's really time to leave, the most dangerous moment of any situation being when a stranger is owed.

Clambering out, I thank the man. He scowls at the onion peels stuck to my tunic, as if he has caught me stealing them, and stays stubbornly watching us even after I've helped Penelope out.

Despite a fresh-looking coat of paint, the squat door at the address we've been given looks like an afterthought in the old stone wall, as if the men who built the place realized only after they completed their work that they were trapped inside.

Penelope knocks on the doorframe, checking her knuckles. She looks back at the man watching us from the street. After a while she knocks again.

"Maybe she's out," she says.

"Or else perhaps we are unwitting subjects in a cruel trick."

She never looks at me when she speaks. "Let's just wait a moment."

"A mystery with no real conclusion, asking the audience to sit with their disappointment and enter into it, to imbibe it, and in doing so, creating the least popular exhibit of art to ever exist—"

"All right, Isadora—"

At that moment Madame Candemir opens the little door. She is not a tall woman, but the doorframe is so short it obscures her face entirely. "Thank you for coming," she says, ducking down to greet us. She frowns when she sees the man on the cart, and lifts her hand to cover her mouth.

Seeming satisfied by her discomfort, the man continues up the hill, looking back at us as he goes.

"I'm sorry," she says, lowering her hand after the man turns the corner. "Won't you please come in?"

Travel allows the most indulgent narcissism. The little goat on the shore reminded me of California, the hotel skylights like a pair I'd seen in Moscow. This strange door is like nothing I've ever known, and so it becomes all of Constantinople to me, all of Turkey, and experience only serves to further flatten the world. It's a shameful practice but most tourists do it, making the world relate to them instead of the other way around, and avoiding the trouble of fitting themselves to anything new at all.

She takes us through a narrow hallway made narrower by thin tables laden with an estate's worth of teacups and leaded crystal, a pile of folded linens uniformly browned by a weeping stain, wineglasses full of buttons, a shoe box full of matchbooks, and thick jars of preserved fruits. Next to one of the tables, a waist-high stack of windowpanes shifts uneasily as we pass.

The sitting room is more of the same: baskets of scrap fabric, photographs spilling from hatboxes, hats lining the windows, piles of mending. The chairs are covered in old newspapers, their pages seeming to have been soaked and dried many times, making a kind of shell for each seat. Every inch of wall space is occupied by heavy-framed paintings of famous rivers. I recognize the Arno and the Danube, and the Seine of course, and the Yamuna from the Taj Mahal rising at its bend, and many others I cannot identify. Even the dull and lesser streams and what looks like a few examples of ambitious paddock runoff are framed in ornate carved gold, each whorl cupping pocks of dust. In one corner sits an empty birdcage, large enough to hold Madame Candemir if she was so moved, a few framed canals stacked behind it. All this makes me think of my single trunk with its costumes, my sandals puckering at their mended points tucked by the door. I have known the false-familiar feeling of hundreds of rented rooms, their clean floors and impartial shade, and I envy a well-cluttered home.

Our hostess walks a thin path through the clutter and takes a seat. "I'm working on a project," she says, gesturing at the pile, and though it is unclear what sort of project she is talking about or which of the assembled she might employ in its creation, I appreciate her optimism and like her more for it. She asks us to call her Ilgın. After we sit, a girl brings in a tray of tea and salted biscuits, balancing it on a stack of books. The room is south facing, but the open windows allow in the morning's hot breeze, giving every object a resonant heat, like the air an inch off the forehead of a fevered child.

"Your home is beautiful," Penelope says.

Ilgın looks around at the thin upholstered chairs, brought years ago from her family home, chosen over her mother's dappled kidskin couches, which were destroyed by her sister's cats within a month of the funeral.

"I hope you are enjoying your time in Pera," she says. "There are a number of fine shops and cafés if you take the time to explore, many Christian houses of worship and synagogues in the neighborhood, and you can find French and German shops." She says all this to my hair, which bobs my chin in a truncated wave.

Penelope asks her something in Turkish, but Ilgın looks at me and frowns until she asks again, in English: "What was this place before you lived here?"

"It was a private residence also before," she says. "Before that, I am told it was a shop selling materials for the purpose of horses."

"What was it before that?" I ask.

"Farmland, I believe."

"And before that?"

"All right," Penelope says.

"Water under the bridge," Ilgın says with a thin smile. "The reason I came to call on you is that I wanted to ask for your help. For you see, my son is gone, and I fear he will follow his brothers."

It takes a moment to register—the mind tapping a pen absently on the marble as it waits—but yes, the man Raoul, her son beside her on the dock. "With the epaulet," I say to Penelope, who glares at me in a way that suggests she has either already come to this conclusion or didn't want to.

Ilgın gazes up at a painting of either the Amstel or the Rhine, hard to say, there is a windmill.

"Where did his brothers go?" I ask.

"They went to death," she says. "I buried them both last week."

Behind her winds a placid tributary of the Nile, down which Moses as an infant floated in a basket. It is presented in a burnished black frame, the river looking thick and sodden. Wouldn't Moses's mother have been worried about the basket staying afloat, given the integrity of the reeds which comprised it? Perhaps she secretly wanted to drown him so she could go live her own life, but didn't have the courage to hold him under and so sent him floating away.

"How terrible," I say.

Penelope looks at me curiously, but it's impossible to explain this line of thinking. It's something she will learn in time; her own helplessness is only months from being revealed, the feeling of living with a second beating heart outside her body, a thin ribcage the only protection against the perilous world.

"Was there an accident?" Penelope asks Ilgın.

"They died by their own hand," she says, expressing as much and as little as possible in a manner designed to deflect further questions. Penelope frowns but keeps quiet, picturing the ropes and knives.

"Raoul will have gone to Ayastefanos," the older woman says. "To our old house. He said he wanted to be alone. I tried to save his brothers, but I failed. An oracle said I brought a spiritual illness upon them. Their ghosts hold me back from Raoul."

"Oracles will tell you anything at all," I say.

"Not this one," she says firmly. "The house is set close to the water. Tell the ferryman my name."

"You want us to go after him?" Penelope asks. "Madam, neither of us are in the proper condition—"

The current takes the mother's second-best basket, catching for a moment on a low branch and half tipping before righting itself and bobbing nearly out of sight. The mother watches, holding her breath.

"He spoke of you all the way home and again in the morning before he left," Ilgın says, reaching for me. Her hands are cold and feel full of loose material, as if they hold the disjointed bones of her sons as well. "He despised himself for not making your acquaintance. There was something he wanted to tell you, and he feels he lost the chance."

"You see," Penelope says, leaning forward to physically insert herself into the conversation. "We would very much like to go, but you must understand, I am experiencing a difficult pregnancy, and Isadora not three months ago has—"

"I'll go," I say, and Penelope's sputtering only steels my resolve. "I will leave straightaway."

Ilgın nods once, as if my choice was foretold.

"May we have the name of your oracle?" Penelope asks at last.

Max spends the afternoon looking for a woman who has been doing her best to avoid him

He was in a charming mood, which was wasted on the students. Remembering Elizabeth's exhortation that they discover themselves more truly, he went off in search of the piano teacher. She wasn't sitting behind any of the pianos in the building, not the good piano in the recital hall or the comfortable ones in any of the rehearsal rooms. This confused him, and he nearly called the whole thing off, when at last he found her on the porch with her sewing kit, a child's costume draped over her lap.

"Frau Venneberg," he said, bowing slightly.

Trella gave him an expressionless glance, moved her kit from the bench beside her, and went back to mending.

Taking a seat, Max stretched one leg and then the other. The porch looked over a moderate fenced-in garden and a quiet side street beyond, which saw only the occasional young mothers walking with their babies. Most of the children seemed to prefer the tree-lined path behind the school, and the older women tended to stay indoors, scrubbing various low corners and doing the wash. On that particular morning the only movement was that of the leaves of the young oaks and a little girl crouched on the ground, organizing a line of acorns along the fence.

"She has been out there for an hour," Trella said, "preparing for the parade of forest queens. Now you must stay and watch."

"I'm not obliged, she hasn't seen me yet."

"She expressly asked me to retain any guests who arrive in advance." Her words might have been mistaken as a flirtatious advance, but Trella delivered them in a serious way that made it clear she was only following orders.

The costume she was mending was from their solstice recital. He remembered the moment during the reception—the girls running wild after too many cakes—when one of them caught her foot up in another's long skirt and tore a long strip from her golden veil. Both girls wept over the garment and had to be individually consoled. They seemed to be always falling; perhaps they could add some instruction on how ladies might more carefully walk. He remembered Trella promising them both that she would mend the veil better than new. And now here she was, true to her word, making careful stitches in thread she had found to match the fabric. She would someday become the type of mother who would devote endless affection to her children, gathering them up all day and crouching by their little beds at night to catch the scent of their sleeping breath, emerging with a sighing smile before delivering one chaste kiss to her husband before bed. Max thought of the relief that husband would feel at this reception, the ease of becoming a pleasantly mundane constant, with a woman looking at him the same way as she would a dog or a particularly useful shelf, reserving her praise and scorn for others.

Trella was watching the girl, who had brushed the dirt from her hands and moved into position in the center of the sidewalk. The girl saluted up at them, and Max lifted his hand in return.

"I hear you are not pleased with my improvements to your course," he said to Trella.

The girl in the street began spinning in place, making the occasional tremulous pause to ensure they were both still watching.

"I'm not sure what you mean," Trella said.

"Elizabeth tells me you mentioned it."

The girl threw an imaginary baton into the air and executed a series of spins and slight kicks while it floated, weightless, outside the narrow scope of her imagination.

"I didn't think she would tell you," she said. "I wish she hadn't."

He appreciated her tone, which he took as an apology. "It would help me work more efficiently with your concerns if you expressed them directly to me," he said. He would remember later that she had in fact spoken to him, had brought it up after dinner one day. But it was important to keep the idea constant, and he was glad he didn't remember this when he was correcting her, as the point stood.

"I will remind you that in the absence of the Frauen Duncan, I am your superior," he said. "I'm looking forward to working together to bring the most adequate education possible to the young ladies of the Elizabeth Duncan School."

"Of course," she said, adjusting her gloves.

Max was disappointed in himself, ashamed that his attempt at seduction had turned so quickly to discipline. Wasn't that always the way! He hadn't taken Elizabeth's request seriously when she first made it, assuming it was the old subtle competitive sense that roared up whenever Isadora was involved, but now that Elizabeth was home, she was locking herself up in her room at night, and Max was forced to confront the idea that she had taken a lover. He tried to remind himself of the freedom this gave him, but the feeling was quickly subsumed by the dread of its undertaking. Here he was, forced to learn an art he had never bothered to study when it was most relevant, and now he was failing the tests.

He wasn't even cross with Trella, not really. It was Elizabeth driving his concern, her meddling that had inserted herself into his relationship with the young pianist. Every night he dreamed of a heroic class of women bearing the banner of the new age across their breast, each of them beaming. He was so close to making this dream a reality. If these two had their way, however, the next generation would come to inherit the very brand of weakness they themselves had suffered all their lives.

But he couldn't think like that. The women would eventually find his ideas to be right for the course of the school and very fashionable with new trends. Soon enough, they would all thank him.

The girl in the road had transformed from marionette to bandleader. He watched her conducting the birds.

"Tell me of your family," Max said.

Trella shook her head once. She kept one gloved hand pressed to the costume in her lap as if it were gauze over a fresh wound.

"Come now, don't be obstinate. My theories are meant to only benefit our students. They are standing at a real turning point of human civilization, with the opportunity to take the most modern course. If you would take a moment to consider the potential—"

"I live with my father south of the city," she said. "He worked as a prison guard until he was injured and couldn't work. My older sisters live in Berlin with their husbands. Our mother died when we were very young."

"Fatherhood is a precarious thing," Max said vaguely, though he didn't believe it. Fatherhood actually seemed fairly straightforward. He thought of his own father, who stocked his grocery in keeping with kosher law, with the exception of a daily tray of cheese bourekas, which were so unpopular in Vienna it was a mystery why he kept ordering them. He was a stubborn man and unadaptive to change, and he was not well liked by his customers. Fortunately, of all the lessons he learned from his parents, his mother's uncompromising vision was the most salient.

Trella didn't respond. The girl on the street had become a dancing bear, waving her paws in an inarticulate way. It was important for children to have an early sense of fantasy. Perhaps they could incorporate some element of imaginative activity into the curriculum. The women might be happier with the strength course if the children completed it tumbling like circus acrobats, and the girls' roles could be assigned in a way that challenged their weakness.

Max hated feeling beholden to the women. He worked so tirelessly for their success, and they fought him at every turn.

He stood so quickly the bench rocked back, startling her. "You will appreciate my changes to the school or seek your employment elsewhere," he said.

Trella tipped her head to one side. "Yes," she said, only slightly narrowing her eyes to his back as he walked away. She had been enjoying the morning alone with her thoughts before Max arrived. Once he was gone again, she found herself thinking of her family. She returned to her favorite of the four precious memories that remained of her mother, the one when they were making nut breads for the Advent and shaped a small cake—a secret cake, unknown to the others—which they topped with thin-sliced apricots. Mother served a slice to Trella, her youngest, the one who seemed so disappointed in the world, even as a child.

Upstairs, Elizabeth works herself into a minor frenzy by considering the artistic eye

If a dancer's whole body is her instrument, Elizabeth figured the sculptor's instrument is more potent, distilled as it is into the hands. Romano had lovely thin hands, but the rest of him was an inarticulate afterthought—a pouch of fat behind his knees, rings so deep under his eyes they could be mistaken for a pair of subtle bruises. His hands were as soft as powder, discerning in their function, scrubbed palms cool to the touch, every nail trimmed to a gentle half-moon. She felt the inquiry in his hands, when he pressed her hip to find the bone.

Elizabeth examined her own hands, pink and swollen with the heat of the afternoon. The girls had lost interest in the school's little courtyard when the weather had gotten too warm, and so she had it to herself and could spend the entire morning out there, half-reading the paper and sweating under her light dress. She found that if she circled the small space three times while envisioning the perimeter of a desert island, she could usually generate enough luck for everyone to leave her alone most of the morning.

The social columns included a number of birth announcements, which gave her the chance to think of Romano as an infant. She imagined herself as his mother, stroking his chubby legs and making wishes for his future. Motherhood for Elizabeth seemed imbued with mystic properties that alternately frightened and fascinated her. She didn't understand children, save for their mercurial nature, which she envied more than anything. Once, one of her students shoved another into a doorframe, bloodying the younger one's nose, but it was the older girl who was inconsolable long after the injured one lost interest, weeping through the lunch hour. It escalated until she was found lying prone on the ground, asking God to strike her from the earth. When Elizabeth slipped the girl a piece of candy to cheer her up, she dug a hole out by the fence and buried it.

Elizabeth could remember feeling this way. As a little girl, she peeked during a game of hide-the-thimble and was told by mother that cheating would ruin the game for everyone. At this, she crawled into the bathtub and tortured herself with thoughts of what she had done to a simple afternoon. She remembered wanting to start over entirely, to take the lessons she had learned and apply them to a new family—though surely none would take her in, knowing her history of ruining things. She decided to find a home on the street. She left notes of farewell on her siblings' pillows that evening, with sincere apologies for ruining the game for everyone, and Mother found her at the end of the block, carrying a wedge of cheese and five books wrapped in a cloth.

Isadora, on the other hand, lived a wholly blameless life. She would shrug it off, rejecting the claim like a government official sending back an order that possessed some trivial flaw. Once Deirdre was born, it took only a few months for the rest of them to abandon the fantasy that the child would unearth in her mother some healthy sense of right and wrong, some element of guilt. That was Elizabeth's hope, anyway, and it was dashed early on: one day around lunch, the baby was pulling on the tablecloth when she upended a bowl of soup over herself. It was Isadora's soup, and she had certainly placed the bowl too close to the edge of the table to make room for her writing, but she only watched the scene as if it was happening onstage, sitting in silence while a nurse rushed in, tore off the screeching child's dress, and hauled her into the kitchen. After they left, Isadora shook her head as if she were clearing a web and returned to her notes.

Elizabeth imagined that Romano's mother would have kissed and caressed his knees and ankles, his belly, which then would have been soft and blooming with infant flesh. She had read that true artists had use of a third eye, which they employed to know the world. Romano's third eye wasn't behind his knee—she had already thoroughly prodded both—but she hadn't had a chance to check his armpits or between his toes. Maybe it rested on the domed muscular plain between his scrotum and anus, rapidly blinking in the bath or staring rueful into the toilet. Perhaps the doctors found it when his appendix threatened to burst and they opened him up to save him. She imagined a surgeon discovering the furious eye, agonized in the fresh light of the operating theater. The surgeon would have to work around it to remove the appendix and then tuck the eye like a child into the dark warmth of the body.

It had to be somewhere, anyway, for Romano was a true artist and had earned her respect with the reverent way he spoke about his work. He was most interested in bronze, and would cast flat slabs to reveal their texture. He loved to talk about his favorite pieces, the way each reflected and radiated heat and how one might change when grouped with others, how each took on a kind of charge. While she lay around, thinking of him, he was surely doing something far more serious. She wondered if he drank coffee with his mother in the afternoons, if he read the paper in Italian or English, if he ever thought of the woman who walked into the sea, if he might someday change his mind about Germany, and if he thought of her fondly, if he thought of her at all.

Isadora takes a short trip up the coast with the goal of helping someone besides herself for once

The ferryman used a javelin to shove off the stone, and the two of us held the rail until we got going. The Bosporus is so clogged with steamers, each making its own choppy waves, that the two of us have to constantly brace against the ragged wood paneling on the side of the boat to keep upright.

"Ayastefanos," the ferryman says.

Penelope had been all set to forbid my travel, but in the morning she found herself hunched and glaring at the toilet bowl. When I was pregnant with Patrick, my gut would always soothe with a tablespoon of brown liquor, but when I offered the remedy, she waved me off. And so I finished my morning ritual: until a few days ago I had been sprinkling just a bit of ash from the wooden box over my breakfast. Once I ran out of lighter ash and the texture bore larger grit, I had to start taking the larger pieces and swallowing them like pills. As of this morning, about a quarter cup remains. Soon I will have consumed them both.

I thought we might head a little farther out to be free of the chop, but the man keeps the boat huddled close to the port wall, shoving off it at times with the javelin. He scratches a jagged scab on his forearm, bracing himself as my balance goes off, which sends my left foot across the right into a funny curtsy. He stabs the wall, bucking us in the other direction, and my right foot crosses the left, bending at the knee. The ferryman smiles broadly at the sun.

Penelope by now will have drawn the curtains and called for a seltzer. Perhaps she is afraid I will curse her, and her child will be born with raisin eye. I could lay a powerful curse indeed, but in many ways the work has been done for me.

The ferryman points his javelin at the house, set close to the water. The house looks as if it were transported on a barge from Alamo Square, flanked by palm and pine and creeping jasmine, a sweet lattice lifting its gables like a sugar shell. Shutters cover each window, and everything but the stone roof is painted a blinding shade of white, reflecting the sea painfully on itself. The strongest fortress is a mirror, no doubt, but this takes it to an extreme. Shielding my eyes, I cross the yard to explore it.

Ropes of jasmine hang from the front eaves, cooling the porch. Back on the water, the ferryman watches in bored amusement. He'll obviously stay there until I come back to the boat. To avoid him, I'll have to live here in Ayastefanos forever; after a few years I might recruit some local women and set up a musical series at the Russian monument. We could take donations. Of course the local women will have to do their part to establish an audience from their own social circles, begging friends and family to arrive and support them, an endless cycle of debts without a significant return to warrant the work. Not too many go in on artistic greatness when they realize the effort involved.

I'll look into the various halls in Ayastefanos soon enough. For now, there's a man who needs my help, a man prepared to perform violent acts upon his own body if I do not intervene. His mother knows it to be true, which means he's passed the subtle stage and time is precious indeed. The front door pushes open when I knock. Hearing nothing and with no cause to delay, I enter the house.

I find myself standing in a great and airless hall. Someone has gone to pains to absolve each room of the sentiment that might attend color, and I find myself surrounded by stark white walls over floorboards painted black. After the slight latch of the door behind me, the sound of gulls vanishes and the house is silent. I feel a pulsing pressure circling my skull, as if my ears have been steadily boxed by invisible hands.

The silence drives me to speak.

"All men are my brothers and all women are my sisters." My voice makes a pathetic small quiver at the end.

There is no response, save the floorboards squeaking with my footsteps as I walk through the entry hall. This hall would make a fine small performance space, empty as it is. The local ladies and I could start our series here.

"All men are my brothers and all women are my sisters," I say again, stronger a second time. The hall leads me into a kitchen, which seems to have never been used for cooking; the smell of fresh paint is the only sensory element of the whole place.

Through the kitchen is a dining room, empty save for a marble-topped table with a single white lily ludicrously displayed in a delicate crystal vase. The flower browns from its petal fringe, orange pollen drifting into an ordered pile.

"All men are my brothers—"

Through a wide marble archway on the other side of the dining room I find Raoul. He is laid out on a white chaise, dressed all in white, a white suit and shoes with a white pocket square camouflaged in his pocket, all clothes he must have purchased specifically for this inaugural and determinate use. His arms are crossed, and a revolver rests under his folded hands.

The room throbs around him, drawing me close. I find myself leaning over him. "The lily is a little precious," I say.

He opens one eye. "A field of lilies fling open to the sun," he says. "White flags aloft. Death is one act with no second." His eyes flutter closed. There is no sound, save for the metallic sound his revolver makes as he gently rolls the cylinder between two fingers.

"That's all very good, but since you obviously practiced, I wouldn't mind giving you a few notes."

"Go ahead."

"You should be nude, for one."

He opens one eye, frowning, but doesn't interrupt.

"If you are supposed to be exiled from a place, you can't wear its uniform. The lily is supposed to represent you, isn't it? You don't have it dressed in a dinner jacket. And I have to say, the gun is a nice touch but could go somewhere a little less conspicuous."

He sits up to remove his sack jacket. "On the mantel?"

"Christ's sake, under the sofa, something your audience would find at eye level but wouldn't be so present in the narrative. That's the problem with the scene as it stands, everything is placed just so. It's too much."

Once he removes his jacket, I smell the liquor on him. "Pardon me," he yawns. "I must insist on my personal creative process." But he lets me ease the gun from his hands.

It's as heavy as I remember. Mother kept one at her bedside when we were young, and I well recall the feeling of it, like lifting the corner of a bookshelf. I crouch down and place the weapon under the sofa, pushing it just out of reach. He lies back again but makes room on the couch for me to sit beside him.

"Out of sight, out of mind," I say, tapping his temple.

Like all boys careening about inside the bodies of men, he is soothed by a simple phrase. His thumb twitches, and I can tell he wants dearly to suck it.

"Your mother is worried. After what happened to your brothers. We should go to her."

"She cannot know my pain," he says, this and similar, on and on. He eventually works himself up to weeping, very dramatic. It reminds me of Deirdre at the grocer, reaching for an apple at the bottom of a barrel but not well grasping it and slipping to her knees to scream.

"Hush now, I can help you." Like a country doctor who can name the beast by its bite, I have learned well enough the scope of grief to know its subtleties. There's something here beyond even the pain of death. "What is it truly?" I try, simple ideas often yielding the best results.

Suddenly despondent, he turns his head to the side, the look of a man forced to face two different kinds of suffering and remember that his is the lesser. I once saw the same sour look on the faces of a group of white women who had accidentally arranged their rally for the vote across the street from a freedman's hospital.

"It's all right," I say. "You can tell me."

"Sylvio," he whimpers.

Young love. "Did she leave you standing in the rain?"

"He is in Saranda with his mother." He pouts, watching the wall.

"A gentleman," I say, employing the wonder he wants to hear in my voice.

"That's right. There now, you despise me."

"My dear, *Phaedrus* is the most exquisite love song ever written. Come now, it's not as bad as all that."

"Not as bad? It's impossible!"

"Anything's as possible as you want it to be. Bring him to Paris and begin a new life."

He laughs, a sharp laugh. "Yes, we'll get a little house."

"Maybe not in Ayastefanos. But in France, you'd be surprised." I stroke his sweet thin hair. "You underestimate the pleasures of the progressive artistic class."

"And you underestimate the pleasure of being executed in the street."

What a little saucepot! I like him more already, almost enough to forgive him for not allowing me to solve his problems.

"Diaghilev kept a lover, a lovely man. I can't say much for his talent as a dancer, but people seemed to like him personally."

"Yes, I know the story. Diaghilev was destroyed when Nijinsky took a wife, and if you can name only two moral perverts, you're not working too hard to find them."

"I'm naming the famous ones to hearten you. There are a great many—"

He leapt up. "Thank you, I'm very heartened. Perhaps this lifelong trouble of mine is all a misunderstanding. If only I had you to come and simplify it for me years ago, I wouldn't be in this mess."

"There's Oscar Wilde also, if you don't know."

"Good!" he says, placing his palms over his eyes. "Good. Let's dig him up."

"Raoul, be reasonable. You only have to come back with me to the hotel, this will all be sorted out."

"But why do we have to go, when you've come and sorted it all out already?" He takes my hands. "If you could only change Sylvio's mind things would really be sorted. He says I cannot possibly love him as much as he loves me, and so the whole thing is off."

I make a play of considering this. "That presents a real challenge," I say carefully. "Your lover may have found the truest form of love and heartbreak both, and meeting that call requires true bravery. But you two are very lucky. Let me ask you this: Can you even imagine how many millions of people are fated to find love in lesser measure and then marry young, live well, and die? Can you think of anything more earnest and ordinary?"

"I would have liked that," he insists, but he already sounds unsure. The romantic poets nearby got the best of him, but I learned this trick years ago when a landlord who found me weeping on his stairs declared that my heartache was a rare gift, and that I had a duty to bear it to the whole of Eastern Europe. I did not die in his stairwell as I declared I would. His wise words inspired me through the rest of my tour, and I earnestly worked to lay my heart bare to the world. Much later I realized that old landlord only wanted me out of his stairwell, as my groaning was disturbing his other tenants.

Since then I have employed this tactic to great effect, first to a stagehand who couldn't bear to lift the curtain and then to Teddy Craig, despondent over a snip he met staging *Hamlet* in Stockholm. Of course, then Teddy and I fell in love and the tactic was lost to me, until a police officer, finding me despondent over Teddy, used it to coax me off a railroad track. Raoul here clearly feels as if he is at the bottom of a terrible well of pain, that nobody has ever fallen this deep, despite all the handprints in the mud.

He dries his eyes with quiet dignity. "Will it ever release me?" he asks.

"In truth it may not." Though of course it will—one day he will happen on a picture of a ram and think of how stupid Sylvio was for confusing rams and goats, despite growing up on a farm, and he will realize he has not thought of Sylvio in many months and will shortly forget him for years, saying farewell to the sole passenger on a ship with a route as wide as the world.

But of course it is important now for him to believe that this emotion has no end, that this brief and common madness bears some essential significance to his life.

"We should go have a drink," I say, squeezing his arm. "Your mother is sick over this."

He allows me to help him up. "I should stay," he says.

"Nonsense. Come now, fetch your things."

It isn't until after we've settled in at the bar that I remember the revolver under the sofa and wonder how long before the caretaker finds it. If Raoul has thought of this as well, he doesn't mention it, but rather gazes at the dregs of his whiskey cocktail, his grand love melting away.

At Oldway, Paris avoids the loudest of the renovations, which sound like
a team attempting to tunnel through the entry hall

They had been treated lately to some terrific storms. The girl doing the shopping returned with hailstones snug alongside the bottles in her basket, and a lightning strike split the big whitebeam and set the tar of the new road ablaze.

Fortunately, there was no damage to the girl, the road, or the hangar under construction on the far side of the property. Paris was glad the structures were spared, though it would have been some fun to see it all ripped apart. During the worst of it, the sea came in from Tor Bay and eddied harmless around the hangar frame, tossing up a bit of sand and burying a wheelbarrow one of the men had failed to secure, but otherwise leaving no trace.

The storms were a blessing because they kept him inside just as he was starting to see Napoleon Charles out in the world. He glimpsed the boy from the painting first in print advertisements, then in the schoolhouse windows and the faces of the children he saw on the street. He was wary to greet the young mothers walking their children down the lane, sensing a terrible potential within each of them to spontaneously create another doomed boy, if Paris only willed it.

Stuck inside with the rain, there was a much lower chance of meeting ghosts. He turned his study to Hortense de Beauharnais, Napoleon Charles's mother, who was wearing a blue dress that would have brought out her eyes. At first he couldn't bear to look at her for longer than a moment, something about her expression. He turned to look at the ladies in the papal chorus, but after gamely trying to imagine each of them receiving confession, he returned to Hortense. He felt her grief and feared her uneasy gaze.

Paris saw the people of the world as falling into two categories: creators tasked with making the world, and consumers, who would take and ruin all that had been built. Sweet Hortense obviously fell into the latter category. She looked up at the crown as if it were already locked away. Soon enough she would outlive her use to the history of the world, yet she would continue to exist, in flesh and then in oil.

He saw some of his own mother in her, a woman who made it her duty to use up the estate's surplus of food every month in feeding everyone who entered her home. She constantly monitored kitchen activity to see that there was an abundance of food for her family and their guests, the kitchen and cleaning staff, the gardeners and the men in Isaac's garage, the patent men who arrived daily, and even the fellow who delivered the truckloads of flour and meat, accepting his cart of raw materials and sending him away with roast beef in sandwiches and fruit for his children. She wasn't happy unless people were eating the fruits of her husband's labor. She had a supply of small pies made on the days she went out, which she would distribute to children she encountered on the road. She cast herself as a kindly benefactor to the unfortunate, the type of character usually depicted in her favorite serialized orphan stories as a moneyed older man, and she made sure to care so well for such a broad population around them that her own children were often left picking among the scraps.

From the days of his early youth Paris was naturally suited to enjoy the offerings his father provided, and he had come to expect such gifts from the world. In that way he became a member of the consuming class, though he bitterly fought the distinction.

When Isadora came along, he jumped at the chance to serve as a conduit for her work. He marveled at how she produced and consumed in vast quantity and as a closed system, rushing across her rehearsal room in the tenth hour of self-directed practice with the same look of keen pleasure she brought to endless lazy afternoons reading poetry in the bath. She stayed in bed for three full days and spent the fourth writing enough lecture notes to fill a laundry bin. She was neither the flighty dreamer he had imagined she would be nor the miracle of the generative earth she seemed to like people to believe she was; she was something enticingly other. Her only desire was for control of the bounds of her body—this put her in stark contrast with Paris, who wished to control the acreage plans of multiple estates—but she was insatiable and uncompromising in this small window, in a way that made Paris feel amateurish and forgetful in comparison. She seemed unimpressed by praise and unmoved by sentiment, though she always liked the flowers he brought her, and so he chose to keep his praise of her astonishing skill to a minimum; he could lay gifts at her feet, but then he would be no different from the others at her altar, those false friends who waited outside the funeral, trying to get a better look at her as she went inside. Paris prided himself on a better understanding of Isadora than most would ever know. She worked to resemble a figure on a vase, but she was more essential than the figure or the vase itself, or even the museum in which the vase was displayed. She was a tower, a spire, a gleaming copper steeple forged in fire and rising from chaos to spear the cloudless sky. He would hardly admit any of this to her and thus suffer one of her weeklong preens, but it was true enough, and she knew it.

A letter arrived from her one afternoon, greeting him as "Lohengrin" and going on about her time in Turkey. She claimed to dream of him! He laughed aloud, and surprised himself at the echo the hall produced. The gallery of the Coronation seemed startled as well. If Isadora had her way, she would be Napoleon and Josephine both, kneeling before herself and raising the crown for her own bowed head as Paris stood along with the other ladies in the gallery, trying to catch a glimpse of her robes.

His resentment would burn off when she returned. She had a way of making even his most deeply held beliefs seem petty and malformed, and never ceased to be relieved by her visits, despite the fact that he had no reason to seek her blessing in the first place. He was ashamed by the pride he took in standing beside her; it seemed that in his study of the painting, he could bear daily witness to the coronation of an empire felled by pride and not take from it the slightest warning.

He looked one last time at Hortense. Though her boy tried his best to pull her closer to the activity at the center, she held back. She was comfortable where she was, standing and smiling as if she had been paid to stand and gamely smile. He tried to remember what happened to her. Napoleon's favorite was the other one. Surely Hortense was buried in France. He would have someone look into it.

Elizabeth recalls a memorable performance in London from Isadora, who was always memorable for one reason or another

Elizabeth remembered with fondness the week she stopped speaking. The silence began as a subtle act against her sister, who herself tended to speak only on the subject of her own successful auditions or long lunches she had with men who might book this venue or that tour. Isadora didn't even notice the silent protest until the third morning, when she looked up from a long one-sided conversation to find her sister stone-faced over her oatmeal.

It might not have impressed her sister, but Elizabeth saw an immediate improvement in the attention she gave to the world around her, finding that within the quiet meals and long walks were hidden images and half-considered phrases, things she would have otherwise missed. She found old thoughts rising to the surface: one memory of a group of filthy children staring out a warehouse window at a dead horse, another of a lady gathering her skirts to drop from the Windsor's seventh floor, and then later, after a long and quiet day, the image of her father, hollowing out half a grapefruit in the doorway, the light around him turning him to shadow, an outline of himself. These pictures came and proved to her that they had always been there. The world she had seen never left her but was etched onto a limitless plane.

On that third morning of silence Isadora threw down her fork and declared that since Elizabeth was sick enough to lose her voice, she shouldn't come too near the rest of them lest she infect them with whatever it was she had. Elizabeth responded by crumpling up a page of choreography, then wept and raged with such a rare passion that Isadora got up and left, flouncing down the stairs and slamming the door behind her without another word.

The argument put them all on edge for the rest of the day. Elizabeth found herself worrying about Isadora: was she truly upset? Had this been some kind of last straw? She might be out there spreading evil gossip to their mutual friends. Perhaps she would leave the country and tour in Russia. Elizabeth spent the day walking up and down the streets until she was lost. Too embarrassed to ask for help, she walked on until she found she was coming up on a concert hall, where, as luck would have it, Isadora was performing that night.

It was early still, but Elizabeth went in and sat to get out of the weather. Eventually the rest of the audience joined her, and the lights dimmed once and then twice. They were seated and waiting for an hour all told before they heard a stage door opening and slamming, followed by the sound of shoes being kicked off, then bare feet padding softly and then louder, and at last Isadora emerged, thrust into silence by her own halting momentum. She seemed surprised to see everyone, but recovered quickly enough and breathed out, her face and shoulders relaxing almost imperceptibly with every step. In the center of the stage she planted her feet, flung her head back, and stared at a point hovering five feet above the back hall.

She began with the Tanagra figures. They were simple poses—in one she adjusted her sandal strap, in another she bent to pick a flower—but her confidence and grace in movement transformed them into a kind of living statuary. Elizabeth could hear the audience gasping, transfixed, as her sister's body and bearing distilled and seemed illuminated in museum light.

She chose a peasant mazurka next, a minute-long piece meant to evoke an ancient harvest, and moved through it with an elegant lightness, as if each act—of washing, crushing grapes under her feet, then fanning forward to greet the harvest—was being presented in its ideal form. There was something fundamental about her, something at once so beguiling and accessible, so tantalizingly human, which seemed to imply that her audience had this grace within all of them, just under their inarticulate skin. The audience forgot her late arrival, and tossed roses and sentimental items onto the stage.

It was mastery in restraint, sublimity in action, and only Elizabeth knew from her sister's slight tremor and sway that she had just come from a ripping drunken spree. During the second half of the mazurka, Elizabeth saw, she caught herself stumbling and just barely recovered, translating the forward lunge into a half curtsy, drawing her hand extemporaneously to a perfumed letter that just happened to have landed at the edge of the stage. She touched the page to the tip of her nose and tucked it into her tunic band. Nobody else could have known that Isadora had gone out and drunk heroically to soothe her sorrow over their argument. But Elizabeth knew, and she took a strange comfort in it. This was as close to an apology as she would ever get.

At the Pera Palace, Isadora and Raoul languish in bed after a weeklong jag, there being no rest for the wicked and not much for the good

We have lost the morning, talking of love. I ran my fingers through his hair while he spoke of Sylvio's beauty and bravery, and he refilled our glasses while I told stories about the children. He had brought just one sad bottle of port from the house, so we were forced to order three cases of champagne and two fine crystal tumblers, a third when Raoul broke one in a fit. A telegram from Eleonora Duse was turned away unopened, the bellhop invited to return once he got his wits about him and lost the silly cap. We have been going on for days! With any luck we'll go forever.

Raoul's head rests on my belly, and mine is nestled in a pile of embroidered pillows that we ordered at some point to make the whole thing feel more like a harem. The only thing missing is satisfying sexual congress, though we certainly tried. Raoul goes on and on about Sylvio.

"The perfect face!" he says. "A miraculous face. A wrinkle between his eyes makes him look like a puppy focusing on a blade of grass. Oh God, he hated when I said it. I would laugh and laugh."

The headboard from my position half hanging off the bed resembles the trellis of a hanging garden. "Plato says there would be no philosophy at all if Athens had not known such beautiful youths."

"He nearly left me right there in the restaurant. For laughing! Nothing worse. But he was always so severe. I would have followed him anywhere!"

"No philosophy at all, can you imagine?"

"After dessert he was scolding me, demanding to be taken more seriously, but I just kept laughing. My God. I tried putting my face into my wineglass to mask the sound, but it only amplified it, you see! It only—here, I'll show you—it made everything worse. He turned a bowl of ice cream onto my lap. Oh, it was worth it."

An entire lineage of Athenian youth, eyes aflame with that most dangerous brand of aimless vigor. "You know, I'd like to visit the cliffs of Manisa. Have you ever been to Manisa, by the sea? Eurydice threw herself from the stone. I mean Niobe. I'm only curious to see."

"One afternoon Sylvio and I were having a picnic by the strait. He stripped down to his shorts and swam for so long I lost sight of him. I finished our lunch and fell asleep waiting and he still hadn't returned when I woke again. By the time he found his way back to shore, I was practicing his eulogy. *Such a romantic end! The very spirit of the earth poured into no nobler frame!* You can imagine my relief and annoyance both when he arrived asking for a towel." He reaches to stroke my cheek and finds my stomach instead, amiably drawing his fingers across it. We removed our clothes hours ago, after a discussion about the physical ideal. Penelope left for tea with her aunt and is now almost certainly downstairs staring at a wall.

"My cousin is pregnant," I say. "My brother's sister. My brother's wife. With a child, you know."

"When we traveled together to see Sylvio's sister, she was pregnant. We had a suite with a door that we unlocked at night. Can you imagine the tantalizing dimensions of that door?" He was crying again. "I tried to write about that weekend again and again, but it was never right, I burned it all."

He goes on some more about carrying the ashes of the poems to scatter in a garden and how that garden grew the most beautiful flowers, which would die if they were admired for too long. I think of the children in the wooden box. "My attention was a killing force," he moans, the words echoing into his glass.

"You know, I've long thought that anyone could alter the course of another person's entire life with only their thoughts. But you either have to be very powerful or you need your thinking to match that of a thousand others, a kind of amplification of sentiment."

"Surely not."

"But think of my premieres, my tours, every small success documented. Once I started being written up in the papers, I handed the literate population of the world the power to destroy my life."

He sputters incidentally—wine being difficult to drink from a supine position—and sits up, setting his glass to the side and wiping his mouth. "Ah, well then," he says. Standing, he holds the quilt to steady himself. "We should find something to eat."

"It's very simple. I'm saying that people I've never met or known may have injured me with their thoughts and affected my life as a punishment meted from a place of their own jealous desire."

"Can they bring us some bread? All I want is bread and a little butter. The butter they'll bring you here, if you haven't tried it yet, is a little sweet. People find it sweet. They'll bring you clotted cream if you ask." He drapes the quilt around his shoulders. "I'm a scholar of continental terms," he declares.

This morning he anointed me with the children's ashes while I lay in the bath. He offered to dump the remainder into the water, but I couldn't stand the thought, and from a practical standpoint, the larger bits might clog the pipes.

"Penelope consulted the oracle your mother suggested. She was told that she wishes for a little lamb, but her wish will not come to pass, and that in an elevated place, her life will end after a final meditation."

He stops his preening at the mirror. "The oracle said all that?"

"Come back to bed and let's never leave."

"Tell me what she said."

"I already did. But you don't really believe in all that, do you?"

"An oracle once told me I would find everything I wanted and then lose it, and now look what's happened," he says, taking a long drink from a teacup on the windowsill. "They're very accurate in this region—have you been ashing in this?"

"She only made the appointment to learn her future child's disposition. Now I think she's very bothered."

"Mother has good taste in oracles. She relies on them because most of our family is in the other world. You're right, we really should let her know that I'm safe; she's probably spending all her money on them as we speak."

"Will you be very reasonable and come back to bed?"

"Let's see the oracle," he calls out from the other room. "Maybe she will say something for us. What if she can commune with the dead?"

I find that if I squint deeply into the shadows of the room, they are there, holding hands.

"There's no harm in it," he says.

"Come back to bed, you're making me beg."

He finally acquiesces and crawls across the covers, kissing my cheek and weeping again. Raoul has more than enough tears for both of us. I have a deep love for him, a protective feeling. "Let's have the oracle in," he says.

"Fine. She can speak to us generally and we can draw much from her malformed claims."

He cheers immediately, wiping his eyes on my hair. "Good then, it's settled."

"Nothing is ever settled, my dear." Reaching to ring the bell, I start thinking about the order for lunch, but before I can ask his preference for meat or fish, he's already asleep.

Max fantasizes about his movement but swiftly finds he cannot do it alone

His lecture on termites had gone very well. The girls had made grand gestures of their boredom and rolled their eyes while he spoke, but the whole thing had been written to serve them in the world and he knew that, someday, they would wish they had paid attention. As adults they would see their every effort crushed by the whims of circumstance, and they would try to recall his conclusion—that patient mollification was effective against any barrier—but come up empty. They would flail and fail in short order, and years later he would read their obituaries listing them by their husband's name and naming their children as well, one by one, with no hint as to any larger purpose to their little lives. Max knew with the certainty of his own strong heart that he would outlive each one of these girls, and some of their girls as well, and that some years in the future he would open the newspaper on a park bench and read the stories of their lives in past tense—more accurately, the stories of the lives they supported, the triumph of the living on the work of the dead— and he would remember with satisfaction how they had made such cruel fun of his speech about termites.

Elizabeth at the very least should have been galvanized by his lecture. He was expecting more than her usual cold kiss on the cheek after he descended from the stage, a murmur that she would be in her room. The distance between them was growing, and though Max believed it was best not to force issues of the heart, he found himself made nervous by it. Trella brought her afternoon class to the lecture and gave him a small wave as she walked them out of the auditorium, and this slight attention thrilled him to the point of distraction through his usual post-lecture ritual of standing in the street behind the school and delivering a few feints and jabs to the late-morning air.

He was working on a new theory in his spare moments, during the lunch hour and his free afternoons. It first occurred to him in conversation with a man of science, who impressed on him the idea that the truths of the world were made true only by observation and that supposed theories beyond that were only a mix of conjecture and superstition. This started Max thinking about ideas he had taken as fact, realizing that everything was riddled with assumptive constructs.

Death, for example. Max knew something of death—his mother and father had passed away, and a classmate in an accident on holiday, also once a neighbor's dog—but despite these observed events and the easy extrapolation possible, there was no definite proof that he, himself, would die. He began to fantasize about an eternal life, the first years of which would be spent attending the funerals of everyone he ever knew and then adapting to the comforts which awaited him in the future. His own persistent heartbeat would be his only companion, carrying him into a new age, where he could see his ideas manifested at last. Real change required time above all else, and it wouldn't do at all to have a bus accident or a pandemic spoil his patient plans.

He knew that Germany had the ability to rise and distinguish herself. She had the science and the talent and was building up the strength and reserve. The nation was shifting, he could feel it. Soon enough, there would be a World's Fair on every corner, a cultural revolution every other weekend.

And what's more, he reasoned, the women would lead them. While the men were tasked with putting body and mind toward pursuing the empire abroad—peaceful missions, to be sure—it would be the women inventing the future in bedtime stories of worlds built to shelter their children and support their every effort, tales designed to inspire a sense of nationalist bravery, to pluck the little vanguards from their cribs and introduce them to power.

He knew he was in the right place to make it happen. Before he even saw the worn copy of *Zarathustra* that Isadora carried around—the binding split as if she slept with it splayed open under her pillow, just as he did with his old copybook—he made the educated induction that she would have a similar idea of the future. It was strange that they had never had a proper conversation, given the position they no doubt shared. He had met her briefly in Vienna, with Elizabeth after a performance, but he was only a child then and eager to agree with everything she said. He never had a real opportunity to share his ideas with her, but perhaps that was for the best. When the time was right, he would get his chance.

Still, Max couldn't help but feel a little disappointed in himself for failing to take the famous dancer to bed. He had been looking forward to working alongside her, and truth be told, spent many happy nights planning their love affair. They had such similar notions and would flatter each other. He had a particularly satisfying fantasy of holding her after a successful lovemaking session and speaking of his concept of the bodily ideal, and maintained this fantasy while pursuing Elizabeth, who would surely understand if there needed to be a change of plans.

The last time Isadora visited Darmstadt would have been a good time, but he put it off again. She had just returned from tour and was distracted during their afternoon chat over his tea collection, staring at the wall as he worked to illustrate the irony of improving the individual through group training. She reached for a third cookie as he laid out his plan to remove nine or ten girls from the core programs to favor the most promising few. He had just begun to wonder at the use of appealing to the pedagogical logic of a woman trained by her mother, and had in fact begun to entertain the idea of traveling to Moscow to entreat Fokine at the Ballets Russes, when she heaved an intensely expressive shrug, the motion beginning at the collarbone and rolling through her shoulders and arms before it reached her hands, where she waved it off with such a conclusive bodily effort that he expected the thought to condense and drop to the floor at her feet. She told him to handle it, and when he asked her to clarify, she rolled her head in a slow circle and told him to find the most promising girls and make an experiment of it.

And so he chose his six: Anna, Therese, Irma, Lisa, Margot, and Erica, all of them perfect in their proportion, gazing at the world with such a fearless variety of innocence that he found himself resisting the urge to fall to his knees before them and repent—though for what, he couldn't figure. They were between four and seven years old at the time, their fathers largely ill or absent, and Max found himself spiritually moving into the role, arbitrating their little fights and dispensing advice. There were no other men among the instructors, which gave him an automatic ethos he enjoyed immensely. They all spent long evenings working over sacred arias, and then he watched over them with some satisfaction while they braided each other's hair.

He noticed how each girl casually feared Elizabeth and how she seemed to appreciate their fear and cultivate it. He found her most attractive when she was feeling confident, and their happiest romantic episodes often tended to come after she had just finished disciplining the girls. Elizabeth was a strong woman, and when he lay in bed with her, he was reminded of his reading on the earliest days of man, the tribal squabbles solved by combat. She was in many ways his physical ideal, and he found it interesting only in passing that she was also his opposite, for he was a small man and often sickly.

The Constantinople jag reaches its peak with a visit from a mystic

Another telegram arrived from Duse, stacked with the first and slipped under the door, sounding plainly annoyed: QUIT CASTING ABOUT EUROPA. Tucking the card under my pillow, I dream of touring villages on a white bull, flowers draped across his flank. I'll send a response when absence turns my memory of Duse a little gentler, though such a resolution could keep me off for a while. Despite a sweet and plaintive face that charms all she sees, even the resting heartbeat of Eleonora Duse has an urgency, insisting that everyone keep strident pace. A simple meal with her is exhausting, and my energy lately is in short supply. Still, I should go and see her soon or else she'll never speak to me again, a condition which could last upward of six months.

Raoul prepares the room. He decided earlier that the jeweled tone cast by a goblet of wine by the window imbued the room with certain mystical properties, and began to fill every vessel with wine to its trembling brim—an ashtray, a crystal vase—and align each to catch the light. He filled a glass jigger and moved it from the dressing table to the bureau, then emptied the salt and pepper shakers from breakfast, topping them off and arranging them to diffuse the pinks across the far wall.

"That's enough, dear. She's coming soon."

He takes up the bottle. "If she is going to the trouble of a house call, we should make the environment ideal."

"You've got the idea of it, don't you think?"

"The idea," he sneers, plucking a cigarette out of the ashtray and examining it pinched between his fingers before filling the ashtray with the last of the bottle. I remember that look from Loie Fuller, who could stare at any stage for hours, chewing on the insides of her cheeks before digging through her suitcase of gels and slides for the colors to display on her costume. She looked like a traveling salesman selling rainbows, which I suppose she was, in a sense.

Penelope enters without knocking, appearing very much unlike an oracle with her hair slicked back with sweat. She holds her belly, looking about, as if she suspects someone is going to take it from her. She hasn't slept well on the couch in our two-room suite but refuses to share a bed with Raoul.

"Good afternoon," Penelope says.

"Hullo," he returns, turning his back on her to open another bottle.

"Raoul," I say genially, "come have a conversation." It's important that he show her some deference. He was advertised as a scholar of broken hearts, but when he ignores her, the currency of his heartbreak loses some crucial exchange rate in the open market. We've been enjoying wine and sandwiches at her expense, and if she really likes him, she might go in on the fortune-teller as well.

He returns with the petulance of a spoiled child and lifts one hand to take hers, the other occupied with a soap dish full of wine. "Hello, love." he says. "You had a productive session with the Madame?"

"Very productive," she sniffs. "She said I would lose my child and my husband soon after, and that my own life would end after a meditation. You haven't yet met with her?"

"Wonderful, just wonderful," he says, setting down the soap dish and picking up a wine-filled pint glass. "How very romantic, how affecting." He arranges the pint glass to catch a shaft of light on the floor.

Taking her by the fatty part of her arms above the elbows, I draw her close. "He has been preparing all morning to hear news of his love;

you'll have to pardon his excitement. You know how the romantics are always gazing into a mirror."

She looks as if she has just dislodged a nib of last night's steak from a rear molar. "I should go," she says. "I thought I stayed away long enough to avoid her."

"You most certainly should not go. We need your support."

"You'll do fine, I'd rather go. It was difficult, you see."

She pulls free from me and makes her escape, but just as she opens the door, she cries out to find the oracle herself, wrapped in shawls despite the heat. Serves Penelope right for trying to escape.

It's the oracle's youth that surprises me first. With a teenage self-assurance she unpins the veil over her mouth. She wears a linen dress in brilliant red, and her waves of hair are tucked around a comb at her neck. Apparently, on top of everything, I'll have to get used to young oracles. "The world rolls on," I say, embracing her.

She accepts me stiffly, looking over my shoulder to find no fewer than ten perfectly placed glass vessels around a pile of cushions on the floor, over which Raoul holds a deep bow.

"Do you have another room?" she asks.

He opens one eye, looking to find any offensive object that was placed without his knowledge.

"I will not read before an audience like a trick dog," she explains.

"Would the bedroom suit you better? It's a little darker."

"Let me see it."

"Penelope, will you take her in?"

Penelope obeys, looking truly miserable. How tragic for her, to be forced to entertain! She steps over Raoul, who has sat down in the center of his pillows.

"I didn't think of her privacy," he says, balling his fists and pressing them against his gut as if he could physically work the shame out of himself bodily.

"Don't mind a picky girl. She probably sent back her tea this morning because the cup was not aligned with the ecliptic plane. Take heart, love. The artist never knows what she requires until the moment she requires it."

He takes up a bottle of wine, pulling the cork out with his teeth. "You would know!" he says, tipping it back.

Fearing another scene like the one he made earlier while gazing at a photograph of Sylvio he had come upon in his breast pocket—a fit that included him hitting himself with one of Penelope's heavier books on ornithology—I hasten to his side. "That's all right," I say, easing the bottle from his hand. "Everything will be just fine."

"Didn't you see her expression? I've ruined the day. Every spirit she had been channeling took off when they saw what I did."

He obviously needs to be comforted and kissed on the mouth, and I take the responsibility gladly. "The oracle will be flattered to see it worried you so. People only want to know they've had an effect."

He pushes me off, tripping over his pillows but catching himself before he falls on the sideboard. "Woman!" he shouts. The women emerge on cue with champagne, having somehow found the bottle I had hidden in the bathtub. The oracle points at Raoul, who follows her directly back into the room. Penelope sits down with a magazine, holding her glass aloft.

"I haven't seen this level of dramatics since Teddy Craig," I say. "And even he has been distant lately. I suspect everyone matures if you wait long enough, like wine, though perhaps some people just go sour. You know, Paris acts as if he is the arbiter of this entire tragedy, but Teddy was Deirdre's father, after all. As a romantic, he was too devastated to attend the service. You understand."

She ignores me, running her fingers along her belly as she reads a magazine. Penelope would be happier in a different kind of society, where rooms held vast libraries, candlelight flickering to reveal dark paneled walls and brass-cradled models of the planet, their equators sewn with leather thread. But she will never know that society, not beyond what she reads of it. It was her fault for throwing in with Raymond; my brother means well, but at the end of the day, he is only a benign polygamist and a pretender at best. Penelope must have seen his potential as a man of philosophy and art, but Raymond never did develop the skill required of social movement, success at which might have placed them in those libraries and smoking rooms. Penelope should have run the moment he declared that it was a serious goal of his to design a sandal. But then she must have demurred, picturing as women often do the most successful version of her lover's dream—a factory line spanning a city block. We want only the best for the ones we love, particularly when we stand a chance to benefit. But now she must watch the turn on the poor wager she made years ago.

"You wouldn't like to be rid of me, would you, Penelope?"

"I wouldn't at all like that," she says, turning the page. "I hold you as my dearest kin."

No doubt, if we're including Raymond. "Why, I feel the same! I love you as well as I do my own sister, for you are as loyal to me as she always has been."

"It is my only hope that you dance again," she says, squinting at an advertisement for stockings. "When I first saw you in Athens, I knew you would usher in a new age."

She doesn't look up when I settle near her. "Your love heartens me, you are so dear to me."

She holds her magazine so she can keep reading while she leans in to kiss my cheek. I hold still for her until the moment her lips graze my face, at which point I twist my head and snap at her, catching her lower lip like a piece of gristle between my teeth. Clamping down, I hold on, keeping her there despite her shocked sounds.

She claws at me and slaps my face. Face to face, I have a clear look at her eyes, sparkling with anger.

At last I release her, and she falls back against the sofa.

"What is it?" I ask, wiping the line of spit from my mouth as if we have played this game many times before.

"Nothing." Closing her magazine, she lays it between us.

"What's wrong, dear sister?"

"Nothing at all." And she says nothing more, only moves her hand away when I reach for it. We stay like this until Raoul returns. Family time is so dear to me, I wish it would last forever.

Romano Romanelli
cura di Raffaello Romanelli
cura di Pasquale Romanelli
Viale Alfredo Belluomini, Toscana

Maybe you were right about Darmstadt. I can't shake this feeling of anonymous dread. I mean to say dread of my own anonymity, but the dread itself is anonymous as well, a man on the street looking at himself in the shopwindow. I wonder sometimes about the damage of simply living in the world.

Of course, this isn't a problem unique to Germany, as you'd claim. The perfect image of America came as our little boat was leaving the Port Authority. We had almost cleared the break when we saw a man sprint down the pier, leaping like a stag over the wooden gate bounding the dock. It wasn't clear if he was evading an attacker or the police or if he had been caught in some other confusion, but he didn't slow where the pier ended at open water. He jumped and was airborne, arms pedaling in mad circles as if he could wind himself back, hitting the water with a sickening slap and sinking, never to rise. We watched from the deck, and one of the cattlemen said that it seemed about right. Eventually we were too far away to see the police boats, and by the time we landed in Hull, any paper that might have mentioned it had long since turned to other mundane dramas, the problem of the vote and similar. News of the man's leap probably didn't make it any farther over the water than he did.

I had thought that escaping America's endless chaos would bring me a sense of peace, but I found none of that peace once I left. In London my head could have doubled as a shovel, so consistently was it aimed toward the pavement. Though it was a pretty pavement, drifts of fresh coal carved by bicycle tires. If it wasn't so expensive to live there, I would be there still, eating my weight in Dairy Milk bars and treating myself to opening nights at the Palace.

In France the work that satisfied me before began to experience an uncomfortable elevation, a balloon inflated beyond its bounds. I found the city of Paris to be very much like the poet who stumbles into the party and silences the room with his gleaming witness before falling onto a table of champagne flutes.

The city gives you the illusion that you could offer something new to the world, a loathsome fantasy shared by every artist in residence. The shopgirls believe it, too, and the philosophers. Even the thieves work harder in Paris: I can't imagine any of the pleasant young grifters on your standard Italian tourist beach summoning the organizational energy required to steal the Mona Lisa. In Paris you can steal whatever you like as long as you put in the effort to be original about it. It's marvellous to live but exhausting to make a living.

By the time we arrived in Vienna, I had gotten into the habit of taking long walks to get away from my students, and I found the city amenable to quiet mornings and contemplative afternoons. I walked every afternoon into the evening, conveniently missing Isadora's performances. Sometimes I would walk until sunrise, thinking of nothing but the strange way my feet appeared like little mice from under my dress and vanished quick as they came. I stopped in cafés at pure random and gazed at their pastry windows like I meant to buy one of everything on offer but first needed to find the best example of each.

But back to thoughts of you, my dear. I wonder if you would steal the Mona Lisa? Surely you have better taste.

At Oldway, Paris finds the problem with close study lies in what you inevitably find

It happened in the upper gallery first. He was squinting to look at a nobleman when he saw her emerging chin-first from the hazy crowd at the back. After a few days of tickling the ladies' skirts, she appeared in the lower gallery, leaning on the gentlemen to make conversation. Just when Paris thought she surely couldn't be bolder, he caught her winking among the assembled sisters in front, vanishing if he looked directly but reappearing the moment he tried to focus elsewhere; very true to life, he found. She was barefoot, possibly drunk. Teasing him in her ruthless way. He prepared himself for the day she would become Josephine in profile; in fact he was curious as to how she would carry the crown, if she would hate it on concept or allow an exception to her principle against adornment just this once if it meant she could rule the First French Empire.

But Isadora didn't touch Josephine. She left the woman kneeling as she took the role of Napoleon himself, slipping the man around her shoulders and taking on his pose with perfect, sneering ease. She commanded control of every inch of his bodily empire, her eyes wild with power. Paris was humiliated by her impersonation. She remained as Paris drew near, impertinent to his attention.

When he tried to look away, she was everywhere. She was lodged in every face on the canvas, whether they were three tiers up in the crowd or holding the coronation robes or guarding the hall. She became the pope and the marble angels, she became Christ on the cross. His own ruthless mind had exposed him for what he was: a devoted admirer waiting at her stage door with a stack of her postcards clutched to his chest, her every articulation known to him, every one of her expressions lashed to his memory with unbreakable thread. He was a slave to her legion gaze.

It was time to go. He stood with some difficulty, bowing to the painting as if formality might ease his shame.

He avoided *The Coronation* from that day forward, turning his head when he passed. On the opposite side of the stairwell a terra-cotta bust of Neptune caught his eye, and he had to convince himself that under the floating heroic curls, the old man wasn't laughing at him.

His work would be his comfort, now as always. Resolving to dedicate himself again to the study of architecture, he passed more nights in his office, suffering only a few hours of sleep at a time on the reclining chair, which the girls noticed and started making up like a bed. He took a few meals each day there and quit asking after the mail. The cook's maid reported to the buyer that he was drinking absolutely no beer and less liquor as well.

There was work to be done, and nothing so intoxicating as expanding the empire. He wanted something more permanent in France, and he found a new lease south of the Paris city center, a grand old hotel in Bellevue. Signing the papers inspired the freeing sense of a lightened financial load, the excitement of a fresh enterprise, and the promise of the obliterative tide of industry. The property was in an ideal location, among parks and wooded areas, retrofitted for electric light, and included a lovely modern stage. They could open a school there and offer free tuition to urchins or at least employ them in the garden. If Isadora didn't consent to teaching, he would hire Elizabeth and her man Max. They would support the day-to-day fees and advertising concepts and organize performances for the public. Once it got going, it would require very little in terms of his own operational involvement.

The thought began to bore him just as he signed the last of the documents. He preferred to occupy himself with ventures that held a real chance of failure, not this old academic route, its small gains on low risk. Because he enjoyed such a constant cash flow—a figure that could build two new schools a week if he wanted—solvency wasn't important to him. He preferred the thrill of the venture, the success or failure coming in spectacular fashion. He liked to buy mineral rights in low-lying plains, or whole islands that ended up so overrun with pests that everything would have to be burned to the stakes and begun anew. He fantasized about finding himself in a situation where his good business sense would be rewarded, but until then he was trapped in a carnival game as broad as his life, and nobody would ever pity him for it.

The property at Bellevue would be the perfect place for Isadora to return to work. He would write to Elizabeth at once and ask her to set it up and bring her students from Darmstadt, so that when Isadora arrived, she would find accomplished girls and a comfortable bed. From there, she would remember what brought her to teach in the first place, the importance of training the next generation to carry on her legacy. She might not care for her own life any longer, but in the students she could at least see her ideas begin to manifest. That might be enough.

17 August 1913
Teatro della Pergola
Teddy Craig, Direttore
Qualcosa bolle, Firenze

Ted, I'm doing my level best but the dances are coming out all wrong. Dance is a transient art and I am sleeping under its bridges. Consider my staging for *Jeux* the bum rush:

Deux enfants! Deux faunes! C'est Jeux. Fine linen skirts, rackets strung to humming. The world truncates at the edge of the stage in a haze of electric light. In the performance of fantasy one can fill the seats with whomever they choose, and so a group of precious friends shuffle programs as the curtains rise.

Lights on me, dressed and styled as Nijinsky, *sui generis*, heart pounding over stalk-strong legs. My disguise is of a working man with short pants belted, shirt tucked broad into the waist. The luxury of leaping strength! The thigh's coiled spring! I am a wolf wearing the skin of a wolf.

The children don't fit their costumes. Deirdre holds her long skirt up in fistfuls at her waist while Patrick toddles along behind, tripping over himself like an old man in pajamas. Because there is no costumer but my own memory, I can only blame myself; they are so large in my mind, so perfect. I remember the time a wasp landed on the back of Patrick's hand, I caught and crushed it between my fingers before even thinking of the danger, and the barb that embedded itself in my fingertip grew to a boil within the week. But then perfection must be guarded.

(Briefly: we of course are taking some liberty with the performance, which was conceived to be expressed in the bodies of three men, a sensual portrait. Nijinsky wanted the discomfort of held poses to heighten a sense of danger just off stage. The last time he and I spoke he turned a book in his hand over and over as if he was doing a magic trick, that a scroll might fall from the spine detailing the route to a hidden glen in which, under a pile of half-scorched kindling, we might find the location of his truest self. In the course of production this secret garden was paved over, two of his beautiful men became women, the aeroplane that was supposed to crash onto the stage at the end of the third act made a lengthy and confounding transformation into a tennis ball tossed by a member of the crew, whose hand in turn became the hand of God, *évidemment*. He had his dancers scatter as if the ball were the wrenching metal of his fantasy, and it all must have looked very funny but then compromise always does.)

The children fumble through their *pliés* and *port de bras*. My power coiled and masquerading draws strength from the assembled as I breathe into the engine of my solar plexus, warming the heart and gut as if my organs are gathered around a fire, embered ribs forging a fulcrum point. This is a play of human spirit, real and present, a foundation laid at the perimeter of light, a wall against the barren world.

When I finally come to move, I bring this power and bear them with it. As I lift the children onto my shoulders, we become a towering figure of ideal love, a pillar that cannot be touched by any hand of God or man or passing time. Let the water come.

The oracle earns a healthy day rate by assuring everyone of their strengths and ignoring their weaknesses entirely

Raoul emerges, looking as if he has just been alerted to the presence of a set of magical stairs laid into the far wall.

"What news of your love?" I ask.

"Love!" he says, taking up an ashtray of wine and gazing dreamily at its speckled surface before sipping from it.

The oracle pokes her head out of the bedroom. She has the look of a physician attempting to discern which between me and Penelope might be the most gravely ill. At last she points at me and goes back in.

The heavy curtains have been drawn over the bedroom windows, giving the room a material lushness thick enough to trap and hold the day's heat and likewise muting its sound. Anything I say will sink into the curtain and stay there until a maid beats at it with her broom and is shocked by the secrets that drop onto the carpet.

The oracle takes a seat on the bed where, once my eyes adjust to the light, I see she has laid out a handful of bird bones and a crystal skull. She extracts feathers from her bag and deposits them in the center, pressing her palms to them. A fanned tarot deck lies facedown on the dresser. I'm half heartened to find that the room is as empty as it was this morning, no visitors beyond the oracle herself. Still, maybe she will see something I don't.

She gestures for me to join her on the bed, picking a feather from the pile and extending it like an olive branch. I'm grateful she has not experienced my general ignorance on the topic of rituals and the spiritual practice of paganism, which I've always talked about in the same way as a woman who has never been to France tilts her head to describe, from postcard memory, its various historic arches.

She takes the feather back, then places the crystal skull in my hand, looking up as if its weight might register in my eyes. We sit together on the bed.

"You are the daughter of the Sun," she says. "You have been sent to Earth to give great joy to all people, and from this joy will be founded a religion. After many wanderings in the course of time, you will build temples all over the world."

"That's flattering," I say. She's clearly trying to win me over. "I'm afraid you've got old information."

"My information is ancient, in truth."

"Thanks anyway. I do have two questions for you, though. In your opinion, what do you think are the chances that the dead are agonized by thoughts from the living? Or that a dark wish made by an entire population could have some physical effect on its object? That's all I really want to know."

She pulls me back down onto the bed, taking me gently by the shoulders as if I've been talking in my sleep. She traces my collarbone with one of the feathers. "You are the daughter of the Sun."

"I am the daughter of Joseph Charles Duncan of Oakland, California, and I'm looking for my children. Their spirits were quite young, six and nearly three, they passed just a few months ago, and so may still be near. I was hoping you would have some information about them."

She frowns at the door.

"Penelope put you up to this, didn't she? She wants me to go back to work. She is a wicked one. Don't go, I'm only joking. Sit here with me, I want to hear my fortune."

The oracle takes up her glass of champagne and downs it, coughing a little. "*Salak* woman," she says.

"You could at least read my tarot, you have the cards right here. Come, I have something for you." Pressing a piece of folded money into her palm yields no further vision, but when I try to take the money back, she tucks it into her waistband.

"All right," I say, feigning good nature. "You don't have to say a thing about the children. But before you go, you could at least tell me what you told Raoul."

She accepts more champagne from the bottle. "I saw the man on a great stage," she says. She gazes at her crystal skull before kissing its forehead gently and wrapping it in a cloth.

"Did you see his lover? He seemed to be much relieved."

She places the wrapped skull in a case and latches it. "I saw many lovers attending him in the wings and many more gazing at him from the assembled crowd."

"But one in particular? With a certain unique appearance perhaps, some special connection between the two of them?"

Leaning over me, she collects the feathers. "I have built everything I have into my current practice," she says. "Not everyone understands it, I know. Those who are sensitive enough to understand my skill trust that I will give them everything they need." She wedges the cards into a small leather pouch that seems ill-suited for the purpose. "They would never suggest I contrive more detail than I've already provided. Please remember this is a power I have amassed over many years." A baby cuddling a crystal skull in her bassinet. "Over time, I've found that some believe that my vision exists to present them with what they need, a gown tailored to fit. "People don't see the value in this skill, because it works against what they wish. They would rather I repeat the story they're already telling themselves. These people might have more luck with an opinionated washwoman, but they come to me."

I lie down, as this will obviously take a while.

"And yet they continue to come," she says. "They want the security of celestial affirmation. And so the cycle continues, the disappointment continues, and my true clients keep coming back."

She takes my wrist, squeezing the vein in a rhythm to match the rhythm of my blood.

"All these temples will be dedicated to Beauty and Joy because you are the daughter of the Sun," she says.

She leaves me then, in darkness, but I'm not alone for long.

Perhaps they have been hiding behind the curtains this whole time, though it's unlike them to keep quiet for long. I feel them as surely as my own weight on the bed. Patrick comes close and holds my face in his hands as Deirdre climbs onto me, pressing into my belly as if she could absorb herself into me. They talk, but I can't understand them, they speak rapid and backwards. They smell of river stone. The bed is heavy with all the food I had ever fed them: toast and potatoes and strawberries, roast meat, chocolates and cheese and boiled eggs. My own warm milk soaks through the quilt and weighs us down.

Around us, a murmuring rises in the well of darkness. I don't dare look around the room. They loosen my tunic straps and expose my breast. Pawing at me, they nuzzle like pups, their impossibly cold cheeks warming against me. They nurse in icy silence while I stare past the ceiling, through the rafters and roof, until I find myself floating as thin as air above it, daring not to breathe, not to lose them again.

III

Isadora finds herself in the heart of the pine forest in Viareggio with Eleonora Duse, who has lately been considering the romantic idea of an early death

The season ended, as they do, the moment everyone had begun to think it would last forever. Yesterday there was a city's worth of women walking hand in hand, little children running for sweets along the passeggiata, bicycles and laughing men, tea at the Grand Hotel, and the lazy persistence of summertime strangers.

But then this morning came wrapped in winter wind. They brought the blue umbrellas in, and everyone left for London and New York, even the newlywed rich, who had seemed ready to stay forever. Now, the only man in the water walks waist-high through the surf, working a cage into the sand and pulling it up again, sifting for rings and coins the season left behind.

My time with Raoul ended as abruptly as the season. He took his leave while I was in with the oracle, without leaving a note, nothing to show his gratitude for how I saved his life. I suppose when a spell is broken there's no sense in waiting around. I was left to pay the oracle, and while I was at it, I traded her leather pouch for the carved wooden box in which I was keeping the last of the children. Penelope wasn't thrilled with the trade, as it was her box to begin with, but she had to admit that the ashes fit nicely in the pouch and seemed less liable to spill.

Penelope's brother sent word shortly after that, and she went to him, leaving just enough money to cover the hotel. Left in a lurch, I had just begun to worry when a telegram arrived from Duse reminding me of her setup on the coast, two little houses arranged together in the pine forest, close enough to walk barefoot and far enough to offer both guest and host some needed privacy. These messages come right when we need them and not a moment sooner, or if they come sooner, we forget. And so I went at once.

My very favorite squat hen, Duse has retired to a coop of medals and painted plates, nestling among a lifetime of postcards and mementos, dried flowers strung over her counters and scattering their precious petals over all the food she prepares.

She is fifty-five years old and as handsome as a girl, pushing me away without ceremony when I try to kiss her. She spends most afternoons walking along the sea, and never steps outside without her wide-brimmed hat, which is decorated with batting and feathers. My little dockbird, snagged in her own net. Still, I know for a fact that if we had an audition this afternoon, she would be the one called to try another scene while I could count myself lucky to be directed to a pile of mending in the back room and told where to bring the coffee.

The flat morning air suits this numbness that has been building. Every emotion becomes too feeble to go beyond the confines of my mind, born to die alongside weakling thoughts such as my sense of duty to art and life. These malformed thoughts cry for my attention and cannot be soothed, and like any harried mother, I grow simple in my affect and begin to see life as a tourist taking in a roadside carnival, the type where the main attraction is a block of wood wrapped in bandages and presented as a mummified corpse.

After Patrick's birth I had been scheduled to go immediately on tour, but a strange sadness overwhelmed me. At last, the tour manager noticed that my dead-eyed marionette dances were disturbing the audience, and I was immediately sent to a doctor whose office featured a cool stone exterior wall covered in a moss so thick and vibrant I thought I might hear its life. The nurse found me standing out there, pressing my face to it.

I was familiar with neurasthenia and prepared for its diagnosis. The nurse brought me in, and I found myself in the office of a young French physician, a man as thin as his medical license and equally lifeless, seeming pinned under glass. He listened vaguely to my heart and looked at my palms the way a psychic would before he announced that I was well and truly hysteric. He prescribed a rest cure, tapping his pen against a calfskin notebook as he spoke. I asked him to look again, and reluctantly he consented, examining my left eye and then my right with a silver scope and lifting my tongue to see if the answer was perhaps written there. I repeated my symptoms with my tongue pinched between his fingers: malaise, hopeless thoughts. But he maintained his diagnosis, noting gently that I lacked the neurasthenic constitution. He was a young and nervous man, and his hands shook as he fiddled with a gold-plated pen, insisting that I spend three months in bed.

Through my clouded eyes I saw the future: he would tell the tour manager, who would dismiss me; there would be a notice in the paper reporting my inability to keep a simple series of evening shows. My condition would be taken into account for the rest of my life and subtly brought into talk of my salary, my performance and ability. This man would ruin me in a single afternoon.

It was impossible to change his mind, but I had to try my best; he was already pressing the tip of his fine pen to the prescription pad. And so, for lack of a better idea, I stood, stepped lightly to the center of the room, and lifted my arms, palms up at shoulder height.

I wasn't sure what I meant to do exactly. When he asked, I said I was taking the pose of Blind Justice and would remain until my last breath or until the diagnosis rang true to my condition.

His laughter turned to disbelief, then to complaints and pleading as five minutes passed, then twenty, an hour. He never opened the door to his waiting room, not wanting the nurses to see the negotiation. He was stubborn, which I appreciated, though when I complimented him on it, he didn't respond. He said I was only proving his diagnosis and asked me to come off it. I said nothing in response but held my shaking arms in perfect position, imagining in a pleasurable way that I was nailed to a cross. If I were to die, it would be in self-defense.

He began to suggest that he might have me committed to the

sanitarium. I held on, knowing the end was near of either my life or his will. By then he was sitting on the floor, pleading with me.

Finally he had enough. He opened his calfskin book and, with a long and suffering sigh, wrote a neurasthenic diagnosis compounded by the stress of a small dressing room. For treatment, he prescribed fatty meats and bread along with dark beer and regular walks, with only one week-end's worth of suggested rest. *Condition of the artist*. I had him write it in three languages and then brought it to my manager, who sent a girl to the market at once.

The manager wanted to keep the doctor's note, but it was far too precious to me. I tucked it into the stirrups of my trunk to keep forever. I still marvel over it: a single sheet of paper that would speak on my behalf if I lacked the will to speak, which I can cite as precedent for the rest of my life. Of course it's back in France. Separated from it, I feel distant from my saner self.

It's a pleasant walk to the beach. The whole place is deserted, unless anyone's hiding in the striped canvas dressing tents by the road. Though they get dingy quick with sand and sun, I far prefer those tents to the Victorian bathing machines that preceded them. Some of the hotels still keep the old things around, looking like outbuildings mounted on broad wagon wheels and tipped inelegantly to one side. Duse claims she still sees a few of the older ladies using them. The process is this: climb the steep grade of wooden stairs and lock yourself into a room that slants in a perfect diagonal. Once you've got your footing, you must work through every single one of your buttons and garters and belts and straps and yardage and stockings at that perilous angle, hanging it all on the hooks provided or else every delicate thing will fall to ruin. After that, you must hold the opposite walls with spread and trembling arms as, outside, your male companion hefts up the wooden rail and pulls the whole thing down into the water like an eager ox, at which point—if you weren't brained on one of the wall-mounted hooks—you may emerge at the water with your modesty intact. In theory, it saves a lady the humili-ation of being seen in her bathing gear, but in reality, anyone getting carted around in a splintering man-yoked box is going to get everyone's attention. Seems better to stay home, most days.

I'm grateful to Mother, who never went in on those old ideas. We spent long days at Sausal Creek, where she would watch us flailing from her spot on the shore. Calling out instructions only worked when we were above the surface to hear them, and so she started carrying a long metal hook that she used to fish us out if the situation became dire. I hated that hook and feared her for it, but here I am, in the waves. The social page reports that Mother is in Paris again. I'm sure she alerted the paper herself; I can see her frowning at the clock, as if my return is a simple matter of patience.

These months away from my practice have slowed and softened me, and now that I try to use my body again, I find its power has spread to my shivering fringe. The waves slap my thighs like a man's broad palm before I dive in. At first I would go only a few meters out and bob there like a sullen duck, but I ventured farther the next time, rolling onto my back and righting myself again for a slow crawl. Now I have started the work of distancing myself from land. Happily, I lost my old swimming costume somewhere in Albania; those things are good enough for sunbathing, but I would have sunk like a fat stone wrapped in wool if I'd actually tried to swim. My old cotton romper does the trick; it's a larger version of something the children would wear, shapeless but light enough in the water.

The waves calm far enough out, and I find that if I keep my eyes just above the surface, I lose the land entirely. This is where the poet Shelley went over, his friends reaching from the boat as he gazed oblivious toward nothing in particular. My rebelling mind presents an image of the car doors, which must have bowed grotesquely against the river. They say the drowning soul feels no pain. Or so they say, anyway, to me.

Going under, I feel my thoughts compressing between my ears. The water clasps me like a strangling hand, shocking every hair to brittle attention. I swim through its upended gravity, crawling away from sunlight.

I taught them to listen to the pulsing point under their ribs, to unfurl from it like a banner, taught them to run and leap, to make themselves into columns so perfect they might stand forever. I taught them how to consume beauty, to take it in and make the dance it gave them, an art that can exist only as beauty can, as life itself, in a moment. I taught them all of that, but I never taught them how to swim.

In Darmstadt, Elizabeth finds herself with time on her hands and news of the world

It would come after days spent rolling merrily along, the lady observing the passing scene with a cup of tea and feeling more of a stranger on solid ground than in the gentle rocking cars: an accident, the whole world bursting in a magnesium flash as the train bucks like a bull from the rails, earth drawn across the window like a curtain and the lady's teacup stuck bloody in her wrist, her body so soft against the things that once served it, the worst of it not the shock or pain, but the simple realization that her whole world could be tipped from its axis, that she could find herself flung into a new state of being, her legs crushed under a table, the world's blooming orchestra rendered to a tinny buzz. It was how Elizabeth imagined it, anyway.

That sense—that the planet could violently revolt at any moment— was precisely the speculative thrill Elizabeth came to crave when she sat down to read the daily news. After the story about the train derailment, she spent the rest of the morning in delicious agony, fantasizing the feeling of her body being thrown across every room she entered. These brief sojourns into crisis were more tantalizing than fiction and simpler to attain, but she found she slowly grew dependent on them and needed the newspaper more and more. She started milling around the neighborhood grocery until the boy came by with the late edition. When she gave him her money, she would hold one hand with the other to keep him from seeing how she shook with anticipation.

Just the month before, a man in Mühlhausen had taken the lives of his wife and children and then gone on to murder strangers in the street. The unadorned fact was enough to get Elizabeth going, but she was thrilled to find the paper printed every detail: he wielded a pair of army revolvers with two hundred cartridges in reserve; he was calm and smiling when they captured him, though he was beaten almost to death; the children were found bludgeoned in their beds, his wife's throat slit in the hall; he happily confessed every bit of it as the police dragged him away. He was the town's mild schoolteacher and knew most of the children he slaughtered. It was an evil thing that came upon him, but the law could not discern what inspired it, and he wasn't ill with drink or spurred by circumstance. After she read it all, Elizabeth had to lie down, her heart pounding in her chest.

For days, she watched every edition to see if some detail would emerge that might better explain it, but subsequent articles only confused her more. The man wore a veil over his face, in letters he spoke of wanting the Devil; none of it made sense to her. At least when unsinkable ships went down, there were icebergs to blame. Or when the Windsor caught fire in New York and Elizabeth had to run with the children through the throng of sirens, delirious with smoke and fear as ladies fell from the sky like squalling myths—at least with the fire, there was probable cause, a lamp, a drape. These were things she could avoid, lessons she could learn.

But this! She hated the feeling of helplessness, waiting for the lesson that would never come. With the murderer in Mühlhausen, she felt as if she were witnessing the beginning of a troubling modern trend.

Just as the papers seemed to turn from the crime, the airship L2 burst over Johannisthal, killing twenty-eight. Elizabeth exhausted herself, staring at the pictures of the craft's aluminum ribs drilled into the earth, of the bodies of boys hauled off on shrouded sleds. She couldn't look away.

She tried to tell Max about her repulsive attraction. He was usually very understanding of her moods, having often stated that feminine sensitivity was ideal for the creation of great art. Even though Elizabeth didn't see sensitivity as a feminine trait exactly and also did not view herself as an artist, rather as a technician and a teacher, she appreciated his attempt to place her in the constellation of his own theories, finding her in the golden telescope of his intellect and making a note of her as the wayward, looping planet she was.

As it happened, however, Max was the worst person she could have told. He kept interrupting to ask why she didn't simply stop reading the papers, why she didn't focus on softer stories. Eventually, she gave up on explaining herself, and allowed him to pour her a thimble of bitter Underberg. They sat together on the porch and watched evening pass them by.

As she settled more comfortably into a stuffed wicker chair, her mind drew idly to Romano. She wondered if he had seen the same news, of the murder or the airship. Perhaps he had read of something equally stunning closer to home. Tragedy seemed to only attract him. He spoke of how, as a boy, he walked the seawall to see the fresh shipwrecks, enjoying the sound of hulls wailing against the shoals in the persistent tide. Perhaps she could go to him in Italy, visiting macabre sites along the way.

Leaving Darmstadt was her most seductive fantasy, but it was truly impossible. The girls needed someone to keep Max in check; one more long trip, and he would have them marching in lockstep. And anyway, such a trip would require her to accept that the horrors were so near. She was happy to speculate on tragedy but preferred not to be its neighbor. And so she stayed, and read the paper.

Isadora finds water to be a pleasant companion, one that accepts all who are willing to walk into it

An idea was once presented to me by a man in a bar. He was a Christian man and a sailor, and he silenced the room with two hands to announce that we are obliged all our lives to embody only one of three forms: a sea, a storm, or a boat. Obviously he felt that the triumvirate fit nicely into these categories, with God the Storm, Christ the Sea, and the Spirit navigating the twain, but he noted that his idea had a broader application in love and war.

Immediately I claimed to be a clipper ship, propelled by my own agency and guile; this was called down by the assembled, and the sailor pointed out that a boat would never speak first. Undaunted, I claimed the sea next, vast and roiling, a resilient bed for rest and death, accepting the world's comets and slipping cliffsides, its poets and steamships, and holding it all without judgment. They nearly laughed me out of the bar for trying to suggest that I would harbor anything but myself.

And so that leaves the storm! Violent on the liquid plain, wrecking ships and dumping murk without thought or conscience, destroying everything in its path. They say it's your friends who know you the best, but drunks have a way with your worst.

I've lately found it easier to consider more or less impassively the idea of being pulled out with the swells and dragged under, waterlogged and sunk like a true poet, one foot wedged under the wing of a shipwrecked prow, the rest of me prized away by fish and larger creatures. The ocean plays a little sleight of hand as the thought of a peaceful death holds my attention long enough for the waves to bring me back to shore.

Stumbling to my feet, I find myself shivering cold and far from where I went in. My cape is gone and I must walk up the coast in my romper, looking for it. The thing is thick jacquard and should be easy enough to spot, as it resembles a beaded tablecloth. My romper soaked and sticking to me doesn't make life any merrier. If I've walked by the cape already, it already slipped from the rail and was buried under a thin inch of sand. If not that, children may have taken it for a bit of fun, or, worse, one of the well-meaning women folding towels for the resorts weighed the heavy fabric in her hand, figured a guest left it by accident, and surrendered it to her employer, requiring me to approach every concierge desk in order to inquire, where they will naturally have me arrested and taken away, and a journalist will publish a photograph of the saltwater puddle I leave on the court bench.

Before I resign myself to cut a dripping path for the plaza, a man emerges from a covered porch, holding the cape like a banner and shouting his apologies, making a show of shaking it out as he runs and showing me both sides upon his arrival, as if he is about to perform a magic trick. The man is thirty at most, with a slight figure and a nervous facial tic that makes it look as if he is using intermittent pursing pressure to soothe a cut between his lips. He looks guiltily about, and at first I wonder if I caught him in an impropriety with the cape: beating time upon it to accompany a Fillmore march, draping it about the shoulders of a bad dog, shredding its ends to fill an ornamental pillowcase, boiling it in water and drinking its tea or similar. Of course he must only feel ashamed to see me in the romper, which has wedged itself into every one of my wedgible parts. Handing over the garment, he bows and runs away, a loping run across the sand, looking as if he has never run anywhere in his adult life. The whole thing passes without a word between us.

Back at the house, I find three messages tucked into the doorframe from Duse, despite the fact that I saw her already this morning. The wooden gate claps, and I go out to find her messenger boy, stopped in his tracks halfway up the path. When I ask him to tell her to expect me in the afternoon, he drops a fourth letter and runs. It's the second time I've had this treatment today, despite the fact that I have been sober all the while and it is not quite noon. I go to her before she puts the whole postal service on notice.

Duse has her baubles out again. Fat glass drops hang from horsehair thread in the window over the sink, collecting the light and dispersing it in rays: red chases orange across the yellow-hinged cabinets, and emerald takes a seat on a footstool in the blue corner. Her shoulders are pinned by violet. We sit and watch each other in silence, which started as a game and is lately becoming more serious. The violet light grazes her collarbone. Her expressions mirror mine, fading from one to the next.

She has made it her business to know Viareggio, starting with which mothers will spare their sons for little tasks around the house in exchange for her occasional presence in theirs. The boys bring her sandwiches and deliver messages, they tell her the best route to the beach and the busiest cafés. She probably has them spy on me. She wants to know the town because she plans to die here. I've seen her sample the earth, crouching to pinch the sand and observing it like a scientist before bringing it to her mouth. If only we could all be so fastidious.

At Oldway, Paris takes on a new project with the optimistic idea that the occupied mind is never lost

He had always wanted to put the aeroplane hanger in the Balkans, ever since he heard of the danger. Some wartime intrigue would add a thrill to the venture, and even when peace arrived to the area, Paris held out hope that things would go sideways again. As he waited, however, the local workforce petitioned him to stay in Paignton. The men had heard talk of airborne heroes, of wild aerobatics in Russia and record-breaking solo flights in France, and even a pistol battle between flying aces in the Mexican war. They wanted to bring some fame home to their wives. Paris certainly understood the impulse, and so he allowed them to convince him to change his plans.

The local men insisted on framing the steel hangar themselves, promising to save Paris the hassle of an outside contractor. They installed a pair of triple-hinge barn doors that, despite their impressive size, still didn't have the proper clearance. He had to bring someone in to reframe the door and explain the dimensions again to his local crew. The men were unable to believe how wide he kept insisting the aeroplane would be;

each man thought it would be only as wide as the bed in which he lay every night to dream of his future in the air.

Once the proper door was installed and the frame was set, Paris had the first craft delivered, a slim monoplane named *Cigare*. A group of twenty men began arriving daily from nearby farms, accepting apprentice wages plus tea and lunch to keep everything up.

They all wanted their hands on the little plane. Every morning they took apart the entire engine. They worked in silence, oiling and shining its piston bolts, replacing its hinges though the old ones still shone from the last round. They used teak oil to swab the strips of citron wood rolled over the carriage frame, clearing buildup from its fittings. Once a week an old woodworker would arrive from town to advise them where they might add slips and braces to guard against the cracking influence of ocean air. The others would listen as they worked, polishing the steering column or securing the metal trim over the seating compartment. They took long breaks to admire it with the pride of fortress guards around their single beloved cannon.

Paris was charmed at first. Before too long, however, he came to realize that the men had gotten too attached. They had endless questions about the plane's origin and materials and the details of its aerodynamic function, but nobody seemed to appreciate the fact that he wanted to actually take the thing out. Though they had arrived with daredevil dreams, they lost their will to test the craft once they came to know the intimacies of its operation. In short, the men had fallen in love.

Their loathing and judgment only grew once Paris hired an instructor, a Swiss who had been involved in *Cigare*'s creation yet seemed to be refreshingly unromantic about the whole thing. The men were outright hostile to the Swiss and made cruel fun of his punctuality. Paris started taking his lessons in the hangar office, away from the others. They watched him through the windows.

In Viareggio, after a lunch of fried squash blossoms, Duse being very interested in her own garden as of late

Though everyone else has been polite enough to avoid it, Duse assumes her familiarity well enough to assume she can ask after the accident. She has built her career on apprehending and appropriating the pain of others, a hard habit to break among friends.

"The river," she says, trying to prompt some response.

"I'd rather tell you how awful Paris was to come and try to haul me out of Greece. I thought he was a dream at first, but my dreams are never so administrative in their bearing."

She shudders, thinking either of the river or of Paris Singer, whom she hates to talk about. "We should have some music." She had the piano tuned when she learned I was coming, and she also hired a pianist, a nice enough man who is around here somewhere, maybe in the garden.

A bead of indigo light settles onto her torso, eclipsing snout and stomach. She is freed of the corset she worked in for years, sweating in stays under stage lights. Today she is cocooned in ivory linen, with a shawl that drags in the dust as she walks precisely along the line between regal and absurd. Her white collar is attached with three smart buttons up the side of her neck. The effect is of a nurse committed to the very asylum that had previously employed her.

"It is quite comfortable, though," she says, picking through my thoughts like a seamstress rifling through a bin of silk scraps, holding this one up to the light, then dropping it and reaching for the next. "And how was your swim? Buoyed on millions of tears, I assume?"

"I falsely sensed a shoal, and nearly drowned going down to touch it."

"Is that so?"

"In the course of my own movement I confused my direction and dove deeper as the water closed in."

She holds her hand to her throat.

"Only keeping still would save me then, waiting for the air in my lungs to bear me up."

She struggles elegantly to lean forward and I allow her to take me into her arms, wondering how it is we can ever stand to be apart. In times like these I forget our past. In Florence, she was staging *Rosmersholm* with Ted, and they forced me to translate their awful fights, as she didn't know much English at the time and he refused to retain a word of Italian. He would scream that if she interfered with another scene, he would put her in the ground; I would tell her that he was overwhelmed by her talent and would do anything to foster her artistic aim so long as she gave him a moment to think. They would grin madly and go a little longer before breaking down again. The two of them hated each other so much that I was certain they were lovers. Deirdre was there by then, and a nurse named Marie, who had agreed to work on credit and had come to immediately regret that decision. Between Ted's agonies and the daily tantrum from Duse or Deirdre, or both, it was a wonder any love remained at all. But we were younger then, and love could come and go.

"You are very young still," she points out. "And you know I still love you." She loves me still! I feel it in her embrace, in which I smell lavender from her garden. Touching me like a mother and lover both, with an intensity made to endure the whole of life, she loves with the bravery of a war-ballad general; a heroic figure, albeit outnumbered.

"Some music!" she cries, striking the table. She leans on me to stand, pressing my forearms and working up to my shoulders and the top of my head, blessing every part of me before she goes to find the pianist.

In Darmstadt, an extravagant breakfast becomes an opportunity for Elizabeth to claim something of her own

While Elizabeth was away, Max had begun feeding the girls an American-style breakfast. He made the decision after reading an article positing that such a meal, executed with proper extravagance, would shore up one's strength for the entire day. Though he took only tea and a single piece of sour bread for himself—and firmly encouraged this meager meal on Elizabeth as well, insisting it was the only thing for two adults—the girls enjoyed a true bounty, tucking into oatmeal and biscuits with butter and jam, soft-boiled eggs yielding to their cracking spoons, hotcakes bloated with maple syrup, fried potatoes, various fruits in season, and a full five quarts of milk among them. Elizabeth arrived home to find the girls eating meat again; Max had the cook prepare breakfast sausage, ham steaks, and rashers of bacon, which sizzled from the oven and seemed more than anything to alarm the girls, who had been raised good meat-eating Germans but had grown accustomed to the house-standard vegetarian fare that had been Isadora's order.

After everything was served, Max would take a slow turn around the table, examining each plate before anyone was allowed to eat. On occasions in which extra vitality was required, such as recital days, he asked the cook to add a tablespoon of cream to each cup of milk. The woman brought a cold pitcher of it to the dining room and made the supplement as they all sat in silence. Sometimes she poured a little cream into their orange juice by accident, and the girls said nothing, though the dairy clumped at the surface. Elizabeth knew from the way the woman's hand shook on the pitcher that she was afraid of Max, and the girls didn't much care for him either.

Breakfast was a daunting task. To motivate them while they struggled through their plates, Max would stand at the front of the table, telling the story of the food. He claimed that the almonds were from Puerto Rico, the sugar from India, and the jam sourced all the way from California— the home state of your dear mistress, he would announce, a hand on Elizabeth's shoulder. In truth they ate whatever the cook could find at the lowest price, remainders and cracked eggs, everything just this side of spoiled. Still, the girls seemed to like thinking that things had been done specially for them. They had all been taught that ladies should appreciate a man's effort over his results, and so they took seconds and thirds, stuffing themselves like little queens. After the meal they eased themselves from the table with a collective groan, waddling to their first calisthenics class, where one or two would invariably vomit.

Once everyone had gone, Elizabeth was left with a table of scraps. On Max's request, she took her notepad and walked from plate to plate, making a record of which girl had left food behind. She was supposed to hand over the list in the afternoon so that Max might study it, noting which nutrients each had missed and how the deficit affected their attitude and performance throughout the day.

Ordinarily she would have refused this request and reminded him whose name was on the door, but she soon learned the task's hidden benefit: she was alone with the food.

Elizabeth went to work. She ate quickly and greedily, hunched over each plate, her eyes snapping left and right like an animal assuming quick predators. She took down Therese's half grapefruit, using a steak knife to slice through the shallow wounds the girl had made with her serrated spoon. She stuffed herself with the curled bacon fat Lisa left at the edge of her plate. She drank every drop of Erica's milk, licking cream from the rim, and swiped her finger through the melted butter from her plate as well. Irma never left anything behind, but Margot made up for it, leaving whole bowls of oatmeal and stewed plums, glistening untouched slabs of ham. Margot's plate kept Elizabeth so sated, it was as if she had eaten the child herself. The others were harder to predict but she soon learned that everyone left something behind. She was very happy for a time, and hid happiness from the others so they wouldn't suspect her for it.

In Viareggio, mounting clouds suggest a storm of many days

The sky over the beach is clear and fine, but Duse suspects a storm, point-ing to a series of clouds on the horizon hanging like a wall of old ball gowns. "See how they persist," she says.

"I wanted to tell you, I've worked something out."

She frowns at the rack of clouds, as if my theory will arrive in the rain.

"I believe that there is a collective energy, that enough people think-ing the same thought has the power to alter the physical world."

"A democratic congress of thought," she says. "Very American of you."

"I mean to say a kind of system of—how do you say it? When there are smaller creatures and larger, and some will move to eat the others?"

"Ecology."

"An ecological system. There are strong-minded people—like you, my dear—who over one act can bend her audience to her will. And then there are weaker creatures who couldn't save their own mothers' souls if they spent every day at their bedside."

"Admitting to souls at last?"

"Don't be such a Catholic. I'm trying to make a point."

"Christ is a strength you will not even have to pray to," she says, looping her arm around my waist. "Thereness, my lass."

Viareggio has been left to the locals. Since yesterday they've pulled down the awnings and shuttered the promenade. The temperature has fallen by discernible degrees. The only sign of life on our walk is a man standing at his window on the second floor of one of the pink gabled houses. Before I can get a good look at him, he goes back in.

"And so you believe a group can change the course of fate," she says.

"I believe in a power, driven by a collective thought, that could alter the course of your entire life."

"How could that be, though?"

"Describe your life four years ago."

A thin vine of lightning transpires across the horizon line, too far off for thunder. "I left the stage because I had no use for it," she says, "and because I had fallen in love with Lina. We moved into the little house in Florence, and there was no pleasure to compare with what I found in love."

"Yes, and before that happened, you wanted another production with Teddy."

"Of course I had to put all those things on hold."

"And between your desire for a production, I remember, there was the profile of you in the *Times*, the one that called you a tragic genius."

"I always thought that phrase was a bit much, but of course I liked it."

"I'm saying that profile altered your fate in ways you may not have realized at the time."

"What do you mean? I don't understand you, say it in English."

I hate it when she pretends not to understand my Italian, which is very good, but I obey her. "People began to think of you as a tragic genius, and it so happened you started behaving very strangely after that. Remember when you left a set of keys dangling from your front door and lived in constant fear for weeks that thieves would make legal entry? Or when you gave your last performance in Pisa? You came out for three encores and then forgot to remove your stage makeup for weeks. They called you the Madwoman of Crespina."

"Angels of rain and lightning," she says, watching the clouds.

"Pay attention. Something threw you into a love that was fated to be tragic." The wind tries mightily to work through our clothes. I draw her close, kissing the place where her jaw meets the flesh of her neck, just above the ivory button of her collar.

She coughs in response and shrugs me off. "Your point that the hand of God intervened."

"I mean the very opposite."

She gasps. "Very Catholic, indeed!"

"Not God or the Devil, but an earthly power drawn from a simple desire, from men and women seeing your picture in the newspaper and wishing you well."

"Well wishes cannot change the world!"

"It was desire, as real as your hand, made manifest in your life. Every time the paper prints your name, you must contend with tens of thousands of desires tipping the scales for or against you according to the whims of the culture."

"You're saying that tens of thousands of people wished that I would quit acting? I'm well aware I'm not universally loved," she says, switching back to Italian, working a stone into the sand with the toe of her boot. "But I would think I have more friends than enemies among readers of the evening edition."

"It's not quite so simple. Think of the fable of the children who found the creature in the sand—do you know it? They found a creature and wished upon it, and their wishes were ruined by reality. They wished to be beautiful, and their friends no longer recognized them, or they wished for a castle and were besieged."

I had used the wrong Italian word for *besieged*, saying rather that the children in the castle were delayed, as if by a train, but she seems to understand. "They were all wishing me well," she says, frowning.

"Precisely right. Everyone who read your profile piece and looked at your beautiful face in profile and read of your tragic genius, they closed their eyes and wished that you would find love and comfort."

"But they didn't realize that love and comfort removes the tension that puts me onstage—"

"—and love is the ruin of all, precisely."

"And you believe the fate of the children was brought about in this way."

"Or similar."

"What could anyone wish that would have caused this?"

"I don't know. That I would create a series of funeral dances, or that I would write entertaining memoirs. Everyone loves a good story. Nobody would have wished the children dead, but we so rarely understand what we are asking for when we make a wish."

"I don't know."

"When I was deathly ill on Corfu, I later learned, the papers were reporting my plans for a triumphant return, they said I danced at the funeral. A waltz! If your happiness could be altered by well-wishers, imagine the ruin that could come to pass from their judgment. If enough people choose to wish me out of existence, I might as well vanish."

"They said you were dancing?"

"I couldn't believe it myself. Can you imagine me choosing a waltz? I would have done a processional if anything. There's no accounting for taste, I suppose."

"This is all rather mystical," she says in a way that suggests she has not fully dismissed it.

"Nobody wants to live in a world where children can drown. You'll see. They'll wish they never heard my name, and I'll never work again."

"Look there," she says, pointing to the lightning at the edge of the sky. "It's Shelley's ashes flashing. Do you see? He is walking over the waves." The lightning does resemble a man, a bodily current. Curtains of cloudbanks drape either side. She tucks her chin over my shoulder, watching him. "Life goes on no matter what we wish," she whispers. "It goes on just the same."

In Darmstadt, Max and Elizabeth put their distance aside in the name of business

Singer had written them both to say that he would appreciate their presence with the girls at the new school in Bellevue. It was unusual of Isadora not to send word herself, and Elizabeth wondered if perhaps it was because she hadn't yet returned to France.

She didn't think much of it; there was too much to do. Arrangements would have to be made with families of the six girls Max had chosen to bring with them to the new school. It was a monumental effort to take all six of them on, even without considering the instruction and boarding fees they lost when they made the transition from students to employees. They needed costumes, sandals, and supplies for travel; Paris insisted on paying for six ludicrous sets of matching luggage, but Elizabeth was the one who had to fill the order. But she was glad for the girls, really. She could see how each of them played a willful and necessary part, and losing any one of them, even the youngest, would do something to destroy the larger whole.

Dealing with their mothers was another problem entirely. Elizabeth handled them all with separate conferences, in which most of them came around to see her points. She decided in the end that if Margot's mother maintained her hysterics and wanted the girl back, they were only a day away by train. There was the usual hassle of arranging the lesser dancers with the lesser instructors and encouraging everyone to achieve their dreams no matter what the reviews said. The chosen six would perform one last recital before they left, which Max arranged to inspire the others to work harder in their absence.

The morning of the recital, the cook was trying to get rid of the surplus of food, and the girls' plates were piled so high that Elizabeth was sick for the rest of the day. But she ate, feeling that she might not eat that well ever again. A rotten foreboding sense had attended her for weeks, one that hadn't been chased away with her usual calls for good luck. She tried to wash it down with milk and ham steaks.

They opened the auditorium, which was usually shuttered owing to the expense of light and heat. Elizabeth had the furnace started at dawn, but the room still retained the traces of chilly air that made it feel more like a library or a mausoleum than a performance space. They had a heavy curtain arranged as a backdrop, and the velvet seam opened to a window facing the street.

The girls were accompanied by Miss Venneberg on the piano, her long neck tipped thoughtfully to the side as she played, glancing up at her charges and matching her tempo to their expression.

Elizabeth noticed a lot of improvement among the six, though they still tripped around like enchanted sprites without sense or direction. Serious Irma led the group from its center, drawing from a power in her core body so evident it seemed nearly to glow, and the older girls were patient with Margot, holding her hands. There was an instinctive feel to their leaps, as if the girls had descended from a race who used such movement as language or currency. Of course, this play at spontaneity had been whittled from their own wooden limbs. She had to admit that in her absence they had found an ease she had not been able to teach them.

Max leaned over. "They are very strong."

"Frau Venneberg plays well," Elizabeth responded before she realized her own passive insult. But he ignored her, and she hoped that perhaps he hadn't heard. She watched as his right hand minced across the crease of his trousers in time with the treble clef.

The whole thing was over in fifteen minutes, the girls having completed three ensemble dances and one solo each. Irma arranged herself and the others in a line to take their notes.

Margot was distracted by the window, where outside, the gardener was smoking a cigarette in full view. She was troubled, remembering how her mother once said that a man smoking a cigarette was no good and to tell her if she saw one, and then she told Mama right away that she had seen a man smoking just that morning by the fish market, then Mama said she was speaking of a certain man, and Margot ran all the way back to the market to ask the man if he felt certain or uncertain, and the man took out his thing and showed it to her, all to say a man smoking a cigarette made Margot very nervous indeed.

After notes, Max and Elizabeth walked back to her room. She let him go on about the recital, though she preferred to leave such things behind, thinking of how many recitals she had seen and how many still to come. She was grateful that he wasn't upset over her comments during the performance; she tried to prepare herself to defend them just in case, but found she couldn't remember what they were. As he talked, she changed clothes for the evening, and though they didn't touch each other, she appreciated the intimacy of the moment. She saw in the slim mirror how her belly strained with the big breakfast, and resolved to take the long way to the grocery for the evening paper. Max went on about each girl's contribution to the dance, the energy from one guiding the innocence of another, and so forth, as Elizabeth lay back on the bed, buoyed by the cakes and milled grains and meat, cream lapping at the tender ridge of her gut. He was still talking when she fell asleep.

Off the coast of Viareggio, Isadora takes a swim and meets an unlikely friend

After two days of rain, it's hard to know if the sky is falling into the sea or if the sea is spiraling up into the sky.

I escaped my leaking cottage to find Duse still asleep in hers. One of the boys was hanging around, and I had him find my friend's rain gear, pinning my skirt up around my waist and forcing my feet into her rubbers. He found me a charming parasol, which swiftly flipped upside down in the wind and ripped clean in two before I had even stepped off the porch.

The storm has erased the distinction between the sky and its stage. Everything is upended; cloudy water churns a ragged ridge of sand. One of the old bathing machines snapped its axle and lies half buried, its door wagging in the high tide.

Planting the broken parasol like a flag over my discarded clothes, I enter the sea in bloomers. The water is strangely tepid, as if it wishes to impersonate my body, and my lungs have improved enough to plunge under far longer than before, suspended alongside the waterborne sand. I rush and retreat in an endless leap, the movement upending me, as I am twisted two ways, drawn out by the whim of the world as above me the rain holds constant, a fluid sense extending miles above. Distant lightning startles the fish swimming circles around me; we feel the tingling electricity muted by miles of water. My senses could use a good shock, but swimming closer to the horizon doesn't seem to boost the charge. Still, I swim and swim until even the storm can't keep up with me and turns back to the beach.

I feel closer than ever to the children. They stand behind a wall of flesh thinner than an eyelid. They grasp and beckon, their hands wrapping around my wrists. Desire is nutrient to my blood, and it is desire that takes me to a place, as truly before me as the sea itself, where the poet Shelley reclines on a deck chair, turning the pages of a waterlogged folio. The rain patters meekly around him.

"The storm is overpast," Shelley says, looking up at the clouds. He regards me in a pleasantly distant way, as if he has been expecting someone, but not me exactly. Thin waves wash over his pantlegs, and his hair has dried in a wild curl. One of his shoes is stripped of its sole and wrapped with seaweed, and the other is missing entirely. I can't seem to find the shoal on which he has balanced the chair and so I paddle around him like a happy dog.

He seems like a man who knows his manners but might easily forget them. "I sat and saw the vessels glide over the ocean bright and wide," he says. The shoreline is hidden, which makes it seem as if Shelley has found the last land on the planet. He offers the bare foot and I take it gratefully.

"I suppose we're supposed to hold out here until our hearts mend?"

He shrugs. "I have neither hope nor health."

"My boy lost his shoe as well, patent leather with a calfskin sole. We had bought them the month before, but they were already pinching him. You know how quickly children grow. Have you seen it out here?"

"The tempest is stern," he says, patting his breast pocket and then the pocket in his pants, stretching his legs and coming up empty. "Great and mean meet massed in death."

"It's no matter, Patrick hated those shoes. He threw a fit when I put them on him that morning. He must have kicked it off in the car. Perhaps Annie was fussing to find it on the floor when the brake slipped. Can you imagine, all this over a shoe?"

"Our sweetest songs tell of saddest thought," he says, finding his pen tucked behind his ear and taking up his papers again. "On a cheek the life can burn in blood, even while the heart may break."

"But I'm tired of heartbreak. I only want to join the children."

"Chained to time and cannot thence depart."

"You don't understand—"

"Chained to time," he says, "and cannot thence depart." The rain starts up again, and he seems only vaguely annoyed as the papers on his lap are drenched. I try for one quick glimpse of his work before he kicks me off, sending me backward into the raging storm.

The sea takes me under at once. Cradled in waves and swaddled to them, my legs pinned together as I breathe the water in and spit it up like a baby at the breast. In glimpses I see the shore, where the children have a stormy seaside day. Patrick leaps to plunge a short spear into the sand as Deirdre walks on the tideline, gathering stones in a pail. I can hear their happy cries, the cracking echo of the stones.

The water pulls me down again, binds and strangles me with my own thin clothes and drags me across the rocks. My own weight returns all at once. Without a bit of strength remaining, I have to admit the sea has killed me, but at that moment my head rears back above water as my hands find the cold sand of the beach. The sea is furious at this turn of events, grinding salt water into a thick gash on my thigh as if it could force itself into my veins, to prove what made me.

The rain stops above me, and I see a man leaning over, the water running in dark-haired channels to fall in a halo around my head. From my position he resembles a figure in contemplation on a ceiling fresco, or perhaps a coroner at the morgue. My bloomers clutched around me have torn in places, blood winding sharply down my leg, my hair tangled and sticking to my face. He shivers in his shirt; farther up the beach, his coat and boots rest a shy thirty paces from my clothes, the parasol standing between them like a referee. Between my wet bloomers and his bare arms, we are a decency crime needing only a witness.

"Did you see the vastness?" he asks.

"I don't follow."

"The vastness. Did you see it?"

"I saw Shelley—"

"Tell me what he said."

This man is clearly ill, with the look of a mad scientist watching his monster come to life before him. I think back to the pages in Shelley's lap, which held every line of his careful writing, the ink indelible.

"Madam," he says, his voice fighting waves I would be happy never to touch again. "Madam Duncan, what is it you need? Is there something I can do to help you?"

How strange! This man's very soul is plain to me. He stands between the sea and the world. I will not force the world to cross our paths again.

"Save more than my life," I say. "Save my reason. Give me a child."

Without another word, he gathers me up. Or he tries to, anyway; I have become a sopping pile and he is not a strong man from the sound of it. He falls to one knee, his mouth pressed to my hair. When he tries to stand again, he makes it halfway up but loses the strength in his legs, and I hit the sand rolling. If he had aimed to carry me heroically to his flat, he abandons the plan—most of us do give up when faced with the true weight of things—and instead guides me to stumble across the sand until together we fall hard against a surface that shudders under our weight and threatens to splinter. He tries to brace against it, but it angles itself away from him; it is one of the old bathing machines, the one with the broken axle, the thing rolling haplessly back and forth on its unburied wheel.

He pries the door open, and we find ourselves in the funny little room canted hard to the side. We are sweethearts in a fun house, hanging onto each other. Under his thin shirt I find a long raised scar running diagonally across his gut. I can see him circling another man, describing blades in quick half circles, protecting his heart; I feel the corset pinch, every woman on the street bound in boning; the dueling men thrust and parry, the plunging blade; the stage the bed the empty stage; the wheel turns, the bulging door, water seeping past the ledge; the heat, the heart, the craven center of the very world; the consummate act at season's end; he says his own name and repeats it, Romano, lips set against my skin to brand it; the burning earth, the ash, Romano Romano; my whole body willing a child into being; a baby, shocked and screaming to wake the world.

The man bows his head, his fist landing on the wall hard enough to drive it through the wood. He extracts himself, staggering back and out the door, falling into the rising tide that lifts all ships, the water that seeks me no matter where I go.

Splashing to stand, he looks back. I feel a tenderness for him, a sensation I hardly recognize for its rarity in my life; a warmth, before the silver-streaking pain of the splinter that found the very meatiest part of my ass.

On receiving word from Paris Singer that he is needed in France, Max pushes aside the idea that he has never really been needed anywhere

That wasn't exactly true, anyway. There had been plenty of episodes in the not-too-distant past when his skills and services had been requested, if not demanded. He had always been well liked by soloists in Frankfurt for his good attitude and late nights, often insisting that a rehearsal was not finished until the artist was satisfied. Elizabeth counted on him as a contributing leader of their school, though she had been a little distracted lately and hadn't shown her gratitude in her usual ways. The girls mostly complained about all the hard work he put into nourishing them, but they all looked up to him, he knew.

He was sorry to leave Darmstadt just as his work with the six girls had gotten under way. It was important to respect the conditions of the experiment, which meant the worst thing any of them could do would be to pack up and head to France, where conditions were fully changed and where none of the calisthenic equipment could be transported, being too heavy to move without a surplus charge that Max could not find in his budget. The girls seemed to like Isadora more than they did him or Elizabeth, whom they teased relentlessly, calling her Tante Miss as if she were their old-maid auntie. Girls could be so cruel, and so accurate in their cruelty.

He wouldn't allow himself to be discouraged by the move. The foundation was there, after all; they were perfect physical specimens and sweet girls all told. His legacy would be built on their backs.

He would work harder to improve Elizabeth as well. He could look a little closer at her diet, ensuring that she was eating well and properly. They could take more walks together, and he could listen well to her dark stories about the news. Perhaps Isadora would have some advice about her sister if they ever got a chance to speak; Elizabeth often complained of how critical she was, which meant Max might find in her a kindred spirit.

There would need to be some changes. Elizabeth had been mooning about, sleeping late and staring into middle distance. She ignored his efforts and dismissed him daily. Max felt mired in negative feelings. He found he was coming down with something, and wished there was someone to care for him as much as he cared for everyone else.

*On Viareggio, Isadora discovers the trouble with spontaneous action
undertaken in a wooden structure ignored since the Victorian era*

The splinter carved a formidable slice that bled all the way back, making me look like I had been shot in the hip; fortunately, nobody but Duse was outside to witness when I came limping onto her porch. I tried to convince her to let me keep the wooden piece as a souvenir; I wanted the wound to bloom into a gory cushion, infection working black rot through my veins. How brave I would be, showing the physical proof of my own neglect to the world rather than keeping it hidden like everyone else. But she bent me over her couch, and now I have to wait for her to get her kit as, meanwhile, my ass makes a fine white altar jutting into the naked air.

"You behave as if sadness will pursue you forever," she says, putting on her reading glasses to examine me.

"You're right." Outside her window, the grass is tamped down clear into the woods. "Perhaps it is only a bear."

"Here it is," she says, a flash of pain confirming her tweezer.

"Could you dig a little deeper? The tendons down there could stand a snip."

"Hold still."

"You should have seen him, lifting me like a god and taking me so boldly. We could have been caught at any moment! The passion!"

"Won't you shut up and hold still—"

"His face was so familiar to me, more dear than one of my own dear brothers. I would not have been surprised in the slightest if we had clasped hands and become a wheel to show humanity the meaning of human connection. All right, that's enough!"

She gives me a little slap on the ass. "If you would keep still, I could concentrate."

"Be quick, then. Oh darling, his body was a taut band stretched over a spare frame, pure and efficient. There was a power in his demeanor, and a violence. Very sensual. He had a scar on his stomach, lateral from the navel—nick in the notch, watch it!—a short scar, as if he had been wounded in a bladed duel."

"Ah," she says, working her hand under me to press my belly. "His scar was around here?"

"Precisely there, yes. You know it?"

"I've heard the tale."

"A rumor!" I can hardly keep from bringing both hands to my mouth in glee. "Was the duel for love or money? Did he kill his enemy and go to prison for his crime? Stripped to the waist and glowering in some dim cell, with only his mind to occupy the days? Tell me nothing but the truth! I can take any story of violence."

"I know the man," she says. "His appendix was removed when he was seventeen. They all gathered in the square to see him loaded into the train to Milan because they were all certain he would die. It was rare at the time, very rare indeed, the first anyone had known of such a procedure down here. They still talk about it in town. His father was beside himself, making plaster-cast models of the boy. And then he returned and showed everyone the place where they worked on him, right there. I've never met the man, but I know his father is an artisan—"

"You brat!" I cry, kicking her off. "Spoilsport, leave me be. What use is there to life and love without the mystery of circumstance?"

"Come now, I'm sure he's a nice man," she says, holding her arm where I've kicked her. "We could go see him and his mother for tea."

"I'll never speak to him again, and you'll never speak of it either. Imagine if he went to the press. 'She Bade Me Love Her.' Anyone with a constabulary license could ship me to a sanitarium on an indecency charge at the very least and the charge would be warranted. And you, quit laughing! They would throw you in too for your part in harboring madness."

"All right, all right." She takes her tweezers up again.

"Anyway there's no use in keeping up with him now that his purpose is served. It would be like writing daily letters to the physician who palpated my broken ankle after the series in Nice. *To My Dear Doctor, thinking of you with every step.* Christ's sake, woman, slowly!"

Duse extracts the splinter with a merciless, searing pull and shows it to me—a short piece, and thinner than I thought for the pain it gave me and the blood.

"That should fix it," she says.

"I wish you would have left it until it worked its way into my heart. Think of the fortification!"

"And you're very welcome," she says, turning a bottle of champagne over her handkerchief. She pats the wound with the cloth and presses it there, bracing against me to push herself up. "You can't avoid him, you know. Your mystery man enjoys three meals a day on the passeggiata. A confrontation is inevitable."

"I'll go in the morning to Milan and points north. You'll only need to drive me to the train and you'll be rid of me."

"And another man chases her from the scene," she says, carrying her kit to the sink.

"You're so cruel."

"Have you sent word to Singer?"

"I told you, we ended poorly in Corfu."

"That's right," she sniffs. "You came to me, after all."

"Come now, darling. Trot back over here and be held. Be reasonable, don't be angry with me."

"I'm not angry," she says, plunging sewing needles into a bar of soap.

"Please, love. I have nothing but my arms to give you."

For a moment I fear she'll ignore me forever. But she returns, wiping her hands on her dress.

Later on in bed, she wraps her arms around me, lips to my sunburned cheek. We look out the window at the rain. "Each night gets a little bit colder," she says. "Soon it will be too cold to walk barefoot."

"Once I leave," I say, "I cannot return."

"Isadora, don't be dramatic."

"The train will release a ball of flame, glassing the beaches and outraging the summer-dry trees, their ash falling to settle and float on the bay's wretched eddies. Men and women will burn in their homes clawing the walls, the plaster melting to brand their blackening skin."

"Thank you, that's much less dramatic."

"I'm telling you now, to warn you. Simply wear your nice brocade coat for fortification. You'll find yourself in a charred glade, sparks framing your lovely face. Don't bother looking for a parasol, those silly old-fashioned things."

"You know," she says, easing her arm out from under me. "I met an old man who lived to one hundred years old on coffee and beer. He never took a drop of pure water since he was a child. He claims he drank one glass of milk in his twenties but never ventured to another, said he didn't trust it."

"That's because every glass harbors the mediocre." Turning to face her, I trace the line between her eyebrows with my thumb, the slight ridges of muscle from tempers well and subtly honed. One bears surprise, the other makes the frown.

"You need to go back to work," she says.

"You know, I've worn out my welcome in many homes but never in yours."

"You're unwell, you talk in the most troubling way." Her face is lit by the window's perfect cloudbreak light, wild hair cascading about her shoulders. "Anyway," she gives me a cheery little shake, "you have too much pride to ever retire."

"Can we go for dinner?"

She cinches her gown, getting up. "There's plenty to eat downstairs. Come on, let's look."

Downstairs, we find a few pickled things and cheeses, but we're nearly out of champagne, a true shame, with so much to celebrate. She finds a boy hiding in the mudroom and sends him into town. The rain has come in to rot the windowsills, which she left open for the smell of the storm.

She tilts her head, as if reading something carved over her front door. "You should take them out of Europe," she says. "Your girls in France. Now is the time. They should see their debut in New York, and from there you can go to Moscow."

"There's no taste in New York. Did you know they threw Raymond in jail for wearing his sandals on the street?"

She arranges a plate and pours me a glass of milk. "Don't be intimidated by their intrigue. There's no more valuable commodity to a New Yorker than something he hasn't seen before."

"Also it's too expensive."

"Then you've never gone on Andrew Carnegie's dime."

"Capital plan! We can gather round his desk. If we're lucky, he'll give us a hot meal before he shows us the door."

"I'll write you an introduction," she says, rapping on a loaf of bread before slicing it. "He would be well-advised as a businessman to book your return."

"Last summer, Paris took us out on the water for weeks at a time. Did I ever tell you?"

"You haven't told me a single story about the man that I have enjoyed in tone or substance."

Loosening the leather pouch, I extract a few pieces of bone. The last few bits have been large enough to etch down my throat in a satisfying way, but now they're large enough that it's best I take them with milk. Duse notices but doesn't mention it. "We had some idea that we were bedouins, and we outfitted the yacht with carpets and thick sheets that we had hung around the cabin on the nights when we slept above deck. The children slept together in a bathtub we filled with the softest cotton batting, and each morning the two of them crawled into bed for a cuddle. We would land at some place or another and I would give a spontaneous performance. It was all so wonderful, so perfect. But something began to shift, and though Paris and Deirdre played pat-a-cake over their breakfast trays, though Patrick laughed so often we began to think he had a medical condition—as he nursed, he would spit up for laughing—though there was joy all around me, I felt a mounting dread.

"I felt it building. I thought for sure we were going to sink, that there would be some accident, and I became terrified of every swell and sick with worry overnight. I would sit up all night watching the horizon, as if I could stop any monster that came on the waves.

"The feeling grew and grew, and I finally realized the source: it was coming from the captain and the mates, the cook and the nurse, everyone working to serve us. They smiled and cleaned up our crumbs and made pleasant conversation, but I realized true as morning that they hated us all the while. How could they not?

"Finding the source of the feeling made it impossible to ignore. It was baked into the bread we buttered for lunch, it shone from the deck they scrubbed after the children's scuffing games, and it fluttered from our clothes pinned to the starboard wire. The polished silver was so hot with resentment it ought to have burned us."

"Poor dear! Loathing in your soup."

"I was afraid! Don't laugh at me. I felt the fortune of my birth and couldn't escape it. I knew my station was determined by chance. Their loathing flattened me, and my art became something they could work up in their spare time if they were only so luckily born, so starved for fame as to spend their hours preening, if only they were as cruel and selfish as I. They made me into a paper doll with tunics and sandals to attach or whip away."

"Perhaps you were flattening them as well, my dear."

"I counted the hours until we could get away, but the feeling was even keener when we landed. The landlord, the nurse. The cord the postman used to bundle the mail was threaded with resentment thick enough to strangle me.

"And that was Europe, where class is so fixed. Now imagine what I would find in New York, a city that doubles as the world's longest dinner table, everyone turning in unison to stare down the stranger at its door? They threw Raymond in jail. I cannot bear to think of what they'll do to me."

"And so—"

"And so no, I will not go to New York, not for Andrew Carnegie and not for you."

The rain starts up again. Hopefully the boy fetching the champagne will find us another parasol. "Your mind is set on France," she says, watching the rain on her sill.

"My mind is set. If everyone so desperately wants me to go back to work, I will go back to work and make a new dance to attend it. Paris is the only place. There, my life was burned to dust. What better stage for a revolution than on its ashes?"

IV

At the new school in Paris's Bellevue, a family reunion presents far more trouble than it solves

Mother arrived before the ice and complained so heartily that everyone else came to assume her bad attitude had conjured it. We were trapped together, a feeling that transported me back to childhood. The support staff had gone to be stuck with their own families, and the girls mostly kept to themselves in the bedroom they shared, all six of them lined up in an extravagant bed like girls in a fairy tale. The school in winter really feels like the abandoned hotel it is. Mother quarantines herself at night in the east wing, her bed padded with cards and sweet letters from her Oakland friends.

To pass the time in the later evening hours, the adults go around the group and tell stories of other awful holidays. Elizabeth remembers the year she exiled herself to New York and spent the season warding off the attentions of the father of one of her charges, culminating in a New Year's party where she had to remove his hands from under her dress. Mother tells a charming holiday story about Father making love to a banker's wife in order to secure a loan and how the banker arrived at the house that night to both personally reject the application and to punch

Father in the mouth. Elizabeth's strange suitor, Max, speaks at length about how he was never allowed to celebrate the New Year as a child and how even as a young man he was sent to bed early, including a meandering detail about a gift of tobacco he once bought for himself; he could have saved us all the agony and passed on the question.

We have burned through the firewood and most of the pantry, and the fear is it will be days before they dig a path in to save us. Of course none of us ever think to save ourselves, but were happy enough to complain. I can't think of a worse New Year's than this one, kitchen rations and no liquor, and six girls who are strangers to me. But I don't want to be cruel, and so I make up a story about starting a jealous row with Paris while the two of us were dancing a waltz.

After that game is exhausted, I try convincing them that everyone should set their own personal New Year. Only the poor idiot who slipped on ice in the middle of a depressing January night might mark the day he cracked his hip and was required to keep completely still for months while his desperate wife dug snow from the garden to uncover frozen patches of thistle she might boil for their supper. Perhaps this is the old Father Time we hear so much about.

Elizabeth, on the last of the port, declares that 1914 will stand as a monument to all the years before and past, and the few who don't feel optimistic about the future should keep it to themselves. I'll toast to that!

This blizzard has been a real bell jar, but seclusion has its benefits; most importantly, it gave me a chance to consume the larder without witness, first the bread with jam and then crackers and figs and hard cheese and then a jar of crème fraîche, which I ate with my fingers at precisely the time Saint Nicholas was crooking his staff around children's stockings all over the quiet city.

The snow outside mutes every sound and the house sleeps deeply, which means that I can wander the halls without having to run from them. I walk all night sometimes, rolling a single chunk of bone across my tongue like sweet sugar.

Finally we hear a shovel scrape and frantic knocking at the cook's door. Two men from the city had been trying to dig us out for days, handsome fellows and very cold. The path cleared, the others arrive with mutton and jam and sacks of cornmeal and goose fat and champagne and eggs and enough kindling to light the whole place up. All three jars of the good crème fraîche were long gone by then, much to the dismay of the cook, who had been planning a crepe. Once they clear the electrical box and start lighting the halls again, it feels as if there are far too many people and everyone is far too illuminated, so I make a quick retreat to the darkness of my locked wing.

It is good to lie on the marble floor and feel it against the exposed bit of skin at the nape of my neck. It feels so very good, so clean and cold, that after pulling off my dress, I lie on my side to feel more of it against my body, which shudders with picky sickness at the temperature change. This child, which began on the beach in Viareggio, will bring me a New Year in August.

You must see them, comes a voice from a hunting portrait, from the portrait itself. *You know well enough they have come for you.* It's coming from the dog at center, a pointer; and there's the pretty doe the men have found collapsed in the brush. The dog's eyes water at the scent of his own loyalty. *I cannot hold them. You must let them come.* The wide-eyed doe in the grass is a living corpse for their taking.

Watching this charming scene, I feel my lovers past and present grasp my hands and caress me, taking up my arms to nibble my fingertips. When they see their own greed in the others' eyes, they try to pull me off to consume me in private.

My family gathers around my head, to kiss my temples, whispering platitudes and truths as they stuff themselves with my hair.

My students crouch at my feet, filling their cheeks with my bones, chewing toes and knobby ankles as they try to enter through my veins, to grow strong and vital there before they gnaw their way out.

It is an agony to endure until I feel my two babes nestling at my breast. I murmur down to soothe them, but this is different from before. They hunch over me, sucking with all their might, furious by the failure of their effort. They sink their teeth sharp as sawpoints and rear back blood and flesh. They thrash against me, digging to pry open my ribs. But still, I bear them gladly; if this pain has the power to destroy me, I welcome it to my breast.

Max attempts to practice the life of the mind in order to forget he is trapped with Elizabeth and her terrible family

The whole sad story of the accident was a real distraction for Max. In Germany it had been easy enough to ignore, but avoiding the idea was impossible in Paris; the river was close enough to Bellevue that it could be viewed through the slim windows flanking the top floor even without going out on the balcony, which seemed to Max unstable. Though he had no business above the ground floor, he ventured up a few times to peer at it through the dusty glass.

Their poor nurse had died that day as well. Annie Sim was her name. Max found himself thinking of her often and pitying her, for he knew that everyone else dwelled on the unknown potential of the children. But this woman Annie Sim—who reminded him of his long-suffering mother and slightly resembled her from the picture he saw, the same hardness in the eyes—had lived and known her own full life, had surely known heartbreak and shame, and enjoyed the attention of a fellow at school, and snuck a half glass of beer from the bottles littered about the kitchen after her parents had gone off to bed. She had cared for and soothed the two children in her charge and maybe even loved them and entertained the fantasy that they were her own. She must have often fantasized that she was the famous one, that every evening would find her onstage, performing for a breathless gathered crowd.

How the woman died was not as important as how she lived, Max told himself. It would be an insult to reduce the woman to the moment of her death, a moment she hadn't chosen and one in which she was not even present, not really. He hated the thought of the crowd at the riverside, waiting for the bodies to be dredged out. He tried to imagine Annie Sim's personality from photographs he had seen of her. Max felt a real kinship to the woman. If she was still alive, after all, she would sleep a few doors down from him in the employee wing. She would sit at the edge of her bed just as he was, in a bedroom appointed in the same spare way; Singer had only had a few pieces of furniture installed.

Perhaps Annie, brushing her hair while sitting on the very edge of her bed, which was made up with a plain white coverlet, might feel the same longing he felt. Perhaps, he dared to believe, she might unfasten her skirt and run her fingers across her soft belly, touching the mark the garment had made. Max thought of her soft skin and abused himself with a guilty fury, spitting on his hand.

When he was finished, he felt such a wave of revulsion that he stumbled to the corner of the room and forced his fingers between the bars of the radiator grille, gritting his teeth as the pain absolved him. He slapped himself briskly in the face and went down to breakfast.

At the table he found toast and coffee and an egg dish that he wouldn't touch. When he asked for tea with cream and sugar, they brought it already prepared, a tannish mix.

Elizabeth and her mother had come to the point of their morning argument where they were addressing each other by name. Max was annoyed to realize that no matter where he chose to sit, he would be forced to place himself between the two of them.

"Dora, dear," Elizabeth said, "would you pass the butter?"

"Of course, Elizabeth," her mother returned. "Do you need the salt as well?"

He thought about how strange it was that old Dora Duncan had given her own name to Isadora, a convention he had previously seen only among men. Max himself had always been told he was named after a member of the Austrian navy, but on her deathbed his mother confessed that they had actually named him after a favorite dog. The original Max was a schnauzer and a good boy by all accounts.

They ate in silence. Halfway through the meal Max was startled by the sound of a woman crying out. Isadora was keening again and wanted them all to know. Elizabeth grimaced at the newspaper folded primly on the table beside her. The sound extended to make itself known and held to the ragged end of the performer's vocal ability.

"What on earth?" Max said at last. The women looked up, one frown repeated on the other's face. Dora's thicker skin slackened around her jaw, which was at that moment working industriously at a piece of ham steak. She had been reading the social pages, fashion and petty crime.

"Shouldn't someone go and quiet her?" Max added, realizing too late that the question might have implied an annoyance he hardly felt and certainly hadn't intended to express. A maid came to offer more tea and left without even a moment of corroborative eye contact.

"She's fine," Elizabeth said. The two of them went back to their reading.

The wail started up again, as if to contradict her directly. Elizabeth took a piece of toast spread with a lemon marmalade the cook had found in the market earlier that morning. The cook, it seemed, was awake at all hours. There was an unsubstantiated report that she slept standing at the larder, her face pressed onto a side of beef.

"Apparently the education board and clergy are considering substitutes for the tango," Dora said. "They visited the École Massillon and found it vulgar among the students. They very much enjoyed the perigon, though." She looked up. "Should we teach the perigon to the girls? I enjoy nothing more than pleasing a man of the cloth."

"Try as I might," Elizabeth said, "I can't imagine anything less vulgar than a bunch of twelve-year-old girls fumbling through a tango."

"But what will you say to the clergy, Elizabeth?"

"They may visit and judge us all they like as paying guests of our next performance, Dora."

Her mother gave a humorless little laugh. "I hope I'll be here to see it."

The wailing continued, attended now by a muted thumping noise, as if she were beating her fists against a wall.

"I really am concerned," Max said.

"Go see for yourself," said Elizabeth, sliding her keys across the table.

"You locked her in?"

"More likely she locked us out."

Max goes on a journey to save a woman and to say maybe just one thing about his own ideas

He needed to think strategically; this was his moment to realize a plan that had been in motion for years, a journey that began the day he met Elizabeth in Vienna. Here he was more or less at the center of an artistic movement, with a chance to see his theories honed by willing subjects.

He had always heard that Isadora tended to run in extremes with children, first doting and then shrugging them off. He sometimes found old lecture notes of hers tucked into books in Darmstadt, but nothing made sense to him. *The joining of the child's life to Nature's,* one of the lines read. *Every child's love for music.* There was no organization to her thoughts, no central idea.

The walk to Isadora's private wing required passing through an empty hall, cold and unfamiliar. Rooms flanked the hall, full of furniture under protective cloths. The first was draped in ivory, the second in black, and so forth, reminding Max of zoo animals sleeping in their pens.

Elizabeth's keys were lined up on a brass ring like a warden's set. As he unlocked the big door to the wing, he was startled to hear a roaring like a car engine, though they were far from the road and the sound came from directly overhead, so close that Max crouched down until it faded, fearing the whole place was coming down. The door swung open into darkness, and his eyes strained to adjust.

Isadora appeared to him in silhouette, seated on a velvet bench like a girl in a museum, staring at the painting on the far wall. She was stark naked, her clothes in a pile at her feet. Max stood at a distance he deemed respectful and averted his eyes. On the walk over, he had thought he might offer himself up romantically to her, but he changed his mind seeing her posture, which was unnaturally straight in a way which seemed mildly possessed.

"Madame might join us for breakfast," he said.

She made no response. It occurred to him that between the formality of his question and his pressed white shirt she might confuse him for a member of the staff. If she failed to recognize him in daylight—as she had failed, on his arrival with Elizabeth to Bellevue—she would never know him here. The hall was lit only vaguely by a window far down the hall, around the corner. It was even colder than the others, the marble like ice under his feet. His eyes grew accustomed to the dark, and he saw that she was patting the bench beside her. Obediently, he came and took a seat.

"There is toast and marmalade," he said. "Something the cook brought up from town. A lemon marmalade." It was a small bench, with more room for carved wooden filigrees than for comfort, and they were forced very close as a result, their arms touching. She must have been cold but he didn't dare move to warm her.

"Did you hear the aeroplane?" she asked.

"Your mother sent me to check on you."

She didn't respond. He hated himself for lying, and hated her as well for inspiring the lie. His intentions had been muddied, he meant to show her simple human kindness, but she was cold to him and the whole thing was ruined.

Desperately he tried to assure himself that this was the last place to be ashamed by his own emotion. He was an intellectual artist, after all, and had once developed an interpretation of Beethoven's piano sonatas that spoke to the composer's mathematical phrasing. But she didn't think of him as an artist or an intellectual. She gave more care and regard to strangers. Max knew all he needed to know about Isadora from what he had heard of her behavior at parties. She was always trying to reflect herself off flattering surfaces; Elizabeth had a story about her sister dragging a destitute man from his pallet on the street and parading him around a gala, introducing him as a cousin of the Kaiser. She would have looked like a goddess escorting a mortal to his own sacrifice. As an added benefit, Elizabeth pointed out, the others assumed it was the strange cousin who had arrived smelling like a distillery.

"You are troubling everyone," he said at last.

She turned slightly, pressing her leg against his from hip to knee. He saw that she was holding a sterling silver nail file, the kind ladies kept on their dressing tables. She turned it over in her hand. Max decided she was either about to murder him or invite him to her room. Or she might do both, asking him in for a drink and making her deadly intentions known only once he had settled himself on her bed. The interaction's dark potential troubled him, but Max reasoned that he could be flexible in his response.

He needed only to turn slightly in order to take her in his arms. She was waiting for him to act on his impulse and would thank him heartily for it.

"The meek," she said, "shall inherit precisely nothing."

"What's that?" He wasn't meek at all; he was strong and certain and had come to comfort her as a man comforts a woman. And here she was, as naked as the day and trembling. Max stared straight ahead to keep from seeing her. Perhaps he was the one trembling, but still it charged the moment.

He considered the angles. There was the fact of the nail file, which she was pressing at indeed a rather sharp angle onto a vein at her wrist. It occurred to him that she might stab him in the throat.

There were ways he could use such an attack: gesturing to the file sticking out of his neck, he could make the assertion that the girls needed to build short and stocky muscle that would make them more likely to defend against such crimes.

It was time to act. He would take Isadora into his arms and pledge his life to her. She would yield to his touch, and they would kiss, tasting the tears that flowed freely from them both.

It was time, it was past time. She had gone.

He watched her walk away, her dress forgotten on the floor. Her bedroom door echoed when it closed, and he heard it lock.

She had left the silver file on the bench. Max regarded it warily for a moment before slipping it into his pocket, looking around to see if anyone would catch him. He felt foolish taking it. He hadn't believed in magic since he was a child.

Teddy,

Consider the tale of Iphigenia, murdered by her father's hand:

Because the fawn was cut in the wrong glade, the idiot boy upending the map until peaks toppled into valleys and muddied all the dale— because Artemis, picking her teeth with the point of a silver dart, espied this folly and truly was annoyed—because she stilled the winds through the strait, slouching sails upon the rig—because the men on those ships were glad and ready to die—because for Troy, the Argans needed men and ships and wind and the favor of the gods—because of all this, the firstborn girl would have to go.

Curtain rise on Agamemnon promising his girl another show of swords and oaths and a hearty meal after in exchange for her attendance at the sacrifice. Tricked by his love and attention, Iphigenia goes along with it, wearing a coat of feathers lashed with fine golden thread, one of her very finest garments, because she has been promised a good seat at the show, *One of the best!* he says, gazing off strangely at nothing.

They hold hands along the path, walking as they did when she was a girl. He feels the fault in the deal he has struck with the gods, trading the life of his child for a bit of wind. Surely there is a lesson to be learned, the weight of war or fleeting life. He doesn't see reason quite yet. He thinks of his men sweltering in the bay and how his choice will ease more pain than it brings.

The usual blank-eyed women crowd behind, their children in rags. Every night they dream the same terrible dream: a wall of death bearing down, the blood of their babies cutting paths in the dirt.

The girl picks her way among them to find the seat her father gives her, in the center of the stone broad enough to lay her head. She settles into dread, knowing what it means if you look about for a sacrifice and cannot find the fawn.

Let's make it quick from here: draw the chorus forward like a wave and back to show the girl in her father's arms, throat clean slit, head turned from the blood that soaks her feather coat.

The chorus stands in silence, waiting. Is the miracle supposed to arrive straightaway? The wind could pick up a little at least.

Agamemnon watches a single feather ease out and fall like an arrow, marking with blood the spot where he traded his love for love of country, where he cut open his heart and found it as empty as the eyes of dying men, as empty as their sails.

In the aeroplane hangar at Oldway, Paris prepares to break a few hearts

The local men arrived even earlier than usual, coming up the road before sunrise. They stood around like grandmothers, stepping forward now and again to stroke *Cigare*'s hull. They tried to ignore the Swiss instructor, who wouldn't even look at them as he made the last operational points to his student.

Someone passed around a box of cigars, and each man took one but it felt far from a celebration. Paris considered giving a speech about the glory of the modern age but decided against it and strapped himself in without fanfare.

As they rolled him into position, Paris had a chance to wonder at the purpose of humility. Was the goal to eliminate pride from one's life entirely, or to simply remove its more boastful displays? Perhaps the goal varied based on one's spiritual belief. The Greek gods seemed to really have it out for pride and vanity both, but their mortals rarely had an internal life to scrutinize; as a result, there was no way to know if the error was in the display of these flaws or their simple existence.

The engine started without incident, and soon enough he had *Cigare* rattling across the field toward the line of oak trees his father planted fifty years before. The unplowed field was rougher than he thought, and the tires jammed into ruts and gopher pots, splintering off pieces of well-loved wood. Just as he had begun to fear he was too weighed down, the whole thing lifted with a miraculous shudder and Paris was airborne, flying against sense and reason. It was a wild ride, the craft shaking so heartily that he was sure the whole thing would disassemble in midair. But the bolts held, and he shouted with joy, gloriously aloft in the bracing wind. He watched his father's tree line turn puny, a line of noble matchsticks he soared over without another glance. His property was a lovely green postage stamp, beyond which lay Paignton, the bay and Channel beyond. He felt like a ghost or a god, soaring to greet the sky.

The local men watched in hard silence below. They grimaced every time the plane pitched too far, as if they were standing on a wire that shocked them in unison. Half of them removed their hats. One of the younger men broke down weeping and had to be helped inside and given a glass of gin. The others remained stoic, smoking their cigars and watching Paris circle back.

He landed harder than he had intended and heard a crunching sound that came from either his neck or the engine block. The men ran after the plane as it bounced across the field, trying to track the path of gleaming bits that flew off into the grass. At last *Cigare* came to a stop against a low bank and sank deep into the mud, and extracting it would require the rest of the afternoon.

Paris eased himself from the cockpit, relieved to find his neck sore but not broken. A few of the men clambered up to open the engine hatch, but he called them off. He wanted a few moments of victory to himself, and he would enjoy it, even if someone had drunk all the gin.

Despite low winter clouds, the future looked bright. He would chart the *Cigare* north to cross the Channel, following the rivers and roads he knew, coming into the field at Issy-les-Moulineaux. From there, he would find his way to Bellevue and to Isadora, and they could have a revival of their old selves, taking to heart the fresh feeling of a new year. It would be a year of invention, of progress and healing. She was back to work at last, and would be glad to see him. Perhaps he could even take her up in the plane. She was a brave woman, an independent spirit, and he missed her by his side.

He thanked the men for their service which, he added, was no longer needed. They left, casting back sullen glares, but he didn't mind a bit. He would have his grand return into France, where he and Isadora would finally sit and talk like the sweethearts they were, a man and woman who had fallen in love and created a child in the course of desire. It would absolutely be that simple.

The ice melts enough for Elizabeth and her mother to go out for lunch

Mother, it would be known, was not interested in speaking French. Of course she knew the language perfectly well and had taught her children enough that they would never struggle to understand any Parisian's praise or scorn. Sitting in a café and acting as if she didn't understand was only her idea of a good time, and she seemed to like it even more when Elizabeth was visibly uncomfortable.

She flagged the waiters down and asked for their preference on lunch, demanding to know the intricacies of every dish and correcting their English before choosing the opposite of whatever they recommended. The waiters scowled and hated her and one even spat at the back of her chair, and still she pretended not to know that they were wondering aloud to each other where a pig had found such unfashionable clothes.

Knowing that something like this was bound to happen, Elizabeth had chosen a café outside the neighborhood, but she was still ashamed to see the Parisians making note—literally, she observed with dismay, in little books. And it wasn't just the waiters passing judgment, either. After Mother demanded ice in her water, one of the patrons took out his sketchpad and set to work on a series of comic illustrations, portraying in colored pencil the old woman styled as a needle and Elizabeth as her faithful haystack.

Mother was only getting started. She was in good humor, making the waiters repeat the tea service again. "Look at those gossips," she said.

"Stop pointing, Mother, they can see you."

"That one just said that he hopes there is enough room in Hell for the fat." She laughed, licking her lips. "How I hate them!"

"You're certainly breezy this morning," Elizabeth said, hoping a subject change would distract her.

"My dear! You're only as bad as you feel."

"I was worried about you last night." They had all been having a perfectly lovely dinner conversation about termites when Mother interrupted with a coughing fit, looking clammy and pale, as if she had risen from her own casket and come up for a meal. Making hasty apologies, she asked that the digestif be brought to her in bed, and she looked so bad that the maid wrapped a scarf around her own face before she went in with it. And now here she was, tucking into her second plate of bread and annoying the staff with her usual enthusiasm.

"Do you recall the principles of energy conservation?" Mother asked, spooning jam onto her plate. "Hopefully, you didn't forget everything I taught you. The energy bounded by my body holds no rank over that which is found in trees and lightning, and other bodies, and in the air. I simply decided to pull my strength from these forces and heal myself in the cosmic world." She leaned in confidentially. "I suspect if I can keep vigilant to this practice, I might never die. What do you think about that? Your sister might even have to see me, considering how I would be a miracle of science by then."

"You've seen her plenty at meals, Dora."

"And I'm only asking to be granted audience in her room, dear Elizabeth. Why doesn't she want to spend any time with me?"

"She's not sure you didn't bring a pox with you on the *Olympic*. We have to be very careful. The illness on Corfu nearly put her down."

"A pox on both your red rumps! I know them well. Please pass the butter."

"You must give her time," Elizabeth said. "After all she's been through."

"If she can make the arduous trip across the hall, I would appreciate it. My word, I might as well not have left Oakland."

Elizabeth could picture the old house: bedrooms shuttered and barred, a single chair by the parlor window, a cup and saucer balanced beside the sink. As children, they had tried using one of the delicate cups from the tea set to cover a lamp in order to provide soft stage lighting, but they soon discovered that the hot glass had burned the china in a ring. Fearing a beating, Elizabeth buried it. She wondered if it was still in the side yard.

Mother stirred her coffee with a silver spoon that she slipped into her purse. "Can we talk about Max?"

"We cannot talk about Max."

"My dear—uncross your legs, you'll burst a vessel—I only want to present the argument, from the old-fashioned set, that if your man has not yet expressed the desire for marriage—also, your shoulder blades should find your chair, for posture and cardiovascular health—if your man doesn't want to marry after all you've been through together, you may as well look elsewhere."

"The fact that you're lecturing me about marriage after everything Daddy put you through is a true shock."

"You are forty-three years old."

"I'm forty-two, and I'm—"

"And you're old enough to know how to manage your life. And yet here I see poor posture, a bad diet, rejection of stability, and an ignorance of the daily benefit of routine."

"Max and I are fostering a house of girls and preparing for an international tour, which means pursuing venues in New York, Chicago, and Moscow. We're organizing the travel for a house full of performers and support staff, managing the instructors and curriculum of two schools, and planning a performance series through the end of the quarter."

She made a face. "Why would you leave Europe?"

Elizabeth started to answer, but realized she didn't have a good one. Isadora had suggested that she look into New York, and Elizabeth took it upon herself to make the inquiries, confused all the while, as Isadora had previously made her thoughts on the city clear.

"And so," Mother said, "there's no time for a wedding."

"We are so legally and professionally entrenched in each other's lives that neither of us has grounds for insecurity. There is no chance of dissolution, even if one or the other of us desperately wanted it."

She grasped her daughter's hand. "Anything in the world can fall, you know. That's a lesson we learn from gravity."

"I'm familiar with gravity, Mother."

"But what about the law of universal gravitation?" She waved off a waiter who had arrived to curse her. "Every particle in the universe attracts every other particle with a force proportional to the product of their masses. You are composed of these particles, and he is the same, and the earth below you is the same, and it's as simple as that." She extracted the porcelain sugar spoon from its bowl and held it thoughtfully to her lips. "Laws of science are much more real than your funny thoughts and feelings could ever be."

"I take it you're still spending your afternoons with that old scientist?"

She tucked the spoon into her purse. "One would hope that you might also find a friend who offers you such comfort as Elias, who is not so very old. Will you look at those waiters? See how they line up and scuff their boots against the wall like boys. Come over here, *misser*, and bring the butter! Look at this roll. This is my body, broken for you."

The waiter dropped the cheque and removed the silverware from the table.

"We need to go," Elizabeth said, counting her coins. "Before they put a mouse in our kettle."

"I'd be grateful for any flavor it lent this awful tea."

"Come on, get your wrap."

"But we aren't done with our bread." She pouted but obediently took Elizabeth's arm. "Young people are so decadent," she said, pressing her face against the matted fur of her daughter's coat.

"I thought I wasn't so young."

"You are young at heart, my dear. Isn't it wonderful to be young at heart?"

At the train station in Paris, Max and Trella go to greet a shipment
of weights

Trella frowned, looking from the platform clock to her own watch on its delicate silver chain. It was nestled between her blouse and her new leather gloves, which she had bought the week before as a treat to herself. Her watch was fast, and she set her bag down to adjust it.

"Don't touch it," Max said. "They're slow."

"But why?"

He shrugged. "Some Parisian mix of pride and incompetence."

Trella accepted this without comment. She found it entertaining to pretend to be a bored aristocrat in situations such as this one, when things weren't going her way, and it seemed as if Max was playing along without her even asking. "Their stations are clean enough," she said. "I can say that much for France."

They must have seemed a dour pair, looking often enough at the time to make it clear how little they cared for the chilly afternoon. She extracted a handkerchief from her bag, tucked it delicately around her nose, and blew.

Max watched her, enthralled at the way the embroidered wisp covered one little nostril and the other. He marveled at her productive exhalation. Anything could be beautiful from the proper source. He felt the sharp point of the silver nail file at the bottom of his coat pocket.

"It's too bad they couldn't deliver the weights directly to the school," she said. Her dress was stylishly hemmed to the lower calf, revealing a length of stocking and a smart black boot. Despite the low rise of her shoe, she still stood a few inches taller than he did, and he was pleased to see her crouch a little in deference when she spoke.

"Yes," he said. "It's too bad."

Without a second thought, he reached out and took Trella's hand. They stood there waiting for the train like a charming young couple. He pictured the pale features their children would have, and he was working out their names when she wiggled her fingers from his grip.

She tucked her leather-tipped finger into her cuff to look at her watch again. "The trains," she said.

"I told you. They're slow."

"You said the clocks were slow."

He realized the fatal mistake he had made in reaching for her. Though the action had laid just one thimbleful of power on her side of the scale, it had been more than enough weight to tip it in her favor. He hadn't known the measure until he exceeded it. He wanted to apologize to her, to be forgiven, and he hated that impulse in himself.

He would have to tell a joke in order to save the balance. He would tell a good joke, she would laugh, and all would be well. He only needed to think of a joke. Something about the time. Better not to overthink it.

"They say everything is slow in France," he said.

She sighed. Before he even saw the look on her face, he felt it. In her sigh he heard the history of his own failure and the future of it.

It was all such a drain on the spirit. Max blamed the train station for giving him a feeling of malaise. It only reminded him of what a homebody he had become. He wasn't a young man anymore, but he would make another trip, eventually. Perhaps to Vienna, to visit his mother's grave. He would sit and tell her the story of his afternoon at the train station and the failed joke, and his theories as well, and she would listen with the half smile she always wore to hear his fantasies about the future, the plans she always knew were beyond him.

20 February 1914
Firenze, Pergola
Teddy Craig, Direttore
Pieno come un uovo

Teddy—

I've locked myself in again, this time saddled with child. It saps my strength and blood to make its own, a tiny capitalist within me taking an hourly wage in pounds of flesh. Truth be told, I am thrilled by this weakness for what it means: this child has the power to conquer the whole ruined city of my heart.

I'm certain you can appreciate the feeling of gestating an idea expelled whole. I believe sincerely that if men could give birth, there would be many fewer novels and fewer operas too, perhaps more poetry but no plays at all. You would forget the stage, surrounded by a brood built and warmed by your very own flesh. It would be only natural.

Everyone here is ready for winter to end, but I hope it stays forever. I'm grateful for the ice and cold, grateful that you haven't yet responded, though of course I was furious when that card came from old Harry Kessler—*Thinking of you in this heartbreaking* &c. You can imagine

Harry holding the evening paper at arm's length so as not to catch any transmissible element of our tragedy. Of course I looked carefully among each one of his words for penciled dots in case you had sent me a code to break. I thought you might have wanted to convey some earnest thought, hidden as the best thoughts are, something to prove your heart was as freshly carved as mine.

But there was nothing there, and your feelings on the accident remain a mystery. Perhaps you can't bear it and May is keeping you from rafters and sharp objects. Perhaps you've locked the thought of it away, like the door to a particularly untidy cellar, ignoring the crying down there until it stops. Or perhaps you only blame me.

For a time, your silence was my greatest daily interest, though I wouldn't admit it to anyone here. Of course I knew you would avoid the funeral—I would have escaped it if I could—but then I didn't hear a word from you. I thought of asking after you among our mutual friends but imagined Ernst and Magda and even Charles staring into middle distance as if they were trying to place your name. I couldn't take the humiliation.

Eventually, though, your silence became a comfort. Everyone else had reached out in some way to pay their respects, with enough offers to comfort and hold me. After wading through all that ordinary love, I was grateful that I could assign something more meaningful to you. No postal service could reach the depths of your experience, where you grieved alone. You were suffering in a way I didn't have the courage to even imagine. In this way, I forgave you your silence.

Writing these letters has given me comfort and I hope comfort is what you find in them. I am the lighthouse to your wayward ship, beaming a welcome and warning from home.

The weather improves enough for Paris to make a decision that proves risky

The new runway was fresh and keenly poured, and *Cigare* carved through it like a fingernail through a tray of oil. Everything seemed sturdier the second time around; the plane was as heavy as a banker's desk but simple to maneuver, wheeling on the whims of air as they cleared the field. Paris grazed the low-lying fog as old Compton Castle emerged, its fortress walls a dry dam restraining the landscape. He was so taken with it all that he found he had angled the plane toward the stone walls of the castle and had to pull the nose up at the last moment, whooping with the rush to his senses. Right then and there, he decided to alter his course, to fly the Channel from Torquay to Auderville rather than going up to Dover and then over the water. He would see more familiar sights that way, town and country, the Paignton Pier, and the Channel beyond. He might even see the homes of the local men who helped him with the hangar and craft. He could wave down to them.

He hadn't done the calculations on this new route, but figured it would be simple enough, a little less time over land was all. It was a smooth ride at first and a beautiful one, with a lovely view of the pier. Then the land gave way to the Channel, and he felt the air change as he came out over brackish water the color of a woman's eyes—of Lillie's eyes, he thought, imagining her peering down at him as she stroked his hair, his head in her lap. In early days she wore a linen shirt to bed and pinched his ear when he teased her for it. How young they had been. In the rare times his wife appeared to him, she usually took the form as when he last saw her, disappointed in the door to his study, asking for his return itinerary though she knew he didn't have one. This memory with his head in her lap must have been in London, before they went back to New York and everything fell to pieces. He was disgusted with himself.

To distract himself from his own failure, Paris turned his mind to the failure of others. There was the time Isadora accused him of flirting with an actress at a party and made a scene everyone talked about for months. The actress had been wearing a delicate silver tiara, and Isadora pulled it right off her head, too drunk to be coy about it and laughing in the shocked silence. She wore the tiara arched over her shoulder like a spangled epaulet and was later seen kissing the consulate general. Paris liked to pull that one out when he felt especially bad about himself, and he spent a moment enjoying the memory of the poor girl cowering under her gloves, trying to cover the fresh bald spot where some of her golden hair had been snatched away.

It was darker over the water than he thought it would be. He held *Cigare* steady below the thick clouds, but it was difficult to see where the water met the sky. Paris began to realize the risk he had taken. His altimeter jostled among the other things in the waxed linen bag on his lap; a pride in his own bearing had stopped him from installing the device on the dash. And now it was too late; he couldn't spare the attention it would require to find it and read it. He had no choice but to hold steady to his own waning conviction about his coordinates, to his sense of direction and elevation. Conviction, he tried to assure himself, was more important than certainty. He hoped his pride had been punished enough.

He tried to picture the suburb around his destination at Issy-les-Moulineaux, which he remembered as being quite posh. Once he landed, he would hire a car to take him to the Bellevue school, where he would find the students scattered like new fawns across the lawn, running to embrace him, their very first patron. He hadn't met this new crop but trusted they would be good girls like the ones who had come before, earnest and serious, and kind to their friends. They might have an impromptu recital in celebration of his arrival, and he would sit at the right hand of their founding genius and watch the slow smile play across her face as the night progressed.

The wind over water lulled him into thought. He found himself entertaining an endless receiving line of thoughts, arranged in his mind like the funeral crowd when Isadora locked herself in the cremation room and left him to deal with the reception. A few of the women spoke of Patrick in an attempt to explain their special window into his grief; the papers wouldn't list him, but the gossips could do whatever they wanted. A journalist from the Arts section found it was an appropriate time to ask him Isadora's opinion on other forms of new movement, free expression in the American South, and certain Gypsy modes, and he found himself appreciating the man's insolence and wanting to take him out for a drink. The truth was, Isadora had no interest in artistic citizenship or civility and hated anything that didn't spring from her own mind. It was a trait Paris couldn't understand; as a businessman, it was important to lay the foundation of common ground in order to make it possible down the line to buy the competition out.

The funeral felt like a government function, for all the dignitaries there, and the artists looking for free sandwiches. Ted Craig had been unable to find the courage to attend, so Paris took on the role of Deirdre's father as well. He remembered the little woodland plays the girl had invented. She would declare Paris the Forest King, draping him with garlands and taking his hands to show him her dollies arranged as ladies-in-waiting. He thought of her inventive plays as he stood at the head of the reception line and listened to each stranger tell him how beautiful she was. It would be another hour before he realized that Isadora had gone home without him. He returned to the flat to find her with her siblings, all of them devastatingly drunk, having finished the week's liquor along with the cooking wine and an ancient-looking tincture of opium Raymond had found in the back of a cabinet. "All the men and women of the world are my children," Isadora was saying, her eyes miserably crossed, tumbling into a heap of silk scarving. "All the dark matter of this earth extends from me." Elizabeth was smashing plates in the sink, her hands a bloody mess, and Gus was asleep in the bathtub, facedown in an inch of water that would have killed him if Paris hadn't pulled him out. Raymond sat in the corner and wept.

A gull screamed above, its call lost in the wind. Paris was gripped with the sudden fear that he had arranged a subtle seabound bearing that would soon send him into the water. Digging in his instrument bag, he found the thermometer, then the balance gauge, and finally the altimeter, but it was no use; even if he could make a proper reading, he would need to figure the conversion from hectopascals to meters above sea level.

He put everything back and focused on soothing himself. The Channel below was undistinguished by chop or vessel but seemed far enough away for comfort. Everything was probably fine, and if it wasn't, there wouldn't be much fuss to it. He laughed aloud to think he had wanted to try for a distance record.

Just when he had made peace with the likelihood that his adventure would end more gracelessly than planned, he saw in the distance the craggy line of Sainte-Anne and blessed Auderville beyond. The sight of land startled him, and he pulled back so suddenly on the elevator that he thought for certain he had broken the pulley and was done for, that he would stall out and tumble, like one of the opera's paper programs he had folded and flown to make the children laugh from their box over the orchestra level, all of them watching its glide to the stage and ducking when it inevitably fell into the orchestra.

But the pulley caught and hauled, and *Cigare* ran true, nosing down as gentle as a calf, and then he was back on course, following a rail line, the roads and spires simple to gauge with the naked eye. A few hundred kilometers of easy navigation remained to the trip. Soon enough he would be in Issy-les-Moulineaux, with its shops and cafés. If it was warm enough, he might walk to Bellevue, picking up a baguette and something to drink along the way. They would all stay up late eating and talking. Though perhaps it was too cold to walk; he remembered he had read in the paper that winter in the capital had been so bitter that a starving wolf running through the streets had slaughtered a schoolgirl in broad daylight, leaving only a few bones and part of her pinafore. No shortage of surprises in the modern age.

Elizabeth takes her seat to enjoy the first recital at Bellevue

It was a stunning hall, with a freshly painted stage. The theatre at Belle-vue had previously served the lobby of the old hotel, and beautiful velvet seats had been installed where the guests used to take their tea. The ar-chitect had decided to keep the massive check-in counter intact at the back of the house, and Elizabeth half expected to find the girls back there, playing concierge and advising one another grandly on imagined day trips around a city they wouldn't have a chance to explore.

But of course the girls wouldn't dare fool around. They were back-stage with Isadora, who inspired in them such a serious nature it made Elizabeth question her own skills as an instructor. She had to admit that Isadora inspired respect; or perhaps, six mothers had impressed it on their girls. Either way, Isadora was the one who would turn them into dancing stars if only they worked hard enough and prayed to her every night.

Mother and Max had taken their seats before the others, so were forced to speak to each other. Elizabeth sat just in time to hear Max start in on the female body, using his hands to illustrate thick calves and broad shoulders. Any other woman would have been mortified, but Max was lucky enough to find Dora Duncan an easy audience, and as Trella arranged her score, he was engaging the older woman in his basic strength test, where she worked to press down on his outstretched hands. "Very good," he said. "Very, very good."

Someone clapped briskly backstage, and the performance started at once. Trella started with Chopin. In the first piece, all six girls played spirits made wicked by the night, rushing around in a coven. Then while Margot skipped among them, the older girls stood as sentient columns, animating one by one to follow the sprite. After that, they executed the Tanagra figures with a grace and patience beyond their years. Irma still led, but each girl's personality had begun to take shape. They turned from mood to mood as easily as laying out a deck of cards. Therese stepped as light as batting to cross the stage, turning at the waist to call the others, and Elizabeth had to resist the impulse to leap from her seat to follow; it was a perfect articulation. It was desire they inspired, not sexual, but bodily, an idea they had all been working toward for months.

Partway through the peasant mazurka, there came a noise at the back of the hall, an inarticulate banging as the door was forced against the thin locks straining to stay it. The girls stopped onstage, then the music, and the little audience nervously turned to see the door wrenched open to reveal Paris, windswept and worse for wear, beating the ice from his gloves against the concierge desk at the back of the hall. He held a valise and a wide canvas bag, and he ran his shaking hand through his hair. He looked like a traveling salesman who had been forced to work through a holiday to meet his quota and had reached his wit's end in the home of his largest client.

Trella stood from her piano, but Paris pointed at the stage until she sat and returned to the score. The girls scrambled to find their marks again as he came down and took a seat on the other side of Max. Elizabeth found it interesting that Isadora hadn't come out to check on the noise, which meant she either knew he was coming or didn't care.

Mother made a chuffing noise and leaned stiffly to allow her hands to be grasped. It occurred to Elizabeth that it was the first time the two had met; Mother hadn't left Oakland in ten years, and Singer had had no interest in traveling to California, feeling business prospects west of the Mississippi tacky and faddish. Elizabeth watched as the two of them whispered years' worth of condolences and congratulations and remarks on the weather, which, judging from the man's appearance, had taken a swift turn for the worse.

Irma and Erica made an arch with their hands, stretching as tall as they could. The others ran through one at a time and paused at the edge of the stage, lifting their arms as if they had just realized that they could not possibly continue their destined path on the planet and would have to ascend into heaven. And then, as if the sublimity of the moment was too much to bear, each of them withered and fled to the upstage curtain.

They came through a second time, and lined up for a third when Irma broke the arch to hear something that had been called out from the wing. She whispered to the others, who stopped where they stood. Trella held a minor chord as if she were waiting for someone to turn her page. None of them moved as the chord dwindled to nothing.

It was in total silence—her dancers still, her audience breathless— that Isadora made her return to the stage.

She entered, gallant in a crimson mantle, a robe regally wrapped around her body. Her hair was bound up with flowers and cords of thick red rope. The girls wavered in their positions, watching her steady step. Even the curtains flanking the stage swayed toward her as she passed.

Ceasing her movement upstage, she signaled to Irma and Erica to lift their arms again. The others dropped to the floor and lay prostrate in wonder. Isadora stepped under the trembling arch. The moment she passed, the older girls fell to the floor as well.

She spread her arms wide, holding out her reaching hands to take in the warmth of the light. The goddess had come to take dominion, to bless and destroy. Her eyes glowed with redemptive fury as the mantle parted to reveal her tunic, where the swell of her pregnancy had come to strain against the cloth. She lowered her arms and cradled her thickening body, her cheeks flushed by the lights. Isadora spoke, saying:

"It is a new Era."

Mother shrieked. "My child!" she cried, running for the stage.

"Mother!" Isadora returned, coming to her knees at the edge of the stage.

"My darling girl!"

"Mother, my dear Mother." Isadora took her mother's face in her hands and kissed her tenderly again and again on both cheeks. They held each other, weeping. The girls lay prostrate around them.

The rest of them watched from their seats. Paris shoved something into his valise, and before he closed the hasp, Elizabeth saw that it was a paper bag holding a baguette.

Max leaned over. "I don't think she's really crying," he said in a whisper.

On closer inspection it seemed he was right; Isadora seemed to be only mirroring her mother's expression, her open mouth trembling in the same precise way as she stroked the woman's hair.

"We should go," Elizabeth whispered back. She considered bringing Paris along but decided to leave him be.

Elizabeth and Max eased themselves from their chairs, waiting to see if anyone would notice. They left, holding hands.

It was cold outside, still snowing, but neither seemed to want to go back for their coats. Max put his arm around her as they walked.

They had almost reached the road when he doubled over, clutching his chest.

"What is it?" Elizabeth asked, alarmed.

She couldn't tell at first, but soon it was clear; he was laughing. He made a few constipated snorts and tried to straighten up. For a moment he controlled himself, his shoulders shaking, before he gave up with a snort, pressing his hands to his knees. He laughed, pounding the snow. It looked as if he might collapse.

"My word!" she said. She had never seen him like this, and the sight of it mystified her. She glanced back at the school and was relieved to see that nobody had followed them out. Unsure of what else to do, she reached out and patted his back.

He howled, senseless. Tears streamed from his eyes, but he made no move to wipe them away. She waited while he got it all out, holding himself against one of the brick pillars bounding the property.

"What is it?" she asked at last.

"She thinks," he said, gasping for air. "She thinks it is so easy."

The charm of a second ice storm is lost on the group

After a week without newspapers we've resorted to reading the old editions aloud to one another, changing the names to try to keep some mystery about it. None of the boxes on the third floor held any books, and we found the library shelves were bare except for a heavy set of texts describing varied financial systems in foreign lands. Paris picked up Afghanistan-Andorra and excused himself to his office. He's angry with me, of course.

This time the staff is trapped as well, and the cook has kept us all more or less happily alive with a series of indistinguishable meat pies. The girls and I can focus on a performance which will usher in the aforementioned new age. They anticipate such pleasure and love from their work that they beg me every morning to teach them more complex methods, as if I have been keeping a tumbling course from them. Irma seems particularly keen on perfecting herself and the others, which gives me a chance to relax and lean against the wall, the mirror a cool hand on my neck.

Right before the second storm, word came that Gaston Calmette was dead, killed by some awful woman. I wish I had paid him a visit the day

I returned to France! My last memory of him will have to be of his kindness at the children's service, where he kissed my hands and wished me peace again and again with such vigor it was as if he could brand me with the sentiment.

Calmette had been a gentleman of the finest sort. The woman shot him over some question of her own romantic life, the details of which nobody at all would even care about after a few boring afternoons listening to her go on about it. She had found him in his office—the very worst of all places!—and after it was done, she didn't flee, but waited for the police to pick her up, wrapping the pistol in a square of white lace while the poor man bled and died. She must have thought herself very clever to bring the lace.

There was a long piece about it in the newspaper the morning of the storm, so now we're stuck with the story. It has been torture to hear it again and again, and Elizabeth hasn't made it any better with her morbid speculation about who came to clean the carpet and what menial tasks the doomed man might have been pursuing at the moment Death arrived for her appointment.

Mother attends my rehearsals, and though it was a happy diversion at first and a chance to show her all I've learned, her presence wears a little thin. At the very least, she's agreed not to wear shoes in the room. She sits beside me in her stockings, holding her skirts off the polished floor as if the shine might muss them, and though her milky eyes can't distinguish the actual girls from their reflections, she smiles cheerfully and nods to keep time with the piano, more or less.

"That's quite well," she says.

"They're only warming up."

"Eight lovely girls who each hold a piece of the same soul. What a blessing to have such sweet souls near."

"Well, and there are six of them."

"Such heart," she says.

The child has begun to assert itself inside me with a ticklish feeling of soap bubbles bursting. Mother may not have seen it at the recital, but Elizabeth surely caught her up. Paris and I have settled into a situation in which he ignores me in favor of Antigua. Earlier we had a ripping fight about Ruthie Denis, that little snip from Newark who saw a tintype Cleopatra on a box of cigarettes and decided to model her entire career after it. Paris pointed out that I had an Oriental phase myself, and it was off to the races. It's good to have him here to fight whenever I like.

"No time like the present," I say. "Let's get started. The polka, ladies." The girls stop along with the pianist, a dull-looking German girl. They all stare with the same slack expression.

"Whats'it?" the little one asks.

"Don't be impetuous."

The little girl bursts into tears. She's a sickly one and too delicate. Each of them is a lovely green thorn to me.

Enough of this! I start the piano up again. "Watch them," I call back to Mother, who jerks her head in my direction, smiling.

Paris spends each morning in his office, a room set with old pieces. I recognize the carpet from the boat, something we kept on the bed on colder nights. The chaise from the old flat looks so comfortable that I fall onto it in a trance, listening to him complain about Elizabeth hoarding all the newspapers.

"Feeling a little tired?" he asks, startling me from the half sleep that could have lasted a minute or an hour. He's wearing a tan suit belted at the waist and tall brown boots.

"You look like an archaeologist."

"And what would I find in you, my dear?"

Stretching, I beckon him over. "Any number of things just below the surface." Taking his hands, I press them to my belly, where he holds them for a moment before he gets my meaning.

"Of course," he says. "Our love has led us to tragedy. My last goal was to create this school so that we might make some beauty on this sad earth for others."

"That's somewhat formal."

"Are you aware," he says, "of the funds I've put into the building alone? The underground plumbing was all rooted through, there was mold behind the kitchen walls. The whole place was bizarrely wired for electricity, a spider's web of wires behind the plaster. Switching on a bathroom light could send the whole place up. You don't save a second thought for the dangerous world, which puts these thoughts on the rest of us. And obviously you wouldn't appreciate that rushing a retrofit in the cold season has been an incredible expense. The electrician is working his way through the attic right now, and you had better believe he's charging by the hour day and night until the moment the path is cleared enough for me to kick him out. Last week I called on my contacts to enroll their daughters, but they were turned away, informed that you're taking only six girls this year. How do you expect to turn a profit?"

He never loses his strange smile, as if financial ruin is thrilling for him. Of course, the money talk has its usual humiliating effect, but if he notices my shame he doesn't attempt to ease it.

"And that's all before I hire a single staff member beyond the skeleton crew," he says. "None of the maids in this city will come to an interview for fear of a curse on their children. Everything has really spun out of control. That bastard Merz has the girls running the world's fastest mile, your mother follows you around like a blind shadow, and I really do think your sister is sneaking laudanum into her room for how she's behaving."

"I would love to see you try to prepare a meal yourself."

"Of course, it's fine," he says. "Do whatever you wish. You always have and always will. Only you have a hell of a way of showing gratitude."

"You were done with me! I thought certainly I wouldn't see you again—"

"Casting about Liguria like a bitch in heat—"

"—I wouldn't see you again, and you would have cast me out for entertaining the thought of another child with you, so it can't be helped that I went elsewhere. Also, it was Tuscany."

"Do you remember Lillie's eyes?" he asks.

That one sets me back. "Who the hell is Lillie?" There was a girl in Athens who made us each a crown of laurels and laughed like the villain she was when Paris consented to bow low enough so that she might pin it to his hair. She would have climbed onto his back the moment he offered his hand.

"Lillie," he says, "my wife."

His wife! Of whom he has not spoken unprompted in years, of course. A party guest mentioned her acquaintance once, and Paris turned the conversation to architecture so quickly that everyone assumed she had died, and a week later he found himself puzzling over a set of condolence cards from everyone in earshot.

Trying to recall Lillie's eyes, I think of our first and only meeting, at a party before there was any weight between us.

"They are gray," he says. "Like a dark sea."

At the party, she plucked a grape from a vine decorating the bar and excused herself to the other side of the room to sit and eat it. "I remember them being rather blue."

"I know the color of my own wife's eyes."

He must be readying himself to return to her in Florida, perhaps to take residence nearby, to begin courting her again in the respectful manner she would want and deserve; or maybe he only wants to remind me in insinuation of his living children, his girls, each as lovely and serious as her mother, four silent reminders of happier days. He has an easy avenue of escape while all I have are the little dancing plays I can fund with the last of my allowance.

"Go to your wife if you wish."

"What are you talking about?"

I glare at the whites of his eyes.

"You think you can dismiss me," he says. A slick of oily hair aggrandizes his ears. "I'll remind you, this is my property."

"This school bears my name, not yours. You may walk the grounds but the movement is mine. And I may occupy only one line in your obituary, but you will not appear in mine at all."

That sneering smile. "You don't suppose what will happen once I withdraw funding from this venture one month into its restoration?"

"I don't need a building to house an idea."

He sighs, returning to his desk. "Most women make an attempt to become more charming with age, Isadora. Did you consider that your own potential as an investment might not exactly appreciate over time?"

"I existed before you, and I will live long after your death. I will find new life for centuries to come!"

He picks up the finance book again. "Try not to be so predictable," he says.

There's nothing so promising as a chastening tone after a good bridge-burner. If he's still telling me what to do, he has to care enough to do it.

"You should try harder to be interesting," I say.

He grunts, turning the page.

"Darling," I say, "I'm tired of fighting."

"You're tired of it."

"Come here and kiss me. You're so handsome and easy to get along with."

"Stop it," he says, but he puts down the book. "Don't you have an afternoon class?"

"They'll be all right, they're afraid of Mother and the pianist is there too. Come and kiss me."

"Wasting an afternoon is no way to build a legacy. You've already invested"—he glances at his watch—"twenty minutes into this argument alone, and for nothing."

Hardly nothing! Rolling from the chaise, I find that the tendon has grown to bind my hips, wound tight from my spine. Crouching down, I rub the sore spot on my hip.

"You're out of practice," he says, offering his hand. He is most striking from above, a monolith of a man, a vertical field. "I would hope you would dance again for me sometime, if your condition can bear it."

Taking his hands and pressing them onto my hip bones, I show him where to apply a massaging touch. I wonder if he could squeeze me tight enough to unhinge my bones from where they lock together like thick wooden puzzle pieces. Patrick as a baby would take great pleasure in gumming a puzzle piece before throwing it clear into another room and, crawling for it, would cry the whole distance he had made; I know the feeling.

Paris pulls me close. My body shifts in contrast to his, shoulders and arms arching forward. My hips bear up under, guided by his hand. He could change the very course of my blood, damming the channels here and forcing its flow there, sending life through switchback veins. I hold myself painfully against his thumbs, which push into me so firmly it's as if he means to hook them into the scooping bone of my pelvis. If I were a mountain, he would set the drill to fix eyebolts for his hands and feet. I would shudder and drop a season of snow.

Releasing me, he turns away. "Tell your sister I need an invoice written for costuming and sundries."

"If you could just—"

"Thank you, dear." He's done it on purpose! The awful man. He waves me off, work to be done.

But I'm obedient about it, thinking of the gift he has given me in simply staying, though later I recall that the storm has locked us all in. He couldn't leave if he tried.

Paris watches her go, thinking of simpler biblical times and envying Job in the ash heap, his whole life around him a smoldering ruin

At least it would have been warm.

Isadora is surprised by Mother sitting patiently in the hallway, smiling at all who pass

"You should marry him," she says, speaking in the blithely pleasant manner of the insane.

"I told you to stay in the rehearsal room."

"He wants to support you."

"Were you spying on us?"

"And he loves you, despite your tendencies and everything you've done to him." She takes my offered arm and we walk together. "Think of it as a way to thank him for his service."

"Mother, I am not a war. If anything I am a lighthouse, beaming a—"

"You are such a war that I'm surprised there isn't a draft, but that's not my point. Look at how unhappy your sister is. Her friend Max is more interested in training the girls to lift barrels over their heads than in making her the center of a happy home. Moreover, he's pursuing the pianist. You two have it backward: a happy home lays the foundation for good work. And now she's preoccupied with lucky fortune and you've come to think that readers of *La Revue* can change your life."

"You're saying it's not possible?"

"If it were, your father would have dropped dead eating an ice-cream cone."

The sound of footsteps pounding through a far hall must mean the girls have been released early. Turning away from the sound, I guide us toward her room. Mother will want a rest before dinner.

"The press has changed me."

"The press makes too much of your affairs," she says. "They comment on your physique and coloring like you're a plucked hen in a shop-window. Do you enjoy that treatment? Do you think it enhances your legacy?"

"If only I had a simple old mother who would only pray for me."

She laughs heartily. "I'll pray to whatever god you like if you'll keep a good tall man. I'm sure Paris would be happy to intimidate any reporter if you only let him. He told me so himself."

"Could you stop consulting with him? I'm not a child."

"You are my child, though. They say you've gained weight, you know, they speculate on your diet."

"There's plenty meat to go around."

"And larger by the day," she says firmly, flicking my stomach. "I only want them to adore you as much as you deserve to be adored." At her bedroom door, she takes my hand. "Come and brush your mother's hair."

At her mirror, she removes the pins and bands and thin ribbons holding together her chignon, plucking each one out by memory and arranging the tiny arsenal on her dresser. Her hair eases out of its confinement and falls well past her shoulders. "It's tender," she says, handing me the cushion brush. "Now tell me, what do you think of Max? Don't you agree he's wasting her time?"

"I'll miss you when you've gone home, I really will."

"He's a sneaky little man. I thought I was alone in the library for upward of ten minutes before I realized he was in there with me." She grits her teeth as I work the brush through. "He was sitting in one of the high-backed chairs, staring straight ahead as if waiting to be called. Do you think he is mentally balanced?"

"Somewhere along the way he picked up the idea that he could alter my curriculum."

"He wasn't even reading a book, just gazing at the wall, a strange look on his face—oh, I said that's tender—there's something about him, don't you think? All his funny ideas. I liked him at first but he wears on me now. If our family could be collected into one breathing body, he would be an extra thumb somebody tried to sew on near the wrist. It looked well enough for a time, but it's not a healthy bond, and likely to infect."

"Paris might feel himself in the same position."

"That man is bound to us with stronger stuff, Patrick saw to that."

It's strange to hear her say his name. "I'm sorry you never got to meet the children, Mother."

She starts to cry a little but sees my strange expression and stops, touching my hand. We stay like that awhile, looking at ourselves in the mirror.

"Did I tell you about Elias, my dear friend back in Oakland?" she asks. "A fine man, a man of science. Every year he runs an auxiliary luncheon that funds the school for the entire year, and then he dresses up as Santa Claus and gives out gifts, sometimes during Christmas but sometimes in the middle of July, just for fun. And everyone does laugh!" She goes on like this for a while as I brush and plait her hair. "He reminds me of Paris. A kind man and well read. You owe quite a debt to Paris in the literal sense, in cash I mean."

She must hope against reason that Paris is the father of this child. I consider the many and varied ways I might correct her. I could start with the story of the moment of conception, stripping to the waist to act the scene out. Elizabeth could come and play the part of the bathing machine.

"I went swimming every day in Viareggio," I begin, working a strip of velvet through her hair. "It was a morning ritual."

"Too cold," she grumbles, as if she's put one toe in the Mediterranean since her honeymoon forty years ago.

"I liked it, though. I met such fascinating people. One man in particular—"

"I found Viareggio to be very dull, and the shops were all closed. Of course, we were there in November, because your father wanted to save on the passage."

"There was a real community of artists. Eleonora says the painters enjoy a special kind of light that comes off the water. And there is such a sentimental feel to the region. They cremated Shelley on the beach, you know. And there was one man—"

"How awful!" she says, reaching back to check my work. "A bonfire dirtying the sand. You always did have a knack for finding the least romantic image. Listen, I'll tell you about romance: picture your tall, handsome father walking down the passeggiata in Viareggio."

"Mother—"

"He would step the length of a lesser man with every stride." She dries her tears with her own braid, which makes me see her first as a young married woman and then as a child, then as a baby placed on a parcel of dried grass on her daddy's land, the world a marble blur to her infant eyes. "Poor Shelley, though," she says. "Poor Shelley!"

Romano Romanelli
cura di Raffaello Romanelli
Viale Alfredo Belluomini, Toscana

R—

How can I put this delicately? Isadora is suffering from a condition she picked up on the road that will show its symptoms for a few more months before depositing a tumor on the rest of us to raise. She has been very vague about her season after Greece but Penelope writes to report she converted a suite at the Pera Palace into her personal harem. I know that otherwise she's been running around with Duse, in Florence last I knew, and good riddance to them all.

I'd like to start showing myself a better time. I paid my own fare to the Jardin des Plantes first, in which they have a lovely series of animal exhibits. The girls are all saving their pocket money for the promised tour and said they would come with me only if I paid their way, a trick they must have learned from my sister, which didn't work on me. Max said he was too tired, I can't take Mother anywhere, and Paris has locked himself in the library. They're all a fantastic disappointment, but I decided I would still like to go and be my own best company.

It was a jungle scene at the Jardin des Plantes, kept very warm with torches. I saw glass-walled houses of great blooming trees fawning to the floor and rows of flowers I could never have imagined even if I were given a trunk of colored pencils and a long weekend.

The animal enclosures were even more fascinating. At the center of the park is a series of great walled pits, and in each pit, an animal stalks the ground: a black bear or buffalo with his snout in a trough, a pair of lions, a tiger. All in separate pits of course, or else they would have all torn each other to pieces. I can think of a great many political events that could have found rousing success from this method.

I spent most of my time watching a great-maned lion, in a pit broader and more deep than the others and surrounded by heavy iron bars. Though I stood in a large crowd of ladies and gentlemen a few meters above him, he kept his eyes trained on mine. The creature paced, fixed on me all the while, making his displeasure known with roaring that vibrated the bars I clutched.

Standing over him, I felt an insane urge; I wanted to climb over the gate and drop down into the pen with him, to take his mane up in my fists and hold him before he slaughtered me and feasted on my body. They might write about me in the paper and some mild woman would lose her appetite over breakfast. In a thrilling moment, I knew my life's true purpose.

A policeman standing by mistook my desire for trepidation and assured me that the lion's teeth had been removed long ago, and even if he got hold of me, his jaws would only gum and suckle like a cub. I burst into tears and the officer turned and walked away, satisfied. Life will defeat us all!

Elizabeth folded and sealed the letter and addressed it in her wavering script before tucking it into the stack with the others. None of her letters to Romano had come out quite right, and she decided to wait until she had precisely expressed herself before making her thoughts official by mail. It had been almost a year since she last saw him, and she certainly wouldn't send anything less than the best.

Isadora entered as she was putting away her supplies. "You would not believe," she said, her eyes darting strangely about the room.

"Believe what?"

"Oh, only Mother." She waved it off. "I meant to read the paper, but Paris said you had them all."

Elizabeth pointed to her bedside table, where the whole collection was stacked, a month's worth, with extras on the floor.

Isadora picked one from the top of the stack. "Have you memorized all the rapes and murders?"

"Some of us would like to have a fuller sense of life than what we experience firsthand. The fact that it's mostly horrors is tangential."

"It all makes for a fine distraction, I'm sure." She tossed the page onto the bed. "Elizabeth, I've been thinking. We've spent so many years together, and countless hours of labor. We manage a business, and both of us contribute equally. Isn't it time to call a truce and allow a friendship to grow between us?"

"I wasn't aware we had been feuding," Elizabeth said, trying to sound casual. Was her sister accusing her of some betrayal or questioning her commitment to the school, or was there some other complaint, far more insidious? There was no way to know the angle Isadora would take in an attack, and this idea of truce was a new strategy, one she didn't know how to defend against.

"I'm extending an olive branch. All my life you've been older and wiser, and in my own way I've always followed your lead."

"Mother must have really worked you over."

Isadora didn't respond. She was standing over the desk, flipping through the envelopes addressed to Romano and the humiliating drafting pages underneath.

"Romano," she said vaguely.

Elizabeth held back the impulse to run to the desk and throw herself over the letters, an action that would only implicate her further.

"Yes," she said. "Actually, you're right. Let's be dear friends."

Her sister looked up. "Something is changing."

"What's changing? What are you talking about?"

But Isadora left without another word, walking briskly in a way that struck Elizabeth as very uncharacteristic, seeing as how she never seemed to care if she was late for an appointment. It was only after she left that Elizabeth realized she had walked out with the most recent letter to Romano, as if it were her own.

Isadora loses her temper with the girls

The worst thing is their preoccupation with their own bodies in the mirror. Irma looks as if she is plotting out her memoirs, and the others skip from one side of the room to the other, not even skipping in the right way, putting all the weight on their heels as they stare at themselves. The silly ribbons they've wrapped around their wrists and ankles make them look like marionettes clipped from their strings.

I have to knock on the piano lid to get their attention, rousing the pianist from her nap.

"Focus! Nobody will pay to see six girls playing pretend onstage when they can look out their windows and get the same show for free. You are tasked with sensing and describing with your bodies the very future of the world. Gather round, I have a new lesson for you.

"A mother dies of sadness. The only proper way to understand it requires a long evening, after six hours on the floor, a bottle of wine tethering each hand to reality. But I will do my best to give you the sense of it regardless. Fraulein?"

The pianist looks up from her gloved hands, which have been resting in her lap.

"Play 'Death of Ase.'"

"We're not doing the Schubert?"

"'Death of Ase,' Fraulein."

"Which key?" she asks. I can already picture her waiting to board the train back to Darmstadt, looking at her cheap watch, a costume piece fashioned after a Moser and affixed on dyed pasteboard.

"I don't care which key, the original key."

She watches as I crouch and then sit, then lie flat against the floor.

"The original key is C minor," she says once I'm settled.

"Nice and slow, please."

She begins the movement. From a flat back I roll to one side, lifting my spine bone by bone and twisting subtle against the ground, as slow as the movement of the earth itself. At the fourth phrase from the end, my cheek presses to the ground. As the next phrase opens, I release the tension in my body, allowing it to move subtly closer to the floor. Breathing out, I find an utter stillness for the last two notes—an ominous sound, the very last on earth.

The piano's hammers thump as she lifts her foot off the pedal. We take residence in the blank silence that follows, until someone sighs and the moment is over. I open my eyes and see with satisfaction that the pianist is crying; this will serve as my lesson to the girls.

"Listen well, all of you." I address them still resting on my side. "In order to express grief, you have to physically enter the emotion. One way in is to recall some moment of loss from the past, but such a tactic only produces a result the size of your body, and nobody more than ten feet away will feel it. In order to affect the room, therefore, you must seek out the grief in the room and draw it into your body. It won't destroy anyone else until it threatens to destroy you. Your audience should be made afraid, they should wonder on the walk home whether they have been drugged and transported to a foreign land. This"—here I point to the pianist, who removes her gloves to wipe her eyes, humiliated—"is the purest experience of art, and it is your only goal."

Irma raises her hand but lowers it without asking a question.

"In order to understand the greatest joys of life, you must do more than open yourself to its greatest sorrows," I say, "you must invite it to join you in your home and beguile it to stay. You can live well enough, strolling by the shopwindows of grief and going in before the rain. But you will never know the true beauty and brutality of life, and you cannot be a true artist.

"If I were your mother, I would want to shield you from these things. But as your teacher, I want you to experience it all. Protecting you would be doing you a disservice, and you would grow to hate the protection I tried to give you out of love. Do you understand?"

The girls sway like tethered airships. "May I use the restroom?" one of them asks, the one without good sense.

"You needn't ask. Do you need to be shown the way?" After she goes, I turn to the rest. "I will bear us a child," I say. "When I was beaten down by the waves, a man came to me and together we made a child, a son. My body is nothing less than an act of faith in the loving world. You will care for this child as your own, for he will be your very own; I have created him as a gift to our movement. Through him you will come to know the joy and agony of motherhood as I have known it. You will meet in flesh the new era set to burst over these dark and ordered days. Even now I can feel it building. Come, approach me."

They queue up to receive a kiss on each cheek. As I hold each of them in turn, I finally come to know them. These girls are precious to me: born in this century to die in the same, these are the girls who will dance at my funeral. These little ones will carry my message to every part of the world.

The gentlemen enjoy an argument

"Well now, that's too much," Max said, but when he looked up to remark further to the group, he found that only Paris remained in the library. Max had been so absorbed in his reading that he didn't notice that the women had gone up to bed. Paris looked up, waiting to hear what was supposedly too much, in order to speculate on what could be done about it.

Max would have preferred to have a larger audience, but the other man was waiting patiently, and so he continued, annoyed. "It says here that the gale last week in Lyon destroyed aircraft hangars worth eighty thousand pounds. What is that in marks? That can't be right."

"Hangars are an incredibly expensive proposition," Paris said, closing the book he was reading without marking the page. "I happen to be an expert."

Max settled uneasily in the chair and accepted the teacup presented to him by the butler Paris had hired that morning; a large, silent man who returned to his position by the window.

"Consider your standard barn-size object," Paris said. "Simple enough, yes? But this is no standard structure. First, you must make all of it using steel, which should be double- or triple-layered to prevent and control moisture. That's going to be heavy, and will require bracing and support strong enough to bear the weight, along with specialized bracing. The roof needs to be layered and insulated, and that doesn't even take into account the ingress, which will be a nonstandard height and placed on casters, like this." He set down his scotch so he could demonstrate with two hands. "Then of course, if you're keeping more than one craft, you're dealing with an additional expense in expanding both your ingress and your floor plan. At that point it's almost simpler to build a second hangar, and then you have multiple pieces of property and multiple contractors, most of whom have to be trained. So then, naturally, the structures themselves are divorced of any binding logic. They take on individual personalities."

Max considered taking on another personality to stop the man's speech. He couldn't decide if it would feel more natural to interrupt with political conjecture or to stand and run from the room.

"Distinctive characteristics," Paris said. "And plenty can go wrong. One has walls that sweat in the cold, and the other harbors ants that will destroy your instruments. And you have to keep up with all of this, or else you risk the loss of your larger investment, the aeroplane itself, which has its own troubles—"

Max held up his teaspoon as if to interject, but there was nothing he could possibly add. He tried to remain engaged as Paris launched into a history of industrial construction along with a colorful sidebar on the labor habits of the residents of Paignton.

"Have you toured the field at Johannisthal?" Paris asked at last, and Max was so distracted by his own boredom that he almost missed the question.

"I have not," he said, just in time.

"You really should. It's fascinating. Unparalleled construction and workmanship."

"I haven't spent much time in Berlin."

Paris moved his head and neck in a way that made him look rather like a startled bird. "Why, it's the jewel of your empire," he said. "I have to admit I didn't quite understand Berlin myself at first, but a fellow convinced me to pay a visit to the Wertheim department store near the Potsdamer Platz before I made any decision.

"I arrived on a Thursday afternoon to find a temple to commerce, pardon my sacrilege, strung with pneumatic tubes and dressed for the Christmas season as a gold-gilt fairy kingdom. The very sight of it immediately expanded the bounds of my imagination, doubled it at least. I passed many pleasant hours in the winter garden and bought a few things here and there for my girls. This was when I was a younger man, you see." He narrowed his eyes, as if the younger man in question might be leaning against the far wall. "They had an extravagant display devoted to our sewing machines, with a seamstress there assembling a gown from scraps of fabric, a patchwork of silver and silk. It was something else entirely. I asked my host to sketch the seamstress and went off to wait. Hours later I woke in a display of feather coverlets. It was embarrassing, but the man they sent to watch me assured me it happened all the time. I bought him a pint, good man. He had a wife in Rostock."

"You're saying, your opinion on the entirety of Berlin is derived from a department store."

Paris took up his scotch. "It is no small feat to work in the retail sector, you know. You have to romanticize for people the act of buying fine things. Not the things themselves, but the act of purchase. Very tricky indeed. It requires the invention of desire and the placement of that desire in physical bounds. It's very difficult to reliably house desire. It requires serious work, particularly during the Christmas season."

"To tell the truth, I don't much care for Berlin," Max said.

"Now I doubt that sincerely. Other than the Zionists, I found it to be a deeply inclusive and modern place." He had the easy assurance of a wealthy man. Max couldn't place it in the moment, but he realized later, while draping his socks over the radiator to warm them before bed, that Paris had the same tone of voice of a certain boy Max remembered from school who would recite his multiplication tables while administering beatings behind the gymnasium.

He tried to ignore his nervous dread. This was only a debate among grown men in a library after dinner, the kind of thing he always imagined he would enjoy. "I own shoes older than anything you could find to love about Berlin," Max said, "including your Wertheim's."

"Why, you're not a true German."

Max lifted his chin a little. "I was born in Vienna."

"That explains it. Miss Duncan loves Vienna, but I find it overall a little smug. Do you know what I mean? And driving in Austria is a nightmare. I pass through half a dozen towns where I'm suddenly on the wrong side of the road."

"Vienna is beautiful." It was strange to hear him call her Miss Duncan, as if she were a charge or a child. "And it was an inspiring place to grow up."

"Left side, right side. No warning. Again and again, the officers would stop me to address the flow of traffic in dialects I couldn't possibly understand. I had to start carrying a roll of notes just to buy them all off." He smiled as if he had just claimed an ability to survive a winter on flour mixed with lard.

"I'm certain you could," Max said vaguely. "Trella mentioned you had a chance to observe a calisthenics class?"

Paris shook off the memory of his season in Austria. "That's right, I was meaning to mention it. You're having the girls run the length of the hall forty times, yes? And then lifting iron weights?"

"They've grown quite accustomed."

"Right. The thing is, Miss Duncan doesn't like it at all. Too much thoughtless movement confounds the body and removes its discipline, she claims. Perhaps she has already spoken to you."

Max set down his cup. "I'm sorry, which one of them doesn't like it?"

"Why, Isadora. She explained it to me. Apparently the balance is all off in their legs. Too much strength takes the power from their solar plexus, rather like weighting an engine at its furthest point. It throws off the whole works, from her perspective."

"And what do you think?"

He frowned. "It's not my area of expertise."

"But you've sat through enough performances to stage your own. Surely you have an opinion."

"And see, there's something I've been practicing." Paris lit a cigarette, which he had extracted from a silver box presented by his butler. "You perfectly illustrate it here. The cobbler knows his leather, and so when my shoes are brought in, I trust him to determine the best way to repair a grommet. The machinist knows the works of the engine more intimately than he knows his own body, so if he sees this gasket or that fitting should be recast and replaced, I'm happy to go along with his recommendation. As the head of a number of households—personal, industrial, and fiduciary—I've found it's important to respect expertise. It's the mark of a good manager. And so when it comes to instructional or artistic matters of dance, I find it's best to defer to the greatest dancer the world has ever known."

"You regard her very highly."

His smile vanished. "And you don't?"

Max was surprised to realize he hadn't thought about it. "I mean to say, you must not have seen Nijinsky or Pavlova. Isadora is a fascinating dancer, to be certain. But the greatest? In terms of technical skill or invention? Or are you referring to her lectures or—"

Paris flew across the room like a shot. Before Max knew what was happening, he had been hauled up to standing, the other man's big fists balled together to grip the collar of his shirt.

"She is your employer," Paris said. His voice was calm, but Max felt the hands against his throat shaking with fury.

Max squirmed against the man's knuckles pressing individually to his throat. He smelled scotch and the chocolate trifle they had both enjoyed for dessert just an hour before.

"Of course—" Max sputtered. "Yes, of course she is."

Paris released him and walked to the bar cart as if nothing had happened. He looked like a muscled dog, a bulldog perhaps—Max didn't well know breeds. The butler was waiting with a fresh glass nestled in a hemstitched napkin. Paris took the drink and used the napkin to dab the spittle from the corners of his mouth. "It's important to know the hierarchy," he said.

"Yes, of course."

"Social, physical, spiritual. These are levels at which each of us operate independently and together. An intricate system, if you think about it."

"But that's just what I'm saying—" Max hesitated, making sure that Paris wasn't going to come and throttle him again. "Our students could stand at the apex of the physical hierarchy, the top of the charts. They could usher in a new age of womanhood, a physical ideal."

"But they aren't women. The Isadorables are little girls."

"The Isadorables—I don't much care for the name."

Max crouched protectively when the larger man walked over to him, but Paris only extended his hand.

"If we're selling the concept of them dancing in unison, the market demands a charming name," Paris said as they shook hands. "Members of the press always appreciate when you do some of the work for them."

Now that the fight was over, Max wished that he had brought his old tobacco tin into the library, and moreover that he had learned to roll and smoke cigarettes. It would have suited the moment very well indeed. But the moment was over, and Paris walked to the door.

"Good night," Max said.

"You'll have to broach the issue of strength training with Miss Duncan, though I'm afraid you may have already lost the battle. She is shifting to a method a little more"—he placed his glass lightly on the offered tray—"comprehensive."

The butler rolled the cart behind him as they went. Max listened to their footsteps recede along with his hopes of founding a theoretical movement. Once again, the momentum he had carefully gathered around his ideas was stripped away.

He thought of Isadora's shoddy teaching theory. She would have the girls lie like corpses on the stage, then send them squealing across the lawn, banners flying from their outstretched arms. They were forced to memorize sequences by watching her repeat them, arguing the moves among themselves while she went off for a nap. There was no method to it, and she was apparently cruel to Trella as well, a woman who deserved only protection and love.

He knew one thing for certain: Isadora Duncan didn't care a bit about the girls. When it came to their training, she offered them scraps, as if they were kitchen dogs. Meanwhile Max was laying out a full meal to no notice. Isadora had a career beyond the success of the girls, but the success of the girls was Max's only interest and the culmination of his life's work as well.

He wouldn't have minded her criticism had she been open to his ideas in the first place. But the moment he had presented a way to improve them in every element of their training—a theory, but a damned good one—the opportunity was taken from him.

He felt as he did as a boy, standing over Benjamin Franklin's tiny grave. He had assumed that when he attached his name and talent to the institution, it would mean adding his own voice to its progress. In the end, everyone seemed happy enough to ignore the very world he intended to improve. And Singer was the worst of them. His father would have been ashamed.

Max picked a volume from the bookended line on the desk, something about merchant figures. Opening it to the center, he poured the last of his tea into it, aiming for the center of the spine. He watched it seep into the binding before he closed the book, used the edge of it to brush the excess liquid onto the floor, and replaced the book on the shelf. In the morning he would speak with his employer.

Romano Romanelli
cura di Raffaello Romanelli
Viale Alfredo Belluomini, Toscana

R—

When I think of you, I think of breakfast. I remember how you took your coffee and the distracted way you would read the same paragraph over again, your dog-eared pages, your pastry on a plate. From these crumbs I have created a constellation of certainties between us. My fantastic mind conjures hours of talk about the world, bloody as it has become and spinning out of control. My mind is charitable enough for joy as well: a home in the country, a dog warming our feet. At times I conjure up a child in a high chair between us, some sexless thing mangling a strawberry in its fat little hands. Are infants allowed to eat strawberries? I don't care.

I thought I saw Mother standing in the garden the other day, but it turned out to be a rather large stone vase. Soon enough I suppose she'll take her things and go, leaving her goodbyes with the maid. She doesn't have the energy to make a good scene the way she used to, and I think that depresses her. It certainly depresses me.

As for the others: the girls are well enough, talking often of New York. Paris is having some men in Issy-les-Moulineaux make repairs on his aeroplane, and he threatens to take us up in it sometime, the horror. Isadora reminds me of a priest with the serious way she walks all night through the halls.

Max had been sitting in on all my classes, watching the girls and taking extensive notes, refusing to remove his street shoes, though he knew I hate it. He was making the girls terribly nervous and put me in a bad mood as well, bringing in photographs of gymnasts for us to study. Finally I banned him after the tension became too great and I couldn't get the girls to stop crying long enough to listen to me.

All he wants is a chance to make himself heard. I pity him and want him to have his say, but it's already too hard to claim a piece of land for ourselves to worry about someone else's plot. Mother goes on and on about her Oakland acre, but digging into the garden she claims to own would yield the bones of men who laid their own claim in blood long ago. It's the same way for the rest of us. The earth harbors history's warbling tide, impossible to chart a reliable course and foreign even to the stars. But I will say this: when he doesn't get his way, Max is no fun at all.

Isadora charts her own course

I took a rare walk to town for some breakfast and met a doorman who told me a woman demanding the vote in London attacked a painting with a cleaver. How strange! I'd prefer to let the men destroy themselves with such games while the women live in peace. To me the vote looks like a passion play of equality, a screen to hide the smoke. But I might feel differently if I was making someone's dinner.

The doorman also said a volcano erupted, though he couldn't remember where, and when I said I hoped it was near enough to see the city covered in ash, he only tipped his hat. The world is just as strange as ever and no darker than before, despite what Elizabeth says. Soft gray ashes, fluttering along the way! The children died a year ago, and last night I swallowed the last of their ashes and licked the pouch that carried them. For the first time, I miss them, though I only have to cradle myself to hold them near.

After I saw the doorman, I bought a warm bun and a newspaper. The Champs-Élysées will put on *Lohengrin* in August; by then the child will be born and I should be up and around, and perhaps Paris will join me in seeing the show.

Walking home, I think of Viareggio, the current there and the man. People must have read that the Duncan sisters were convalescing in Greece and everyone made a wish that the two of us would find many things in common and grow closer than we had ever been. How fortuitous! Now we have Romano.

Back at Bellevue, I take a daily practice alone in my room: I lie on the floor with my legs straight in the air; then, rolling my ankles to keep the blood flowing, I stretch my legs wide. My bones have softened enough to allow this tender pose, legs spread to bear the world, hips arched to kiss the floor.

This child is kinder than the other two. Patrick at this stage liked very much to huddle up against my spine and kick gleefully at its vertebrae.

It was during a long performance that he most memorably asserted himself. I was employing my greatest skills as a mother by ignoring him to pose as varied figures on a vase and then creating with my body a sense of the vase itself, so that my audience might feel intimately connected with the antiquated past. Something about my position or the lights or my pride itself must have inspired him, the vengeful little god. He made a brilliant extemporaneous attack on my sciatic nerve, leveraging himself against my ribs to strike the worst of the blows. He seemed to be gnawing on my spine. For the finale, he delivered one sharp kick to my bladder, which released a strong and glorious stream of urine down both my legs. This would have been a terrific scandal if it hadn't come at the precise moment I was turning the vase as if to upend it over my body. The crowd gasped to see the water flowing down my skirts and slowly across the floor. Such magic happens when the people have a little faith!

Lately our morning rehearsal lasts six hours before we break for lunch, coming together again in the afternoon. I have them bring reams of paper. All of them gather around and spend the first hour sketching me, noting the rise and fall of my costume with my breath. The smallest details make the whole.

This morning I asked them to bring empty crates from the larder to give me a short platform, an altar. As they sketch, I try to create in my own body the memory of the children laid out in their burial clothes—a vibrating stillness, as if the particles that gave them life felt a common regret in leaving and thus lingered as long as they could. When I have the girls try to create the pose themselves, they mistake it for total stillness, though Irma tries to shiver some at least.

We work like this for hours, locking the doors against interruption. The scullery maid leaves a pot of tea in the hall and throws pebbles at the outside window when she goes, thinking us overserious.

When Irma goes to fetch the tea, we're all surprised to see Max crouching to lift the tray in a sad attempt at gallantry that places him on his knee, in deference to us.

"Leave it," I say, from my position on the altar.

He sets the tray down and goes back for his valise, inviting himself into the room. The girls sit and drink their tea, watching him in silence.

"Good morning," he says. "Could I perhaps observe?" He is a small man who wears a suit in the size he wishes he was, making himself appear even smaller in the process.

"Of course," I say, hardly able to conceal my annoyance. "Only keep quiet."

He makes a strange little salute and goes to one of the corners. I can hear his dress shoes on my floor, and it takes some effort to push away the image of the shallow half-moon shapes they are pressing into the soft wood. At last he is still.

This is the mourning sequence, which I have blocked as a processional. The idea at first was that their arms would be held in front of them, facing the sky, as if they have brought ghostly branches to lay at my head and feet. In the course of rehearsal I found the girls quickly fatigued holding their arms like that, which I thought at first suited the anguish they should be experiencing and asked them to continue, but then Therese lowered one shaking arm a little and I found I liked the effect, which appeared as if she was carrying a swaddled child. In the course of our study they became spirits laying infants around the altar of the eternal Mother. I knew we were on the right path because their movements began to deepen, as if they had earned some purpose. They cultivate a vibration in me, the sense of a tuning fork pressed to my sternum making an echo in my chest.

We're running this very sequence when Max starts coughing.

How strange it must feel, to lose control of one's own body! The cough might have begun as a subtle gesture of displeasure or discomfort, but soon enough he can't stop himself, and hacks away like an old man, pressing his palm to my mirror. The girls stop and stare. On my gestured command, one of them trots over and pats him perfunctorily on the lower back as he gasps for breath. The others hold their pose, arms frozen in place.

"Forgive me, girls," he says. "Forgive me. I only hoped to see a little more movement. This is a very slow scene. Is there not typically music?"

He waits for a response, which does not come, and the discomfort of the silence starts him coughing again.

"Ponderous," he manages.

"It's a funeral," Irma says.

"It does seem so, very slow. Not much to it, physically. And then I imagine there will be a rebirth?" Extracting a cloth to hold across his mouth, he points at me on the altar, seizing as he tries to stifle himself.

"We're not certain," says another.

"You're not certain?"

"We haven't decided."

"Teacher hasn't decided," says Irma.

"I see," he says. "Teacher has the final say on a variety of topics." He swipes the cloth across his mouth. Would that all his shored-up liquid coalesce and dissolve him.

The girls watch me, waiting, each of their arms still obediently lifted. Margot holds her pose. Even the child inside me stops his movement. Only Max continues, folding his cloth and placing it in his pocket.

"Final say," he repeats. "In fact, Frau Duncan, I came to address this very topic."

Lifting myself elegantly from my wooden altar is no small order, but the simple act of placing my feet back on the floor gives me the strength I need to continue. It's a nice reminder that he walks the same earth as I do, yet he chooses to live this way, as a coward. I raise my chin, regarding him through eyes slightly narrowed by an absolute disdain for his presence.

"Get out."

"Fraulein?" he asks. His face blanches as if I have physically reached into his body and pinched off a vein to his neck.

The girls look from him to me, eyes wide with anticipation.

"Go and get your things," I say. "Collect your books and your lecture notes, gather up your inability to communicate directly with any human, take your chippy pianist, and get the hell out of my school, forever."

"But my philosophy—"

"Watching your piggy lips sputter has been reward enough for months, but now I want you gone. You think I could not see you scheming? How dare you. Take your place in the anal tendon of artistic merit, you disease. You don't have a bit of philosophy you didn't scrape off the shoes of greater men, and there is no greater man than me. I am your very own father and mother both, and I am putting you out on your ass.

"You humiliate me with your very presence! Go on, this instant. Go ply your sad trade elsewhere. Try your hand in a college or carnival. They can come laugh in your face instead of only behind your back. I haven't wasted a moment of concern on your half-bit ideas. I know everything in your mind, you staggering shit, and I hate it."

He reels back in surprise, his shoes leaving a thick black streak on the wood floor. The girl who was comforting him during the coughing spell takes off in a sprint to the other side of the room.

"All right," he says, holding up his hands. "All right. Only one thing, my theory—"

"I know your theory, you idiot. And your opinion on my method, though you have not been brave enough to express it directly. You are so deeply tucked into the pocket of my good grace that I must dig you out with the crook of my finger in order to flick you off like the offending chunk of wet garbage you have become to me. Go back to Darmstadt and mind some failing farm. Make your lectures to a cow. Write letters to my sister if you want, she will use the pages to steady her desk."

"I'll leave," he says. "It's all right." In grasping for his valise, he nearly tumbles, looking like a fawn slipping on black ice.

"You hack! It is not all right. You have failed to see how each planet in my orbit is lashed to me with diamond thread. Your lover, your students, your confidante men; they would each of them betray you in a moment, and they have. Everyone in this school has given you up for fun. Every subtle thought you've had was transmitted to my ear before you even finished thinking it. Now go on, get out of my sight."

He doesn't wait another moment, bowing as he runs to cross the studio, his bag banging against his thigh.

In an act of genius I never would have thought of myself, Irma unbuckles her sandal and throws it after him. It hits him flat on the ass as he grapples with the door, causing him to leap as if one of us has flown over and bit him. The girls burst into wild applause as he flings open the door and slams it behind him, and they keep up their clapping for Irma's sandal on the floor as if it might animate and provide an encore. And so I have one less mouth to feed.

Max is obliged to take his leave

Elizabeth was finishing a letter at Max's desk when he burst into the room.

"I wanted to use your desk," she said, folding the letter into a book and turning to another chapter.

Ignoring her, he went for his old leather suitcase, picking it up with such force that one of the handle's fasteners split and wagged against his thigh as he transferred the suitcase bodily to the bed.

"What's going on?" she asked. "Where are your shoes?"

"Your sister," he said. He balled up the shirts that had been delivered from the laundry and stuffed them into the suitcase along with his note-books, shaving kit, picture postcards of Darmstadt, his velvet pencil pouch, and a button that had sprung the previous day from his vest. On top he arranged his books, six large volumes of study on the subject of the human body. He latched the case and tightened two large leather straps around it. "Your sister is a God-forsaking, linen-draped nightmare."

"Are you crying?"

"She's dismissed me," he said, leaving a streak of pencil lead when he wiped the tears from his face. "She said she knew my thoughts, my theories and opinions. How did she know, Elizabeth?"

"You broke your old suitcase. Here, let me have a look—"

"Don't touch it!" He threw the case down and leapt at her, finding the thin collar of her robe and pulling her forward. "Answer me! How did she know?"

Elizabeth remembered all the times he had lost his temper during party games, the rage that filled his red-rimmed eyes. She thought she had seen the extent of his physical malice, but this was different. He was on her, and she was afraid.

"I don't know what you're talking about," she sputtered. "I haven't the faintest idea."

She heard the material of her robe straining against his fists, its delicate thread snapping stitch by stitch. She found herself hoping that he might rip it so that he would see what he had done, and be sorry. "Please," she said, her voice shaking.

He released her and got down on the floor to reach under the bed, coming back with one of his slippers, which he flung against the far wall. He looked up at her, crouched like an animal.

"I don't know where your other one is," she said.

"Women should be strong," he said. "Think of Cleopatra, of Catherine the Great, Joan of Arc at the stake. Imagine if they had possessed the physical strength to match their will. The Blessed Virgin, heavy with child, holding out until they reached a proper town for her to labor on clean linens; think of the order such an action would bestow upon the faith, the palliative sense of comfort. Physicians would be canonized with the saints they treated.

"Imagine Marie Antoinette fighting off the mob at the Tuileries, burning the place to embers, and emerging from the smoldering frame with Louis-Charles on her back. Her monarchical might dominating France. Can you imagine what it would do for the empire?"

"If you—"

"Shut up!" he shouted over her. "Shut up! I'm not speaking just to please myself! You can't possibly understand what I'm trying to say if you don't listen long enough for me to say it. Otherwise you are only employing your best guess, which, I can assure you, does not match my theories, not even remotely." He pounded his fist into the floor to emphasize his point. "There is absolutely no reason why Isadora wouldn't embrace physical strength as a female ideal."

"It contradicts her artistic movement," Elizabeth said. "To find the beauty of life and to express that beauty in the body."

"To hell with the artistic movement!" he looked at her, his weak chin lifted. "Also, Singer is a godamned anti-Semite."

Elizabeth did remember some ugliness coming from Paris at some point, but she had heard Max mention his childhood faith only once, in passing, and she was surprised to hear him fall back on it. She supposed shame was as good a reason as any.

Spotting the other slipper under the desk, he went to fetch it, picking up the first by the toe, as if it might be required to make a positive identification. "We'll leave on the evening train," he said.

"I'm not going anywhere," she said, surprised at this sudden allegiance. "Listen, Max, be reasonable. We could go talk to her together. Maybe when she knows you better, she'll allow for your ideas. I can act as intermediary."

"I mean to say, Trella and I will go."

She stared at him until he looked away.

"You can join us when you've wrapped things up here."

He put on his slippers and buckled the straps across his bag, tucking it under his arm to keep the broken handle from coming all the way off.

"Good luck with the grand artistic movement," he said.

"And to you," she returned graciously. "Give my best regards to Trella." She crossed her toes, holding in her mind the image of the two of them trapped in the wreckage of a burning car.

And with that, he was gone. The room fell silent, and she listened for the sounds from outside. In the hall, Max struggled with the bag as he walked. Someone in a far wing was knocking at a door, and she heard the girls playing in the garden. She even discerned the slight, soft padding of Isadora's bare footsteps going back and forth in the rehearsal room, a sound she could recognize anywhere.

Max was gone. He had left her alone with them.

On an unseasonably warm spring morning, three eat their breakfast
at a table set for twenty and read of an accident at sea

There numbered two hundred and sixty-nine lost souls, all drowned
with the *Empress*. Nearly every woman had gone down with the ship.

Though Mother wanted to know only the morbid details and Paris
turned to the heroic tales of gentlemen and brave sailors, Elizabeth
couldn't tear her thoughts away from the women who died. She gazed at
the ordered line of names in the newspaper column, their ages floating
beside them in parenthesized lifeboats.

As she went down the list, Elizabeth tried to imagine each of the
women from their names and ages, to invent a story in order to human-
ize each of them in her mind. An older woman became a glamorous
French widow who showed kindness only to birds. Another became in
Elizabeth's mind a lovely girl, traveling for language study abroad. Another was worried about her marriage prospects in Canada, but would
have found herself with plenty of suitors had she only lived. And another,
not so young anymore, had a limp and a secret diary in her trunk detailing scandalous affairs drawn from her own naughty imagination.

Elizabeth realized halfway through that it would be bad luck to stop speculating and forced herself to continue: one was an amateur astrono-mer and was walking the deck when it happened; another was asleep in her second-class cabin, dreaming of a buttered roll. One of them just had a shot of whiskey and blamed her own drunkenness for the sudden strange angle of the ship's floor.

"Most of them sleeping, poor souls," Paris said, his own copy of the paper spread across the table before him. "Hard to fathom when a ship goes down."

"Hard to fathom indeed!" Mother said. "Very good."

"I know one thing for certain," he continued. "I would have been up on deck with the first fog whistle, calling for the boats." He tapped the image of eight bespoke men in a lifeboat. "I would have toiled to save the ladies in the lower classes, unlike these lads."

"How could you have been up and down at once?" Elizabeth asked. She imagined the old French widow breaking away from her nurse as they waited for rescue and diving into the water, swimming an elegant crawl around Paris Singer as he read the British news alone in a trembling lifeboat.

"Don't be so disgusted," he said, turning the page.

"You don't know what you would have done."

"I can't see a thing!" Mother shouted.

"At the very least, you could come sit with us, Dora."

"I am happy by the window, thank you, Elizabeth. This room is over-warm."

It was too warm to work indoors, and outside it wasn't much better, humid without much of a breeze. On the lawn, Isadora and the girls were running back and forth in the garden. The large American meal had gone with Max, and Elizabeth missed the bacon most of all.

"Read it to me," Mother called out. "It's impossible to fathom from so many leagues!"

"Would you like to hear it in French?" Elizabeth asked.

"I'll give you the basic facts," Paris said, finding the paragraph. "'Di-saster has overtaken the fine Canadian Pacific liner *Empress of Ireland*, which sailed from *et sea* at *et sea*, was due to reach Liverpool *et sea*, first reported to have collided with an iceberg, later messages show the disas-ter was due to collision with the collier *Storstad*.'"

"An iceberg!" Mother said. "Imagine the rotten luck. You know, I considered the Canadian Pacific line but determined the White Star third class was finer. How close the calls can be sometimes."

"It wasn't an iceberg," Elizabeth said. "You know, it was not a close call for many souls."

"Shall I read you the list?" Paris asked. Elizabeth liked Paris on this trip and found him to be a useful friend to her.

"Read it to yourself," Mother said. "Tell me if there is anyone on it from Oakland."

"Toronto, Toronto, Winnepeg, London. A Japanese man. How far is Okinawa from Quebec, do you think?"

"Or San Francisco, thank you."

"If anyone could align a tragedy to reflect themselves, Dora, it would be you."

Mother gave a start, dropping her butter knife on the floor. "Be reasonable," she said, reaching for a replacement from another place setting. "Why else would you read the papers in the morning but to work its lessons in relation to your own life? You can claim to pity the souls all you want, but you're the one imagining the feel of the water around your own waist. I don't know how I raised such selfish girls."

"Selfish? I've devoted my life to my sister's artistic movement. And if she was truly selfish, she wouldn't be out there teaching six little girls to be wood nymphs."

Mother arched an eyebrow. "I suppose you'll always defend her."

"I won't," Elizabeth said, hating the plaintive sound of her own voice. She noticed Paris laughing to himself, writing something in the margin beside the list of shipwreck dead. She hated them both intensely.

"The father of her child is a stranger to her," she said. "The girls told me. Just so the both of you know."

Mother took up a hard-boiled egg that had been rolling about her plate and cracked it with her butter knife as Paris turned the page to the financial news. They were quiet almost long enough for Elizabeth to feel bad.

"No news from Oakland?" Mother asked, after a while.

"Nothing from Oakland," he said, "or San Francisco either."

"You don't mind, then?" Elizabeth asked, incredulous. "Neither of you mind?"

"You always were a hateful child," Mother said.

"I'm merely relating facts to help you make the best decisions. She has spent so much energy playing you for sympathy or plying you for cash, and though you each have better places to be and better people to be with, you insist on standing beside her as she runs off with some strange Italian." They looked down at their plates but she continued, emboldened by their shame. "What do you have to say for yourselves now? How will you justify this?"

A kiss on the cheek startled her, and though the arms thrown around her kept her from turning, she knew the grip and squeeze, the softness buoyed by solid bone, the smell of sweat and hair, of dark beer, and perfumed soap. "I didn't mean it," she said automatically.

"Who means anything," Isadora said lightly, plucking a roll from the basket at the center of the table. She took a hearty bite and put the rest on Elizabeth's plate. The others said good morning and she returned the sentiment sweetly, rubbing her sister's shoulders and kissing the crown of her head.

"I'm glad the three of you are here so I can tell you at once," she said. "We are having a special recital tonight for the movement, and I want you all to come. When the girls and I undertook this endeavor, it was with the plan that they would be dancing my work without my direct involvement on the stage. In essence, they would be having a conversation with me, but that I would not be able to answer in turn. This is the closest I have come to my own death. We would greatly appreciate notes from a thoughtful and supportive audience, and I cannot think of a more suitable trio than my mother, my lover, and my dear, darling sister." She fondled Elizabeth's hair where it was knotted at the nape of her neck.

"Eight sharp, in the hall," Isadora said. "I've prepared brief remarks. And then afterward, the girls have requested ice cream and I thought it kind to oblige them. Do you mind?"

"I'll make a note to the cook," Paris said.

Mother worried the corner of the tablecloth between her fingers. "How can I help?" she asked.

"You just make sure to arrive on time. Perhaps Elizabeth can brush your hair. Would you, dear one?"

"Of course," Elizabeth murmured.

Isadora kissed her sister's cheek and straightened up again. "The Italian is called Romano," she said. "I know him well."

And then she was gone. The air returned to the room and flushed all their cheeks red, but Elizabeth found she couldn't catch her breath. Paris rolled up the newspaper to swat at a fly. "This heat," he said.

Isadora makes an introduction that naturally upsets all in attendance

They hired a stagehand to operate the new lights, but he seemed not to know quite how to do it. Elizabeth decided against going back to help. Paris brought a lantern into the dark hall, setting it at Mother's feet like a glass-walled campfire as she went on about parties back home. She had insisted on having a set of orange silk flowers pinned to her hair, which, in the low light, made her resemble a sea creature.

"The Colonel has the entire neighborhood over," Mother said. "It's mostly ladies and older couples these days. But he has the most wonderful side yard and garden, with room for long tables and a stage. His Civil War function is the greatest night of the year. Elias escorted me last year and we had such a wonderful evening." She held a stack of loose pages on her lap featuring inarticulate sketches of the girls. "The Colonel has three or four tables set up with linens and silver, and he dresses his waiters in bonnie smocks. He has a few of them put on a show of plantation melodies, just the most charming music you'll ever know, performed by the nicest people, all of them."

"How droll," Paris said, examining the wick on the lantern flame before taking up his drink again and returning to his seat.

"It sounds dreadful," Elizabeth said.

"Listen to the little queen!" her mother said, tapping the lantern glass with her toe and casting shadows on herself. "Bored of a home-cooked meal."

"Your friend dresses his servants up and makes them do a number at his charity functions. You don't think it a little tacky?"

"The queen, the European! He doesn't force them to do a thing, they're as free as any of us. You obviously haven't read any of my letters to you, but I am a progressive woman." She busied herself violently with the little program the girls had made, which included their names and an abundance of biographical notes. "I hope I haven't missed the whole season," she said. "The Colonel was planning the greatest night of the year and I don't have too many more of those to work with. Oh, I hope I can get back in time."

"No time like the present," Elizabeth said, picturing her mother's progressive friends. She hated how heartily they all congratulated themselves on their own expired ideals. Max was a bit of an absolutist and had his cruelties, but in fifty years, people would be calling *him* progressive, not Mother's old friends.

"Don't rub your face, Elizabeth, you'll fold a new wrinkle."

"If you're worried you're going to miss a party, Dora, maybe you should take your leave."

The older woman was quiet, and Elizabeth knew she had gone too far. Motherhood might very well be a gown that fit anybody willing to squeeze into it, but Elizabeth wasn't without sympathy for her mother, who was more or less trying her best. She leaned over to kiss her hairline, the orange flowers tickling her nose.

Beside them, Paris watched the stage attentively as if the performance had already begun. "All right," he said. "I think it's about to start."

As if on cue, the new footlights illuminated like a row of flashlamps. Mother cried out in terror as one of the bulbs burst onto the proscenium stage. The stagehand cursed backstage as the smell of burning hair drifted through the auditorium.

The stage was thrown into a stark and terrifying contrast that eased only slightly as their eyes adjusted. The bright lights looked all wrong to Elizabeth. They were clearly dangerous, though candlelight had its own hazards; she thought of the time Isadora convinced her to hold a pedestal candle during an impromptu performance behind a restaurant for the man who would finance Prague. Though the candle had burned too quickly and its wax ran rivers down her bare arm, she held it, eyes welling with tears, knowing the trouble she would be in if she stopped.

Paris remarked half-audibly on the dove-gray velvet curtains that had been installed that morning, saying something about eyes.

The girls came in from stage left and scurried back and forth, their feet making the same imprecise sounds as a timpanist before the violins begin to tune. But there was no orchestra, and Trella's piano sat empty beside the stage.

Elizabeth wondered what her sister had planned. It had been a while since she had seen her perform. She was expecting the usual flirtatious disinterest, her whole false act of quiet gratitude, but was not prepared for the Isadora that emerged.

She was cradling herself, as if her body were a precious stone. Walking toe to heel, she stopped to turn at the precise center of the stage.

She moved with a very purposeful subtlety to balance out the obscenity of her body under her thin tunic. Pregnancy had infiltrated areas previously thought to be private property, spreading to her arms and neck, the flesh at the base of her neck, her hands and jawline. She held her head back, breathing through her nostrils like a thoroughbred horse.

The girls tried to mimic her movement as they walked to their marks, their arms in first position, in line with their navels. They squinted in the light like rabbits on a country road.

The girls held their positions. Contrasted with their stillness, Elizabeth saw Isadora's subtle movement. She drew her shoulders down and back, lifting her chin. The tendons in her neck began to lengthen and define themselves, and her chest seemed to broaden. Her jaw lifted as if the room was filling with water. Her feet charged evenly from the points of her hips. It was a full reversal of the curving pregnant posture that had defined her only a moment before. Her belly eased upward to fortify her breast. She transformed from the raw materials that comprised her to an elegant effigy, an idol poised and ready for their worship.

Paris worries for a moment that Isadora might injure herself in the rafters before he realizes that she is not actually ascending

He would never admit it to a soul, but attending years of Isadora's performances had the effect of blending them all together. He was no scholar of the arts, and found the dances pleasant but largely indistinguishable. Before the accident he had actually gotten a little bored of the whole venture and had taken to working out anagrams among the program names. But this, Paris knew at once, was something else entirely.

He followed the vector of her lifted arms as they reached for the rafters and stretched above her full height, growing before his eyes as the girls rushed about her in a circle. They were working without music, and their padding bare feet was the only accompaniment. Isadora in the center lowered her arms to mid-shoulder and stretched them wide, bent slightly at the elbows. The pose made Paris wonder if the ancient Greeks had practiced crucifixion with the same gusto as the Romans, and he was just making a note to check when he heard a whining noise generated in the back of Elizabeth's throat. She was rigid, her breathing shallow, and when he touched her shoulder he found it cold as porcelain. He worried that a pin snuck into the new seats had jabbed her into a state of shock, and he shook her arm to rouse her until she slapped his hand away.

"That's enough now," he whispered. "We'll get you some air shortly."

Isadora pushed her arms slowly upward, pleading with the gods or lifting some physical element of the sky. The girls began humming "Ave Maria" in a breathless, strange way, more or less in unison. They broke into a run as Isadora took one step forward and then turned a slow circle before sinking to her knees.

She unfastened her tunic to expose her right breast and then wound the cloth of her garment around her body to shroud herself. She lay down on the floor and covered herself with the cloth, head to foot. The girls, running faster, made a melodized groan.

Paris looked to his companions. Dora was fussing with her program notes and looking around as if she meant to leave but needed to sort out one small idea first. Elizabeth was gripping both sides of her seat so hard that her fingernails were ripping diamond-shaped holes into the arm-rests. He had shipped the material just the other week from London, choosing the plush velvet over the standard variety on the recommendation of the shopgirl, who had pressed it against his cheek.

"All right," he said, lifting her hand. He tried to keep his tone agreeable, though Elizabeth never listened, none of them did.

At that moment the girls ceased their singing, froze in position, and dropped to the stage. Paris was struck by the sight of the six small collapsed forms, their teacher shrouded at center. From under her shroud, Isadora cleared her throat to speak.

Isadora speaks

"All men are my brothers, all women my sisters, and all the little children on Earth are my very own. What flimsy thing is art in a world where children die? My babies were brought to me holding hands.

"To slip the river's grip I had to thank it for what it gave me and ask for more. It gave me all of life just as it appeared to be taking life away. Death taught me that there is no malice in a river. And so I learned, as a child learns, word by word: the world doesn't take a thing from us, only holds what we hand it. When the children died I learned that all the rivers on earth are my children.

"Life is a glorious beast, the sea its Leviathan eye. I stand worse for wear before you, wearing the world, having done battle with this animal, but now I know to ride it. I pull myself as close as I can, I take its fur by the root as it runs and hold my head up as we go, because life is a beast bucking mad to crush its cargo, the journey's only purpose caught in glimpses along the way."

Paris is obliged to take his leave

After the performance Isadora refused to see anyone but him, and only if he brought her some seltzer. He always knew it was time to go when he started doing her bidding.

He found her backstage, squatting with her back pressed to the wall by the low table where the girls kept their ribbons.

"There you are," she said, reaching for the glass. "I hope you put some whiskey in it."

Handing it to her, he lit a cigarette. "You must hate getting back-aches. How mortal of you, how deeply ordinary."

"It's my hips," she said. "I'm dizzy. Will you put that out?"

The blisters on her bandaged feet had taken to weeping, making her look like even more of a martyr than she intended.

"Max forgot an old package of tobacco in his room," he said. "I would guess it's twenty years old. The maid brought it to me after he went away, she found it in the armoire. The lid was stuck, but I had the boys pry it open. It was still wrapped in wax inside, totally untouched. Twenty years old at least. Can you imagine?" He picked a thread of tobacco from his tongue, examining it before flicking it to the floor. "It's awfully stale."

She eased off the wall. "Mind where you put the cherry, they just painted the stage."

"I won't insult by suggesting you should rest, but you should go and talk to the girls. I can hear them crying in the hallway. I think they're quite exhausted."

"They ought to be. If they don't leave every ounce of themselves on that stage, people will wonder why they're on the bill at all. At this point I'd do better rolling six handsome potted plants around on casters."

"Show them a little kindness."

"You cannot even imagine what I am forced to go through for this performance. At the very least, they could hit their marks."

He smiled from one side of his mouth. "I can imagine it, though surely not as well as you, my dear."

"You know, Gus made the same face for months after he fell asleep next to an open window."

"If you're looking for forgiveness," Paris said, "you won't find it from me."

"Forgiveness? Why, whatever for?"

"All that you said about the river. You really are a heartless thing. The rest of us were sick with misery, we quarantined ourselves for months. Meanwhile you took a trip to Greece. You had a grand old time. Family in Albania, intrigue in Turkey. A right proper Italian holiday. You met new friends."

"You're being ludicrous."

"The river gave you a gift, it seems. It gave you your life back and your freedom. All it took from you was your work, and now you've got that back as well."

She swirled her drink, and he thought for a moment that she might throw it in his face. "You fear life and shrink from it," she said. "You come to me in witness of experience, having forfeited your own."

"All right," he said, standing. "All you want is an argument, and I won't give it to you, so you might as well leave me be."

"You would be so lucky to ever possess even a handful of what I want," she said.

"Some sense of legacy? The invisible result of your invented ideals?"

They smiled at each other, sharp enough to crack each other's ribs.

"At least I have a legacy," she said.

"Woman, my legacy was established before you were born, with a product that ushered in the age. Every garment in the modern world bears my mark."

She stood, bearing full scorn upon him, and he stood to match her.

"But you didn't invent the sewing machine," she said.

"And you didn't invent the goddamn concept of dance."

He threw down his cigarette and left her to sort it out. For all he cared, the whole place could burn to the ground.

15 July 1914
Romano Romanelli
Viale Alfredo Belluomini, Viareggio

Romano,

Progress comes all at once! Mother took a week to mind the schedule of crossings, discussing the merits of each ship before deciding on the *Adriatic*'s first class from Liverpool. And then, surprising us all, she allowed Paris to fit her in a toque and goggles before serving rather poorly as his flight navigator across the Channel. He wrote to say that he turned back to check on her after they landed and found her grinning like a girl and slapping herself on both cheeks and calling out the landmarks and major roads.

Max sent me a birthday card three months too early, noting that all was well in Darmstadt and that I "should stay and help with Isadora's delivery." It wasn't clear if he meant her child or her artistic method, but I doubt he reserves any tenderness toward either one.

Lately I feel more urgently that the girls and I should leave. I feel a tingling at the back of my neck, the feeling before an electrical storm.

Paris offered us a place to stay at Oldway before we prepare to go to New York. Isadora insists on staying on here, so I'll leave her to work out the delivery herself.

She came and found me in my room this morning. She seemed as pleased as a summer cat, and despite her bodily resplendence leaned gracefully down to kiss my cheek, frowning at the clippings I had spread across my dressing table. This week I've started pasting selections together, favoring full-page images of violent events juxtaposed with mannered portraits of the living. More interesting stories are covered by different papers, making it possible to collect images and ideas in order to create a fuller picture from it all. For this method I find the larger and more violent events the most attractive, as there is the best chance of total understanding simply from the sheer volume of information. Or that's how it feels, anyway.

Tragedy is a comfort to me now. The stories remind me of the small earthquakes we felt every now and then in California, when Mother said the earth was finding relief. Build enough tension and the fault lines come to crave it; survive enough upheaval and even the children lose their fear.

Isadora arrived just as I was finishing my work on the assassination of the Archduke and his wife. I've had more to work with on the topic than anything yet. There are my favorite pieces: a photograph from Sophie's younger days, the pearls cinched tight around her thin throat; an official portrait from the same time, where she appears to be rising head and shoulders above a taffeta cloud; a picture of her in a garden, her lap piled with a spray of buttercups and whitebells, her gaze serious and intelligent; one with a tiara on her heaps of auburn hair like the sugar trellis of a cake; another official portrait with the children, Franz in the background like a museum docent. For the backdrop, I used a large image of the mourners at their funeral and affixed the whole thing to a pegboard I found out behind the kitchen.

Isadora skimmed a piece from the scraps about conflict with Germany before setting it aside. She frowned over the artistic rendering I found of the assassination itself: a furious-looking Sophie holding on to the side of the car, glaring at Ferdinand's ludicrous feathered general's hat as if it were the reason for the pinprick bullet on its fateful path toward thin lace making a pathetic shield across her breast. Our womanhood won't protect us, no matter what they say!

She leaned into the side of the desk to work its corner into her hip. I suffer her, if not gladly, then with the knowledge that the suffering is mutual. I know for a fact that she didn't keep any of the articles covering the children's accident, preferring to draw her lessons from her own mind rather than outside expertise. I hear her through the walls at night, talking to the river.

She turned a picture of Sophie to examine an advertisement on the verso, a woman wreathed in flowers over an article on the uses and benefits of cold cream. Looking up, we met each other's eyes in the mirror, the two of us appearing in the low light as young girls. We stayed like that for a while, and I found myself afraid to speak.

At last she went away, but before she did, she said one thing: that this is an essential labor, and that I play an essential part.

I said nothing in response. I've never meant a thing to her.

Isadora finds herself alone, though she is never alone for long

The simple strangeness of pregnancy carries me through. With Deirdre, I became a tree, carved out and filled with black sand. With Patrick, I was a quarried stone shot through with champagne bubbles. Today my body is a birdcage tucked too high into the rafters, old news lining my arching ribs.

Mother and Paris have gone away, failing even to say goodbye. Soon enough, Elizabeth will take the girls while I pursue our next iteration of glory alone.

I went looking for the girls, wandering Bellevue like a ghost, burst blisters leaving a trail behind me. I'm too tender lately, out of practice, but I'm glad to lend my blood to the revolution which bears my name.

The girls aren't in their rooms or backstage or in the rehearsal room, aren't outside playing badminton or sunning themselves. Finally from the lawn I spot them standing in a line on the highest balcony, four stories up, shading their eyes to see something far away.

It's so unbearably warm inside and out and now they send their poor teacher up four flights of stairs to see them. The baby saves his strength, making small and subtle movements.

The heat gets me so dizzy I have to clutch the rail on the final flight, easing myself closer to the cool stone wall until I'm strong enough to walk again.

A trail through the dust of a shuttered ballroom leads to the girls on the balcony. Outside, the iron slats groan gently underfoot. All six of them hold the rail, as if inviting a lightning strike. They're looking at the dark clouds over the city, far enough away that we've felt nothing of the storm except this sticky heat.

I wish they would stay here in France with me through August, and I nearly say so, but it's too late. Everyone took such care to ensure they wouldn't be involved in the next grand movement in our artistic lives; Paris arranged a doctor and two nurses to stay on with me at Bellevue, and Elizabeth is making preparations to take the girls to New York via Torquay by the end of the month, staying a while at Oldway while she gathers their supplies. I don't have the energy to fight any of them.

The girls make room for me on the balcony. "You don't belong up here," I say, cupping my hand at the nape of Margot's neck. It's possible to span the curve of her skull with my palm. "It's not safe."

"We will miss you," Irma says. The others murmur their agreement. A bit of cool air blows in from the storm, and I lift my chin to feel it.

"We'll be together again soon. And if you haven't kept up your drills, I'll see to it you won't miss me after that. Now let's go inside, we're about to catch a real storm."

"It's war," says Margot.

"That was over months ago," I say, remembering the man lighting Catherine wheels in the strait.

"The older girls say so."

"You've been taking your cues from the older girls? That explains why you're late to all your marks. What if the older girls told you to eat your slipper with gravy and bread?"

A few fat drops of summer rain begin to fall, marking their presence on the rail.

"Teacher Merz sent us a letter," Irma says. "He says we should leave Europe at once. There is a conflict, he says."

"Germany will soon be securing her place in the sun," Erica says. "Teacher Merz says so. He wrote us all letters. Our mothers don't want us to come home either."

"Don't you feel it?" Irma asks.

"I feel a storm coming that will ruin our day, but I can use my eyes and ears for that. You shouldn't accept any letters from Teacher Merz. He is only trying to tease you."

"Look!" Margot cries, pointing. "Down there! They're taking away the flag!" She dissolves into hysterical tears, burying her face in my dress.

Across the river, two workers are taking down the decorations that had been strung up for Bastille Day. One of the men scales the lamp to undo the knots up top while the other waits on the ground with a basket.

"You should come with us to New York," Irma says.

Margot sobs, clutching me. "Won't you come with us, Mother?" she sobs. "Won't you?"

"Now see, you've worked Margot into a frenzy." I crouch down, bracing against the rail. "It's nothing," I tell her, holding her close and kissing the tears from her face. "Do you want to know what you're really feeling, my darling? Look at me. It's not any kind of war. Stop crying, and I'll tell you what it is."

She wipes her face with the tail of her sash like a lost orphan in one of Deirdre's little books. They are all orphans, their own mothers pushing them from the nest.

"What is it?" she asks, sniffling.

"What you're feeling, my darling, are the first drumbeats of the artistic revolution, and you and I and your sisters here are the ones leading it. It's the sound of change, you know. Change can be a scary thing, and sometimes feels as if it's spinning just out of your grasp. Do you understand? That's what gives you a bad feeling. You hold the future inside you. Soon enough this glorious new movement will arrive, casting light onto everything it touches. It will sink its teeth into you and eat you up, and you will become a part of it, just as it now is a part of you. There now, don't cry. You will be carried by a familiar beast, and your reward will be a yearning that will die with you and a legacy you won't be here to enjoy."

Margot weeps more earnestly than before. Irma gives me a dirty look as they take her inside, but the rest of them seem lost in thought. It's best they all learn now what lies at the end of this path. The more they know to dread, the less they have to fear.

30 July 1914
Romanelli
cura di Viareggio

I know there is no connection between us, subtle or otherwise. Though I trusted my desire would find its way to you somehow, it was only rolling from ear to ear in my own head. Still, I need to share the truth of things with you. You'll wonder over this letter most seriously, I'm sure, as it will be the first you've heard from me since our last morning on Corfu, but as you wonder, know this: I hope you are well. Ever so.

Before the girls and I left for the train, I brought Isadora a gift. We've never much cared for birthdays, and Christmas has always been eaten up with preparations for holiday shows. But when I saw it in the shop-window, I couldn't help myself.

I left it in a box at the foot of her bed while she was sleeping. She's never liked to say goodbye and will fight anyone who shows her kind-ness, and so it is best this way. When she wakes up she'll find it: a scarf as red as the blood between us and long enough to wrap her and baby both. If she tied it at her neck it would unfurl like a banner behind her, reading *Sans limites!* or *Je vais à la gloire!*—I couldn't guess, as her whims change by the hour.

She thinks that her suffering will be rewarded with glory, that joy and pain will be balanced on a scale the size of her life, but she's wrong. Happiness is not earned. We fall on it like drunks, then pick ourselves up and stumble away, looking for all the world like we're dancing.

In Bellevue, a child is born

I'm afforded a good view of the mobilization from the balcony where we all stood just a few weeks ago. A line of men cross the length of the bridge, waiting to sign the transport roster. The men are flanked by glinting silver cavalry and autobuses stretching around the bend. If the girls were here, we would bring the men flowers and dance for them. But the girls are gone. This whole time I thought a new era was building; now I see it was only a war.

Watching the first buses pull away, I feel a thin internal stretching followed by the sound and sense of a cracking knuckle as a thin stream of water trickles down one leg. I wait as long as the pain allows before I ring the bell and the child waits patiently with me, having one last word with the universe; the same conversation we all had, which vanished the moment each of us was born.

Once I ring the bell, two white-capped nurses come running from some recess of the house. They wheel a hospital bed right into the center of the dusty ballroom and set to preparing it without comment. How they got it to the fourth floor in the first place is a mystery to me. Paris spoke of the bed's expense, so I'm disappointed to find it's only a padded

metal table glorified with levers and cranks and a pair of white cloth re-
straints affixed for the obstinate, and a length of white muslin sufficing a
cushion, the whole thing on casters. Terrifically advanced, I'm sure. The
nurses bring in trays of silver tools, a pair of high chairs, and a white
enameled bucket, all of it looking as if it fell this morning from the surface of the moon.

The doctor enters, pulling on his white coat. My medical staff has
gotten accustomed to pinochle and late nights in their guest rooms and
seem annoyed that they must get back to work. One of the nurses un-
folds a white linen shade to protect the privacy of the bed from the ghosts
that roam in the building while the other tries to coax me from the window. I press my wet forehead to the glass, trying to find the river in the
activity around it, the men and horses, the dust they raise. I wish I could
see to England; Paris sent a picture postcard of the Paignton Pier with a
colorful caption in his script—*WISH YOU WERE PIER*—and the girls'
names signed like an attendance roster underneath. My darling girls!
Life is such a sparkling thing, and their toes have only just touched the
water.

The nurse goes to get me a seltzer in exchange for my obedience,
and I have just enough time to make a sad farewell to my body. Holding
the window frame, I point my left toe and describe a circle, as soft as a
breath, to the wall, then float it up and back, hips wound to strangling.
I focus steady on my pain until it bows to me.

They guide me to the bed, which has been lifted to its highest point,
forcing me to heft myself up. A series of needles are presented with great
aplomb, but the one I pick seems too large for my vein. By the time the
nurse is finished, she may as well have attached a button. She goes to work
on my undercarriage, pulling off my wet bloomers. I remark to the doctor
that the child has been baptized already in his own water, but the man
doesn't have a thing to say in response. He cleans his glasses, the way
Gus does, while the nurse makes endless slight adjustments to my body,
swabbing my skin and pinning my clothes, binding my legs to the stirrups
and draping a sheet over it all, as if my lower half is a table on which
the doctor has been invited to dine.

The other nurse returns with the seltzer. She places it on a pedestal
just out of reach, and I can only watch with helpless desire as its lemon

sinks to the bottom of the glass and bubbles back up. The doctor affixes a cotton sling over his mouth and nose.

A rumbling on the street startles everyone. One of the nurses goes to the window and returns saying, "*C'est la guerre*," as if the war were a man outside with his hat in his hands, waiting for us to be done.

The doctor ducks under the sheet and says something I can't quite hear through his mask. Before I can ask him to repeat himself, the old ignoble pain rips through. This time it won't be bowing to me.

Pain can claim so many pounds of happy flesh, and still it keeps coming, spiked and serpentine. The doctor's muffled "*Courage, Madame*" rises from between my legs, and his words become a set of waves I can duck under and swim. Tongs and forceps sink around me, spitting bubbles in their wake.

The doctor rests a moment against my leg. His forehead fits on the ball of my knee, which becomes a joint lubricated by our sweat. The nurses assure me when I cry and call out for Paris that the city is with me now.

Pain is a landscape. They have spread me out like a picnic, with iced drinks and sandwiches, cheese plated on paper, the nurses tucking into fruits and bread while the doctor jabs inelegantly in the crook of a nearby tree. One of the girls has lovely red hair, which I wind around my fingers as we walk, finding a pond tucked among the high reeds and sitting down together to watch full life-and-death spans of foreign creatures. She tells me stories of childhood in this country, where she was raised to always trust that if she did her best to be a good and ordinary girl, she would have a good and ordinary life, that if bad days came, she would weather them knowing that things would go back to normal soon enough. In living like this, she found that the bad days became ordinary in their way and in hindsight seemed not so bad after all, and eventually those bad days came to be the most natural course.

She tells me all this with her head nestled in my lap, raising her voice to be heard above the sound of a transport train picking up speed, every car packed with boys. The engine man squints at the track, but with the dust still settling from the last train, it's impossible to see ahead.

Either another doctor has arrived or the first one has taken on the expression of an entirely different man. This new man is more serious and upright, frowning from one side, as if his face were painted on a half-drawn curtain. He removes his mask and speaks to the nurses in a regional French so rapid that his meaning is lost on them both; they call to mind a pair of ducks, one and then the other bobbing under the sheet to have a look. His second round of commands sends them running for strange objects, ornaments and goose feathers and rum. There are more of them all of a sudden, the women tripling to complete their tasks. One of them rolls a thin glass cylinder from its place in the corner, but when I try to turn and follow her progress, another pair of hands holds my head away. I warn the first that she'll need a broom if it breaks, though I can't think of where to find one. One nurse pinches my cheeks hard and runs away before I catch her. Another plunges a spoon into a slouching bag and pulls out soft gray ash, packing the wound the man has sliced between my legs. Another plays a madhouse tune on a toy piano, rolling a ball of yarn between her stocking feet.

These are my girls, I realize, my dancing darlings. The real nurses must be tied up in the pantry, kicking at the door. *You naughty girls!* They wink and laugh. *There's nothing to it*, one of them says, and another says *The war! The war!* A fist pounds against a metal door. One siphons a bottle of rum into my ear. My hands are caught in metal cuffs; the knocking is my head against the table.

The doctor taps my tender sex with a pair of forceps to show me where I need to tense myself, but fatigue keeps me from knowing the muscle to order it into action. I bear down with all my might. My heel slips the stirrup and jackknifes into a nurse, a hard kick to her breastbone. She holds her chest with two hands, leveling her full scorn and hatred at me, as strong as ten thousand good wishes; she will read news of my death years from now and have a second serving of cake.

Of course my own body would keep me from delivering this child. Of course I would die here after a life spent learning the personality of every muscle. The body is all that fails me here, and all that saves me as well. There is no white light, no kind eyes, no angels here to bow their heads. Pain is a man in the room. The mind slips its bounding rail, and time steps aside to watch it fall. Only the body remains, failing and riding through failure.

The nurse I kicked reels back into a tray and sends the cart on casters spinning, its silver crashing across the room, a sea of scalpels and forceps and fine-tooth saws, silver-plated speculums and pins and long-eyed embroidery needles and shaving blades and steak knives, sharps tossing to bed themselves into skin and soft wood, the nurses crawling to escape with needles in their hair. The one I kicked got the worst of it; clean red blood seeps from her leg, sliced neatly mid-thigh by surgical steel, her stocking slick with blood, both nurses screaming to see it as the baby, with no better fanfare than total disaster, falls into the doctor's hands.

The doctor catches the slick body around his head and waist and holds him steady through the struggle of his stretching arms. *This one is too young to go to war!* We need to be ready when the enlistment man comes. *Too young!* My boy's eyes are wetly sealed, he hasn't seen a bit of this world. Send the enlistment man away, keep my child close for all my days so that no matter where life takes him, he will be near. If he goes to war, he takes me with him.

The doctor licks his thumb and swipes the baby's face to clear the blood. He hands him to me and crouches beside the screaming nurse, leaving a bloody print on her cheek when he slaps it. Her eyes roll back as she faints and the other two carry her away. The afternoon has gone with them, and the men onto their buses, and the sun sinks past the treeline. My child and I are alone.

The cord still connects us, its use to him fading. He struggles on my chest, seeming troubled by the fact that the material that warmed and held him is swiftly chilling to a sludge.

But the blanket doesn't soothe him. He tenses and grasps, twisting sightless in my arms like a bisected worm. His hands ball into two fists and then stretch wide, and either he is silent or the world has become silent in witness.

I pull my tunic down and hold him against me. He is as weak as an old drunk and beats my breast with his tiny fists, rearing back and bucking his head. His skin seems stretched over a wire frame.

"Mamma's here," I say. "Hush now, I'm here."

He goes still when he hears my voice, then lifts his tremulous head.

"That's right, darling."

One of his eyes unseals and then the other. He stares at me with two black and boundless pools. They gleam in the fading light.

Transfixed, the last strength of my body draws him closer. "Who are you?" I whisper into his perfect ear. "Who are you, Deirdre or Patrick? You have returned to me—"

I bring him close enough for our lashes to tangle. The whole world rests in his endless eyes.

He strains to speak, and I ache to hear, but when he opens his mouth, I see that his throat is closed off, and no air can come or go. It is sealed like a tomb by skin as soft as lambskin leather. His perfect throat winnows to nothing, his lungs twin thumbprints of contorted flesh. When I try to push my thumb to break the skin that seals his throat, he jerks away. The place is malformed and strung with nerves. I feel it too, for his pain is mine.

He seizes, overcome. Our eyes meet again, and I see that he knows me as I know him. I see Patrick's energy and Deirdre's attention, the pride of their fathers. I see my mother's love and my father's, Elizabeth and my brothers. He has my very own will to live, beating his fists against life itself. And then there are parts of him I don't recognize—a peace wholly foreign to me, and courage I have never known.

His love is a gleaming thing. His eyes, the endpoint of a dark wire connecting him to the universe. He knows the past and future, it is etched onto his bones. I fear him, this germ of the world, but he fears nothing, not joy or pain. His body relaxes as he rests his head on my breast, so gentle, and dies.

In the blue light of evening I feel every agony of my life compounded: the pinch of a door, a stinging slap, blisters and jammed toes. An arm broken ice-skating, scalding drops of cooking oil. The children drown again and again. His body in my arms is the color of an oyster's shell, his temple smooth against my lips.

The world at last has burst me. My bones are winched apart, and from every porous place streams a triple fountain of blood and tears and milk. The three rivers drain and pool onto the floor.

My life has been staged for all to see, with no wings in which to wait and not a moment of rest. It is a performance of a lifetime. And though I thought I was alone, my audience was with me all along.

Men and women line the walls in silent witness. They are naked, without a stitch to cover them, and I see all shades of human skin, a statuary of the young and very old. Standing shoulder to shoulder, they form a line of flesh, a gapless human wall. Before I can speak to greet them, they come forward together as a wave and pull away my robe and tunic, leaving me as naked as the rest.

They were with me all along! They look at me with love, as if I am not plagued by the dead. They hold their hands on me, and I reach to hold them back, to touch their thighs and paunching breasts, their speckled necks, their pocks and puckers, swollen lips and hips, all of them thrumming with life. They are my body, I am their dark heart beating, and all of us are naked as the day we came screaming into this world.

ACKNOWLEDGMENTS

Thanks are owed to Emily Bell and the whole team at FSG, including Debra Helfand, Rachel Weinick, Abby Kagan, Maxine Bartow, Na Kim, Sarita Varma, Maya Binyam, and Jackson Howard; to Claudia Ballard and the team at WME, including Laura Bonner and Caitlin Landuyt; to those who offered thoughts on portions of the draft, including Summer Block, Steph Cha, Maggie Evans McGuinness, Sasha Fletcher, Susan Quesal, Lee Shipman, and Timothy Small; and to Ashley Warren for archival research.

A number of texts helped to support this novel, most notably Charles Emmerson's book *1913: In Search of the World Before the Great War* and Peter Kurth's *Isadora: A Sensational Life*. Special thanks are owed to Mary Sano and her Studio of Duncan Dancing in San Francisco, which keeps Isadora's method alive with a great sensitivity and devotion, and gladly offers lessons even to the gawkish.

I'm grateful for the institutional and financial support from the New York Public Library, TBWA\Chiat\Day LA, Texas State University, Vermont Studio Center, and the institutions and events that have hosted me. And lastly, gratitude to Lauren Goldstein and Cassie Riger and to my family, near and far.